Mavis Cheek was born and grew up in Wimbledon. She began her working life at Editions Alecto, the contemporary art publishers. After Alecto, she attended Hillcroft College for Women from where she graduated in Arts. After her daughter Bella was born, she began her writing career in earnest; journalism and travel writing at first, then short stories, and eventually, in 1988, her novel *Pause Between Acts* was published by Bodley Head and won the *She/John Menzies* First Novel Prize. *Yesterday's Houses* is her twelfth novel.

Mavis Cheek has been described as 'Jane Austen in contemporary dress', with a 'sharp ear and a wicked eye for the discrete lack of charm of the bourgeoisie'. She now lives and writes in the heart of the English countryside.

by the same author

PAUSE BETWEEN ACTS
PARLOUR GAMES
DOG DAYS
JANICE GENTLE GETS SEXY
AUNT MARGARET'S LOVER
SLEEPING BEAUTIES
GETTING BACK BRAHMS
THREE MEN ON A PLANE
MRS FYTTON'S *country life*
THE SEX LIFE OF MY AUNT
PATRICK PARKER'S PROGRESS

MAVIS CHEEK

Yesterday's Houses

faber and faber

First published in 2006
by Faber and Faber Limited
3 Queen Square London WC1N 3AU

Typeset by Faber and Faber Ltd
Printed in England by Mackays of Chatham, plc

A CIP record for this book
is available from the British Library

ISBN 0–571–22423–7

2 4 6 8 10 9 7 5 3

For the Jacobs family, robust friendship of great longevity

. . . and so help each one of us to see in the half-glimpsed truth about someone else's life, the truth about our own.

Paul Scott, *Birds of Paradise*

It is never too late to be what you might have been.

George Eliot.

A hill is a house for an ant, an ant.
A hive is a house for a bee.
A hole is a house for a mole or a mouse
And a house is a house for me.

Mary Ann Hoberman,
'A House is a House for Me'

Marianne Flowers went to a party when she was seventeen. It was held in a very big house in a quiet suburb of London: a house with a long front path and big bay windows and a double front door with a stained-glass window panel at each side. The front garden was big and overgrown but – oddly to Marianne – it did not look unpleasantly neglected; it looked interesting and slightly mysterious. Where she lived, if a garden was neglected it meant it looked shabby and mucky and shameful. This garden must belong to what her mother would call A Better Class of Person.

It was early in the year but already there were shrubs with dark green shiny leaves and white or pink or red flowers. They were as pretty and exotic to Marianne as ballerinas in their tutus. Later, when she came to know about such things, she would discover that they were camellias, and that it was a beauty tinged with sadness, that they were made famous by Greta Garbo in a romantic film in which a brave courtesan dies sacrificing herself for her lover. Marianne would begin her adult life thinking how romantic such things were and grow into thinking that it was yet another example of foolish womanhood martyring itself on the altar of the feminine ideal. But for the time being the flowers and Camille were mysteries to her and she simply responded to their exotic puff of petals by picking one of them and tucking it into her long hair. These were the days of such things. Flowers. She was also wearing beads and strings of seeds so she tucked another couple of the lovely things into these, too. Disappointingly the flowers had no scent. That seemed a crying shame in something so pretty. She would learn, also, that the world was full of such disillusionments, major and minor, and that having few expectations was best.

She rang the doorbell which was loud and long and made her jump. A bold sound. An announcement that could not be ignored.

Marianne shrank into herself a little. It did not do, so she had been brought up to think, to draw attention to yourself. She hunched in the doorway and waited.

The house, like the garden, had a run-down, dingy look about it, which was intriguing but also a little unnerving. If Marianne were an educated girl or had read *Northanger Abbey* and *Jane Eyre* she would know that the house had a Gothic Air about it. But she was not yet educated and all she could think was – Ooh – spooky and – Ooh – spiders. Marianne had never been in a house like this for any social reason (though her doctor and dentist had their surgeries in such places when she was growing up) and she was quite in awe of it, quite tickled to be there as a guest instead of as a patient. These were the kind of houses Marianne walked past and wondered about and which often had interesting people with lots to say for themselves going in and out of their solid front doors. These were the people who did not look respectable, as her mother might say. People who did not hang *net curtains*.

As she waited for the door to be opened she felt a flutter of excitement. Marianne's life had been quite dull, quite mundane (a word she had just learned and liked) – until now – ordinary: what she would one day come to hear called 'respectable working class' and 'suburban'. Entering this new world of what she would also come to hear called 'the Intellectual and Bohemian' was exciting. Different. The porch in which she stood and waited, for example, was nearly as big as her back bedroom at home. She could judge the desirability of this new world only by such things. Yes, you could definitely get a single bed in the porch.

The reason Marianne was at the house was because someone she had met at a bus stop in Kingston upon Thames had kissed her hand and said that there was to be a party at number 3 Laburnum Grove, and he would meet her there. He was small and blond with a pair of mustard-yellow stacked boots and a lilac floral shirt and he, like the flowers, was exotic-looking. She forgot to ask his name so that when the door to the house was opened and she was asked whom she was with she could only shake her head, but then the girl with the long dark hair and bare feet who had opened the door seemed to lose interest and drift away. So in Marianne went. Even she knew enough to compare what she felt with Alice's experience of Wonderland. And if she had read *Through the Looking Glass*, she would have felt it was like that too.

2

She marvelled at the hallway and the long flight of stairs; she marvelled at an old mirror which reflected her as a girl with a flower in her hair, flowers at her neck, and several alarming black spots all over her face. In years to come she would learn that mirrors were silvered, that old mirrors lost some of their silvering, and that caused the reflected one to look spotty. But for now she put her hand to her face in wonder, but found that when she moved her reflection the spots stayed in the same place. This was a big relief as Marianne was worried that she might have contracted something on the bus coming over. Then she wondered again why, although everything was clearly old and not in the best condition, it did not look tatty like the worn-out furniture back at home. When that caught a scuff or a bit dropped off it looked awful but here in this hallway the mirror, the chest of drawers, the straight-backed chairs, the brightly coloured carpet runner – all were marked or worn or a little broken, but all looked just right. Later, of course, she would come to learn that a mark of quality is the ageing of something that lasts, another is patina, and that there is no shame attached to a mid-Victorian chaise longue if a bit of its carving has been knocked off – perhaps in a fit of Bohemian pique. Whereas she would also come to learn that there is every amount of shame attached to a piece of second-hand deal furniture that collapses when you sit down a little too heavily upon it. This was quality; she began to feel it in her bones, and she liked it.

The hallway fascinated her. It was high and arched and painted in yellow and white (not papered in something bright and floral) with a steep, wide staircase. Although the party noise came from the room immediately to her left, into and out of which people drifted with glasses of wine – red mostly, very sophisticated – or cigarettes, talking and laughing and holding each other, quite wonderfully careless of what anyone thought: one man in particular had his hand down the front of the dress of the girl he was with and the strange thing was *she did not seem to notice* – how very cool that looked. Marianne made a brief note to herself to stop all that silly stuff about removing wandering hands in future – it was tiresome anyway and they always crept back. She did not quite have the courage to go into the party room immediately. Instead she went up the stairs, passing one or two smudgy-eyed girls and shaggy-haired boys with silk scarves knotted round their throats. Someone remarked on her dress – they liked it – and Marianne smiled at the girl who had spoken but the girl had

3

already looked away. That, too, seemed the ultimate in cool – to be so detached from everything. Marianne would come to learn this trick, too. That it did not do in the blossoming age of existentialism to be like a floppy puppy and rush up to people and be bloody well nice and expect a pat for it. But for now she was finding the whole thing something of a dream and she felt honoured to be there. Nevertheless a welcome note of physical practicality struck because Marianne needed the bathroom – what she referred to in those days as the lavvy or the lav but which she would one day come to learn was called The Lavatory, or The Loo, and never, ever The Toilet. Unless you were being ironical.

She tried a number of doors on the pale-yellow landing, causing some rufflings as she disturbed the various bedroom activities, but eventually she found the right room and in she went. How it took her breath away, this bathroom and lavvy combined. Now this really was bigger than her bedroom at home. It was tiled in white and black and it had walls of a strange pale-greenish colour that ought to have been vomit worthy but which looked just right. Later she would learn this was called eau-de-Nil and was one of the great art-deco colours. She sat on the high square lavatory with its wooden seat (not plastic, then) and felt the warmth from the enormous, chunky radiator creep all around her. There was something so *indulgent* about having heating in the bathroom instead of gritting your teeth at the removal of each garment as the air stabbed at you with its icy little pickaxes. How she longed to get into that huge white bath and see how it felt. How magnificent it looked balanced there in the centre of the room on its grand clawed feet – like a supine lion offering its body to be entered. It was luxurious by any stretch, thought Marianne, and when she pulled the long chain and the water cascaded perfectly (unlike the one at home which needed a *knack)* she did dare to climb into the white belly of the sleeping creature. And it was comfortable and big and generous and for a moment or two she pretended that she owned such a wonderful bath and she lay there staring up at the ceiling mouldings (slightly grubby but pretty fruit and flowers) and thought how desirable this room was compared to the cramped, cold, lino-covered bathroom at home with its teensy frosted-glass window and its pink candlewick toilet-seat cover and matching (ugh!) drip mat. This was the kind of bathroom she would love to have. It was the first time she had ever understood that a room could

4

be more than its function, that a room could be a kind and thoughtful and comfortable friend. She lay there and she dreamed.

Someone rattled the door handle and her heart nearly exploded with guilt as she hopped out of the bath, smoothed down her dress, touched the flowers in her hair and at her neck and opened the door, blushing at the uncool idea of being caught lying fully clothed in a stranger's bath. It was a tall, thin boy about her own age, leaning against the wall as if he might fall down, and wearing a pink shirt with huge flowing sleeves. He had a Zapata moustache and black curly hair in what her mother called a mop. He was absolutely gorgeous and a very odd colour in his complexion. Something like putty. She put on her snootiest air and walked past him. 'About bloody time,' he said. And as he pushed himself upright he winked at her – with one rather bloodshot eye – and tickled one of her cheeks. 'Sweet little thing,' he said, cool as you like. But as the door closed behind her she heard him throwing up.

She never forgot that bathroom. It was not the bathroom she would choose to reproduce but the feeling of it. Warm. Clean. Kind. Caring. Indulgent. A place where everything worked and where it was nice to spend time. Somewhere for thoughts and dreams and the passing of hours. A haven.

Descending the stairs, head up, back straight, she smiled at the girl who had commented on her dress, who very coolly did not smile back. The doorbell rang again. Magnificent sound. Someone, not the same dark girl, opened it and walked away, leaving the grand door to swing to and fro. Someone on the stairs called out, 'Anthony! You're here.' And there was the boy from the bus stop. 'Obviously,' he said and stepped into the hall. Marianne smiled at him and she thought he really is a bit short, and he has freckles and his hair is thin and he looks more like a pixie than a boy – what could I have been thinking about? But Marianne went on smiling, despite her disappointment, because she knew that was what you must do. But curiously he was not smiling. If anything he was looking extremely embarrassed, cross even, and as the door swung right back, Marianne saw why. He had his arm around something that at first looked like a large dog, but which turned out to be a small, pretty blond girl in an Afghan coat. 'This is Harriet,' he said. 'Hallo, Harriet,' she said back. Harriet gave a very high-class whinnying noise, and they both disappeared into the room containing the party.

5

Marianne, partly relieved and partly cast down, followed and it was only when she was on the other side of the door, swirled and buffeted by the throng, that it occurred to her that this was very awkward. To be invited to a party by a boy and then find him arriving with another girl. In fact it was totally and utterly unacceptable and so, *so* wonderfully careless. She had no idea what to do about it except Rise Above which was the only bit of advice her mother ever gave her. Whenever the world gets you down – rise above. From grazed knees to getting blamed for something you did not do. Rise Above.

'I got told off for wearing plimsolls to school today . . .'
　'Rise above.'
'The boys won't let me have a go at their football rattle. They say my arms are too skinny because I'm a girl.'
　'Rise above.'
'I told Miss Bishop I can't stay on because I need to get a job.'
　'Rise above.'

Marianne's mother could not abide strong winds. One day when they were walking back from the shops together and their hair was being blown about and her mother was holding on to her headscarf for dear life and getting crosser and crosser and finally said, 'Drat this bloody wind. I can't stand it.' Marianne said, 'Rise above.' And got quite a slap for it, on the back of the knee. So that apart from Rising Above she also learned from that to bite her tongue and not consider herself on the same level as her elders and betters. Of which latter there seemed to be quite a lot in this room . . .

She attempted the proposition now, Rise Above. Her chin went even higher and her back even straighter and she wandered over to where a few bottles and some plastic beakers stood in among some fascinating china and brass objects and postcards on the mantelpiece. Marianne was at a loose end in a room full of people she did not know and the temptation was to leave. But how lovely and strange to her was the house. She did not want to go away from it yet. Everyone at the party was young and everyone was talking and laughing or talking and looking serious and stylish and they were all so different from any group she had ever known. They probably all went to grammar school or university.

She would stay. She picked up a beaker (not daring to rub it on her hem even though she was sure it had been used already) and was about to pour herself some red wine (a new and daring colour for her) when a voice said, 'Hey, flower girl. Allow me . . .' Across the crowded and smoky room she saw the boy from the bathroom, his Zapata curling as he called to her. She would come to know that he was called Charles Legg. Never Charlie. That he had indeed been to grammar school. And that he was about to go up (Up!) to university to read (Read!) chemistry. He looked clever and handsome and a great deal better that he had looked waiting for the bathroom. Pink rather than putty coloured. Marianne thought again how attractive he was. So confident, so funny, so clever. Somehow he seemed to fit in this elegant house: he looked relaxed, as if he belonged. As he filled her beaker to the brim, Marianne thought he was the perfect dream of a boyfriend and as she did not have one of those yet (obviously the boy at the bus stop was a non-starter) she decided to ask him out. Before anyone else did and once she had got the beaker of wine inside her, of course.

She said, 'Is this your house?'

And he said, 'No, I live at number 14.' And then he asked where she lived and she told him vaguely, but not specifically. 'A couple of miles away.' He seemed happy enough with that. 'It's walkable,' she added. 'Or you can get the bus.'

Then she said, 'Will you give me your phone number?'

If he was surprised he did not show it. That was sophistication for you. He nodded and said, 'If you'll give me yours.' To which she had to say that she did not have one, not having a telephone installed at home *yet*. She said *yet* more out of hope than belief. In her house they were a long way off such a luxury.

'Playing hard to get, huh?'

She let him think so.

He put his finger into one of the crocheted spaces of her dress, quite near to her tummy button. She laughed. He said, 'And where do you go to school?' To which she said, 'Oh no, I go out to work.'

His finger stopped for a moment and he looked up at her. He seemed very surprised. 'Work?' he said.

'Yes,' she said firmly, because she was quite proud of getting a job somewhere so prestigious. 'I work in Brightley's of Bond Street. Cosmetics.'

'Nice dress,' he said. 'Sexy.' And he resumed his attack on it.

She knew that it was a nice dress. She had saved for it and it was from Brightley's and it cost about two weeks' wages. It was a stretchy, white, crocheted copy of a Mary Quant and beneath it she wore a skin-coloured leotard, which was very daring. So she felt good about herself in that department at least. Something had already told her that it was sexy – well obviously – because it looked as if she was naked beneath the open crocheted work, but as yet she was unsure what being sexy was all about. If you had to feel sexy before you could look sexy then she had not achieved the state of sexiness. However, she could be wrong. Rise Above. Anyway, it was nice that he thought so. That was the point, after all. It was not to do with how she felt in the dress. It was to do with how any He that came along felt when he saw her in it. And this one approved. Good. He looked, she thought, exactly like George Harrison.

'Are you asking me out?' he asked. There was a very slight edge of disapproval.

'Yes,' she said. She began to wonder if it was a very bad thing to do but – Oh well – it was too late now. She had done it.

Suddenly he pinched her quite hard through the leotard fabric and she squealed with the pain. 'Did you like that?' he said. He looked dangerous and definitely like George Harrison. She nodded. She hadn't liked it all but it was interesting and unusual and very different from those endlessly boring wandering hands. And she'd have said yes to anything because she felt so elated by this new world set out before her. She really wanted a boyfriend very badly. Without one you were a bit of a failure, really.

'Usually,' he said, 'it's the boy who asks the girl out.'

'Not in Spencer Park,' she said, with spirit, abandoning the notion of keeping her address vague.

'So you come from there,' he said, as if she had mentioned a zoo. 'From the other side of the tracks?'

There was a railway, certainly. Her geography was uncertain but it could well be the other side. Best keep quiet.

So she just smiled and shrugged and drank her red wine (pleased that she had asked him before she was too drunk to get her tongue around the words) while he wrote out his telephone number on the back of a cigarette packet. She felt no embarrassment because in those days, as with big indulgent bathrooms and the words loo and lavatory, and the follies of boys at bus stops, Marianne Flowers did not know the rules. After she became Charles Legg's girlfriend, and later his wife, she soon learned.

HOUSE NUMBER ONE

80a Dragon Street, London

On their wedding day, in early October, the sun was shining and the air was warm as they emerged from their damp, dark flat beneath the pavements of the eminent central London borough. Once upon a time their subterranean accommodation provided the kitchen quarters, the Downstairs to the Upstairs, of the Gentleman's residence so grandly porticoed above them. Now, fifty years on, the basement from which they emerged was damaged space; the range ripped out, the butler's pantry torn down, the flagged floors dull and begrimed from years of neglect. Only two of its three big rooms were habitable. The third, at the back, where the light-well let in its miserly light, was without electricity and grew greens and yellows of some strange, soft substance on its walls. They never ventured in there. The other two rooms made up a kitchen, dark as death her mother used to say when she visited, and a bedsitting room which looked up to the front railings and never saw the sun. Charles said it was fine. Charles said it was cheap. Charles said it was central. Marianne followed his reasoning and so they moved in.

At the far end of the flat, next to the unused room, there was a bathroom – of sorts – containing a stained enamel bath and a geyser of ancient lineage which farted like a heedless old man. Marianne hated that geyser, hated that bathroom. Never felt clean. Charles laughed at her distress. Baths were not for luxuriating, after all; baths were for hopping into and out of before a quick rub-down with a towel. Silly creature that she was. If she had known the word *sensual* she would have told herself that it was what she was, and he wasn't . . . But she didn't so she couldn't and that was that.

Well – even on your wedding day – you certainly hopped in and out of this bath. Horrible, horrible place. Worst bit of the whole flat if you didn't count the no-go back room. The bathroom walls were cream-coloured and thick and scabrous with the paint sloppings of countless careless tenants and the floor was covered with cracked brown lino. Just as it had always been at home, taking a bath was a necessity and never a pleasure. Perhaps it was her destiny to have a horrible bathroom? When she lived at home she bathed once a week in two inches of lukewarm water, in a green copper-stained bath, rough to the skin from too many years of hard scrubbing. The idea of luxuriating (like the advertisements for Camay and Lux soap said) was quite out of the question. It seemed unlikely that she would have been allowed to luxuriate in all her growing-up years even if they had owned a lovely bathroom. Being clean was a respectable pursuit and not a subject for pleasure.

When – if – Marianne ever complained of the cold her mother inevitably told her to Rise Above. Which was not hard to do. You got into two inches of lukewarm water, and you bloody quickly rose above out of it again. A wartime bomb had displaced the bathroom window and her mother was not fussed about getting it mended so Marianne's one abiding memory of childhood baths was the feeling of cold. It was a great disappointment to Marianne when she and Charles came to see this basement flat and she opened the greasy door to the bathroom. The only consolation here was that it could not be draughty, horrible as it was, because it had no window. She had still to make up her mind which was worse. So she got on with it, made the best of it, hopping in and hopping out, just as she had always done at home. And while in the process of hopping she dreamed of a beautiful, clean, sweet-smelling bathroom in which she could idle her time in scented peacefulness. One day, one day . . . Maybe, she suggested to herself as she gave her unrelaxed body a quick rub-down, maybe getting married would change it all.

One day a month or so before their wedding and mindful of the occasion to come, Marianne picked up a pair of multi-coloured checked curtains from the junk shop at the end of the street. They were newish and pretty in pale green and pale blue and pale orange and she thought they were lovely. The man in the shop, who was entirely yellow from nicotine and – as he said – past caring very much, sold her the curtains very cheaply. Buoyed up by the bargain (and doing something entirely on her own initiative) she had an idea. She called into a paint shop on the way home and came out smiling, smiling, smiling.

When she finally got back to the horrible flat she sewed curtain rings on to the curtains and strung them up along a piece of washing-line wire. That shut out the horrible dark well at the back of the flat. Then she hid a carrier bag in the dark back room, and waited for Charles to come home, eat his meal (bits-and-pieces risotto, her grim speciality) and go out to his evening class (which he referred to as his further degree and which she could never remember not to call his evening class). He did not object to the curtains as they were very cheap and needed. 'Well done,' he said. And she thought, with plea-sure, you wait until later. Home decor had never been part of her life, but she saw no reason for it not to be.

Once Charles left she placed their three rickety wooden kitchen chairs on to newspaper and took three small pots of gloss paint from the carrier bag, and a brush. She then began to paint. And smiled some more. She was homemaking. Each chair would be a different colour to match the curtains. True, by the end of the evening the chairs and their paintwork looked a bit gloopy (for the first time she realized that paint did not necessarily have to be old to look lumpy and rippled) but they would have to do. She had been over them twice and she could do no more. It took such an age to dry, paint, that she had painted over the first coat when it was still wet in each case. The man in the shop had told her to be sure to put on two good coats. Oh well.

She left them to dry and went to scrub off as much of the paint from her hands as she could. Then she went to bed, having set the chairs around the table. Charles would be impressed.

Charles was not impressed. Or rather, Charles, who drank very little alcohol nowadays, on coming home having finished a rather good tutorial and therefore having indulged himself in a rather necessary pint or two with his tutor, was aware of a slight nausea. He therefore entered the kitchen for a glass of water and, not wishing to wake Marianne, he did not turn on the kitchen light (the hall light was always on, day and night, which gave enough illumination to find the tap and a mug). He then sat down at the table to drink the water. In one of the kitchen chairs. The pale green one.

Some minutes later Marianne was woken by a horrific roar – in her dreams and before she surfaced she wondered if it was a jungle ele-phant in pain – which turned out to be a cry of rage from her soon to be husband. When she ran into the kitchen she found him standing – mesmerized – at the sight of a chair that was partly pale green and

15

partly – mostly in the seat area – of original wood. His best Levis were, she could see as he bent over and tried to look at his bottom, covered in pale, smudged green. She said – thoughtlessly – 'Oh my lovely chairs . . .' Charles said, 'Oh my fucking Levis . . .' Marianne then began to laugh. Charles did not. It was the first time Marianne had a sense of foreboding about her forthcoming marriage. She instantly dismissed it. Charles had a black look about his forehead. Charles was angry.

'You've got to see the funny side,' she said.

Charles did not think so.

She made a cup of tea, panacea of all ills, and he drank it, cold-eyed, still standing, still wearing the jeans.

'Never,' he said, 'ever do anything like that again, Marianne. Leave the do-it-yourself stuff to me. You are not capable.'

'Sorry,' she said. She was rubbing hopelessly at his Levi back pocket which had taken the brunt of the paint but it was no good. Really all she was doing was moving the mess around.

For years and years afterwards it was these Levi jeans that Charles wore for his do-it-yourselfing. A reminder, for years and years, of Marianne's inadequacies in that department. And in many others, as she would come to learn.

When they moved from Dragon Street the gloopy chairs were flung on to a skip, where they lay, legs up, their rumpled paintwork another reminder to her – and the world – of her first and only attempt at solo decorating. The experience was a profound one. It was, after all, men's work.

They were the first couple out of all their friends to get married and the only couple, it transpired over the years, to stick to their principled guns and not get married in church. No sumptuous white dress and little bouquet of roses for Marianne. No buttonholes for the family. No pretending you wanted God's blessing or that you had any truck with honouring and obeying anyone. In an ideal world you lived together and had nothing to do with such bourgeois stupidities. So said Charles, and so said Marianne – if a little wistfully. This marriage was not being made for romance; this marriage was being made for very practical tax reasons. One rose above romance. Charles was very firm on the bourgeois concept of marriage, outmoded institution that it was. He had been brought up to think liberally, with liberal parents who embraced the unconventional from the comfort of a good education and a sound bank balance. He also embraced the unconventional. One lived in sin. Only now that they needed to get their foot on the housing market, and save hard, marriage was preferable. You could get a mortgage with a marriage, banks were kind to you with a marriage, and the Inland Revenue positively rained indulgences upon you if you tied the legal knot. On being told all these things, Marianne could see the sense of it.

In the hour or so before they were to be wed, Marianne was so nervous that she was practically queuing with herself to pee. Not her usual way. She usually held on to it for as long as possible when she was in the flat because the alternative, like the bathroom, was so unpleasant. In her dreams a bathroom held both a bath and a lavatory. But not here. Here the lavatory was in the oubliette beneath the street at the front of the flat. Successive tenants had attempted to hold back the wetness of the walls with various do-it-yourself solutions. A single bulb revealed tar-backed paper, waterproof coatings, sealants of every variety. None of which worked. Using the lavatory in this place, like taking a bath, was never a pleasure. And as there was no wash basin in either place the shaving of chins and washing of armpits in the morning rush took place at the kitchen sink. How the serving incumbents of bygone days would have recoiled to see such brutalized activities in their domestic domain.

All in all, the basement in Dragon Street was a filthy hole. But – yes – definitely cheap. And that counted for everything. Saving, saving, saving was the watchword. For the duration of their tenancy they were saving, saving, saving. The cost of the wedding was minimal. 'Who needs fancy trappings?' Charles said. And she agreed. Though it did feel – when they made a shopping list the previous Saturday and ticked off onions, potatoes, carrots, cauliflower, bananas, wedding ring, two pounds of mince, six rashers of bacon, eggs, bread, toothpaste, tea, coffee, butter, half a pound of cheddar, Branston pickle, digestive biscuits, tin of tomatoes, spaghetti, and a few other things she could recite in her sleep – that it would have been nice to have gone out specially to make the purchase. 'What was a wedding ring?' he said. 'Tribal, really, Marianne.' Well, quite.

Now, on this bright October day, like a pair of gaudily dressed mushrooms, they emerged. White-faced and pale-skinned and blinking in the brightness, as if they had been away from the sun's radiance too long. She wore a long dress in purple velvet with a ruffle round the hem (not new) and trimmed with gold braid (which was) and he wore a pair of tight, lilac-and-white-striped Loons. There was a green silk scarf knotted at his throat, his hair curled over his high collar, and on his feet he wore red Chelsea boots. Her hair was long and fell on either side of her face like a pair of perfect curtains. She had borrowed a gold necklace, and she clutched a tiny bouquet of white freesias. She tucked a couple of the flowers into her hair and remembered the night she and Charles met. Somewhere she had kept one of the camellias, pressed between the pages of a book, but she could not remember which book. Such sentiment, apparently, gave away her class, according to Charles. Marianne did not yet know enough to say that it gave away no such thing, that it was a method of token-keeping that lovers had used since the Greeks and before, that it was a symbol of love and that love had no class structure. She knew nothing of this and duly accepted the statement as a bit of a rebuff. He smiled as he said it, though.

The two of them looked the part as they walked to the register office, which was the poshest and most famous in London, which for some reason pleased Charles. He was not usually given to condoning snobbery of any kind but it was true that Elizabeth Taylor and Richard Burton had only recently been married there (for the three hundredth time it seemed), so that did make a difference she supposed. Neither of them felt as nonchalant as they said they felt about this marriage thing but Charles was better at dismissing it than she was. Marianne was still struggling a little with dreams. On the other hand, practical or not, a dream or not, it was still marriage and a legal contract that bound them to each other and it was therefore an immensely grown-up, major step. No turning back now. The prize would be their own house. Eventually. The saving had gone very well. She managed to stick to the housekeeping budget that Charles set for her and it was agreed that any birthday or Christmas money was not for the pot but for their own personal use. It made buying new things just about the best treat in the world. Occasionally the urge to buy something nice became too much, house or no house to save for, and sometimes Marianne would crave a skirt or a pair of shoes so badly that she would buy them and then fib and say that a purchase had cost a certain amount when it actually cost a great deal more. Somehow she always managed to make up the difference. It was, she knew from women's magazines, a little deceit that wives –

and presumably girls who lived in sin – were good at. Living in sin struck Marianne as rather disappointing. She imagined – well – something wicked and secret and full of colour and smells but it didn't seem to be any different from the way properly married wives lived. If anything she and Charles had mince more often than properly married wives cooked it.

And that was what she was about two hours later when they emerged from the register office. A wife. The friends and family who came back to the basement enjoyed cheap wine and French bread and cheese. Simple fare. And cool. It was no good Auntie Min asking for a nice sweet sherry or a bit of fruitcake. Or looking askance when the tea she requested instead of the cheap wine came in a blue-striped mug. This was the new world: youth ruled. Cups and saucers were things of the past. Marianne's mother had provided a turkey which sat in its ripped and shredded carcass state because it was bourgeois to carve it. Auntie Min looked at it and blenched and declined to have a nice little slice after all. Marianne's mother was deeply offended and said she'd have brought a carver if she'd been asked and took the bones away to make soup.

They had saved very hard. And their reward was to enter the ranks of what they once regarded as filthy capitalism. They had been offered, and had accepted, a *mortgage*. This was being properly married indeed. The days of political protest and Property is Theft were over for them. Now Property was (or would be) their unassailable home. No longer would they call people with private incomes Running Dogs of Capitalism (which Marianne always liked the poetical sound of and the dramatic picture it conjured). In future – instead of voting Communist – they would vote Labour. Though Marianne had not, yet, quite had the opportunity to vote for anything, being just twenty-one. But Labour it would now be when she did. An honourable shift and a sign of maturity.

The house was chosen, the sale was going through nicely, and after the marriage ceremony they could spare the time to go to Cornwall on a little honeymoon break which her very nice parents-in-law paid for. Indeed, Marianne's mother-in-law, Jean, whose persona seemed to be somewhere between Gracie Allen and Lucille Ball but who – Marianne was beginning to realize – was no comic fool, insisted on their honeymooning. She did not always approve of the way her son was all work and no play and quite often told Marianne to stick up for her rights. 'A honeymoon is absolutely essential,' said Jean, and Bernard, Marianne's new father-in-law (who was nothing like either George Burns or Desi Arnaz) agreed. So Cornwall was paid for and they went.

They did play a bit. Some of it was quite surprising to Marianne. In the hotel bedroom Charles produced a pair of quite alarming-looking handcuffs – real handcuffs apparently – which he wanted Marianne to wear. Truth was, as he moved her body this way and that on the bed and slapped her here and there and got thoroughly excited by it all, she had to concentrate to keep her hands in the cuffs because they were really too large. When he asked her if she was frightened of him she said that she was, very frightened, and prayed he wouldn't realize about the unsatisfactory nature of her fastenings. It would be all too easy to slip out of them and prove it all to be a charade. Later she would come to know that this activity between them was known as Bondage and – even later – she would come to think of this particular incident with the over-large fastenings that appeared to be insurmountable but which she could slip out of at any time as a metaphor.

Charles said that she should write all the postcards because she was good at that sort of thing. He sounded slightly surprised to acknowledge it but Marianne didn't mind. She *was* good at that sort of thing, she enjoyed it, there was something about putting words down on the page that allowed you to think and organize what you wanted to say to its best advantage. People always said they liked getting letters from her, which was one of the rare compliments she was paid and which she therefore decided meant very little because she did not find writing things down difficult at all. She made up a poem for each of the cards. The one to her mother said:

> Marianne is on the Beach
> Charles is in the Water
> Both are having a jolly time,
> With love, your new-wed daughter.

Back they came, delighted with themselves. They might be Mr and Mrs Legg but Charles said that he hoped she didn't want to change her surname because that was unnecessary and patriarchal and she should remain Marianne Flowers. When Marianne asked her mother-in-law the exact meaning of patriarchal in that context, it occurred

20

to her that Legg and Flowers were each as good a surname as the other since the former was Charles' name and the latter was her father's. If anything the Flowers was the more patriarchal of the two. Jean laughed and said she was quite right and why on earth Marianne never went to college beat her. Which made Marianne feel strangely warm inside because – well – no one ever had suggested it before. The feeling of warmth was about as far as she could go with the suggestion, however, as they now had a *mortgage* to pay and her salary was required.

When she asked her mother if she liked her postcard, her mother said it was a nice picture. Oh, thought Marianne, and the warm feeling about college died away a little. Probably her mother was used to Marianne's playing about with words.

Number 23 Eastbourne Road, the chosen house, was on the fringes of Putney and a very acceptable, if dull, address. With a sweet little bathroom and lavatory combined which needed decorating in a more modern style – but Marianne always remembered entering it and breathing deep and enjoying the brand new smell of cleanness. It had white-painted walls and net curtains. Well, she would change that. She would put up wallpaper for warmth, and a window blind with pink swirls, and she would make that bathroom, once it was theirs, a little palace. She was quite content with the white bathroom suite, though her mother thought it a shame it wasn't coloured.

Charles was rather sorry that they could not go on living in the heart of London. Or The King's Road. They had become used to being at the centre of things with a postal district that was the same as the Queen's, but as Jean pointed out to her son, very crisply, they had lived like struggling fungi for far too long and it was time to come out into the sun. 'You can always get the train up to town,' she pointed out. 'And quality of life is important Charles, for both of you.' He opened his mouth, Marianne guessed to say, 'Oh, Marianne didn't mind a bit of damp,' but seemed to think better of it.

Later Jean said to Marianne that Charles had conflicts in his nature (they were sipping sherry in the kitchen, just the two of them, and Jean was being remarkably chatty – presumably this is what you did when you had a daughter-in-law proper) which meant that, despite his socialistic urges, he actually put up with the nasty basement place because the address made everyone sit up and take notice, it being so central and fine-sounding and near Buck House. But it was only impressive until they visited them, said Jean with a knowing wink. After that the visitors would scuttle back to their nice semis in places like Twickenham and heave a sigh of relief for decent plumbing and a bit of garden. 'The point is,' she told her new daughter-in-law, 'that the kind of people who owned that big old London house originally had places in the country to go to. But for God's sake don't point that out to my son or he'll begin saving up for one of those as well. He's an aristocrat *manqué* at heart.' Marianne asked what *manqué* meant. Jean said it meant wanting something you didn't have the where-withal – spiritual or physical – to achieve. Marianne laughed and said she was pretty *manquée* in every department, then, at which Jean grew serious and told her not to believe in such nonsense and that she was a great deal brighter than she knew.

Jean's view of life was the opposite of Marianne's own family's. There the work ethic was vital, oppressive running dogs of capitalism or no oppressive running dogs of capitalism, and you were grateful to be employed, with the rent paid. Jean, on the other hand, whose deceased father was a liberal judge, said that life was too short and youth was for living. She and Charles's father Bernard were separated in the early days of their marriage, within a week of the ceremony, by the war, and she said it gave her a very clear view of priorities. 'When Bernard came back and before Beryl came along' – Beryl being Charles's older sister – 'we had the best year of our lives. We had fun. And so should you two.' Then she patted Marianne's cheek and looked at her as fondly as anyone had ever looked at her (including Charles, oddly enough) and told her that she was a good girl. Too good, actually, she added. Later she gave Marianne a book by Simone de Beauvoir, called *The Second Sex* which Marianne read but which she felt did not apply to her, she being neither old, nor intellectual, nor French. Besides she was too busy with the moving plan (Charles's moving plan, a countdown chart on the wall) and thinking about wallpapers and pink blinds and sweet smells – and saying goodbye to horrible, scabrous bathroom walls.

Charles had completed his degree and he had a proper job now. He worked for a government organization called the Building Research Unit and as far as Marianne could make out what he didn't know about pre-stressed concrete and extruded aluminium could be written on the back of a sixpenny piece. As he pointed out, it was a good starting salary, thanks to his degree, and that was the reason they could get a mortgage. Obviously selling cosmetics for a low wage scarcely impressed the mortgage-lender, who happened to be the local council and therefore even more inclined towards disapproval, which Marianne understood all too well. As a job it didn't impress her very much either – but it hardly mattered because one day she would have babies and then what her job was now would be irrelevant. She would be a full-time mother and she was looking forward to it so it was just as well that one of them was a success. Her mother, though not one to approve very much of men, agreed that Marianne had married well.

Charles was now, as Marianne told anyone who asked, a research scientist. The term research scientist covered a very broad church and she was seldom asked exactly what he did, which was just as well. All she knew was that he was sure of a job for life if he wanted it, that he would have to do some travelling for site visits and suchlike, and that his salary, on appointment, was twice what Marianne earned and within six months he had been given a rise. Certainly she had married well. Future assured.

A house of their own. How much they had given up for it. How many of their friends looked on with envy, criticism and amusement, as they saved their pennies and lived so much of their youth in apparently dull and cautious lives. What Charles meant by 'living at the centre of things' meaning the Dragon Street basement, had Marianne wondering. After all, what was the point of living in the centre of London if your only social outing was for half a bitter at the local and the occasional – very – trip to see a film or a play? Unless one of their friends took them to a restaurant they never went near such places – and the centre of London was full of them – all looking really inviting and exciting and exotic with steamed-up windows and dishes like spaghetti Bolognese and sole Normandy written on the windows. Marianne craved such places but she knew better than to suggest eating in one. Sadly, and it did make her feel sad, they were here only to look. Charles might wave his arms around and say that they could walk back home from Soho easily – but really, what was the point of going to Soho if you only got there, turned around, and walked home again, pausing, if allowed, to look at some of the wilder seductions on offer; Charles did not really like her peering into the windows of the sleazy shops but given the chance she always did and it always made her laugh. They sold the proper kind of

HOUSE NUMBER TWO

23 Eastbourne Road

Nicely presented three-bedroomed property on the fringes of Putney close to the main railway station, in a quiet tree-lined cul-de-sac. Small kitchen, newly decorated, with cupboards and stainless-steel sink unit leading to a dining room of good proportions with door to garden. Front sitting room with stripped-pine floor and open fire. Small garden, about three feet deep, mostly paved, to the front, containing a mature laburnum tree and shrubs. Back garden mostly laid to lawn surrounded by borders. Area at back measuring thirty feet by eighteen to kitchen and dining-room windows. Brick under a weatherboarded upper elevation and hipped pantile roof. The interior is in good decorative order throughout but is in need of updating. The house would benefit from the installation of central heating. Otherwise it is in very sound condition and early offers are recommended. Starples and Co., sole agents.

The new house came with fitted floral Wilton carpets to the hallway, sitting room and stairs – classy but old-fashioned and quite unlike the cheap, brownish flower-patterned runners of her childhood. Charles put newspaper down at every opportunity to save them from being worn out. They had paid the vendors extra for them, within something called fixtures and fittings, and even though they did not want them they had to pay up or the sale would not have gone through. Odd, she thought, to cover them up when carpets were made to be walked on. Even odder as they did not like them very much (floral not being the modern, Habitat way). When she commented on this, quite light-heartedly, her new husband merely snorted (he had taken to snorting rather a lot recently, as if he had become a different, more serious-minded person) and he went on covering them up with the *Observer*. 'I don't trust any of our friends,' he said, 'because they are still renting and doing things like using the banisters to prop open windows and peeing in the sink. They don't understand about ownership. They'd probably stub their fags out on them, spill beer, vomit even, and those carpets represent a substantial part of our investment.' When it was put that way she was bound to agree, the word investment holding deep and unfathomable meaning.

Eventually Charles stopped putting the *Observer* down largely because he ran out of excuses for their increasingly sceptical visitors. It was a relief all round. Initially their friends were somewhat perplexed, rapidly turning into offended, at there always being newspapers on the floor when they came to visit. Though Charles was inventive in his excuses – the sweep called that day; the French windows leaked; been walking in the woods and got mud on our boots (to which Ginger, who graduated with a chemistry degree and was now doing mysterious things with something called PVC said, 'Oh, sod off, there *are* no woods round here . . . ') – he had to give in.

Marianne's mother, who had never had proper fitted carpets in her life, thought they were lovely. Which just about summed them up, really. Lovely in a way that was entirely reactive to the bleak 1950s and had no, absolutely no, interest in the post-Conran metamorphosis. Charles not only cared for them, he decided – after seeing *Don't Look Now* – that they needed to be christened. Marianne was perplexed until he showed her what he meant. She kept looking at that particular place on the carpet for days afterwards and blushing. Charles was *so* advanced and free. She had a rubbed bit on her bottom that Willa said was Carpet Burns. Willa seemed to know all about that kind of thing. She, Marianne, must follow suit, she must, but it was hard to get enthusiastic about such a noisy, wet, unrewarding, *grunting* business.

Sex was very tedious in Marianne's opinion though, like most of her opinions, she kept it to herself. Whereas Charles never seemed to tire of the idea and the action, though to spice it up a bit (and if she thought about it at all, which she seldom did, she could see his point – it did need a bit of oomph since the handcuff game was becoming jaded), he suggested that they bought a magazine called *Forum*. It had vaguely rude and very badly drawn pictures of couples on the front which she decided to take very seriously. *They* certainly looked serious about it so she must too. As far as Marianne was concerned, it was serious. It was, after all, what you did in order to be living in that heady old thing called *sin* – and apparently it was what, if you *didn't* do it, you could use to get out of being married. So it was very important. She needed to get better at it, concentrate, and it was no laughing matter. (Though the pictures did sometimes make her want to giggle. The couples in them looked more like athletes concentrating very hard on a particular movement than lost in pleasure – which is what you were supposed to be. Or at least, Charles was. One of them had to be, and of the two in a marriage, if only one was going to get lost in pleasure, it ought to be the man.)

The problem with the magazine was that Charles either placed it on the pillow to follow instructions, or on some as yet unneeded part of her recumbent body, or he held it in one hand and read it while twiddling at bits of her with the other. They *both* took it all quite as seriously as the couples in the illustrations. It seemed to her that it was exactly like the way her husband did his cooking (which was not often and greatly admired on completion), propping up the recipe book and peering at it intently at each new stage. She could never follow recipes. Rather as she approached cookery so did she approach sex: just get it done with the best and most economical ingredients as possible – and wash up afterwards. If such things went through her mind at the critical time, she was wise enough not to say so. At least, now, she had a beautiful clean bathroom to disappear into when it was all over.

Sex was part of life, of course, and every woman's right, apparently, according to a new set of magazines, some of which had articles like 'How to get an orgasm without a man' on the front cover: Marianne, who did not buy such publications, thought she must have misread the cover tag on that one: 'Ten in a bed – group sex in the Netherlands' was another one. And – oddest of all – 'Food for the bedroom', which actually had a picture of a naked woman covered in bananas and cream. But instead of feeling she had a right to lie down with fruit salad all over her and take it seriously, it only made it seem an even funnier and alien old urge. Sex was never mentioned at home when she was growing up, of course. When her first period arrived and she was mystified at the blood, a book suddenly appeared at the end of the bed called *How a Baby Is Born*, which she flicked through, could make neither head nor tail of (almost, you could say, literally, given the diagrams) and abandoned. Her friend Willa, at school, told her that it would happen to her every month 'from now on until you die' – which seemed worrying. She nodded, thoughtfully, and put on an expression of grave acceptance. At least every one of her classmates was or would be in the same boat. It took some time for her developing body to be noticed by her mother but when, finally, the middle button of her school blouse flew off, right into the face of Mr Pardoe, the music teacher, her mother went out and bought her a cotton brassière and one for spare. Willa, who came from a classier family (her father worked in a bank) than Marianne, had four of the things, which seemed a wonder. 'You can have one if you like,' said Willa kindly, but they were too small. Pity, because they had lace all over them. Years later, when she met Charles and wanted to wear lacy, silky underwear, he said it was not the kind of thing he liked at all. It went with his dismissal of cosmetics as an unnecessary frilly cluttering of life.

'Marianne – I don't like you wearing too much make-up.'

'But it's my job,' she said, rather forlornly. After all, making up her face was something she was also supposed to be good at.

Shortly after their marriage, they were sitting around the table at Charles's parents' house when he said, yet again, that he wanted his wife 'to shake off the feminine chains of the past when such things as face-painting and frills represented the constricting bourgeois view of women as men's chattels'.

'Oh, shut up, Charles,' said his mother.

Bernard said, in gentle warning, 'Jean . . .'

Sometimes Marianne's mother-in-law got what she called the bit between her teeth – and she had it there now. She leaned over and half playfully, half threateningly, tapped her son's hand in admonishment. 'Stop telling Marianne what to do and let her choose for herself.'

Charles's big sister Beryl, finally home from university where she had just completed something mysterious called Post-Grad. and who was also sitting at the family tea table, looked at Marianne as if she thought the possibility of her choosing anything wisely was nil. Marianne was always humbled by Beryl, whom Charles revered.

'Oh, I don't mind,' said Marianne.

'Well, you should, dear,' said her mother-in-law. 'One day I hope that you will.'

Marianne, who always felt a bit more lively after one of her mother-in-law's bit-biting sessions, took another piece of bread and butter and considered pointing out to Charles that she thought the black satin corset with the *superstrong laces for a real snug fit* that he had bought her recently possibly came into the category of constrictingly bourgeois, but good sense told her it was not the sort of thing you drew attention to over tea and fruitcake at your very new husband's parents' table.

Even once she was married, Marianne was aware that she did not know much, but at least Charles was very advanced. This was one of the reasons you had a boyfriend. And why you did that grown-up thing of living together before you were married. It was so you could have sex and get good at it. Do what married couples did. Then, when you had passed with flying colours, you got married yourself. Her mother had been furious with this approach at first, but quickly saw that it was the modern way. She was a pragmatic woman and instead of screaming the street down, she quietly went out to the Co-op and bought them their first double blanket. 'At least I won't have to do your washing any more,' she said with a somewhat tight smile.

Marianne was already on The Pill which was absolutely essential for a girl. Even if you didn't have a boyfriend you took it, just in case you got one.

Everything, Marianne felt with a bit of a heavy heart, seemed to centre around the sudden freedom to have sex but in all the best stories that she read the best girls had the best time of it when they didn't give in. Like Jane Eyre and Jo March. (By now Marianne was reading such books.) They also got bunches of flowers and nice meals out, which Marianne thought would make the whole thing much more fun. But no. Not now.

After the gift of the blanket came some of her mother's old sheets from the back of the cupboard and then Charles's parents donated a double bed which was taken to the basement flat in bits and put up by Bernard and Charles after much debate and mysterious masculine grunting (not unlike sex grunts, actually). Marianne's parents-in-law lived in a big, dusty house (a few doors down from the house in which she first met Charles) which was full of odd bits of furniture in its attic rooms – good quality but a bit bashed about – and they could part with a double bed without even missing it. It was sprung, as opposed to mattressed, and the springs squeaked. The castors were wobbly which made even more noise. And the headboard rattled. But it was big, it was private, it was free – and it was theirs. When they moved it came with them to their bedroom in the new house despite Marianne's yearning for something new and clean and silent (a Dreamworld Divan with underbed storage was what she really wanted) because it was perfectly – as Charles said – adequate.

Not a lot of their sinning actually went on in this bed. Most of their sinning went on all around it: tied to the back of the bedroom door, flung back over a settee downstairs, up against the sink unit in the kitchen. Marianne longed to lie on the squeaking, noisy, rattling sprung thing (without wearing handcuffs) and do the sinning, but it seldom happened. Charles preferred foreign films which also involved quite a lot of being flung over old desks and suchlike or what Willa called 'up against a wall' stuff – and everyone just seemed to walk away afterwards, quite often leaving the girl or the boy crying or the man getting killed.

After *Closely Observed Trains*, in which both more or less happened, Marianne came out of the cinema in tears and not only sorry for Milos who never got the girl yet died a hero, but sorry for everyone,

33

even the lecherous old man with the rubber stamp – because his life seemed so horrible and obsessed. Charles put his arm round her and told her she was a silly thing. Marianne hoped to God he wouldn't take up the film's idea of using a rubber stamp on her nether regions and nodded meekly when he told her he thought the film was very funny and true. Marianne longed to ask him if it was true then, as shown in the film, that boys saw sex in every single object all around them, but she decided – from her own experience with Charles – that it probably was. Which explained everything. With that kind of inner eye he was streets ahead of her. Charles's interest in, and his practice of, sex blossomed. If *Forum* magazine had been an exam paper he would have got top marks. She followed along clinging (sometimes quite literally) to his shirt tails. Years later, looking back, she would laugh about it and think that she could have been an actress winning an Oscar. But for now it was all like a fog to her – this Oh so important thing – this Sex word that seemed to represent so much – liberation, youthful pleasure, fun – she didn't feel any of those things. Well, not yet anyway. It just seemed to make people do odd things, like Charles and his peculiar preferences. As if enlivened (or perhaps emboldened) by the maturity of home-ownership, he had recently taken to smacking her on various parts of her anatomy – mostly her bottom – with a hairbrush, which she found about as exciting as ironing sheets, but which he seemed to find quite stimulating, urging her to beg for mercy which she obligingly did, her mind roving free over such things as whether they had any butter left and would the mend in her turquoise Quant tights be too noticeable for work and feeling deeply ashamed of herself for being so dim.

Now, the hairbrush laid aside, he had started whispering in her ear, late at night, about very young girls – like her niece, who was thirteen – which she found mildly repellent but which she assumed came under the banner of 'anything between two consenting adults in the bedroom is all right'. It was what *Forum* magazine and other pundits on the Joys of Sex called 'fantasy time'. Fantasy time seemed largely to be made up of Grin and Bear it time, which she did. Fantasy time for her was being cuddled and kissed very gently. She managed to sink into this image occasionally, particularly during the fantasy time in which she was required to shave herself *down there*. That wasn't so bad, but the growing it all back was murder. She supposed all this went under the other banner of 'keeping your man

34

happy' which was vaguely disquieting as a premise – but only vaguely. From shaving *down there* she developed the most terrible itch and often had to excuse herself at work to lock herself away in the Ladies for a really good scratch. So driven was she eventually by the discomfort that she rebelled.

'I'd rather not shave myself again,' she said after one particularly difficult, warm day at work. 'If that's all right by you. I've been scratching all day.'

He winced.

Firstly you did not discuss bedroom activities out of bedroom activity time. And secondly, since she had, he was quite unsympathetic, saying that, after all, *he* had to shave *every morning*. She took this to heart and bought him an electric razor for his birthday, the first birthday to be celebrated in the new house, and he was terribly touched. He remarked on how thoughtful she was in which compliment she took great delight, so rarely did she seem to live up to his expectations.

Marianne then prayed that he wouldn't suggest that she used the razor, too, but obviously that was a step too far and eventually the bald pubes fantasy faded away. Well, that was a relief. She might have told Jean about it, signalling it as a little victory in standing up for herself, which her mother-in-law would like, but yet again it really did not seem quite the done thing to talk about explicit sexual fantasies to a mother about her son. Especially not those ones. Boys and men, Marianne was beginning to realize, were extremely different. They had needs, as her mother once said when they were discussing Uncle Ray's annoying finger-pinching interest in her mother's bottom, and those needs, it was quite clear, were best sated. As her mother implied, once they were sated you could get on with the rest of life.

For Marianne the single great attraction to sex was that it was the way you had babies. Apart from that she couldn't get the hang of why it was so important. Here she was, just out of her teens and it was all a mystery to her. So much was written about it, so many jokes made about it, so much interest shown in it and so much disapproval attached to it – and yet the process was really very odd. Dull. Very dull indeed. She got more excitement in the Big Wheel or a high swing-boat. Babies made sense of its existence, though. She was glad that something did. In the meantime, as a respectable married couple, they carried on having sex in Charles's increasingly bizarre choice of location. Wrapped round the banisters during the day – or up stepladders, under the table, over the sink. And sometimes wrapped around the plum tree in the garden at night. The only place Marianne avoided was the new sweet-smelling bathroom. Once Charles had suggested that the bath would be exciting, all that water and soap and stuff, and Marianne obliged – but afterwards it made her less able to relax in her own little bathtime haven (which is what shutting the door and lying there idly rubbing herself with soap and dreaming of pink paint and pretty wallpaper created) so she said it gave her terrible back ache being up against the taps like that, and they avoided it in future. She learned that wiles counted for something, for when Charles suggested it again some months later, Marianne swiftly went into rearguard action (later she would learn to call this both a physical and metaphorical allusion) and got him up against the spare-room doorway instead.

The new house needed decorating. There was nothing wrong with the decor as it stood: it was just not to their taste. She longed to begin on the dear, clean little bathroom with its neat white suite and airing cupboard. They would keep the old-fashioned lavatory which had ornate iron brackets and a cistern with a long brass chain. Bought from the Portobello they were told proudly by the outgoing owners. It reminded her of the bathroom in Laburnum Grove, where she first met Charles, and that was a good thing. She dreamed of putting rose-pink carpet on the floor (which was tiny so they could afford it) to match the paper she would put on the walls in something big and pink and floral. But before anything of what Charles called a 'cosmetic nature' could happen, he said that all the floors must come up because the place must have central heating.

'What?' she said startled, 'Even in the bathroom?' It was such an *adult* thing to do. Central heating was what middle-aged people smoking pipes (men) and knitting pale-blue jerseys (women) in adverts had installed. It was what all new houses boasted they offered. And it would be such an invasion.

'Of course in the bathroom,' he said, 'In there, more than ever, you want to feel warm.' He squeezed her thigh. She smiled cautiously, hoping he wasn't going to suggest doing it in the bath again after all.

'What a luxury,' she said. And she thought What a very expensive idea, too. Charles might not have said Yes to going to India, he might have refused to buy seats to see Olivier in *Saturday, Sunday, Monday* (which her parents-in-law saw and recommended) but by golly he was straight in there when a new heating system was called for. He announced, proudly, that he would install it himself. With a little help from his father. Which is how they would be able to afford it. 'Ah,' said Marianne. Thinking Oh and remembering the bed and their gruntings. When Jean heard about it she just rolled her eyes and said nothing. Marianne wondered if she felt cross that Bernard hadn't tried to do central heating for her and said so. 'Good grief no,' said Jean. 'I put on another cardigan and thank God for it.'

Now, Marianne liked her father-in-law, Bernard, but he was a somewhat *instinctive* person (which is what her mother-in-law, Jean, called him). Later Marianne would come to realize that *instinctive* was Jean's polite way of saying *bodging* – that he bungled his way through things. Be it driving to a destination a few hundred miles hence and only having the vaguest idea of the direction and not taking a map (this was known as 'Bernard taking the scenic route') or creating a vegetable garden that did not flourish until he found out that you needed to dig in manure (their garden had been used as a tip by the builder who owned it before them) and then scouring the bowels of every horse known to be living in the vicinity until Jean confessed to Marianne that she thought she could taste more of the horse droppings than the vegetables. So Bernard helping Charles with the central heating would be – well – interesting. However, they were men. And men must do what men must do. So Marianne just said Good, because there was nothing else to say, and trusted her husband.

The idea of having central heating, as a delighted Charles told their friends and reminded Marianne, was modern and sophisticated. Very modern. Very sophisticated. And of course it meant sacrifices, but it was an investment for the future. Marianne decided to think about being warm and having babies as the future and smiled. Her mother tutted at the extravagance. Central heating, according to her mother and other members of the true, blue English working, middle and upper classes, was what gave Americans those flat, pale, beige complexions, while everyone knew that coal fires and draughts allowed the beauty of the natural English Rose to shine in all its pink and white prettiness. An even warmth throughout a house (including, perish the thought, the bedroom, where really you were supposed to have fires only if someone was dying) sent the glow of your capillaries (about which Marianne knew from her cosmetic products) into no man's land. Marianne remembered the wind whistling through the gaps in her mother's bathroom and shivered. Willa said that since Marianne was a Pisces, she was a fish, so it made sense for her to be at her happiest when she was wallowing in water. Which explained everything. She also had a fear of smelling unpleasant, since her last years at school when the weekly two-inch bath was simply not enough and she endured the humiliation of the head-mistress taking her aside one day and telling her 'to wash a little more often, dear'.

The promise of an even warmth throughout the house marked a happy beginning to a long successful married life, Marianne decided. To still be waking on winter mornings, as she had as a child, to find that Jack Frost's fingers had made pictures all over the inside of the bedroom windows was definitely down among the dreary past. A married woman, now – and babies to come eventually (though it did not seem to be happening yet) – she needed to break free of her origins. These were the days of liberation. Marianne was considering giving up wearing a bra – something her mother's generation would find deeply worrying – and therefore it followed that Marianne would no longer tolerate a cold bedroom or bathroom as her mother had done. On with the new and a radiator in every room.

Further, she thought firmly, what was being tied up to the banisters by your husband and smacked on the bottom with a hairbrush – or itching down below all night – when he could install central heating for you? It just did not compare. He was looking after her and you could put up with anything if you were warm. She knew how cold the house could be for they moved in December and it was bitter. She remembered waking one night when Charles was away and thinking that one of her feet had dropped off. When she turned on the lamp and inspected it, the toes looked bluish and she was happy to tell Charles about the experience. Presumably installing central heating was a statement of intent, a way of saying that he loved her and would stay with her and that this was their home to which he would remain forever attached once the radiators were installed – and there-fore he would remain attached to her. This was a relief, as his behaviour, occasionally, made her wonder.

It was yet another aspect of her new husband that Marianne felt she could not share with anyone. Not even with Willa. But at least he did not do such things with her. For Charles had . . . quirks. And the only way Marianne managed to deal with these . . . quirks was to disappear into herself, wait for them to pass, and then emerge when it was perfectly all right again. Mostly there was never a trace left.

Charles's quirk was going after other girls. It was confusing. When he did it before they were married, Marianne thought it was because he was trying to make up his mind about settling down. But when he did it after they were married, when he had definitely and in free will committed himself to her, she simply could not fathom it. It shouldn't happen, she knew that. But at the same time she thought it must be to do with a failing of hers. It was never mentioned between them and nobody else ever mentioned it either, so in a way it wasn't real at all. And if he was planning to leave her he surely wouldn't be putting in central heating. Would he?

Nowadays his quirks mostly happened at parties when he would suddenly disappear with a girl – either outside into the night or upstairs into a distant room – emerging sometime later looking ruffled and a bit dishevelled and quite often with the girl in tears and looking decidedly ruffled and dishevelled herself. Marianne was never quite sure what to do about it. Once she saw him embracing a girl called Isobel in an upstairs room and it was almost funny the way he ran his hands up the side of her dress and tried to grab her bust and she – without removing her mouth, which was glued to his – removed his hands, which then went back to the hipline and tried again. To be repeated and repeated. Up and down, up and down, as if they were pretending to be train wheels. Marianne knew how irritating it was from her pre-wifely days when boys just assumed you were there to be groped.

That particular girl, Isobel, who had probably had a bit too much to drink, burst into tears when Marianne appeared and said, 'Charles, have you got the can-opener – Marcus wants to know . . . ', to which Charles said that he had not, at which Marianne felt in his trouser pocket (quite difficult at the best of times given how tight his trousers were, but made more difficult by the fact that Isobel obviously was having an effect on him), at which Isobel drew the line and said so.

'Go away,' she said, yielding Marianne's husband's lips in order to speak.

Marianne gave her an apologetic smile.

'Who is she?' asked Isobel crossly as Marianne fumbled about.

Downstairs she could hear Marcus calling her and chinking bottles and laughing. 'Well?' said Isobel. Charles was silent, looking cool. So Marianne said – quite calmly – 'I'm his wife.' And finding nothing but a handkerchief and the car keys, left the room. Only to hear – and then see – as she pushed past her on the stairs, Isobel pink and wet cheeked and wailing with mortification. Followed by Charles who said he was sorry. To Marianne, obviously. 'It's all right,' she said. He then put his arm around her and led her back into the kitchen where everything was perfectly normal and their friend, the clown, Danny, was standing on the kitchen sink and peeing out of the window. Of Isobel there was no sign. Marcus said that they had taken their time and where was the can-opener and it didn't seem healthy for married couples to disappear at parties. That was strictly the prerogative of the unwed. Marianne made a note of the word prerogative, which struck her as very impressive.

But of course, if she ever let herself think about it, which she did sometimes, it wasn't really all right – he should stop upsetting girls at parties – but she did not, really, know what else to say. He was not just her first husband, he was her first proper boyfriend *ever*, and in all the stuff about free love and liberation and self-discovery there seemed to be a message that this kind of behaviour was what went on. And she had no experience of how her generation of boys and men behaved – or any generation much since she had grown up without a father and her uncles were somewhat distant, fabulous beasts glimpsed only occasionally, and mostly drunk, at weddings and funerals. Charles never got drunk as it gave him a headache. In that respect, anyway, he was a good man. For all she knew, things like the Isobel incident were the way of things. It happened. They never talked about it afterwards. Marcus didn't seem to do it – he stayed glued to girlfriend Ruth's side (he wouldn't dare, Marianne guessed) – nor – come to think of it, did Bernard, but still . . . Rising above such things seemed the best way.

At least Willa was not like that with Charles. Marianne cared about that more than almost anything else. In this strange and difficult world a good friend was wonderfully cheering. Like holding a mirror up to herself and knowing that somebody – apart from her husband and her mother and her mother-in-law (all of whom *had* to like her in a way) – liked her only for herself. Willa just would not hurt her, and she would never hurt Willa. For half a year, before Marianne and Charles moved into the horrible basement at Dragon Street, she and Willa shared a flat and in all that time Charles never left the room with her friend and she never looked flushed and ruffled with him. Which was a relief but not surprising. Willa was alarmingly free-spirited and dangerous, Marianne thought, and very involved with an older man. The older man was twenty-eight and, apart from not having very much hair, he took exciting drugs. Such wildness and excess hardly compared to Charles's quirks and she was right to forget all about them once they were over. Willa, though the same age as her, was planets ahead in experience and she would probably just laugh.

When they were still sharing the flat – which was in Hammersmith – Willa's older man, whom Marianne privately thought of as the Bald Wild One, took some LSD and had to be walked to Southwark and back. It was frightening, slightly, but also fascinating to Marianne. It was no advertisement for the joys of the drug, that was for sure. The Bald Wild One, in his altered state, was just like the fishmonger's father whom Marianne knew from when she was growing up. Unattractively off his trolley. Mumbling and burbling as he walked along. *Just* like the fishmonger's father in fact. When she said so, Willa seemed offended. 'The fishmonger's father?' she said indignantly, 'He's not old and mad. He's just blown his mind.' She said it as if it was quite an accomplishment.

'Well, he looks and sounds *just* like the fishmonger's father,' said Marianne again, a bubble of indignation also arising in her. After all, spending the night walking with a burbling idiot who might be arrested at any point was not, as Willa seemed to think, the height of Swinging style, surely?

It was quite comic to watch but not at all cool, which was the other thing she said to Willa who looked daggers at her as she helped him down the steps at the Embankment. Here there were one or two dossers who looked – and on being wakened certainly sounded – in much the same boat as the Bald Wild One actually, but this time she kept her mouth closed. Willa was her best friend and if she chose to think this kind of behaviour was a turn-on, then Marianne must accept it. But really, thought Marianne, as they steered him, shaking and slavering round a dirty raincoat that snored, it was comical the way he rubbed at his head with his fingers while walking. Rub, rub, rub – babble, babble, babble, he went – all nonsense. It was no wonder he had scarcely any hair left if he did this sort of thing very often.

Privately she thought, since he was so old and so bald, it was amazing and also a little frightening that Willa, who was very pretty and slim and funny and all that (whereas Marianne was only quite pretty, rather plump and very dull comparatively, she knew), found him so attractive. He seemed a touch too dangerous and unconventional to Marianne, which must be the reason Willa liked him. It was one of the reasons Marianne never complained to Charles about his quirks. Best not to rock the boat or she might find herself all unmarried again, out there and single and dating someone really odd like that herself.

Being single was a very alarming option. Most of the time Willa was in despair about this man of hers. He just did not do the things one wanted in a relationship. Yet she clung to him because he was exciting. 'He makes everyone else I meet seem inadequate,' was how Willa, with envious grandeur, put it. On the other hand, thought Marianne involuntarily mimicking her own mother – exciting is as exciting does. At least Charles behaved properly once they were together. OK, he might be a little . . . unpredictable in the sex department but that was clearly the way boys and men were. He remembered her birthday and went everywhere with her and took all the important decisions and he never went off for long stretches of time without saying where he was going or where he had been – and Marianne always felt she was his special one. After an amount of time being boyfriend and girlfriend they went to bed together and then they lived together and then – inevitably – they married. That was what a relationship was. Not suddenly turning up with no hair left to speak of, dribble on your chin, and eyes that looked like someone had just put out the lights.

Oh, Charles. How glad she was to have him. How good he was. And now he was proposing to heat the house centrally and there would even be a radiator in the bathroom – you really couldn't say fairer than that. Willa was still struggling out there in the wilderness of – as she called it – having her heart broken. The Bald Wild One hadn't been seen for weeks again and did not answer his phone at home and had given up his job in the post office, so she said. Presumably this meant the relationship was over. Mariannne wondered what having your heart broken actually meant. Largely it manifested itself in Willa coming round to their new house and smoking and drinking and staying up late to talk endlessly about it. Then came the tears. At which point Charles went to bed. Marianne just did not understand the tears. The Bald Wild One had never promised Willa anything so why get upset when nothing was given? That was logical, wasn't it? However, she kept this thought and the excitement she felt about the central heating to herself. Instinct, like the Rising Above instinct with Charles, told her that it was not the moment. Instinct told her very firmly that, at this precise point in her life, Willa was not terribly likely to become enraptured over Marianne's new heating system. Marianne told them all about it at work, though, and the girls on the cosmetics counter were really impressed. They all wanted husbands like Charles, they said. Marianne preened herself.

The copper piping and radiators and all kinds of mysterious bends and joints were purchased and heaped up in the hall. Charles sometimes knelt before it and ran his hands through the mound as if it were treasure trove. It made life coming in and out of the house pretty hazardous but Marianne bore it. Then the carpets, that floral Wilton they had so carefully protected, had to come up, which was utterly traumatic . . . Charles rolled the carpets as lovingly as he ever rolled her, she thought. He always showed care and attention to something he viewed as valuable. He taped the rolls down and pulled up the nasty-looking track rods (full of spiteful little nails) and stacked those neatly in the front room and then put notices all over the Wilton rolls saying KEEP OFF CARPET. Then he went away to a factory in Wales and she was left with bare boards, piles of strange plumbing requirements and a vague sense of resentment. When she asked him, before he left, if she could help in any way, he just looked at her, raised an eyebrow, and smiled. 'I don't think so,' he said. 'Do you?' She remembered the painted chairs and felt like a naughty schoolgirl. She did not tell him this, he still being keen on pigtails and gymslips as an occasional fantasy.

It was not just the bits and pieces of plumbing stuff he had left around that made her feel resentful. She did not like it when he went away. Being on her own in the house was not good. Sometimes she stayed late in the West End, wandering into one of the gallery parties that always seemed to be happening. Then she would have two or three glasses of wine and either wander home and go straight to sleep, or once or twice she came home several glasses down and with a young man (she never chose bald wild ones) who was anything but ready for sleep. It was less a case of what's sauce for the goose than a case of it not being very important either way. It was something to do, and it was company. Marianne was a little afraid of the dark.

Occasionally she went to bed with them but always in the spare back room and they were gone before morning. One, called Vincent, who had a lovely smile and a long ponytail, said he could make her really happy if she would leave this suburban existence and come away with him. She was astonished. She was happy, she protested. 'Rubbish,' he said, running his finger over her face in a pleasing way. 'If you were happy you wouldn't be doing this with me now . . .'

Best not think about it. Rise (or in this case, float) above. Somewhere in her stomach, as he caressed her, she felt a little tickling sensation, as if a small flame were licking at her, but she ignored it. Instinct told her that was best. But Vincent had disturbed her, touched her in some way, and it made her unhappy.

From then on she mostly came to her senses and if it happened that she came back with someone, she said it was a mistake and bade them goodbye at the door. None of it meant anything and it was confusing to find herself behaving like that. Besides, after six months or so in the house, and once the central heating was done, she would have a baby. Soon she would stop taking the Pill (Charles said she should go back on it until the radiators were up and working) and then she would really have to stop staying out late and making such muddles. On the other hand, if she came straight home and stayed in she got all twitchy. The solution to this was to buy half a bottle of gin, easing the money out of her account and hoping Charles wouldn't notice, and drinking it until she passed out. Once, not long before this particular night, she was halfway down the bottle and rang the Samaritans, thinking that it would be nice to be one (she had just read Monica Dickens on the subject). When the man answered and asked, very gently, how he could help, she said, very brightly, 'Oh no, I don't need help – I'm happily married – I just wanted to know how I could go about becoming a Samaritan like you.' She was proud of the way she managed to sound so sober and concerned. The Samaritan in question transferred her from the emergency line and went on chatting about the job for ages until Marianne suddenly put down the phone. The Samaritan spoke to her as if she had something to offer and he had not realized she was a bit drunk. She did not know if she felt better or worse about herself after this. So she *could* be clever if she tried. Maybe.

After drinking nights like that she tended to feel a bit sick in the morning and look a bit flushed in the cheeks and watery in the eye and it didn't look good behind the cosmetics counter. Really, the best way to spend the time when Charles was away was to invite Willa to come and keep her company for the night. Especially now that the Bald Wild One seemed to have truly vanished. When Willa arrived, with a bottle of something called Pino Grigio (how sophisticated) in hand and saw the bare boards in the hallway, and then the rolls of carpets with their handwritten notices, she laughed and laughed. 'Your Charles is so *safe*,' she said. And immediately sat on one of the rolls and bounced up and down. So Marianne did too. Now that she came to look at it, the notice did seem a bit far out. She added the word EXPENSIVE so that the notice now read KEEP OFF EXPENSIVE CARPET which for some reason seemed even funnier. Then she put her fingers to her mouth and shook her head and said, 'He'll be really cross,' but there was nothing she could do about it now.

Willa said later, half a bottle of wine inside her, 'He doesn't have much of a sense of humour, does he?'

Marianne, who contained the other half of the bottle, knew that her friend was making comparisons with the Bald Wild One and was indignant. The Bald Wild One would run a mile at the mention of marriage, for example. Well, he obviously had. She rose to the defence of her husband, prepared to defend him to the last – but the words came out all wrong and she found herself saying, 'He's a prick,' instead of 'He's a brick,' at which they both fell off the carpet rolls in aches of agonizing laughter, and the notice, occasioning more head-shaking from Marianne, was torn in two.

Charles did not really approve of Willa. He had certainly never forgiven her – and possibly not Marianne – for the occasion when he and his old schoolfriend Danny were driving them back from Brighton and Danny's ex-post office van broke down. It was part of life, of course. You never actually got into a car at point A and expected to arrive at point B and then get home again without some kind of mishap. All their friends' cars were ancient things and not reliable. This time Willa and Marianne sat on the grassy side of the A23 while Danny and Charles became nothing but a pair of loon-clad bums peeking out of the steaming bonnet. The girls waved at any passing cars with single men in them and pretended to look coy when they waved back. Then Willa blew a kiss and nudged Marianne so that she followed suit. That particular driver slowed and tooted his horn.

When Charles emerged from the bonnet to see why the toot, the girls were looking innocently up at the sky and the car, with its laughing driver, had sped on its way.

'How's it going?' Willa called after a while. They were both a bit bored with the waving game. Danny and Charles, having poked and prodded, stood up with their hands on their hips and pursed their lips and looked serious. 'Not enough earth,' said Charles. And they both disappeared back under the bonnet.

'What?' called Willa.

From under the bonnet and sounding extremely irritable, Charles repeated, 'There's not enough earth.'

Neither Willa nor Marianne could speak. Nor did they need to. They just looked at each other, held their sides with silent and uncontrollable laughter, eyed the scrubby patch they sat on, and decided. Marianne went and found a plastic bag from the back of the van and they proceeded, in between terrible, soundless, weeping laughter, to fill it with soil. Willa then tapped Charles's bottom. He stood up and said imperiously, 'Yes?' And she handed him the bag. 'You needed more earth,' she said. 'And we've been good girls and got you some.'

It might have been all right if both girls had not then fallen to their knees, totally and incapably weakened by how clever and funny they thought they were. Clever and funny were not the words Charles (or Danny) used. And when the car's engine finally turned, the girls sat in the back, wet-cheeked, biting their lips, while the boys drove home in disapproving silence. When they dropped Willa back at her house, nobody spoke, not even to say goodbye. Willa went up to the driver's window and said sweetly, 'Sorry, Dan. It was Marianne's idea. Thanks for getting me home.' But Charles was not fooled. He knew, perfectly well he said, that Marianne would never have thought of anything like that on her own. It crossed Marianne's mind that she had been got at on two levels: one, her friend had dropped her in it, and two, her husband thought she was incapable of dreaming up a joke. It was all a little sad.

Given that incident, which had never quite been forgotten, it seemed best to put the carpets back as best she could when Willa had gone, and say nothing about her visit and the prick and brick incident. Wives must be more serious than that. And she wouldn't want to put him off his plumbing.

When Charles came back from Wales at lunchtime on Saturday, he made unusually brisk love to her in the bedroom (which was a relief as she knew he was taken with the prospect of the small shed in the garden for daylight hours currently and she often wondered rather guiltily what the elderly Mrs Hills next door made of the noises) and then went off to change into his overalls. The installation had begun. He turned off the water.

'But it will be back on in time for my bath tonight, won't it?' she said. But she already knew the answer.

'Of course not,' he said with gusto and joy. 'It will take weeks to get it right . . .' They would be back to boiling kettles again and washing in cold water at the sink. She shivered, remembering Dragon Street.

'But don't you worry,' he said. 'It will add hundreds to the value of this place when it's finished.'

She was not entirely impressed with this argument. Since they weren't going to sell it, what were those hundreds to her?

'How long will it take?' she asked, tentatively.

He sighed in a very adult way. 'It will take, Marianne,' he said, 'as long as it takes.'

'OK,' she said. 'When is it starting properly?'

The doorbell rang.

'Now. There's Dad.'

As Charles went to open the front door it occurred to Marianne that they had done no preparation. Surely they should have packed things away? Of course she waited for Charles's directives in such matters but *surely* some of the furniture and books and pictures should be put safely into the shed. He couldn't possibly install an entire heating system by going round the furniture, could he? But Charles was already letting his father in, there was already the rattle and clump of toolbox being put down in the hall. She was *persona non grata* enough as it was in the matter of this heating thing. Best not rock the boat by making what might seem criticisms. She removed a couple of pictures from the wall, tucked them into the bottom of their bedroom chest of drawers, and stretched her mouth into a smile.

Bernard arrived in a pair of overalls that had once been white and were too short in the leg, so he looked a bit doo-lally, as Marianne's mother would say. He was rubbing his hands. Charles had bought some blue overalls and looked quite dashing in his. He rubbed his hands, too.

'Can I help?' she said, still hoping she could give the place a bit of

47

a whip round. 'Put stuff away maybe? Take down some pictures?'

'Make us a pot of tea, love,' said Charles. Bernard nodded and smiled.

At least there was enough water left in the kettle. If only she had been told in advance she would have filled every saucepan. She pushed down the irritation at such lack of forethought and while she waited for the water to boil she put all the food away in the kitchen. Something told her you didn't leave loaves of bread and open butter dishes lying around when floors came up. Marianne made some tea, put out the reserve biscuits and went off to do the weekly shopping. Charles gave her a peck on the cheek. It was one of his dismissive ones. He told her to take her time. Bernard was wielding a crowbar and a hammer. She was quite glad to get out.

When she came back two hours later, with three bags weighing her down (Charles loved his potatoes) and her fingers nearly dropping off, she had to hand the carriers through the front room window and then climb in. Everywhere was in complete chaos. Floorboards up in the hall, in the front room, in the dining room, and upstairs in all the bedrooms. Everywhere, everything, was covered with a grey dust. Even her clothes, lying over the back of the chair in the bedroom, were covered in a dirty film of grey. And her beloved bathroom was worst of all. When she left the house that afternoon, the floor had been covered with some quite nice vinyl – dark red and clean and properly cut and fitted without any gaps for dirt or spiders. This was now ripped up and lay in pieces. The wash basin held tools and bits of pipe and brass joints, In the bath was the fawn bathmat which was covered in dark greasy fingermarks, the soap ditto, the flannels ditto, the beaker containing their toothbrushes and paste, and all the other nice bits and pieces that made the place so nice and bathroomy were in the bath, put there by someone with dirty, dirty hands. On top of it all rested half a floorboard, splintered down the middle.

'You can still use the lavatory,' called up Charles. 'But nothing else.'

She went out again and closed the door. She felt as if the room were her and she was the room and they were now both defiled.

It went on for weeks. And weeks. It was difficult to get a good run at it, was Charles's excuse, as he was still going away quite a lot for work. Marianne thought, surprisingly sourly for her, that he and

Bernard had turned it into a way of life, a piece of theatre, which they both seemed to enjoy enormously. Bernard was there every weekend and some evenings and Marianne began to feel she was being driven mad. Like in the play *Gaslight*, it really did feel as if they were doing it deliberately. Drive the wife mad then claim her inheritance. There was nowhere in the house to sit comfortably, nowhere to feel settled. Every floor was up, every room a muddle. The dirt, in what had seemed such a pretty, clean little house, was unimaginable. Where did it all come from? When Marianne wept her mother-in-law put her arm around her and took her home to stay for a weekend. 'It's the same when Bernard cooks,' she said, 'or mends the car. When he's finished it's like saying that the Second World War finished in 1945: Tell that to Dresden, London, Coventry, Warsaw . . .'

Her mother-in-law, like Marianne, bore it. But only because she chose to, so she said. In the name of peace and quiet and a contented husband she decided that she could rise above temporary domestic squalor – spanners in the breadbin and motor oil on the fridge. Because, she said, she looked upon Bernard as her third child, which helped considerably. 'But I'm not looking forward to a repeat performance of what you're going through, my love.' She laughed sympathetically. 'But I probably will. Women have always been the cleaner-uppers. Wipe down the refrigerator, scavenge on the battlefields – it's all the same. It's up to your generation to change it.' She looked at Marianne a little doubtfully. 'Unfortunately the male of the species, and I include my son in that, does not seem inclined to give an inch.'

Marianne squirrelled the phrase away: 'the male of the species'. It sounded like poetry and as if you knew what you were talking about.

As far as Marianne was concerned her mother-in-law was wonderful because she knew so much. She wondered if that was why Jean could remain so cheerful. 'I really miss my bathroom,' she said miserably. It seemed such a foolish thing. Jean touched her cheek and looked at her with understanding. 'I'm not surprised after that nasty basement. It's your special place, is it, the bathroom?' Marianne nodded. 'We all need one,' said Jean. 'Mine's the top landing by the little window. No one goes up there unless Beryl's home and has a friend with her. I sit up there for hours with a good book. Every woman needs a room of her own, according to Virginia Woolf. But I've always thought that nowadays every woman needs a house of her own.'

'Who's Virginia Woolf?' Asked Marianne.

Jean told her.

Wincing with the memory of the conversation with her head-mistress about washing and body odours, Marianne was so driven by the need for a bath that she even went home to her mother and sat in the replacement (but still horrible) lemon-coloured plastic bath now installed. The bathroom windows were slightly less draughty but not much, and the water was a bit hotter but not very much either. And as she lay there, feeling uncomfortable, she was back to being a child again and – just as she had done then to blunt the unbearable reality – she was dreaming that she was really a princess, mixed up at birth, and would one day be rescued by a handsome prince. The one she had in mind did not – she was quite surprised to find – answer to the name of Charles, wear white dungarees and sit around endlessly discussing something called gravity feed with his King the Father.

And then – just as she despaired – just as she had given up hope of it ever being finished – just as it seemed that she was living in some kind of masculine cult – Charles's big sister Beryl announced that she was coming home to England for good because she was getting mar-ried. Charles thought it was clever and significant that they should choose the beginning of the new decade which, so Charles said, would consolidate all the changes that the sixties began. 'Especially in the area of women's liberation,' he said. Beryl was, apparently, a leading good example of this. Charles both adored and feared his big sister and thought she was the cleverest, most beautiful, sexiest thing on legs, largely because – so far as Marianne could make out – Beryl thought so herself. And also because she had once run three boyfriends at the same time when she was at university. While Charles thought this worthy of a goddess, Marianne thought it was pointless as Beryl didn't seem to like any of them very much. Not surprising, really. Marianne had met two of the three (Beryl came home from university once in a while) and neither one had struck her to be as attractive or interesting as George Harrison or Mick Jagger, the like of which – at the very least and given her assumptions about herself, as Willa pointed out – was what you would have expected.

It was something of a relief when Beryl finished her Post-Grad mysteries and departed England for Foreign climes. To follow, so she announced, the Margaret Mead path of anthropology. Her mother was never relaxed when she was around (they never had fits of the giggles and sipped sherry in the kitchen while cooking the lunch like Marianne and Jean did on a Sunday), and her father was always having dramatic political arguments that meant no one in the house talked for days. The first time Marianne ever met her, introduced as Charles's new girlfriend, within half an hour of the family Welcome Home Dinner Bernard had left the table apoplectic (Beryl was no socialist and had been expounding the virtues of castrating morons, hunting and private education) closely followed by Beryl – and Charles was white with some terribly mixed-up emotion, his eyes dark as he stared at his sister's huffy, retreating back. Jean leaned over and patted Marianne's hand and said, quite absently really, 'Never mind, dear, Beryl doesn't come home very often . . .' It was only when she was on the bus going back to *her* home that Marianne realized Beryl had never addressed another word to her after the initial 'And which university are you aiming for' to which she replied, 'I'm not, I go out to work . . .' The boiled blue eyes had widened; the mouth had gone very schoolmarmy. 'Work? At what?' 'On the cosmetics counter at Brightley's.' She added lamely, 'In Bond Street.' And down came the shutter. It was as if Marianne had confessed to packing maggots.

And that was that.

Fortunately Beryl was abroad when Charles and Marianne got married so they were able to have their own little ritual in an easy, relaxed fashion. Of course various suggestions were made by Beryl, via letter, some more than just suggestions and more like commands, but on the whole they got off lightly. Somehow Marianne managed to lose the list of *people who must be invited* and to say 'Yes' when she meant 'No' regarding speeches. One of the benefits of Charles going away from home was that he did not always know if a letter arrived and she could dump it. Anyway, she wrote all the replies – because she was good at it (Charles still said that with a slightly perplexed air) – and typed each one so that both she and Charles could sign them so that Beryl would never know that the descriptions, sentiments, family news came from Marianne only. Sometimes Beryl addressed her letters only to Charles so that Marianne felt like his secretary.

A parcel came from an unpronounceable place with their wedding gift. A heavy, white lace bedspread. Marianne hated the thing and even Charles couldn't quite summon up the enthusiasm Beryl might have required. They put it in a cupboard and forgot about it. Marianne wrote the thank-you letter and she wrote such a piece of theatrical nonsense, such a wonderful big fat lie about their first sight of the exquisite thing, made such a story of how they felt when they spread it on their bed that she was almost convinced they *had* done so. Charles was impressed. 'Quite the little story-teller, aren't you?' he said. The letter was despatched, and that was that. The bedspread would have made a very practical cover for the furniture while all the plumbing work was going on, but Marianne didn't – quite – think she could get away with that. Many years later, many many years later, she used it for just that purpose.

Beryl's forthcoming wedding meant, as Bernard said, that it was all hands to the pump. The family had its marching orders. Nothing must get in the way of the organization of Beryl's perfect day. All hands to the pump it therefore was, both metaphorically and literally, really. Pumps being a very necessary part of the operation, as she was told when she poked at a strange-shaped piece of metal on the kitchen workbench and which, on application, she was told sent the water swirling around the central heating pipes. Suddenly it was imperative that the central heating was finished. Marianne stroked the pump occasionally, as if it were an icon, and privately blessed Beryl for her imminent return. At last she would have her house and her bathroom back.

But it was not only Beryl's return that made Bernard and Charles take wing with the plumbing arrangements. It was that Beryl was commandeering Marianne's and Charles's house. The wedding would be in one month's time from her arrival and Charles and Marianne would offer bed and hospitality to some of Beryl's and Richard's guests. And that was an order. There could therefore be no delay in getting the pipes connected, the floors down, the carpets relaid, and the house cleaned. OK? She ended that letter with: 'Trust you, Dad, to do it the hard way. Why on earth didn't you just employ someone to come in and do it for them?' She always seemed to act as if Bernard and Jean had 'family money'. On this occasion Jean said to Marianne that she thought her daughter had a point.

Beryl's husband to be, apparently, did have 'family money' as well as being a Professor of Sociology – Professor Richard Bingham. No one, apparently, was to call him Dick so Marianne and Willa immediately – privately – did so. It was a little rebellion that helped Marianne enormously through the difficult times to come. Professor Richard Bingham's breeding was never mentioned in detail though he clearly had some. Marianne might not know exactly what sociology was (and her mother-in-law said that quite a lot of its practitioners didn't know either) but she certainly knew about Breeding because she served it with cosmetics. Breeding meant you could just look straight through a person if you were so inclined. Breeding meant you could talk in very loud voices about incomprehensible things like stocks and shares and polo, or have your hair highlighted and wear a velvet Alice band to reveal your perfect brow. It also meant you could be terribly, terribly gracious towards inferiors and – if you were the particular inferior that Marianne seemed to be – you could – by being terribly, terribly gracious towards her – make her feel lower than a worm. Brightley's was full of them. Alice bands and Gucci shoes and kindly smiles and twisted vowels.

Willa said that it was almost worth delaying the finishing of the installation so that Beryl couldn't get her way, but Marianne was robust in seeing the silver lining. Her bathroom, her bathroom, her beloved bathroom.

'Oh no,' she said, 'Her horrible guests will go after two days, and then I shall have everything back just the way I want it. It's worth being bossed around for that.'

'All the same,' said Willa, 'we could spice it up a little . . .'

'Do not even think about it,' said Marianne, laughing. 'Charles would kill me.'

'Fair enough,' said Willa. She was a much nicer person to be with at the moment because – Marianne assumed – she had put Gordon, the Bald Wild One, out of her head. Sensibly Marianne asked nothing about him. Willa tended to be extremely touchy about his disappearances even when she was supposed to have forgotten all about him.

When the first radiator was fitted successfully, and Charles and Marianne stood back admiringly in the hall and after Marianne innocently asked if they could turn the heating on now and Charles, smiling with indulgence, said that it wasn't *connected you silly*, and put his arm round her, he said that Marianne should come off the Pill and she did so immediately, the following morning, with great joy. It gave their – necessarily quick due to the requirements of plumbing – sex life much more of an interest for Marianne. Every time it was over she thought *this might be it*. All fear of being provocative vanished in the huge excitement of possible motherhood. Marianne was amazed at the new lease she found now there was a baby in sight. So was Charles.

The day of the wedding guests' arrival dawned greyly. The house was more or less back to normal though the loft ladder was still down in case of any plumbing hiccups. 'That's good,' said Willa, mysteriously, when she rang to say that she and Roger would be popping by as arranged. Last week in true friendly solidarity, when Marianne told Willa how much she dreaded the whole thing, Willa said that she and Roger –

'Roger?

A characteristically dismissive wave of the hand.

'Oh, he's nothing serious.'

A questioning look.

Another wave of that dismissive hand.

'Gordon's gone for good.'

'And?'

'Fine. It's fine.'

Of course it wasn't. She could see it wasn't. But you did not argue with a dumped girlfriend.

Willa suggested that she and Roger would 'just call in' and interrupt the dinner and be amazed to find a family party in progress – and despite the dreaded Beryl's undoubted disapproval, they would stay.

'After all,' said Willa, 'it is your house.' Not at the moment, thought Marianne. 'Why,' she asked, 'are you doing this? You dislike Beryl and you're not very fond of Charles.'

'Because,' said Willa, 'at the moment it helps to go around upsetting people.'

Fair enough, Marianne thought, fair enough.

'Added to which I think Roger may have a little plumbing trick up his sleeve.'

The bedrooms were cleaned and the bed made with freshly ironed linen. Marianne and Charles, at Beryl's behest, gave up their own double bed, to Richard's cousin (who was an Hon) and agreed to sleep in the lumpy bed in the spare bedroom. Marianne tried not to think of it as the room in which she had sex with strangers (or used to), but it was, and something about that thought was pleasing. She had begun to have these little secrets to herself and she found they gave her a very small but enjoyable sense of warmth and superiority. 'It will be fun sleeping in a different room,' said Marianne to Beryl, giving her a particularly vacant stare. 'Like camping out when I was a child.'

Beryl blinked her boiled eyes and said no more. It crossed Marianne's mind vaguely to wonder what on earth her sister-in-law would say if she knew that esteemed brother Charles liked it in the shed, or after a hairbrush whacking and a bit of a chat about young girls – but she thought again. It was just possible, looking at those eyes and the apparent lack of understanding of the word 'fun' that Beryl, too, had a likeness for such things. Perhaps it was a family trait? Marianne's sense of superiority shifted, ever so slightly, upwards.

They were providing dinner on the first night, as ordered. Beryl and Richard would come; the cousin-who-was-an-Hon and his wife would already be there – and Charles and Marianne. That was all. Marianne deliberately misunderstood and invited Bernard and Jean. She did not see how she could possibly get through it without her mother-in-law, who had a way of behaving that was quietly and cheeringly subversive. Marianne had never met anyone like her mother-in-law before. She was so funny, never wore an apron, quoted Shakespeare at the drop of a sherry cork and was wonderfully critical of both her children. It was a mystery to Marianne how Jean had managed to bring two such frightening beings into the world and Jean said, with one of her quiet little smiles, that it was a mystery to her also although she admired them for their achievements. 'High flyers, both,' said Jean. 'It's to be hoped their wings aren't made of wax.' Icarus and Daedalus were then explained to Marianne who found the tale riveting and a very useful lesson. 'Can't beat the Greeks,' said her mother-in-law. 'Best stories in town.' And she lent Marianne a translation that – frankly – made Marianne's hair curl. Agatha Christie was never like this. Jean was so clever and yet she never made Marianne feel wormlike and Marianne had to be very careful not to make her own mother jealous with her praises for Jean. Everybody needed protection from feelings, Marianne thought, except – it seemed – her.

The guests arrived at about seven in the evening. The tall Hon and his short wife were taken up to their room, made nice noises about

didn't quite put it that way. What she said was that she envied Dora her complete freedom to choose. Dora was very sharp on the matter. 'Complete freedom to choose state benefit. Oh yes. Complete freedom to bring in the coal on a shovel in winter. Oh yes. Complete freedom to bake a nice fruitcake and find that nobody comes to eat it . . . Oh yes.'

Such were the words of her mother's that helped Marianne get married and want to stay married for as long as she possibly could. Now that she and Charles had a mortgage she found it wonderfully imprisoning. If ever she thought to herself that she might be a little – well – unhappy (particularly after that experience with Vincent), she counselled herself that there was absolutely nothing she could do about it because of the *mortgage*. The mortgage seemed to Marianne a promise as unbreakable as the law. She was here, she was married, she lived in this house and one day she would have a family in it. And that was the way it was.

So now, Marianne nearly died when the Hon said, with obvious relief and tearing his eyes away from the laburnum, 'So – you have children?'

'Well, no,' said Marianne brightly, 'but we are certainly trying.' There was more silence so she added, even more brightly, 'Oh, *yes*. We certainly are . . .' Even as she said it she realized it painted a picture of persistent sexual activity all round the house. As if to confirm this impression the Hon and his wife looked about them, probably seeing signs of sex everywhere. Marianne just about stopped herself from saying, 'It's all right – we've never actually done it in *here*. Only up against the door jamb outside.'

Charles gave her a ghastly smile and Marianne tried not to remember the night before when, after making love, he had turned her upside-down for ten minutes, which was, apparently, a useful thing to do and something he had read about in one of his guide books on how to get pregnant. She had never felt more stupid that she did lying on the bed with her legs in the air trying to look as serious about it all as he did. Now they were trying to have a baby, Charles took it on in the same way he took on the central heating. He had several manuals on the subject which he studied. Upending your wife after sex was, apparently, recommended. 'It makes sure everything gets to where it's supposed to get,' he said vaguely. Everything, she thought, sounded like an upended trunk. It didn't exactly add to the romance of the experience, though, and Marianne hoped she'd fall for a baby soon so that she didn't have to go through such things any more.

Now she clamped her mouth closed, gave a little compliant shrug, and looked firmly back at the laburnum. 'Ah', said the Hon. 'Well – good luck.' He raised his glass to the road and he went very pink.

'Th–thanks,' said Charles, with understandable embarrassment.

He eyed the Hon's shoes mournfully.

Beryl coughed loudly. And the pink-faced Hon continued to stare – glassily – out of the window. His even shorter wife, with a profile like a chicken, seemed to have found something interesting on the ceiling. But the Hon was from Harrow and knew what England expects. He thought for a moment, pulled at his four-button cuff, and then said how amazing it was that people could get the asphalt so smooth nowadays. Just look at that perfect line . . . Not for nothing, it seemed, did the blue-blooded hold rank over mere mortals. In a million years Marianne could not imagine coming out with something like that. She wondered if she should make some complimentary comment about the brickwork opposite but Charles might sneer. Yet there was her husband now, at the Hon's side, nodding sagely as if he had just found God in the asphalt of Eastbourne Road.

Jean said, in declamatory mode, and with the same brightness that Marianne had used, 'There was an Asphaltick and Bituminous nature in the Lake before the fire of Gomorrha.' Nobody knew what it meant. Bernard broke the silence saying comfortably, 'Oh, Jeannie, you and your quotes. Let me guess . . .'

It was a game they played regularly. Jean the better read, Bernard the willing attempter. 'Pope?' he said.

'Earlier.'

'Milton?'

'Right period. Wrong author.'

Marianne always loved these exchanges, trying to remember everything because it was all so new and interesting. She usually went away to the library and looked up whoever was mentioned. Or made a note of the name and dawdled in a bookshop to investigate. She was much more inclined to do this nowadays if she was on her own for the night. It was much more interesting that picking up strange men and bringing them home. Books were full of interesting facts and she had begun to read fiction, too, much of which was lent

to her by Jean. Currently she was reading E. M. Forster, but only spo-
radically. Charles did not like her reading – he never read novels –
and currently he liked to see her being busy. If she had more money
(Charles gave her what she needed for fares and things and there
wasn't much over), she would have bought books for the few books
she owned she loved.

'Dryden?' asked Marianne.

'Good guess,' said Jean kindly.

Richard said quickly. 'Cowley?'

Jean pulled a face as if to say: How could you think that?

'Better tell us, love,' said Bernard.

The Hon and his wife were staring, frozen now, at Jean. She gave
them a little enquiring look which made them shuffle a bit. They said
nothing.

'OK,' said Jean cheerfully, 'Thomas Browne,' she looked straight
into Richard's eyes.

'Of course.'

The Hon and his wife and Richard all nodded. 'Ah yes,' they said.

'Who?' said Marianne.

The Hon and his wife and Richard – and now Beryl – all looked at
her a little sadly. Their looks said: How Could You Not Know That?

Jean smiled at Richard. 'Tell her then.'

He seemed uncomfortable.

Beryl said, 'Time to eat.' Very firmly.

Jean said, 'No, wait. Richard? Who *was* Thomas Browne?' It was
interrogatory.

To which Richard, looking longingly at the door, said, a little less
loudly than his previous remarkings, 'Yes – I'm jolly hungry. Longing
to eat. Delicious.'

Jean rolled her eyes and let him go.

The relief in the room was palpable.

Later Jean told Marianne that she could not abide people who pretended to know things and that it was far better to admit ignorance
and be glad to have learned something new but that since he would
soon be part of the family she did not pursue it. Jean did not seem to
like her prospective new son-in-law very much.

Marianne thought privately that if this was well-bred sophisticated living and gay conversation, give her their ill-bred peasant ways
any day. Charles, she could see, was worried about the new heating

system (he kept drumming his fingers nervously on the radiator – or perhaps he was just drawing attention to its presence). He was relieved, he said earlier, that since it was late spring the radiators would not be required. He and Bernard had shaved it so close that they had not yet had time to run the system through properly. Willa's new boyfriend, Roger, apparently called round the previous weekend and popped up the ladder to see if he could help but Charles took umbrage and declined. 'I wouldn't trust anyone associated with her,' he said firmly. He had a point. Marianne was sorry she had been out.

The party moved silently into the dining room and, just as they were all helping themselves to the smoked salmon, the doorbell rang. Marianne went to answer it with a smile of relief and happiness. Willa and Roger, the cavalry, had arrived.

He was a handsome, dark-haired man, about their age, and he looked eager to please. Willa was dressed to the nines in thigh boots, floral ruffles and a dress split down to her navel.

'Come in, come in,' hissed Marianne. 'I'm going nuts.'

Willa smiled a wicked smile, kissed her friend on the cheek, and the three of them trotted down the hall trying to look nonchalant. 'Ooh,' said Willa. 'You haven't got the central heating on yet.'

'I know,' hissed Marianne. 'And just don't ask.'

She led them into the dining room saying, 'Look who's here', and thinking as she did so that it was just as well she had never, after all, become an actress. It sounded false as Father Christmas.

Stony faces met her and the new visitors.

'Hi,' said Willa. She certainly looked very sexy as she walked – or swayed really – over to Beryl and kissed her very firmly on the cheek. 'Congratulations,' she said. Beryl looked as if she had frozen over. The icicled impression was complete after Willa turned to Richard and said that he must be the lucky boy and kissed him with even more force. Then she gave Marianne an enormous wink which Marianne immediately recognized as a one-bottle-down wink. And then more loudly she added, 'Hi, all of you – sorry if we're interrupting – she wiggled her hand at them – 'We just called round to tell you that Roger and are engaged.' She kept the smile on her face, the hand aloft, upon which flashed a diamond of dazzling scale. 'Too.' She and her new fiancé paraded up and down for a moment or two and then Roger excused himself to go to the bathroom. He was away for a long time but it scarcely mattered. Willa held the show.

While holding a glass aloft to be filled she continued to tease them with fleeting, but unmissable, flashes of her engagement ring. Big diamonds. 'Carved from the caves of South Africa,' she said, letting her gaze fall to, and immediately move on from, Beryl's overshadowed one smallish diamond and two sapphires. And she chatted away about where to get married, what to wear, the best kind of honeymoon, who should have the wedding list. Jean and Bernard went on munching their way through the salmon and looked bemused rather than affronted. On another occasion they might have reminded Willa that good people did not buy South African goods but there was something in the air that said it was all a piece of theatre and need not be taken seriously. Except, perhaps, by Beryl.

Beryl was speechless but very pink. Matching her Eastern sparkly thing. Really very satisfyingly pink, Marianne thought. Pink ice. And as if to read her thoughts, Willa said, 'Beryl? Are you cold?' And then sidling up to Charles and the radiator which he was tapping as before and she ran her fingers up and down its metallic creases very suggestively and said quite loudly that she herself was feeling a little bit chilly and how about that central heating then? Bernard, who had been longing for just such a moment, put his plate down, clearly delighted, and said, 'Let's try it out, Charles. Come on. It is a bit cool in here.'

'No, it's not,' said pink-iced Beryl. Which was laughable coming from her.

'Oh, let them,' said Jean, as if they were six years old and it was a train set.

And Roger, who had quietly appeared in the doorway, said he would help.

Charles said there was nothing to help with and Roger said he'd come and see anyway. He had already put in two central heating systems he told them, so he knew what to do if it went wrong.

From Charles's expression it was clear that this statement was akin to being told there was a decomposing corpse in the garden. Roger then slapped Charles on the back, which also did not please Charles and which occasioned a look that could be fairly interpreted as if there *were* a rotting corpse in the garden, Charles would quite like it to be Roger's.

'It's all right,' said Roger, 'So long as everything is connected up OK. In the loft?'

Charles bridled and said that it was.

'My hero,' said Willa.

Bernard rubbed his hands and said they'd better check it all the same.

'Not necessary,' said Charles aggressively. 'So who's cold then?'

It would have taken a brave man or woman to answer that they were. But brave men and women there were in that room – indeed the flower of the once chivalrous class and brave to a fault.

'I am a bit, as a matter of fact,' said the Hon's wife, firmly.

'It's because we don't get the sun in this room,' said Marianne. Charles looked at her as if she had just accused him of mass murder.

The Hon then nodded too. They were clearly not of the breed that put on another jumper when the dial hit nought. 'Bit chilly,' he said. 'Just a bit.'

Charles did an interesting thing with his lips. Marianne had never seen them disappear quite so completely before. But he rallied.

'Oh, well, fine,' he said. '*Fine* . . . ' He would go to the airing cupboard on the landing where the controls were housed and he would *put it on*.

All four men left the room, leaving only the Hon. Jean gave him a nice smile and offered him an olive. Roger and Richard and Bernard were practically sprinting up the stairs in Charles's wake for the airing cupboard. Then there was silence, then the murmuring of voices, one of which was Roger's saying 'Are you sure you don't want me to check it over?' To Charles's incomprehensible reply.

There was silence for a while, apart from the muffled sound of their voices from upstairs. A little eating took place but the room seemed, really, to be a room in waiting. Marianne downed her glass of wine and poured herself another. Willa asked to see Beryl's ring and compared them. Unfavourably. 'I quite like small stones,' she said. 'But not small diamonds . . .'

Beryl gave as good as she got and said that she thought large diamonds were vulgar and smacked of Elizabeth Taylor's absurdities.

Willa said she wouldn't mind having *those* – or her knockers. Which definitely seemed to finish the matter.

And then there was a shout from upstairs and the noise of water in the radiator. Tinkle, tinkle, gurgle, gurgle.

'Oh good,' said Marianne, 'it's worked.'

And down came Richard and Charles and Bernard, the two latter

63

beaming with pleasure. Roger followed on a little later. He had a small toolkit in his hand which he slipped into his pocket. Marianne wondered if all men went around ready for plumbing action. Charles looked very peeved but said nothing. 'Pipework's excellent up there,' said Roger. 'Excellent.'

Charles gave a stiff little smile.

Willa said, 'And he really knows, Charles. His flat is beautifully warm. Well done.' She looked at Roger, and Marianne thought that her face held a question which he seemed to answer with a slight nod of his head before he took up his glass and downed it in one. 'Excellent stuff,' he said. No one could be sure if this time he meant the wine or the plumbing.

Tentatively Marianne reached out and touched the radiator. It was warm! Oh joy. 'My hero,' she said to Charles, and kissed him on the cheek. Beryl seemed to wince at the gesture. It began to dawn on Marianne in a profound way that Beryl did not approve of her at all. Not at all. She wondered why. There could not, she thought, with an unusual frisson of pride, be very much about her to disapprove of, could there? She was fairly sure of it. She began to feel assertive (the white wine helped) and she thought: this is my house and my husband and I can do what I like . . . She touched the radiator again. It was *really* hot. 'My hero,' she said again, loudly. 'My lovely, lovely hero and husband.'

Beryl definitely winced again.

Then Willa announced that she was 'just popping upstairs to the er-um-er', and did so. Life was restored to the roomful of people, more food was placed on plates, conversations began and glasses were filled. The air grew warm and Charles leaned over and turned the radiator down. 'Individual temperature gauges,' he said happily, 'for each room.'

As they all beamed at the individual temperature gauge, there was a noise from the bathroom upstairs. A shout from Willa followed by the secondary roar of a lavatory cistern filling. 'Oh my God,' cried Willa from above. 'Oh My God!'

'What is it?' called Charles, alarmed.

Marianne noticed that Roger was smiling, a snide little smile, the kind of smile Charles sometimes wore if he was winning at bar billiards. Roger went on smiling his smile but did not move. Odd, thought Marianne, he seeming to be so fond – if not affianced – of her friend. Willa called out for the third time. If Marianne had not been sure she was mistaken, she would have definitely said her friend was trying not to laugh. 'Oh help, help, help,' came shrieking down the stairs.

A galvanized Charles took the stairs at a sprint, followed by his father (dripping his red wine all over the precious carpets, Marianne noticed, thinking that she could use that if ever Charles complained about their friends again). With that thought she followed her husband and her father-in-law up the stairs. Willa was standing at the open bathroom door with a distraught expression on her face. Behind her the room was filled with steam and there was the sound of hissing from the lavatory cistern from whence rose more steam.

'I just pulled the chain,' she said dramatically, 'and the room filled with boiling water.'

Charles and his father looked at the hot, swirling vapour, looked at the still swinging brass lavatory chain, looked at each other.

'Oops,' said Marianne, a rising something in her throat. She knew better than to meet Willa's eye. 'Oops. That's odd.'

Charles, in need of relief, looked yet another killing look at Marianne. Behind them, Roger arrived. His smile had gone and now his face took on the guise of wonder. 'Good Lord,' he said, and shook his head. By now Willa was staring at the bathroom floor. Her shoulders seemed suddenly to be very wobbly. Marianne was sucking her knuckles and beginning to shake.

'Good *Lord* . . . ' Roger pushed past Charles and his Dad. 'You've hooked up the hot water to the cold water feed somehow,' he said. He was extremely red and also shaking.

Charles and his father were neither pink, red nor moving very much. They seemed, in a very real sense, to be rooted to the spot. Their faces – particularly Charles's – were what Marianne's old granny would call 'a picture'.

The something that wished to rise in Marianne's throat would not be quelled any more. She allowed herself one glorious long look at Willa. And they both burst into unquenchable laughter. It was the release of a thousand pent-up repressions for Marianne – so racking that it could as much have been tears of sorrow as laughter. But laughter it was. More feet thumped up the stairs. Here were Jean and Beryl. Jean, her mouth a perfect circle, made no sound. But there was a distinct look of levity about her eyes as she stared at the steam issuing from the cistern. Beryl's mouth, on the other hand, was more like the harsh opening of a pillar box – and there was no levity remotely connected with it. 'What?' she shrieked. '*What?*'

Roger said, very calmly. 'Got his hot and cold pipework mixed up . . .' He chucked Marianne beneath the chin. 'Hope it doesn't do that in any other departments.'

Jean said, 'Puts a whole new complexion on the term Hot Flush.'

Willa's and Marianne's laughter, like the steam on the landing, swirled and engulfed them both. Even Charles's expression could not still them. Oh hell, thought Marianne, giving in to it. I'll just beg his forgiveness when everyone's gone home and hand him the hairbrush. At least, she thought, she had done something deserving of it for a change.

A grim-faced Bernard, who had done nothing but scratch his head and wonder over and over again how it could possibly have happened, said that he had better take his wife home. And since he had driven Beryl and Richard over, he would take them back as well. They looked as if they had just relieved Mafeking. Jean said what a shame because she was just beginning to enjoy herself. In the hallway she turned to her son and patted his cheek and said, 'Very nice evening.' Then she patted the hall radiator in much the same way and said, 'Well, dear, with these you need "Fear no more the heat o' the sun . . . Nor the furious winter's rages . . ."' And she laughed. Charles looked at her stonily. Marianne looked down at the carpets but couldn't resist saying – in a *very* small voice, 'Um – Shakespeare?'

'Exactly,' said Jean happily. '*Cymbeline.*'

'Who's Cymbeline?' asked Marianne, but everyone except Jean gave her a look of serious disapproval so she did not pursue it.

'Jeannie,' said Bernard, 'we're off.'

Thank God, thank God, thought Marianne as she wiped her eyes and waved at the departing car from their gate. Without Beryl there she felt she could at last remove a corset. I wouldn't be her for a million pounds, she decided. It was a surprising thought. She watched them drive away with Beryl sitting upright and looking – pinkly – like the Snow Queen. Richard sat beside her staring straight ahead with what Jean had whispered to Marianne was His Noble Profile in perfect view. Earlier in the evening Beryl made reference to his connections with something she called The Nobility which put a glint in her mother's eye.

Roger and Willa hung around in the hallway while the Hon and his wife, diplomatically, if not a little desperately, excused themselves – tiring journey, long day sort of thing, wedding to go to the next day – and said goodnight and went up the stairs to their room. After a while Roger said to Charles, 'You'd better warn them, hadn't you?' For a moment Charles looked blank. So Roger made a chain-pulling gesture.

'Oh, *fucking hell . . .* ' yelled Charles – but even as he ran it was too late. They all heard the sound of the cistern being flushed and a little, very well-bred feminine scream. Steam slid from beneath the bathroom door and when it was finally opened a dazed guest appeared. Mrs Hon had just copped it.

While Roger and Charles (in absolute silence) sorted the problem out, Marianne and Willa went up the garden and screamed and cried and ached into the shrubbery. When they saw Mrs Hills staring down at them from her back bedroom, they lay on the ground and hugged and rolled and cried some more. Marianne was fully aware that this was not the correct behaviour for a married woman trying to get pregnant, but she decided to do it anyway.

'I feel better for that,' she said eventually, smoothing down her skirt and wiping her hands over her damp face.

'Of course you do,' said Willa. 'That's what life should be all about. Fun.'

Marianne looked at her friend. She didn't seem, from the sudden change of expression on her face, to be entirely convinced of the argument.

'Are you really engaged?' she asked.

Willa shrugged. Then she shook her head. 'Woolworths,' she said, and held up her hand to the light. The diamonds winked. 'He's very boring actually,' she said. And sighed.

Marianne, thinking of Charles, nearly said, Same Here. But it couldn't be true, could it?

All was done. Marianne thanked Roger as he left. Charles said nothing. He was quite rigid and his mouth had gone odd again.

'Don't mention it,' said Roger. He patted Charles on the top of the arm like a friendly uncle. 'It's easy when you know how. You'll soon learn.'

For a moment it looked as if Charles might punch him. Marianne thought that would be interesting. Charles (and she) were both socialist in politics, liberal in outlook, and punching people was just not acceptable. Aggression was for savages and boxing as a sport was a disgrace, obviously. As Charles said, one could control one's urges, and one should, otherwise one was uncivilized. Marianne (who used to be quite religious) said that Charles sounded like Jesus saying Turn the Other Cheek to which Charles was firmly dismissive. Punching people in a fit of temper was barbaric and so was organized religion . . .

All the same, standing at the front door now she could see his clenched fingers and his wrist twitching, and she thought she could read his mind. She had a strange urge to lean over and whisper 'go on, give him one' which she controlled. She was having these little bubbling moments more and more frequently. Willa, loose and sinewy from drink and wickedness, wound her arms around Charles and clutched him to her with a passionate embrace. Marianne blinked. But she said nothing. It was all part of the continuing game. 'Never mind,' breathed Willa into Charles's pinkening ear. She then kissed him long and hard on the lips. Marianne blinked again. It seemed less part of the continuing game and more like one of those quirks of his. Except he seemed surprised by it all. And not unhappily so. 'My hero,' whispered Willa, and she accompanied it all with an unmistakably sexy stroking of his crutch. This time he blinked. And for a moment he seemed to find it very pleasing. Then he remembered. And didn't. He pushed Willa away. 'Goodnight,' he said, and stepped back from her. The image of their kiss stayed with Marianne all the way up the path to the garden gate. It was still there when she waved to her friend, who winked at her from the car, blew yet another kiss at Charles, and drove off. Marianne felt uneasy. If she hadn't known Willa better she would have said she was playing the vamp with Charles – but with an edge of truthfulness. A Willa bored was not something Marianne wanted to contemplate. Well, certainly not in the area of her husband. Or his crutch. However, she continued to wave and laugh as the car began to move away.

Charles was now white and his lips had quite disappeared again. He gave Marianne a look and she stopped laughing and waving immediately.

'I'll see you soon,' called her friend. 'And you, too, Charles.' Then she waggled the so obviously false ring out of the window. 'She's mad,' said Charles, but there was a definite air of admiration in the way he said it. Oh, thought Marianne.

Back in the house a silent Charles closed the front door.

'I think I'll go to bed,' said Marianne. She was about to say, wasn't it something that she had recognized that bit of a quote as Shakespeare – but decided this was not the time for singing one's own praises, 'Night then,' she said, tottering up the stairs.

Charles still said nothing.

Charles said nothing to her for nearly three weeks. At Beryl's and Richard's wedding he said nothing, in the privacy of their own home he said nothing. At the farewell lunch for the Hon and his wife he spoke not. When the Hon and his wife said their goodbyes and the Hon said, 'Thanks so much for putting us up in your sweet little house', Charles spoke to himself or the walls, not Marianne, when he later said, 'Sweet little house – sweet little house – patronizing bastard . . .' Marianne said that it was – a sweet little house – wasn't it? But he ignored her.

They kept up the regime of attempting to get Marianne pregnant and that was also done in silence. He never said a word as he held her upside-down afterwards, which felt doubly odd. What was even odder was that he did not take up his old pleasure of beating her with a hairbrush. She still thought it was more appropriate than ever as he was so obviously cross. When she suggested he might like to have a go at her with it, after some consideration he deigned to reply. He told her that she had humiliated him and that he could not contemplate – for the moment – anything of a more intimate nature. In other words, he would not bestow upon her such a loving and intimate experience as being smacked.

Well, blow me down, she thought, if life only gets more complicated, not less.

'Sorry,' she said. And she tried to look as if she was really disappointed. She apologized several times more for laughing at him, as she had done every day since the hot water incident. And she realized, all over again, that she never *would* get the hang of this sex thing – it was totally and absolutely masculine and therefore incomprehensible to her.

The decorating was completed – in silence mostly – by Charles, and she cleaned up after him most cheerfully. Apart from not being spoken to by her husband, and not getting pregnant, in all other respects she was happy. Charles would start talking to her again eventually and she was right. He did decide to talk to her again. One evening, when she was lying in her bath, having finished the last little bit of wallpapering above the airing cupboard so that the beautiful little room was now warm, and clean and floral pink and perfect (and flushed only cold water), Charles appeared, late back from work, and perched on the side of the bath as if nothing had happened between them. He asked her how her day had been, as if everything was fine, and he held in his hand an estate agent's particulars. She glanced at them. The photograph showed a three-storey early Victorian house in horribly dilapidated condition – and an address near the river, a couple of miles away.

'Marianne,' he said, 'I've decided. Now that this place is all done up, we're moving.'

It was as if he had attacked her with a knife. Slip, slide, right between her ribs and into her heart.

'No,' she said, '*Noooo*', and she wept.

'You old silly,' he said, and smiled at her kindly.

'Oh please, no,' she said, tears and bathwater streaming down her face. If only she hadn't laughed at this all-powerful husband of hers he would have let her stay. Her reflection was a picture of misery. It would have wrung the strongest heart. Nevertheless she knew as she looked about her at the perfect little bathroom set in her perfect little house, that move they would. She was too weak, too feeble, too cowardly, to do anything else.

HOUSE NUMBER THREE

24 Russell Road, Richmond upon Thames

A mid-Victorian pilastered terrace, on three floors in need of complete modernization. Ground floor: two rooms, kitchen, scullery and bathroom. First floor: two rooms and wc. Third floor: two attic rooms and disused small kitchen. Hall-sized cellar. Outside: small front garden, hedged and paved, steps up to front door. Rear garden mainly shrubs and crazy paving laid to patio area. Approximately fifty feet in all. Sole Agents Johnson and Johnson. £12,500 subject to contract.

The sound of the neighbours' Saturday morning hi-fi thumped through the downstairs wall. Glenys and Bertie Munt (who had lived all their married lives in the house next door, brought up their children in it and seen all three off the premises to be wed) liked band music – Ellington, Basie, Sinatra – and they had no idea that since Charles had stripped the front room floor so that it was now polyurethaned bare boards, the sound echoed through from their house to this as if there wasn't a wall between them. Which, in a way, there wasn't as the houses had air vents that ran beneath the entire terrace. Marianne knew this because Marcus explained it to her. He said that if he had been Charles he would have put down sound-proofing. 'I think', said Marianne, 'you had better not tell him that.'

Marianne did not like to complain. Basically, Marianne did not know how to . . . So now she lay in bed – Charles was out for most of the day – on a Saturday morning, and waited for Glenys and Bertie to turn the sound down. They always did. It began loud and then, presumably, one of them wanted to say something to the other and the volume was damped down and they forgot to turn it up again. It was, really, very boring to know your neighbours' habits so intimately, but practically sharing a room with them, as Marianne and Charles had done for over a year, meant you couldn't help knowing.

Bertie was a bus driver and Glenys worked in a dry cleaner's. Their other neighbour was what you could usefully describe only as an Old Biddy, and she, it seemed, had never married and was once a school dinner lady. This was hardly the exciting life that Charles envisaged when they moved here. He really did think that he was going to mix with fascinating, well-educated people (like Beryl and Richard presumably) and found it annoying to be hemmed in by such small minds. But the house was the right kind of house, in need of improvement and in an area that was becoming what the estate agents called Gentrified. Sooner or later, Charles was certain, they would see the old residents move away and new, bright, cultivated, social and intellectual equals replace them. In the meantime Marianne felt quite relaxed about her neighbours as they were just the kind of people she grew up with. Charles – now on the upper rungs of Junior Management – was away a lot more nowadays and it was Marianne who had to do the stopping to chat on the front path, and the hunting for something to say. It seemed to her that all conversations revolved around no one actually saying, 'When are you going to start a family then?' but implying it in a thousand ways. 'Big house for just the two of you . . .' That was the Old Biddy. 'Lovely area for bringing up a family . . .' That was the others.

'We're still doing it up and we will be for some time I think.' That was her.

They were, most definitely, still doing it up. The previous tenant had lived in the house for forty years. He rented it from the Water Board and the Water Board felt that if the rent was low that was all they needed to do. The old man was happy to be left alone and the result was squalor, but a squalor that meant Marianne and Charles could afford it. Charles said it was something he could really get his teeth into now that he had got the taste for doing-it-yourself and Marianne stamped a bright smile on her face.

When they moved in Charles put on his old paint-smeared Levis (Marianne pretended not to notice them) and immediately set about ripping up floors and taking out old cupboards and removing boarding from chimney breasts. Unfortunately the Junior Management commitments didn't leave a lot of time for putting any of the mess to rights. Nor did the Junior Management salary. Even if Marianne had the skills and knowledge to replace window frames or replaster walls, she was forbidden to do so on the grounds that it would only be those silly chairs all over again. So Marianne continued to live with floorboards long pulled up in the hall, filthy old walls in the scullery and adjoining bathroom (from the bath itself you could practically reach out and fry an egg on the disgusting old stove), bare and dusty floors throughout. Even the ground-floor bedroom – the one room that she was promised herself would be completed – was unfinished. The window glass was still cracked and the door, which was due to be removed and stripped and beeswaxed, had somehow just remained in place. Charles just never – quite – got round to lifting it off its hinges. It was definitely a two-person job or Marianne might have dared to attempt it herself.

In the end, as Ruth pointed out (Ruth had that irritating characteristic of being one who likes to give advice, and one whose advice is usually right), it was best the door remained, really, for Charles had decided to do this really cool, really daft, thing of having their bedroom in the ground-floor front. 'Mad' – as her mother said when she visited – 'People can just look in at you.' Marianne waited for the lecture on putting up nets, which came, and then the pièce de résistance, which hurt because it was true. 'And just what was wrong with that nice little house in Eastbourne Road?'

Well, *quite* . . . It was mad of them to have a bedroom by the front door. 'As if you were a lodgings,' her mother also offered, which did feel annoyingly apt. You heard every street noise and they were surprisingly many for such a quiet residential road – the milkfloat, the passers-by, the trundling and rattling of shopping trolleys, the revving of early-morning engines and the squealing of children going to school. What with that and the neighbours' big-band sounds, a Saturday morning sleep-in was a thing of the past. You could lie in, of course, as she was doing now, if you didn't mind lying in stiff and tense as a ripped-up board.

It was a debatable point whether there could ever be a good time for the bedroom door to come off and get sent to the strippers. Without it whoever came to Marianne's and Charles's front door and then entered the house could not help but look in at their bed and their underclothes and their most private things – and maybe their private moments. A bedroom should be upstairs; of course it should. It did not need Dora to point that out. But Charles wanted the big front room upstairs (which Marianne had looked forward to having as a lovely, big light bedroom) to be a sumptuous drawing room (which, apparently, was what elegant people did) rather than wasted on them sleeping there. 'An upstairs front drawing room', he said, 'is stylish.'

Marianne did not argue. She was at the end of arguing really. She had tried. She had failed. They had moved and she mourned the absence of her pretty little warm, safe house – and its precious bathroom – daily. Once in the new dilapidation she tried to stand up to Charles regarding where they should sleep, and he paid no attention. Only to say to her, ever so mildly, that he did not expect her to be quite so strident about something that was hardly world shattering in its importance. It always did seem to be that argument. Anything she thought would be nice he seemed to think was petty. And he had called her mother a petty bourgeois when she said things like, 'About time you had a decent cooker in here', as if having a decent cooker was the silliest of silly ideas.

Marianne had one more attempt at putting her point of view. The final attempt at a little bit of what *Spare Rib* called 'female assertiveness'. She suggested to him that perhaps they should work on only one room at a time, instead of tearing up floors, taking out cupboards, throwing away old light fittings that left gaping holes in the walls and ceilings in every single part of the house. One room at a time meant they would always have somewhere comfortable in which to sit. But no. On he went. She watched him and it occurred to her that he was enjoying the act of destruction very much: sometimes with his father, sometimes on his own, occasionally with Marcus. Perhaps, being liberal and socialist, it was the only violence he was allowed? He certainly no longer hit her with a hairbrush. Indeed, since their move here and with so many boxes still packed, she hadn't been able to find the bloody hairbrush. They seemed to have given most of that side of things up, anyway. What with his banging and crashing and ripping and the filling of skips outside the front door, there was no time left for anything else. When no baby materialized (just as well her mother said, with the house in such a state – but still) the GP said ,'Relax' – but their way of relaxing appeared to be to stop having sex entirely. It was relaxing for Marianne, but it wasn't likely to produce a baby. Now there was a conundrum. This sex business was definitely complicated. Basically Charles was either away for work, at home beating the shit out of the place or falling asleep in the filthy old bath from where she had to rescue him quite often, with the water all cold. And now? Well, now – the worst thing was that none of it mattered. She did not, really, care where she slept or what she did in where she slept any more, just as she did not really care about the Basie or the Ellington beating its loud rhythm through the walls or the sound of two old biddies having a good jaw on the pavement outside at eight thirty in the morning.

The dream – whatever it was – had vanished – along with the perfect little pink bathroom. Nothing was, nor ever would be, the same. As for the bedroom door – let it hang there off the door jamb with its disgusting old paint. (Why did she always end up in places that had scabrous old paintwork?) Why should she care? She felt a terrible lassitude nowadays – it was like a bruise deep inside her, an ache she could not define, and she did not think that she had laughed for months. In fact, when she tried to remember when she and Charles had last laughed together, she cried, because she couldn't. And this was marriage, this was mortgage, this was being a home owner for the rest of her life. She was trapped and she felt utterly alone, ashamed to tell anyone what had caused this final falling away of herself. It was losing Willa to a kiss. Willa, who had always put her back in touch with what she thought of as the real Marianne, was now lost to her. It was a friendship she could never retrieve and all because of a kiss, a fumble in the dark. Oh, it was not the kiss of the wedding party. That was funny in its way – a piece of Willa's theatre – which, if it made Marianne uneasy, did not shake her belief in her friend. No – this was a new kiss, a Judas kiss, a kiss with malice and intent. Where once she would have felt sad or hurt and pulled herself together – Risen Above – now Marianne recognized these things and understood. She had stumbled into the Wildeian world of those who kill the thing they love. One day she would make the literary connection. For now it was enough that Willa had hurt her deliberately and that because of this she and Willa were no longer talking to each other nor ever would be again. Whatever happened they could never go back to that depth of intimacy and knowledge and private understanding because Marianne's trust in her friend, her only true friend, had gone. All her other friends belonged to both her and Charles. Only Willa was her friend and hers alone, and now Marianne had lost her to a careless, thrown-away moment. All the wishing in the world could not restore it. Truly they would never be the same again.

Willa was not lost in a physical sense. Oh no, indeed not. Willa's clean little flat was only half a mile down the road. Marianne could walk to it. Or she used to. No – she had lost her in the heart of herself, in her spirit. She could barely mention her name, actually, and – though she would not admit it to Charles – she had taken out and torn up her photographs of them together as happy girlfriends, school and all. Oh yes. She had lost her all right. Lost her to the moment of finding Willa and Charles in their disgusting downstairs lavatory together (Marianne had even put a red light bulb in it to make the appearance of something more pleasing – which of course made their faces look even more embarrassed) at their party for Charles's twenty-fifth birthday.

A quarter of a century seemed like a coming of age, which is why Marianne suggested giving a party; well, that and the need to find something in this dead and dreary existence to celebrate. When she saw the two of them standing there, wrapped close together, something profound flipped in Marianne. She was besmirched, betrayed. She seemed to grow about six inches and to say, from her new, imperious height, 'Willa, get out of my house.'

She could still hear herself saying it, picture the scene, if she had a mind to. Willa's surprised eyes, Charles's astonished ones. And her own voice repeating, 'You heard me, Willa. Go.'

But even as Charles removed his hand from inside her best friend's bra strap and stared at his wife, and even as Willa moved away from him, all awkwardness and then that superior smile. Willa wiped her mouth with the back of her hand, curled her lip, pulled down her skirt (which did not, actually, need the gesture but which gave her an enviable moment of *hauteur*) and left. Marianne felt perfectly numb. She knew what Charles would say to her later. And he did. How well she knew this husband of hers. Telling Willa to get out of the house, apparently, and according to Charles the next day, was being over the top, a spoilsport. It was all a bit of fun. It was a party, for God's Sake, a *party* – surely Marianne could have shown a bit of laissez-faire. Perhaps I would have done if I knew what it meant, she thought, making a note to herself, despite the current tensions, to find out later.

Marianne waited for Willa to telephone – or write – or something. Marianne wrote many, many letters to her erstwhile friend. Delightfully vicious affairs that made her heart burn with pleasure. She even wrote a short descriptive paragraph about Willa visiting a hat shop and accidentally stabbing herself through the eye with a hatpin because she was watching someone else's husband in the store. In the paragraph she died. Marianne could not, or would not, save her. It was lovely. In years to come she would use the idea for a wonderfully shocking short story and sell it.

That Marianne's refusal to have anything to do with her friend went on for weeks made Charles angry. It was time, it seemed, that she stopped holding on to her futile anger and apologized to her friend.

That was what he had said to her.

Oh!

She said to Charles that Willa was no longer her friend and he looked at her as if she were a child having a tantrum.

Very well, she thought. Very well. So now, Saturday morning, without Charles until that afternoon, she lay, listening to the beat from next door's music, knowing that later that night she must go to Willa's neat, clean, perfect little flat – and be civil. That was Charles's word for it. Civil. And all Marianne could think of was Civil War. Roundheads and Cavaliers and Biafra and Ireland. What, after all, was a bit of grope and an unstripped door compared with that? Why nothing, nothing at all. It did not, however, feel like Nothing. It felt like fog, with underlying aches. Never had she felt so trapped, so unhappy, so – she recognized suddenly – *angry*. And anger made you do extraordinary things.

As she lay on the bed she remembered the flirtatious eyes of an artist she had met at a gallery party last week. It was her late night at Brightley's. When the store closed and she was out on the street she knew that she did not want to go home. Charles was away, the boards were up, the doors were off, the windows were broken and it was all too depressing and sordid and Dickensian to contemplate. She walked down Cork Street on her way home, feeling the fogginess and the ache that came quite often now and about which she could do nothing except drink until she passed out – which made it worse the next day. She was in Cork Street when she saw a gallery party in full swing. It was something she had not done for a long time but now – with the fogginess and the ache needing balm – she entered the comfortingly anonymous world. She was somewhere between a dream and a nightmare and she just wanted to drink red wine and talk to anyone, anyone at all, who knew nothing about her and would not think that here was a humiliated girl. A married woman who could not get pregnant, who lived in shit, and who could not even keep her husband faithful, nor keep her oldest friend. She was not pregnant, not laughing, not anything much really, and now she was not even happily married. Red wine and anonymity would make it better.

Marianne stood in front of one of the pictures and tried to focus on its grainy surface. Sometimes abstract art (which she did not under-stand but found good to look at) could remove her from reality – but not tonight. It was a painting by Prunella Clough and it was made from collage and aluminium paint – the soft and the hard, the magical and the reality. Too much like her own experience to be comforting. It drew her to it and she stood there, drained off a glass of wine, and tried to become absorbed. She knew, of course, but had forgotten, that if you stood around for long enough in an art gallery at a party and you were under forty and over sixteen, someone would come and chat you up. So when someone did, she was momentarily off her guard.

'Hallo,' he said.

Great opening. She smiled and looked down at her glass, surprised to find it empty. He reached out and took it from her and held it under the nose of a passing waiter, who curled his lip in acceptably camp fashion, but filled it.

'Filthy stuff,' he said, and handed it back to her. 'Whatever happened to the glory days when they bought the best?'

She shrugged. 'Tastes all right to me,' she said, and emptied the glass again. He looked surprised and impressed. They looked at each other with a long unflinching stare.

'What's your name?' they both said at the same time.

It should have made her laugh that he was called Norman. Because she and Willa called Hush Puppies Norman, and it was the name she and Willa used to give to any male that they thought was *just awful*. 'A real Norman,' they would say – and laugh, and laugh, and laugh. No more. In fact, it made her want to cry now. He was looking at her in a disturbing way. Questioning, maybe approving. She looked back at him and shrugged. This Norman had (slightly boodshot) blue eyes that made her want to fall into his arms and cry. They both looked back at the picture and she said that she thought the paintings, by Prunella Clough, were beautiful. He nodded. 'Not bad,' he said. 'Bit girlie. But beautiful surfaces.'

Later, when she repeated the word Beautiful, as they walked around the room together, stopping at each painting in turn, Norman said that she was too. Beautiful. Now that was a new one. Was she? Charles had never said so. Nor, she was sure, had anyone else. And Norman (God help her she supposed she'd have to actually say the name to him at some point) was drunkish. But anyway, it was a good moment to be told that she was. 'What's your view,' she said, 'on hairbrushes?'

He shrugged and took her elbow in his hand and guided her into a corner of the room. It was very gently done. She leaned against the wall and was glad of it. 'Hairbrushes?' he said, tapping his pursed mouth as if contemplating a question of the Universe. 'I don't think I have an opinion . . . And you?'

'I think', she said, 'that I prefer using them on my head rather than on my bottom.'

As if she had invited him he put his hand on that part of her and gave it a little pat. 'On this, you mean?'

But she had long ago given up taking strangers back to her home – that was when she was irresponsible and lived in the Eastbourne Road, days when it all seemed very remote and silly and inconsequential. Now it meant something. Now she had a sense of what betrayal was. And when Norman asked her if she wanted to go to the pub afterwards, she said, 'Oh no, I am married actually.' To which he said, standard response, 'If you were my wife I wouldn't let you out on your own . . .'

She could think of nothing witty to say. Because she wanted to say that Charles didn't seem to care what she did, that out of sight was out of mind. She remained mute, looking deep into her empty glass, feeling the possibility of tears that she did not want to shed in front of this stranger.

'Happily?' he said.

She looked up, said faintly, 'No. I don't think so.' And then gave a little gasp. It was a shock. It was, she saw suddenly, the truth. She had communicated the truth, out loud. 'And now I must go home.'

'Sure?'

She nodded. 'Sure.'

'And about the marriage?'

'Sure.'

Norman took a card out of his pocket and wrote on it. As he bent his head she noticed it was slightly balding. For some reason it made her feel old. When he handed the card to her he said, 'I've got a show coming up in Stepney. An installation. Come along. Or just give me a ring.'

And she left.

An installation? What on earth was that?

Coming home on the tube, more than a little bit drunk, she was astonished to find it was the truth. Said out loud and to a stranger.

She was not a happily married girl. She wondered if she ever had been. She hiccupped and smiled like a baby. She could see herself in the window opposite. She was not happily married, she never had been happily married and at this rate she was never likely to be. And she was, apparently, beautiful. Or someone called Norman thought so. It left her feeling weak. When she got home she fell down a hole in the hallway and twisted her ankle but it scarcely hurt.

Well, that was Thursday. Friday was a miserable hangover, all day, so that she could barely focus on the promotional mascara, let alone apply it to her silly customers. And now it was Saturday and she lay on her bed alone and forced herself to consider The Thing Called Tonight. A mountain of misery to come. A civil meal with her friend when it should be civil war, and with her husband who liked to feel up her friend, and possibly one or two of the others of their friendly circle as well – almost certainly one or two others as well. It was to be hoped they knew nothing of Marianne's humiliation (being far too drunk at the party to make head or tail of Willa's sudden departure) and if they had been told since – it was to be hoped double, triple, quadruple that they would have the wit to stay quiet. It was going to be horrible all round, really.

One thing, however, was good. Charles was out until late this afternoon because he had gone flying with a friend of theirs who was getting his pilot's licence. It was the first time Marianne had felt so glad that he was away from home. She stretched her arms around her on the wide mattress and enjoyed the feel of the space. This was also new. Thinking about all that had happened, Marianne had a sudden cold feeling deep inside. And what was this cold feeling deep inside related to? She knew perfectly, shockingly well. It was related to the fact that she wished – with all her heart and soul – that Charles would fall out of the plane and die. That would solve everything, including the mortgage. And as if all *that* wasn't bad enough, she thought, wondering how much longer the drum solo from Glenys's and Bertie's chosen album could continue, as if that were not *quite* bad enough, Bloody Willa was a much better cook than she was, too. This was not surprising. Bloody Willa had a proper kitchen in her dear little done-up flat. Marianne had never had a proper anything in her domestic life – certainly not a cooker – so how could she be expected to knock up the perfect soufflé?

Charles did not fall out of the plane. Indeed, he returned home that afternoon much enlivened by the experience. She made him a cup of tea in the vile scullery with half the floor up, and he took it into their bedroom, suggesting they sit on the bed because it was the only decent place in the house to sit. He had a way of saying it that sounded as if he disapproved and that it was somebody else's failure creating all this mess. She wanted to scream and ask – since he knew how vile everything was – why he was so utterly selfish as to go out on a Saturday afternoon for pleasure, leaving her behind in this squalor, instead of rolling up his sleeves and getting down to the work so that they could live again. Living had been suspended ever since they moved in here. She remembered living from the brief and happy time they spent at the end of their stay in Eastbourne Road – once the central heating was completed. Sometimes she dreamed of that house, so much did she want to go back to that contented state. It was horrible to be back to the Dragon Street days of begging baths from family and friends. The bathroom here was a hundred times worse than any she had ever known – filthy, rotten and steeped in the horrors of old man's residues. She felt sure his bacteria was all over the place, despite going at every surface with double doses of bleach. She knew that the waste pipes must contain unspeakable human detritus and the cracks in the floorboards would be full of unmentionable substances.

Occasionally she braved it and sat bolt upright in the bath simply because she had to have a bath – but mostly she waited until they were at friends or family. It became second nature to tuck a towel and flannel into her handbag whenever they went anywhere. But it made her feel second class. Why, she asked herself quite angrily nowadays, *why* was she still living in a mess. And what if a baby came along . . .?

Mother-in-law Jean had quite a go at Charles for what he had done, or rather, had not done. 'Ripping up this and pulling out that – and then it gets left. You were born wearing blinkers,' she said. 'But Marianne wasn't. It's not fair on her.'

Charles said that he was doing it as much for her as himself and Jean said he didn't seem to be doing it at all. Mother-in-law Jean had fought valiantly and won the right to have her central heating installed by professionals, citing Bernard's and Charles's disastrous experience when they did-it-themselves in Eastbourne Road. Marianne suddenly saw where Charles got his high ground from: Bernard did not speak to his wife for nearly a week. Jean just winked at her daughter-in-law. 'Means I can get on with reading novels,' she said. 'And then I can pass them on to you.' Then, more confidingly, she said to Marianne, 'Try to relax more. I'm not surprised nothing has happened with all that upheaval going on.' Which made Marianne feel a little better about her total inadequacy in the fecundity department.

Beryl did not want children and was very firm about it. Richard, it seemed, did want children. Marianne had a bet with herself that Beryl would win. Beryl had all the right arguments for abstaining, including – on a mundane but absolutely understandable level to Marianne – the fact that their new house (just like Charles's and Marianne's in style but in a much better part of town) was nearly complete and was done out from top to bottom in biscuit and white. Not sticky-finger biscuit, either, but smooth, pale, warm oatmeal that would show every mark a biscuity finger might make. They paid builders to do it. And then, when they visited Russell Road, they sat around on horrible old chairs and drank from Woolworths glasses and said how wonderful it would all be when it was finished. Marianne wanted to tell them to Shut Up whenever they told Charles that he was making a first-class job of the conversion and how hard it must be for him running both his career and doing all the building work at the same time. While he preened, Marianne fumed. It was, they dared to hint, a great blessing that she was not pregnant given the pressure on poor, hard-working Charles.

Neither was Beryl pregnant, of course, and it occurred to Marianne that this, too, was a great blessing, given the suffering of any baby she might have. But she did not say it. The whole baby issue was one she preferred to stay clear from. She wanted a child so much that it was like a little pain to her, the redness each month. Sex – Oh how to get up the enthusiasm to even pretend? Especially when she spent time alone considering the happy occasion of her husband's parachute not opening?

Surprisingly, Charles wanted to have sex after his second cup of tea. It was probably the flying. All that thin air. Sod's Law, thought Marianne, who could not have cared less. They did so. And it was quite horrible. If he washed his hands a thousand times, she could feel their taint and see them wandering their way around Willa's curves. Why it was very different from the quirks Marianne did not know. But it was. Willa belonged to her and now she had gone from her. And for what? If Charles was telling the truth, then for no more than a quick grope in a disgusting lavatory (which might have led to something more, she supposed). A bit of fun. All the same, now as he squeezed and pulled and rubbed at her she could only see that moment, that vile lavatory of theirs and the two miscreants of lit for ever by the silly red light bulb. She had tried to make less of it later, and she had failed. Yet another failure by Marianne.

As soon as it was over and Charles sighed and closed his eyes, she went to their horrible bathroom to put her raging body into the horrible bath and wash him away. This, she thought, as she rubbed at the hard, cheap soap with her flannel, was the way life would be for ever. No way out of it. Exit barred. Married with a Mortgage – and that meant for always. Even the soap reminded her that there were, and ever would be, precious few rays of sunshine. (Why buy expensive soap which doesn't last half the time? Charles was so fucking *rational* . . .)

But at least she could smile at her one little bit of pleasurable rebellion. She had managed to procure for herself one little ray of sunshine for this forthcoming numinous event (new word, just learned it) tonight . . . Something to shore up her feelings of being a reject. Coco Chanel said, so Marianne read, that it was the quickest way to warm a woman's heart. Marianne had bought a new dress. Her first since they moved here. And warm her heart it did.

The sunbeam in the gloom, the one nice thing that she had to look forward to, and which she had concealed from Charles, was that Marcus, who was really Charles's friend from schooldays, offered to lend her ten pounds so that she could buy a new dress for the occasion. If Marcus knew why it was so important for her to have something new to wear, he made no hint of it. She thanked him, told him to keep it a secret, took the two fivers without blinking, and immediately spent them, for she knew exactly the dress she wanted. It was something called a Dolly Rocker, in unbleached calico with a deep lace-edged yoke, long, lace-cuffed sleeves, and an Empire line. Which emphasized her small bust and hid her more substantial bits. Willa, of course, had a very nearly perfect figure, but – and now it could be said – she was a bit spotty – yes, yes – definitely a bit spotty. Marianne had perfect skin – even if the rest of her was a bit on the lumpy side.

Tonight, Marianne decided, it was time to grow up. Mother-in-law told her, as she did so many interesting historical things, that her

Victorian and Edwardian sisters were not allowed to put their hair up until they were considered to be young women and to have left girlhood behind. Which was rather what Marianne felt about herself now. That she had passed over a chasm of girlishness and reached the bumpy terrain of being a grown-up woman. So up went the hair on to the top of her head in that sophisticated way that models and actresses did now, with lots of curls piled high (you made those by pinning them) and little soft tendrils floating about her ear and fluffy bits at the front to soften the hairline. If she looked different tonight, then maybe she could be a different person. Someone to whom such a sad and dirty thing had never happened. She was so grateful to Marcus for not asking any questions. He had just done the deed and shut up about it. Marcus, dear Marcus, always suffering himself. Perhaps that was what made him so kind. If Marianne thought she was ill used, it was as nothing to his experiences; his first girlfriend, after some consideration and a disastrous attempt at heavy petting, turned out to be a lesbian and his second took his bicycle and never came back. But now he had Ruth who was strong, independent-minded, and neither lesbian nor a cyclist but inclined to boss him about. Which he seemed to like. They were, it seemed, born for each other and happy. Why wasn't she happy being bossed around, then? It dawned on her that Marcus was bossed around because he liked an easy life – and because in the end he was a free agent. When Charles bossed Marianne around, he meant it, and she stayed bossed. What a silly girl, as he so often said of her, she was.

Charles, who had known Marcus since school, argued that Marcus could afford to be kind because he was rich, but she privately thought that was rubbish. You either were, or you were not. Once, years ago, when they drove Charles to the M4 to hitch a lift back to university (Marcus already had an Austin all of his own) and they were on their way back to Dragon Street, he stopped the car and took her hand and tried, very cautiously, to kiss her. 'No,' she said sweetly. 'No, thank you.' As if he had offered her an ice-cream in a flavour she did not like. It was never mentioned between them again and, really, it was probably an action made for a point of honour rather than out of any deep desire for her. Anyway, she liked Ruth too much. And so did Marcus. During the last few months Marianne found herself thinking more and more about what made people do certain things, the way their minds worked, what made people tick.

In the past she used to accept, almost without question, the unfolding of events and actions. Now, for the first time, she pondered them.

If only Marcus and Ruth were coming tonight – but she knew they had not been invited. They would have been her allies, or at least impartial. Whereas Charles . . . No more pretending. There was something very, very wrong in being married to someone whom you did not feel was your ally. If Marcus and Ruth were invited Marianne would have felt protected. You should not need to feel protected from your husband. Or from your best friend. But Willa did not care for Ruth – who did not care for Willa much – and Charles said she had *nothing to commend her*, as if she were a second-rate stately home. More likely Ruth wasn't included in things because she spoke up for herself and – you could honestly say – did not try very hard to look her loveliest for her man – or any man – in her life. 'I like to be comfortable,' she would say of old cardigans and baggy jeans. 'And Marcus doesn't care what I look like . . .' Personally Marianne thought that was a little too revolutionary – to not care at all what someone looked like seemed to smack of, well, just not caring at all. But because things were changing in her head and she was prepared to think she might, after all, be wrong on that. One thing she was not wrong about, she was absolutely sure of it, was that tonight would be full of demons. The butterflies in her stomach told her that.

While Charles scrabbled about looking for his clothes, Marianne filled a washing-up bowl with hot water, stood in it, and washed herself. The bath was too depressing. Then, despite her hands shaking, she coiled her hair up on her head smooth as a television advert. It made her look even taller and her neck looked longer and in the mirror she saw a sophisticated woman – a Marianne who had aged five years and who looked as if she knew a thing or too. Looking was about as good as it got, she thought, for she felt as soft and deflated as an old tyre underneath.

Then came the dress. Once the buttons were done up and the skirt smoothed down, she knew that she looked – well – *something*. It made her think of Norman and it made her wish he could see her now. He had called her a Beauty in her cheap yellow dress from Dorothy Perkins. What might he call her if he saw her wearing this? Ah well. Even if she never saw him again, Norman was a nice secret. Tinged with pain, of course, for the one person whom she could have told and who would have laughed at the name Norman was gone.

Through her many and painful ponderings during the last few weeks, Marianne finally understood. It was like those Greeks in Jean's book – Medea and Clytemnestra and so forth. Willa was angry. Willa was hurt. Willa was a dumped woman and Willa wanted to destroy. Her sigh in the garden, for example, and her urging Marianne to have fun, the fizzing sense of danger that surrounded her since then. It was all to do with the Bald Wild One, Marianne realized. A complete prat had brought their friendship to this. With his drugs and his intellectualism and his extraordinary capacity to remain upright having drunk a lake of red wine he was – monstrously – what Willa wanted. More than she wanted Marianne. This, Marianne realized quite calmly, was very silly of her. Losing friendship was serious. But so it was. Willa couldn't have him and Willa was *very* angry. And when Willa was angry she was dangerous, without a care for whoever got in the way, including her best friend. Marianne had seen it often enough but never directed at herself. Now she was included. Indeed, if Marianne thought about it, it was probably *because* Marianne meant so much to her that Willa was so cruel. Self-Destruct it was called. One of their other friends did it when he was at university; dumped by his girlfriend, he gave up on his work and started taking heroin, and died. 'He was always one for Self-Destruct,' they said over the teacups at the funeral. It was a good lesson to Marianne. Gin drinking until you passed out might be the first step to something much, much worse.

She picked and licked at her curls and hummed into the mirror until Charles had to call her to the front door twice because she was so lost in her thoughts. He was impatient to be off. 'I want to get this over and done with. And she'll have cooked something interesting,' he said, as he closed the gate behind him. 'She always does.' Marianne laughed and tossed her head of curls. 'That's what your mother always calls my cooking,' she said. 'When it goes wrong. She says *Interesting, dear* – and she means it's horrible.'

He looked at her, about to say something, but his voice died away. Instead he blinked and then just about managed, 'Good grief', which he had taken to saying recently. 'What have you done to your hair?' But he added almost immediately 'It looks very – different.' And then he added, 'I mean it looks good.' He nodded to himself as he started up the car. 'Quite a change.'

Then he smiled at her, a nice smile, warm. For a moment she felt they were two adults out together. Evens. 'Makes you look older,' he said. 'Sophisticated.'

She very nearly said that wasn't much of a compliment in the case of his preferences, but she kept it back. No point, no point at all. Instead she concentrated on breathing evenly. She felt nervous but so far, so good. In all the tumble of curls and the sudden ageing process he had not noticed the new dress. As to his smile – why – she could not have cared for it less.

Marianne was glad they drove though it was a very short journey. It meant that the worry of arrival was over more quickly. Charles rang the bell very firmly. He was utterly confident. The door opened, there was a smell of something pungent and good to eat, and Willa stood there wearing black. The kind that Coco Chanel *really* meant when she said every woman should have a new frock . . . A perfect, knee-length, little black dress. The kind Jackie Onassis wore. And she had lightened her hair. Her facial spots were under control, which was a pity, and she looked about five hundred times more grown up than Marianne – and quite friendly. The fizzing seemed to have died away.

Willa held the door open for them and as Charles went in she looked down at the floor, a nicely demure gesture, Marianne thought, wanting to kick her. Willa then looked Marianne full in the eyes. 'Like your hair,' she said. 'MichaelJohn?'

'Marianne Flowers,' she said. And walked on into the impeccable little living room. Clean wooden floor, clean white walls, everything in its place and – more to the point – a place for everything. The small wooden table was laid, candles burned from the mantelpiece, from the bookshelves, from the centre of the table, and already sitting drinking at it was – it could not be much worse – the Bald Wild One.

'Long time no see,' he said. And raised his glass of dark red wine. He was either drunk or stoned or both.

'Hi,' said Marianne and, girding her calico-hidden loins, she went over to him and gave him a kiss full on the mouth. It was absolutely horrible but she kept smiling as she sat down next to him. He tasted of sour wine and smelled faintly of onions (or perhaps it was garlic, maybe he had been away in France). Charles leaned across the table and shook his hand – about as limp as the lips Marianne guessed – said, 'Gordon,' quite curtly, and sat down opposite them smiling with his teeth and not his eyes. The Bald Wild One poured them each a glass of red wine and dripped some on to the impeccable, stripped wood of the table. Marianne watched the pool of it sit there and hoped it would stain *very badly indeed*. Irritatingly Charles mopped it up with his handkerchief which Marianne would then have to wash *and* iron. The thought spurred her on.

She batted her eyelashes at the Bald Wild One. 'You've been out of the picture a long time,' she said. 'Travelling?'

'Nope,' he said. 'Prison.'

'Gosh,' she said, which was an understatement but all she could manage. Sophisticated calm vanished. *What for?* she wanted to ask, but dared not. 'Well, I never,' she said, unable to stop herself. It was the sort of thing her grandmother used to say over the fence to Mrs Perkins. Pinny talk. Charles frowned. Then he leaned across and whispered to Marianne that Willa was in the kitchen. Marianne gave him a look as if to say, So What? He gave her a significant look. She continued to look blank – something that never surprised him and at which she was obviously quite good. He leaned closer and whispered that it would be a good time to get the apology over and done with. Marianne continued to pretend she did not understand and asked for some more wine. 'Sorry,' she mouthed, as she appeared to search the table for another bottle. 'More wine first.'

'Oh fuck!' said Charles, abandoning his careful use of language. He tried to alternate Good Grief with Oh Damn on the grounds that such phrases were more cultivated – and Beryl's husband said them a lot. Marianne found this touch of morality rather confusing since they both roundly disapproved of the yobbish kind of man who refused to swear in front of women but occasionally hit one. She said, 'Oh, Charles!,' overwhelmed with the need to point out his mistake. Indeed, she was suddenly and very keenly overwhelmed to point out *all* his mistakes – for ever. She coughed a little cough and lowered her voice. 'Mind your language.'

He looked at her, his lips first going white and then disappearing. She knew that look. One more push, it said, and he just might dump well-balanced man and go for a more yobbish turn. And then a little miracle occurred. His lips reappeared. He pulled them into a semi-smile, and he said, 'Sorry.'

She blinked.

He then added, by way of explanation, 'The wine's still in the car.'

He leapt up and was down the stairs before Marianne had time to suggest that she would go and retrieve it. She wanted, very much, to get out of this flat and get away from the Bald Wild One – whose finger ends were definitely going to bruise her knee. The thing was – if she left here now – she knew she would never come back. That would also have been very nice. What a shame Charles had beaten her to it.

Willa came into the room with a white dish of very black olives which she placed on the table with elegant precision. 'Sorry there aren't any of your favourites, Marianne,' she said. 'The ones with those little bits of orange stuff in them.' She made it sound as if she were talking about Spangles versus Charbonnel and Walker. 'I love black ones,' said Marianne, which was not true. She took one and braved it. Like eating greasy salt. She took another and savoured it as if it were ambriosal.

We are all acting as if we are in a play together, thought Marianne, looking at Willa's perfect poise, the Bald Wild One's bloodshot and lecherous eyes. And the absent Charles – the hero to their chorus. Jean had taken her to see *Antigone* a couple of weeks previously and she explained the Greek way of theatre to Marianne. The form of Greek drama allowed it to deal with the darkest, most horrible things. It was the form of the thing that protected the viewer and the participants from sinking into hell. Rather, she decided, like tonight. While they were all playing their roles, they could pretend to be saved. The bloodshed had happened nicely off stage.

She took a deep breath, swallowed the last of her wine, and looked up at Willa. Who looked back at her. The eyebrow that Willa raised, and with which they had always had such laughs (you could say a great deal of encoded information with a raised eyebrow) was now turned on her as a weapon. So she made the exchange as straightforward as possible. She said, 'Charles wants me to apologize. I apologize.' And then with great deliberateness she turned back to the Bald Wild One and said, 'Prison. How exciting. What for, exactly?'

But Charles almost immediately arrived back, breathless, and took centre stage by sitting down very heavily at the table and plonking down the wine – Hirondelle – and saying that it was still cold despite the air being very warm for the time of night. Thus, by the Englishness of invoking the weather, did he stop them all in their conversational tracks.

'Saw that girl who's moved in below,' he said conversationally.

'Stella,' said Willa. 'She's a pain. Wears a lot of patchouli and plays the guitar. It's no wonder the baby never sleeps.'

'What does her husband do?' asked Charles.

Marianne was thinking, *baby, baby, baby*.

'She hasn't got one.' Willa smirked. 'Not that she wouldn't like to have . . .'

'Oh,' he said, 'Well, she looked all right. Nice smile.' As if that concluded the matter. 'Here.' He pushed the Hirondelle towards her. On its label is said it was *larger than a litre* – for which Marianne was very glad. She had to give up excessive drinking only if she was doing it *alone*.

'Oh good,' said Willa. 'More wine.' And she ran her fingers up and down its frosty neck. 'Ooh,' she said, with far too much flirtatiousness, 'It *is* cold, isn't it?'

Marianne would have laughed once. Now she felt irritated. Such an obvious, schoolgirl thing to do. She turned to Charles and said, 'I've just apologized to Willa for my silly behaviour the other night. Haven't I, Willa?'

Willa nodded.

'Good,' said Charles rubbing his hands at the prospect of food, 'Glad that's over. I'm starving.' He stood up again and took the bottle from Willa's hand. 'I'll open that, shall I?' he said.

'Oh please,' said their hostess. As if he had offered to personally tread the bloody grapes, thought Marianne, as they went out to the kitchen together.

She and her table companion watched them go.

'Dope,' said the Bald Wild One.

'He is a bit of a prat, isn't he?' said Marianne, with much relief.

'No,' said the Bald Wild One, looking puzzled and enunciating carefully. 'I mean I was in prison for dope.'

'Oh,' said Marianne, and laughed.

But as her laugh died away she heard, very faintly, its echo from behind the half-closed door of the kitchen. That does it, she thought, that does it.

Everything about the evening contributed to Marianne's irritation which the drinking of wine seemed only to make worse. Usually wine made her feel cheerful, or at least forgetful, which was the same. Now she thought about it, that was Bad, wasn't it? Very Bad. The only brightness on the horizon was that Willa seemed to be no happier than she was. And that was good, wasn't it? Very Good.

Every so often Willa shot an anxious peep at her lover and if their eyes met (his swivelled a lot so by the law of averages they would do so occasionally) she gave him a huge and even more anxious smile. It was quite clear that all was not well in that department. Good, thought Marianne. Damn Good Job. Good Grief.

As the wine went down, the Bald Wild One released her knee. She was much relieved at this and hoped he might slide to the floor, he certainly looked in danger of it. But he rallied when the food arrived and gave her another vicious squeeze before tucking in. She yelped but no one seemed to notice. Nobody ever did, she thought.

Willa continued to send the Bald Wild One little glances and to try to make sense of what he was saying, much of which seemed to do with a man called Ron. Marianne looked at the food. It would choke her, she knew. But actually, when she came to think of it, she was very, very hungry. Her stomach always did let her down. How often she had longed to be pale and withering away out of some Great Sorrow Borne – only to smell the whiff of a piece of toast or bacon and pass on swiftly to the realms of being rosy and rounded. The Bald Wild One, having consigned her knee to its mate, said, 'Come on my little duckie, tuck in.' She smiled at him. She picked up her knife and cut into the butter. 'Duckie,' she said. 'That's what Henry VIII used to call Anne Boleyn's tits.'

'What?' he asked, squinting as he tried to focus on her.

'Duckies,' she said. 'Instead of tits. Much more polite.' She splayed the butter firmly on to her bread. Leaving them, once again she hoped, in a confused silence. She began to dine. She did not look up. If she caught anyone's expression, anyone's at all, she knew she would scream.

They ate home-made pâté into which – Charles asked so they were told – Willa had chopped olives and garlic, which was even more irri-tating because it was so good. They drank the bottle of Hirondelle (Marianne could almost smell the sex clinging to its cold little neck) and then Willa produced a bottle of something called Rioja, which she pronounced like a cough, and said that it came from Spain. To which Charles said, 'Clever of you to know all these things.' To which Marianne said nothing and thought much. To which the Bald Wild One said, 'She gets it all from me. Bit of a connoisseur.'

'You can say that again,' said Marianne brightly, and got another leer and a squeeze of her knee for her pains.

Charles was impressed. '*Spanish* wine,' he said, reading the label carefully. 'Hmm.'

Willa smiled and then produced a bowl of pasta which was very oily and teeming with big, fat prawns. It must have cost a fortune, thought Marianne.

'Should really be *tapas*,' said the Bald Wild One. 'Or something that approximated to it.'

Charles nodded sagely. He was good at appearing to understand. Marianne was concentrating on not taking too much, though she could have eaten an entire dishful. 'Only a little for me,' she said sweetly. Willa gave her one spoonful. And then waited, staring right into Marianne's eyes. 'That's more than enough,' she said. 'Thank you.'

It was *sickeningly* delicious. She left a little, a gesture of defiance that finished her off in the irritation stakes. She could have eaten it all up *and* managed seconds. It didn't help when Charles just took her plate and cleaned it with a piece of the exotic seeded bread. After most noticeably cleaning his. She told herself, rather than burst into tears, she could have whatever the sweet was.

The Bald Wild One recovered his powers of speech, not surprising since he ate well. 'First decent nosh since prison,' he said cheerfully and Willa looked delighted. It was a funny old world, thought Marianne, the way her friend had fixed on a man who was – in every way – hopeless. He would never marry – he would never want children – he did not see the point of owning a home. (All these things he announced at the table, brushing the salt-cellar aside as if it represented china mammon.) He considered himself, so he said, to be a Minstrel of Life. By way of illustration, presumably, he began to sing something that Marianne just about recognized as being by Leonard Cohen and – smiling politely at him – she acknowledged the use of her name. He slapped her on the back. 'So longggg Marianne,' he sang, 'It's time we begannnn . . .'

Willa got up to fetch the sweet. *Dessert*, as she called it. Charles made a point of always referring to it as 'Pudding' since that's what Beryl and Richard called it. Marianne knew it as Afters, which she kept to herself. Pudding always made her think of something bubbling in a pot with a bit of old sheet tied over it. The pity of it was that Charles would now require a long debate on the pros and cons of *desserts, puddings* and *sweets* – because He Liked Words and he liked them to be exact. And while he got on with that, as he would do, Marianne would continue to smile at the Bald Wild One in what was probably a lunatic way as he continued to sing and smile beatifically at her. Some sixth sense told her that Best Friend Willa did not like this, Best Friend Willa did not like this one little bit. Bloody Good Job The Second, she thought. She was smiling so hard now it made her jaw ache.

As predicted, Charles would have his pudding debate. It was his way of telling the world that he might be a science graduate, but he was also *cultivated*. Like the French. The French, it seemed, managed to turn out scientists who had read Dumas and listened to Berlioz. Marianne refrained from her usual 'Who?' She wouldn't give him the satisfaction. It didn't matter. She would find out later. A clever debate about language was – in his opinion – a strong indicator of this kind of towering French intellect. As far as Marianne knew, they didn't have anyone called Dumas on their bookshelves but perhaps he had borrowed it from the library? He never went near a library . . . She kept quiet. She'd look the name up. That was where the information about Duckies came from. One of Henry VIII's tenderest of tender letters to Anne Boleyn – written just a couple of years before he chopped her head off.

Marianne watched her husband begin clearing plates. He, too, was a traitor. He never cleared plates at home.

'I'll bring these out,' he said to Willa.

Marianne thought he said it very smugly. But she also felt smug. 'Yes, do help, Charles,' she said with equanimity. 'Do.' She gave him a most brilliant smile. Which she could, now, because she – quite truthfully – no longer cared. How wonderful not to care. She watched him as he followed Willa's elegant form into the kitchen. It would be nice to think that a look of alarm crossed his face as she smiled so brightly but she could not be sure. It didn't matter anyway.

'Ron's been on Highway 61,' said the Bald Wild One, rubbing at his forehead.

'Where's that, Gordon?' asked Marianne politely. He blinked as if trying to remember.

Beyond the kitchen door she thought she heard the faintest sound of a little pleasurable squeak. Charles was obviously up to his tricks again.

'Who's Ron, Gordon?' she said, more loudly.

'Met him in clink,' he said, his voice a little dreamy.

More sounds came from the kitchen. Charles said, Ooh!

Marianne heard her own voice, couldn't believe it, calling out, 'Come on you two, stop whatever you're doing – we want our *sweet*.' That'd stop him mid-grope. She touched the tip of her table companions nose and said, 'Don't we, Gordie?'

And he roared that he certainly did. 'And bring more wine.'

'Yes,' called Marianne. 'Sweet and wine, sweet and wine.'

She rather wished she hadn't been quite so enthusiastic when Willa reappeared, for she carried her baking tray aloft, like an offering to the gods, and upon it, set out in perfect symmetry, were eight perfect little chocolate éclairs. Still warm, it seemed, from the oven, for so Willa smugly told them.

'I just watched her put the cream in,' said Charles excitedly. 'And do the chocolate.' He looked at Marianne sternly. 'Pudding, Marianne,' he said. 'Not sweet.'

'Oh, I always think of puddings as heavy doughy things,' she said. But it was no good. She looked at the perfectly symmetrical trayful. They were perfect. They were desirable. They attested, suddenly, to Willa's absolute command in all areas of her life. Why, she did not even need Marianne's friendship any more. To produce such things – as the Bald Wild One was saying, such *poems* of cookery – was queenly. In their tip of a house, Marianne was still cooking on the old gas stove left behind by the previous owner. If you could call it cooking. Sticking a chicken in the oven for hours and praying it wouldn't be pink when you pulled it apart was hardly gastronomy. Ruth, kind Ruth, as kind as Marcus in her own way, indeed, the kindest of couples really, had come and cleaned the horrible cooker for her (there you are, Marianne, that's how you do it) but even so – you could never produce anything like those éclairs from it to save her life. Or her marriage. The smugness which had been so warm and pleasant drained away. She was nothing.

'Well, Gordon,' said Willa. 'One or two?'

His eyes were pink and and wetly downward as oysters. He smiled at her. 'Hey, babe,' he said. 'You're an absolute doll.'

Willa looked pleased and excited. The first time, all that night, that Marianne had seen her face clear of anxiety. She was like a ten-year-old at Christmas, Marianne thought acidly. So she really cared for the drunken twerp. She curled her lip and wrinkled her Hirondellepinkened nose and found herself saying to the wall straight ahead, '*Babe* and *Doll* strike me as two very demeaning things to call a girl . . .' (Damn, she thought, should have said *young woman*.) 'A definite touch of male chauvinistic piggery, actually. Think of Germaine Greer.'

She plucked the name out of the fuzz in her brain not having actually read *The Female Eunuch* yet – but she knew about it because it was out there, in the ether, if not in her head, and mother-in-law Jean had told her about it and said she would put it in Marianne's stocking at Christmas. To cite it now seemed right what with *Babe* and *Doll* and six different ways to say *Pudding*. Anyway, it was debatable whether or not Charles had read Dumas. Whoever he was. She continued to stare at the wall otherwise she would laugh or cry, she wasn't sure which. It began to dawn on her that she might not need to read the blessed thing after all. She probably *was* the Female Eunuch. Good grief.

The book's title hung in the air. There was a complete and rather wonderful silence. Again. All three sets of eyes were fixed on her. Again. She smiled, reached out, picked up an éclair and stuffed its warm, crisp pastry and its runny chocolate and its perfectly applied cream deep into her mouth. It nearly choked her.

The Bald Wild One suddenly squeezed her knee so hard that half the éclair reappeared through her lips, like a vulgar tongue. 'We pooftahs are like that with women,' he said, giggling quite horribly. 'We just don't give a fuck. Babe, Doll – you ask Ron . . .' He looked at Marianne and gave a game attempt at a wink. 'Does that bother you?'

'What? Pooftahs?' She winked back. Why not? 'Oh no,' she said, munching away happily now. 'I sometimes sell cosmetics to them. They are very friendly.'

Willa was silent and pink-looking. Marianne swallowed the delicious, wonderful éclair, and looked straight into her friend's eyes. 'May I have another one?' she said.

Charles reached out and took an éclair as tentatively as if it would bite him. Gordon reached for one at the same time. Charles flinched but managed not to drop his pastry. Marianne recognized the struggle in him. He was desperately searching around for something Right On to say – after all – he was liberal and socialist and homosexuality was no different from being black or a woman or mentally retarded. Discrimination was fascist stuff. Charles was proud to be free of it.

Marianne helped him. 'We don't have any hang-ups about that sort of thing,' she said, giving Willa a very sweet smile, as sweet as the éclair, and licking the cream from her lips. 'Do we, Charles?'

Willa put her hands on her hips and looked at Gordon. 'Is that a joke?' she asked.

Apparently it was not.

'I've always swung both ways,' he said. 'Darling, I thought you all knew.' He did not sound contrite, merely amused.

Willa did not – it seemed – know. She stood there white and speechless and her carefully made-up pocked skin suddenly stood out in livid, angry pits.

Good, thought Marianne, looking down at the cutlery. She decided to stir the spoon, twist the knife. 'You know, thinking back,' she said, addressing both items, 'The way you behaved and particularly the way you used words makes it all so obvious . . .'

'Such as?' asked the Bald Wild One, interested.

Marianne made something up. She remembered it from school-days and the cutting up of a worm. 'Oh, such as saying all that stuff about hermaphrodites . . .' He nodded. Marianne knew that she had plucked another correct piece from the empire of knowledge that swirled in her fog. She had very nearly said 'bivalves' instead of 'hermaphrodites' but some instinct told her that was *definitely* wrong. The Bald Wild One was many things, but he was not – though he had the eyes of one – a mollusc.

He was about to continue the conversation when, mercifully, Charles interrupted. Presumably in an effort to vent some of his unease and embarrassment, he said, probably with more venom than he actually meant, 'So, my non-academic wife has taken to semantics, suddenly . . .' He laughed awkwardly. Marianne recognized it was some sort of victory for her but since she was not entirely sure what the word *semantics* meant, she just smiled. She would also look that up when she got home.

'Yes,' she said. 'I expect I have. After all, you don't necessarily have to have a degree to do that, now do you . . .?' She prayed that, what-ever it was, you didn't.

Charles stared at her, his half-eaten éclair drooping from his fin-gers.

She smiled at him and stood up. Then, with great deliberation she lifted the hem of her lovely new calico dress to reveal her knees. 'I'll say he swings both ways,' she said, never more grateful for her sensitivity in the matter of bruising skin. For there were the unmistakable imprints of his fingers. 'Gordon,' she said, addressing him as if she were an indulgent schoolteacher, 'Honestly. Talking about your Ronnie while squeezing my knee. Look what you've done.' She shook her head, dropped the hem of her skirt and smoothed it back down, picked up her crocheted bag, finished off the last of the wine in her glass and said to Willa, 'That was really lovely. Thank you.' And without daring to look her in the eye – she left.

Behind her, on the stairs, she heard Charles thumping downwards, and calling her name. The sound of a guitar twanging floated up towards her as she ran. The smell of patchouli was everywhere. On she hurried and this time she did not look back. At the bottom of the stairs the pale face of Stella, Willa's neighbour, appeared at her door. Behind her a baby started to wail. 'Sorry,' said Marianne. '*Sorry*.'

HOUSE NUMBER FOUR

(Rental Property)
71a Redland Road, London, w11

Self-contained basement flat. Wooden steps down to own front door. Small lobby. Sitting room 14 x 9, adjacent corridor space as converted bed area (raised platform bed, clothes storage underneath), lavatory, kitchen 10 x 8, small walled garden. Gas fire. No bath, no shower. Hot water from cylinder over sink. To Let unfurnished. 3gns a week.

Here she was, Marianne Legg née Flowers, back in the bowels of the earth. Living under the pavement. But the house that stands above this basement flat was never as grand as the house that stood above the basement of Dragon Street. The people who lived in this stuccoed house were minor players in the Victorian game of grand living; small-time merchants, clerks, lawyers' runners. The three floors of upstairs rooms were much smaller, the garden a mere yard, the staircases narrow and the mouldings and cornices pretty rather than magnificent. In the end, before it was divided into proper flats, this house was the kind of place where Dickens's Cherry and Merry, those venal sisters in pursuit of Jonas Chuzzlewit, might stay when they came to town. Or a just-about-genteel boarding house for Kipps or Mr Polly. Now, however, it is just as grotty, just as uncared for and abandoned in the matter of its lower colon, as that grander address. If Dragon Street's lower rooms were the working quarters for the servants and dark as death, this small, cramped, damp, dismal flat was designed for one maid of all work and a rat. Shopkeepers' houses, these, respectable tenants bringing idiot girls from Berkshire villages to do for them.

If these walls could speak, thinks Marianne, whose mind is slowly opening to such interesting speculations, what histories they could tell. She imagines how it would once have been for her. Maybe she would have been the maid of all work, the Cinderella girl in the sacking apron. There's a stirring in her as she realizes that she has been given – or she has chosen – a new set of possibilities. As she sits and stares up at the small piece of sky peeping beyond the stairs and railings of this new basement, she is aware of herself as she has never been before. She is no longer an attachment. She is she. Art, history, literature have begun to shed their little beacons in her brain and bits of her have begun to feel alive despite the crushing sense of backward decline moving here has produced. It is as horrible as Dragon Street this basement – smaller and just as grim – and, on bad days, it makes her wonder if it doesn't contain a message. The message being that she is still no better than she ought to be, and this is the kind of place she can expect to live in if she will go upsetting the apple cart of a decent husband and a proper marriage. All those other aspirations such as a nice life in a nice house with a sweet-smelling perfect pink bathroom were but moments of possibility and not hers to keep.

The outlook from the front room windows is just as depressing as it was when she and Charles shared and saved in Dragon Street. But that was a means to an end, at least they had a dream to get out of there and buy their own dear little house with lots of nice dear little ones running around safe within it. There are no such dreams for Marianne here, not even such false ones as the Dragon Street dreams proved to be.

Here in Redland Road the area steps are squeezed and pinched in a tiny, rubbish-filled space and the building is tall and thin and flat-fronted above the one small bay window. She has seen the passage-way in the hall upstairs and it is tiny and thin. The people for whom these houses were built were not meant to be expansive. They would, she thinks, be as small-minded as her own mother and maternal relatives. Secure in Empire and as sure of a place in heaven as they knew their place on earth. Nowadays a few of the houses in the road have been bought by couples and families who are hopeful that the area is on the up but mostly it is still bedsit land. Given that the serial murdering Christie's house is round the corner (though no longer called Rillington Place) and given that there have been extensive and vicious race riots in these roads, this possibility of gentrification is hopeful indeed. There are few signs of improvement and the pub at the junction still has sawdust on the floor. Nevertheless, Notting Hill is lively and cosmopolitan, if a little grubby and down at heel, after the quiet of Richmond. Music hits the air after midnight and groups of all colours hang out and laugh and cause trouble after hours. She likes that; it makes her feel young again. She is twenty-four.

There has to be some compensation for living in this scruffy, semi-furnished hole. If there is, it must be spiritual, for there is certainly nothing in the way of amenities. In 71a Redland Road there is no bathroom at all. Just a sink to wash in and a tiny geyser that decides on the day if it will work or not. When she stands at the sink she often thinks of that paradisaical pink bathroom in Eastbourne Road (sweet and neat, how long ago that seems) and how all the evils that have befallen her were founded in the leaving of it.

Her mother says that whatever she gets, she has brought upon herself and Marianne decides that this could be interpreted as self-determination, which sounds better than Just Plain Cussedness.

Marianne now thinks she should have stayed in the bath on the night Charles perched there, dipping his fingers in the water and telling her that they were going to buy somewhere new, somewhere in need of complete everything. She should have lain there in the scented water and told Charles and his plans to move to Get Stuffed. She might have guessed if she'd had half a brain that he could not make them move from that sweet little house unless she, too, signed the papers. She has been told this recently. She had no idea. She was – maybe still is – a fool. Really, she should also have stood up to Charles years ago only she thought no one else would want her, that she was lucky to have him, that without Charles she would fall apart, be left on the shelf.

Now she is beginning to wonder. She is beginning to wonder about everything. (Not before time, is what her dear mother-in-law Jean says, who thinks her son is an oppressive article.) In particular (and she would not share this with Jean, obviously) she is beginning to wonder if all that being tied to the bedhead and bashed on the bottom with a hairbrush by the usually very proper Charles was normal? And if it was normal, shouldn't she have been consulted on the grounds that it did not do anything for her and she'd really rather prefer not? Or that she might get to like it if she had a cuddle or two first? And if it wasn't normal, would that account for the fact that she did not become pregnant?

Ironically, Marianne's first visit to the fertility clinic at the hospital near her old home is due this week. Despite no longer being in a position (not even tied to the bedhead!) to want to be pregnant, she will go. She has waited, as the doctor said she must, for six months, during which time she left her husband, which rendered the process pointless. Except, she decides, it was not necessarily a waste of time. After all, she was, in the way her mother has of speaking, *trying for a baby* for nearly two years before she walked out. Can she, she wonders, still go to the clinic if she is separated? Now that she has left Charles does she still have the right? Marriage gave you such a leg up in the hierarchical order of things, hierarchical being a new word to Marianne and so much more convincing than saying pecking order. Without marriage (and she has removed her wedding ring) they will probably say she has no right to know about her body's fecundity. There was no one to ask – no one whom she trusted anyway. So she made up her own mind (which felt odd) to keep the appointment. She will decide whether or not to tell the doctor about Charles's preferred manner of sex once she is sitting in his consulting room. It might be relevant and it might not. And it would depend on how brave she felt. She would like to know. After all, she might marry again one day. She certainly hopes she will. Babies and wifedom are her ultimate goals. That and a nice house to live in and a nice kitchen and a lovely, lovely bathroom in which to be clean and pure and odiferous as the advertisements say young women must be. Babies and Wifedom seem very remote now. But she must do something. Apart from any other consideration she has very little money.

Marianne's small and scruffy flat – with slugs that creep about and which creatures she sometimes treads underfoot in the night – costs her a third of her weekly wage and her job doesn't pay very well anyway. You are supposed to enjoy selling style and cosmetics to rich young women and shop girls' wages, be it posh shop or local Co-op, are not very much. You are supposed to get scooped up at some point by a good husband who will make your earnings irrelevant. Well, she has forfeited hers. But she is still paying her half of the mortgage. It was the mortgage that made her delay her departure from her marriage for so long. It was a debt, and a debt was something that her family did not countenance. Debt led the working classes into drink and ruin and the workhouse. Extraordinarily, and even she can see that it was extraordinary, for quite a while she continued to pay all of it – since all of it came out of her bank account on a standing order – until a colleague who was also separated from her husband asked why, if she didn't live in the house any more, she was goose enough to pay her husband's share. Which certainly shone a new and fairer light on things. So she changed the standing order. Charles was extremely annoyed when she reduced the payment to exactly half – and he came to see her. She opened the door to his frighteningly loud knocking and even before he had entered the flat he said, 'You can't go making financial decisions that affect me without discussing it first.' To which she thought, but did not reply, Why not? You always did that for me. She would have said that she couldn't afford it but then he would say that she should have thought about that before she left him. She would have liked to get the words Hierarchical Structure into the conversation somehow, but they did not quite fit. 'Come in,' was all she offered. As usual, when he was angry, less was best.

The first thing Charles said when he had crossed the squalid threshold was, 'That thing's lethal,' pointing at the gas fire popping away in the horrible beige-tiled grate.

'You should see the geyser,' she replied enthusiastically. 'It's like a time bomb.'

He went out to the kitchen. 'Where's the bathroom?' he asked. And then, unable to stop himself, he said, 'My God, this place is a real tip.'

'It's cheap.'

'So I should hope.' And then he rounded on her, turning on his heel, not noticing as he did so that he ground a slug to pulp beneath his shoe. Marianne noticed. 'I'd never have taken on a mortgage like that,' he said, 'if I'd known you were going to leave. And now you won't pay more than the absolute minimum. You are the one in the wrong, Marianne. You.'

Somehow, though quaking in her shoes, she stood her ground. 'As it is,' she said, 'I'm working as a barmaid three evenings a week to manage.'

'Then why don't you stop all this and come home?' But he did not say it with tenderness or love, she felt. He said it more with irritation.

'No,' she said.

'Why?'

'Because I am happier here.'

'Is it because of Willa? It was just a bit of fun. I told you. She still wants to be your friend. She's going to come round and see you and put it right and *then* perhaps you'll come home.'

'Willa,' said Marianne, with spirit enough to make her husband blink, 'can just fuck off out of it.' Twelve years of friendship down the pan – but what the hell. 'Tell her that, please. You can't have a best friend if you don't trust her.'

'You know what Willa's like,' he said, more warmly now. 'Doesn't mean a thing.'

'Well, it means a thing to me.' She folded her arms across her chest.

He looked at her, shook his head at the waywardness of it all, and left saying, 'You are impossible, Marianne.' He was actually growling as he ran up the slimy, area steps.

Later that week good friend Ruth appeared on the same, slippery, wooden steps. She was holding a bag of cleaning materials. And she immediately sprinkled the slimy slipperiness with salt. 'Otherwise you will break your neck.'

'As if they'd care,' said Marianne, only half joking.

Ruth tutted but otherwise ignored Marianne's bid for pathos as if she were a schoolteacher and Marianne had just said a rude word. (Best ignored, misbehaving children.) 'You can take a scrubbing brush to it later.'

How nice was the familiar.

'Haven't got one,' said Marianne happily.

Ruth tutted again.

'And welcome,' said Marianne.

Ruth entered looking grim.

Wherever Marianne lived since she left home there was always a filthy old cooker and Ruth always arrived to scour and rub and shine each one. It was traditional and always unrewarding but this one was definitely, definitely the worst.

'You won't make much headway with this,' said Marianne mildly. 'I think Alfred probably burned the cakes in it.' There was no sense of shame in her where housework was concerned. She had never lived in anywhere that was worthy of a duster and her mother, widowed and too busy trying to scratch a living, spent little time cleaning. Tidying in the home of her childhood took the form of throwing old curtains or tablecloths over piles of junk to make them look neat. 'Well,' said Ruth, eyeing the cooker with disgust, 'I'll have a good go at it.' The implication was quite clear. Marianne had *not* had a good go at it. Which was perfectly true.

Ruth worked away and the smell of ammonia sharpened the mildewy air of the kitchen. Marianne rather liked it. The first hint of cleanliness in the place. Somewhere in the slowly clearing fog of her mind, hazy but readable, was a growing understanding that the world was made up of girls who washed down their walls and dust-ed their skirting boards, and girls who did not. And Marianne – as the mist began to rise from her – realized she was one who did not. And – given the example of her own mother, and her mother-in-law, neither of whom were good home-making examples, perhaps it was not *necessarily* a bad thing. The only thing she did know was that if she had a decent bathroom, she would – like some religious rite – clean it beautifully.

'Can I come and have a bath sometime?' she said.

'Of course,' said Ruth. 'I don't know how you get yourself into places like this. Charles said it was bad but . . .'

'He can talk. I'll bet he hasn't lifted a finger at our house.'

Silence. Marcus and Ruth were determinedly loyal to both of them.

While she worked at the burned and filthy enamel, Ruth kept up a series of sympathetic criticisms. It was quite obvious to her that Marianne was not here because she wanted to be. Notting Hill was a very dodgy area – not good for a girl living on her own – all those black men standing around being idle. (Ruth came from a Colonial background. Spending your first nine years on the Gold Coast obviously made a deep impression. Ruth was always saying, if she made cocoa – and she was the sort of girl to make cocoa – that, 'This is what we used to grow on our farm before they took it away from us.' Or – being of a substantial build – she would say, a little mournfully, that in Africa they liked their girls to be fat.) Apart from these idle black men, apparently out to get her, the area was full of oddballs: women wearing grubby cardigans and men's caps who muttered and drank, savage tramps who just stretched out in a doorway when they wanted to sleep, and dirty long-haired beatnik types, probably on drugs. The drugs that Willa's boyfriend, the Bald Wild One, went to prison for, perhaps? No wonder Willa was feeling contrite. To lose your boyfriend to a man and an ex-con, and your best girlfriend to a quick grope with best girlfriend's husband, must be tough. Especially now that ex-best-girlfriend is living in dangerous and dashing Notting Hill. Providing she never let Willa into the flat she might just go on imagining it like that.

Despite Ruth's views the area sounded a great deal more exciting and dangerous than it really was. Or that Marianne had ever noticed. Because she left for work by eight thirty and spent two nights, sometimes three, working at a pub in Kensington, she had not – actually – experienced a great deal of the local colour over the past few months. But she knew the woman in the cap and cardigan who had aroused Ruth's extreme disapproval.

'You mean Mrs Norris,' she said. 'She has the pots and pans stall in

Portobello. It was her husband's cap. He never came home from the war. I got my pans from her. Very cheap.' Marianne pointed to the three slightly chipped brown enamel saucepans standing on the rickety, scrubbed table. Ruth looked at them with very appealing disapproval.

'When Charles told us what it was like here,' said Ruth, resuming rubbing away at the grease and the grime (she really was a dab hand with a Brillo pad and the ammonia bottle), 'I couldn't believe it. Marianne, you are silly. If you want to make a point to stop him misbehaving, just stop speaking to him. But don't move out, for goodness' sake.'

'Is that what he thinks?' Marianne asked, sitting on the three-legged stool and watching Ruth's labours with fascination, as if she was at the theatre. 'That I'm making a point?'

Ruth put down the soapy pad and gave her what her mother called an old-fashioned look. 'No,' she said, 'It's what I told him. I also said it was about time you stood up to him.'

Marianne said nervously, 'What did he say to *that*?'

'First he cried over your wedding photographs. The ones we've got.'

'Cried?' said Marianne.

'Well – all right – he looked glum over your wedding photographs. 'Then he went out and got very, very drunk.'

If Ruth was about to say something further, she thought better of it, shut her lips, and returned to the stove with renewed verve. Marianne longed to say, for a joke, that she was in danger of finding Australia if she rubbed any harder but there was something very unjokelike in Ruth's manner. She looked, thought Marianne, a bit shifty. 'Ruth,' she said, 'who with?'

'Who with what?'

'Who did he go out and get drunk with?'

Ruth went on rubbing. 'Well, I know who he went *out* with. He went *out* with Danny and Marcus – to the Northumberland Arms – the one in Putney that stays open till eleven. And he got very drunk. The police were called for some reason. Apparently he had a hangover for three days. When I saw him he was still green.'

'If only,' Marianne said to Ruth, 'if only he had done something wild like that with *me*. Ever.'

Ruth, always practical, said, 'Don't be silly, Marianne. He was still throwing up when I saw him. Not the slightest bit exciting, a weak-stomached drunk. I know because Marcus is the same. I never let him have more than a pint and a half.'

'Anyone else go with them?' Marianne wondered where this instinct came from. Maybe her new-found independence was sharpening her senses?

Again Ruth looked shifty.

I'll take the bull by the horns, Marianne thought, her mind playing tricks so that she actually heard Charles saying, 'Cliché, Marianne, *cliché* . . . "Did Willa go that night?' she asked.

'No,' said Ruth, putting down the silly, foaming pad. With a resigned look she said ,'He went round to see her afterwards. Then he came back to us in the morning – and he's been sick ever since.'

Later, the blackened cooker looking remarkably unappealing, though minus several levels of enamel, Ruth and Marianne were sitting on the floor with the gas fire on full blast so that it popped and spluttered very cheerfully. Besides the gas fire, the only bit of liveliness in the room was an Indian bedspread she had draped over a disgusting settee – an item of furniture inherited from the previous tenants. It sagged in every department. 'Just like me,' she said to Ruth, who had the grace to laugh.

'Actually you've lost weight,' she said. 'It suits you.' Ruth eyed her up and down, 'In fact you're looking very well indeed.'

Marianne blushed and immediately turned and stroked the bright coverlet.

'That's nice,' said Ruth. 'Where did it come from?' She, too, began to stroke it. There was something soft and desirable about the weave and the rich gold and redness of the colours. It was exotic and out of place in all this squalor.

'Nice,' said Ruth again. And waited. But Marianne was not going to tell her where it came from. It was her secret and – while she was still a married woman – it did not do to rock the boat – make waves – open cans of worms. The solicitor had put his fingers in his ears and said so.

Ruth's cardigan made scorching smells she was so close to the flames. It was October now and the nights were chill. The cold that seemed to live in the walls reminded Marianne of Dragon Street all those years ago. She shivered. If only she had stood up for herself then. If only she had said that she did not want to live in the damp and the dark but in the light and the air. Jean was right. She had been too amenable, too unsure of her place in the world, and Charles had not exactly taken advantage of it, but had taken charge. She could only blame herself for being so pale and unassertive. Only herself.

And then, suddenly, the fire died. 'Have you got any money?' she asked, shame-faced. She had used her last this morning. 'I'll get paid by the pub tomorrow. Sorry.'

'Pub?' asked Ruth.

Marianne nodded. 'I can't afford my half of the mortgage and the rent without doing an evening job. But I like it actually. It's full of artists and writers and interesting people and they don't seem to think I'm thick.'

'Well, you aren't,' said Ruth firmly. 'Just badly educated. Like me.' She took a couple of coins out of her purse and dropped them into the meter. What bliss those flames were – like a friendship in the horrible room.

Ruth reached out and ran her fingers along a small bookcase. 'Are these yours?' she asked, surprised. 'They're Penguin Classics.'

'Mostly,' said Marianne, unable to keep the pride out of her voice. She picked up a blue and white paperback. '*Swann's Way*,' she read out loud. 'Proust.'

Ruth looked impressed. 'I haven't read stuff like this since school. Didn't really read it then much, either.'

'Me neither,' said Marianne. Though she knew it was for different reasons. At her school there were no Penguin Classics – not in a moribund Secondary Modern. Ruth went to a small public school where if the books were on the shelves there was little encouragement to read them unless you were super-bright or taking a specific exam. They were both girls of their time and academically expendable. Marianne learned how to make shepherd's pie and rice pudding and iron a shirt, Ruth knew all there was to know about flower arranging, deportment (including getting in and out of a Mini without showing her knickers) and the finer points of napery; Marianne could add up at shop-keeping level – well, just about – and Ruth knew exactly how to address a bishop. Apart from that they emerged from their respective establishments ignorant and unformed though Ruth did, at least, have confidence.

Since Marianne moved here the beginning of knowledge and the outline of a shape seemed to be happening to her. The people in the pub, the ones she served, who looked scruffy and interesting and lived in Chelsea or its boundaries, came in with paint under their fingernails, pencils entwined in their hair, books tucked beneath their arms, and spoke to her as if she knew all about everything. Just as if she were the same as they were – apart from the ogling that often went with the bar talk. There were a lot of men who were regulars – old ones usually – who wanted her to pose for them with all her clothes off. She'd been halfway inclined to do it when one of the so-called painters turned out not to be a painter at all but a man who designed gardens. One of the real painters, with white hair and sharp blue eyes and a love of pink wine, pointed this out. 'Arthur,' he said kindly to Marianne, 'is a hybrid of Gertrude Jekyll, Capability Brown and a lecherous old shit.'

Hybrid, she thought, was a nice, new word.

'He's not a painter. He's playing the fool with you.'

'Thank you,' she said.

'Don't mention it,' he replied, leaning nearer towards her on the bar and promptly asking her to do the same for him. She smiled, said nothing, and went off to serve someone else.

But at least he was an artist and you could forgive artists every-thing – just because they were artists.

'Matisse,' he said later, apparently mindlessly stroking the inner softness of her forearm, 'is not *better* than Picasso, just different. His view of women is softer. Yes? His colours kinder. His light lovelier. Do you agree?'

She nodded. And reluctantly removed her arm. She had heard of Picasso, obviously; Matisse, however, was new to her. She noted down the name on her pad by the till. Everything was new and everything was exciting. Very different from school. She wanted, suddenly and quite desperately, to learn.

'Fuck Pugin,' said a pale youth in very scruffy corduroy.

'Who?' she asked. And she added him to the list as well.

The pale youth watched her. 'And fuck you, too?' He added with hope. 'That'd be nice.'

She served him his light and bitter with a bright smile. 'I don't think so,' she said. He smiled back, quite at ease. 'One has to ask,' he said. 'Obviously.'

'Obviously,' she said, and smiled again.

113

Smiling seemed to counter these awkward moments. She found that she could deal with all kinds of things that would once have unnerved her. An ease had come about now she was no longer connected with husband Charles. With him she always felt awkward and stupid. Here she felt flirtatious and attractive and as if they thought she was worth something in the brain department. Though it was clear that the body department still took precedence after drink was taken. She let her eyes look into the eyes of the corduroy youth so that he leaned his elbows on the counter and asked her if she would fly away with him.

'Perhaps tomorrow,' she said.

'You won't,' said the pale youth. 'You're in love with someone else.'

Some years later she discovered that he was the second son of a duke. Too late by then, though. Too late.

'*Le Grand Meaulnes* is a great and tragic book. Life reflecting art in the author's youthful fate . . .' The woman who said this was an author herself, so Marianne had heard. 'I haven't read it,' she dared to say. The woman answered her crisply, as if it were a foregone conclusion. 'Well, you must. Alain-Fournier,' she spelled out.

Marianne wrote that name down, too. Then she tried a little intellectualism of her own. She asked the Alain-Fournier woman about *A la Recherche du temps perdu* (she had overheard the name and written it down phonetically) and the Alain-Fournier woman said she must read it at once. 'It is,' said the woman, 'a way of getting through the night if you are lonely.' As this was often, though certainly not always, the case for Marianne, she went to order the book in the big department store in Kensington. But she did not have to place an order. It was there, on the shelves, so the assistant told her. All lined up alphabetically, every Classic you could name.

Marianne could not find it. 'Proust, Proust, Proust,' he called, pointing at the shelves. Marianne was looking for Prewst, Prewst, Prewst. The assistant came over to help, and despite his spots and spectacles, he became a superior being as he picked it out from quite the wrong part of the shelf marked 'P'. Marianne did not like this assistant who had a tendency to laugh at her. Despite her penury she bought the entire set, and the Alain-Fournier, too, and decided to worry about the money later. Now she was reading her way through them hungrily. What was odd was that they were not hard to read at all. In fact, they were real page-turners. Like scenes from life. She enjoyed them, savoured them. There was something meaty about this kind of writing – as if she were getting her chops around some good old steak and chips after a limp cheese salad.

When she told her mother-in-law that it felt like a proper meal at last, her mother-in-law laughed and said she thought the authors would be delighted to know that. 'It's a good metaphor, Marianne,' she said.

'What's a metaphor?'

Steak over salad, any day. That was what it felt like, reading her way through Proust. Nowadays only the owning of books felt completely satisfying. She had outgrown the local library except for reference. When the time came to take back the books, it was like handing new friends back to outer darkness. She said this to Jean, laughing at herself for being so silly and Jean secretly sent her some money. Not a great deal but a nice little sum – enough to pay for the set of Proust and a few more besides. She also suggested in her note that Marianne should never stop asking questions. Even of the spotty book-selling assistant. 'Let him think what he likes,' she wrote, 'as long as you have the information you need to move onwards and upwards.' Jean said it was all about digging in good manure. Feeding the mind. Nutrients for the brain. 'That's what girls need,' she said. 'Look at Beryl. University, two degrees, and she'll never look back . . .' They were silent for a moment. Both were thinking, no doubt, that sometimes there were detractions in Jean's theory.

Marianne took to keeping a little notebook in which she jotted down the thoughts and questions that arose from each book. Sometimes she solved oddities and sometimes she decided – rather grandly she felt – that it was a flaw in the novel rather than in herself. In *Vanity Fair* she was so taken with the misunderstanding about dear Dobbin being the donor of the piano to Amelia that she never quite forgave Thackeray his mistake. In *Jane Eyre* she wondered long and hard about where it was Jane travelled in the world later in her life as she declares . . . Jean suggested that Marianne should think about going to college.

'But I'm twenty-five!' she cried.

'Old enough then,' said Jean.

It was only later that Marianne thought how odd this was. Surely her mother-in-law should have said, 'Get back to my son at once.' But she didn't. Her errant daughter-in-law decided not to pursue this but to take Jean at her word. It was too complicated to consider anything else. And this lot was going to be complicated enough. She was afraid of failure as she looked at the grey-spined Forsters and the Eliots and the Woolfs brought back from her second trip to the bookshop. These were real Classics . . . *Classics* and she was afraid she would fail to understand them. But she must keep her feelings to herself. Charles's message, that she did not have the intellectual stamina, had bitten deep. The humiliation of failure was too horrible to contemplate. Not least because she had a good reason in her life to succeed now. Having found her independence and having found her brain and having nearly found her new shape, she had also found New Love. And New Love who also thought she had a brain. She could tell from the way he spoke to her and the films they went to see and the way he stood her in front of his (incomprehensible mostly) sculptures and installations and maquettes and spoke about it as if she really *knew* what he meant. This time she dared to ask questions. She did not know that she had stumbled upon the perfect handmaiden to the artist – a good-looking young woman who is interested in your work and your body; he was hers for ever, if she'd have him. Perhaps she should have thought twice, creators necessarily being selfish creatures in order to make their art – but she did not think twice. She did not even think once. She just said Yes.

The gas fire popped.

'You've gone all odd about the eyes, Marianne,' said Ruth severely. 'Are you on something?'

She must not tell her though she was longing to tell someone. Only the people at the pub knew that she was in love. 'Oh no,' she said. 'I'm being extra careful now because I'm going to the hospital next week to see why I'm not getting pregnant.'

'I should have thought that was abundantly clear,' Ruth laughed. 'It does take two, you know. Living here on your own. It'd have to be an immaculate conception.'

Marianne clamped her mouth shut. The indignation was hot and quick. But no, no, no. Though she longed to tell she must not. Oh – how she longed to.

'Does Charles know?' asked Ruth.

'About what?' said a nervous Marianne, forgetting their previous conversation.

'About the hospital.'

'No –' said Marianne, with great relief. 'And you must not tell him.'

'I won't,' she said. But of course, she did. Being Ruth it was unlikely that she told him in gentle tones that his estranged wife was keeping her hospital appointment and wasn't that forward-thinking of her? It was more likely that Ruth suggested he was a complete rat to let his unhappy estranged wife go through it all alone and that he should get on up to Notting Hill and see her about it p.d.q.

Charles seemed to think he still had claim over Marianne's body. When he arrived he was unshaven and wild-eyed.

'You finally slept with Willa,' was the first thing she said, determined to take the high ground from him. In saying it, oddly, she felt nothing.

He looked ashamed for a moment. Then he said, 'Only once. And it made me feel sick.'

'Sure it wasn't the booze?' she asked.

He ignored this and put on his stern face. 'Ruth says you are going to the hospital for tests. Why didn't you tell me?'

'Because it's my body,' she said. And she thought, *Crikey, where did that come from?*

'You are my wife,' he said.

'You are also sleeping with Willa,' she answered. Suddenly she understood the art of arguing with him. Forget your own transgressions by holding up a mirror to the other party. 'My so-called one-time best friend.'

'She was in a state over that boyfriend of hers turning out to be queer.'

'Was she? How unlike her to be in a state over anything. Good old invincible Willa.'

'And you had left me.'

'So I had.'

He mistook her tone for sorrow and bitterness and made a move towards her, to put his hand to her face. She backed away. That much she could not bear. His voice, usually so grown-up, became like a small child's. 'I have really hurt you, haven't I?'

She nodded. That was easiest.

'Marianne,' he said, even more quietly, 'I am so sorry.'

'It doesn't matter any more,' she said emphatically. 'Please just go.'

She watched his departing back, his head hung low, and she heard the door close softly behind him. Only after he had gone did she ask herself how she really felt about his complete infidelity with Willa. And the truth was, it scarcely touched her at all. She felt an immense power to be free of any deeply painful reaction. It was a fleabite, not the rip of a shark. She would not, she decided, tell her husband. But she would love the opportunity to tell Willa that Charles said the experience of bedding her made him feel *sick*. Very good, it would be, to say that. And she had the opportunity. She might even ask if he tied her to the bedpost as well.

The following evening, when Marianne came home from barmaiding, there was a dark shape sitting on her filthy old wooden steps. Bits of paper and dusty leaves blew about the figure in the autumnal chill but the figure remained quite still. It was Willa. Marianne's first urge was to leave her there. But her past self surfaced, and was polite, and invited her in. 'Charles said you would come,' she said, and opened the door.

When she switched on the two small reading lamps she had brought with her from the Richmond house, the interior of the horrible basement did not, Marianne hoped, look too bad. Nevertheless Willa wrinkled her nose as she sat down on the settee.

'Christ!' she said. 'This really is awful.'

'Do you mind if I eat my tea?' asked Marianne, ignoring the statement. 'I've just come back from the pub and I'm starving.'

There was no point in hiding what it was – Kentucky Fried Chicken – so she put the box on a tray and sat on the floor by the popping gas fire, and began to eat. Willa looked at her with a strange look – half affectionate, half supercilious. 'Men,' she said, and shook her head.

'Which particular one did you have in mind?' asked Marianne, licking her fingers.

'All of them,' said Willa. But the beginnings of her old friendliness died away. She fixed Marianne with a firm look. 'Did it really upset you that much?' she asked.

'What?' asked Marianne.

'That stupid snog we had in your kitchen?'

'You've changed,' said Marianne, studying her greasy fingers and sucking on a bone.

'Did it?'

'It did at first. But now – it doesn't.'

'It was nothing.'

'I know,' said Marianne, making even more satisfactory sucking noises as she put each finger end into her mouth. 'He said that. He said that about the other thing, too. The more recent thing. Have you come to apologize for both?'

Willa's face twitched. The high ground had given way to a definite edge of panic. Caught out. She took a deep breath and said in a shaky voice, 'Other thing?'

Marianne's gaze above her greasy fingers was quite steady.

Eventually Willa said, 'It was just a bit of fun. You know what parties are like.'

'I don't mean the party,' said Marianne. And she waited.

This time Willa said nothing.

'I mean,' said Marianne, 'after the other night. When you slept – sorry – my beloved mother-in-law always says I should say what I mean; for instance, she says, if you want to go to the lavatory to pee or defecate then you don't ask to be excused to wash your hands . . .'

Willa was looking irritated.

Marianne continued. 'So – *not* when you slept together but when you had sex together. That doesn't sound as if it was just a bit of fun. Anyway, my husband isn't known for having fun in the bedroom – sorry – *sexual activity* department.'

'How did you find out?' Willa's voice was almost inaudible. But it seemed to be less from embarrassment than rage.

'Charles told me. And from what he said it wasn't a bit of fun for him at all. In fact it was anything but. He said he felt sick afterwards.' She put down the packet with its happy, insouciant Colonel smiling up so innocently. 'That's not very nice, now, is it? Especially after Gordon? You must be feeling . . .' Marianne looked around the room. 'Really awful.' She looked up at her visitor and beamed.

Marianne was right. It was rage that made the mask of Willa's face. She recognized it from school days. She beamed even more broadly. How much she wanted to reach out and discover this was just another joke between them. But she did not dare. It was no joke, she couldn't pretend. Friendships were built on trust.

Willa stood up. 'Whatever happened to us, Marianne? We were good friends.'

119

Marianne shrugged. She tapped at the empty chicken carton with her fingertip and it toppled over, taking the Colonel's smiling visage with it. 'We've grown up,' she said. 'Or I have. What you did was not very nice, now was it? You chucked our friendship down the drain just because it made you feel better to upset me. Not very nice of you, not at all. I mean, how would you feel if I was caught with Gordon's tongue down my throat?' She put her greasy hand to her mouth and said, 'Oh dear – sorry – of course – I wouldn't – now would I? Who'd have thought it of him?' She had scored a direct hit. She wished she had not said it, but it was a sweet, sweet feeling. Willa flinched and her eyes were like stones. Then the demon in Marianne added, 'I might go back to Charles eventually. And I might not. He wants me to return, he wants it very much he says – and that's very nice. After all these years and he still really wants me. He says he misses me. It *is* nice, isn't it? To be wanted? We'll work it out I expect . . . It would be nice to be looked after again. I expect I still love him after all. Yes, yes, I think that I do.' Marianne had just finished reading some of Dorothy Parker's more demented poems.

Nice. Such claptrap. But Willa looked convinced.

Just for a moment Marianne put aside the joy of having Norman (for 'twas he) in her life and really did think about Charles. Does Absence Make the Heart Grow Fonder? was what she thought, and waited for his voice to thunder through her fog complaining about this even more dreadful use of cliché. It did not. She wondered how she really felt about everything. It was all such a muddle. What she felt seemed to have little relevance to anybody. Not even herself. This must change. She could hear Jean saying it. Love yourself was a very embarrassing phrase but it was also essential. From this evening she determined to try to do so and it would not, could not, involve Charles. But she wasn't going to tell Willa that.

Norman. Although she loved the excitement of it all – the whirling off at weekends when she stayed at his flat in Camden (ever so cool) and their constantly eating out in interesting, un-posh places where the food was nothing like meat and two veg and the drink came in unmarked bottles – she was still finding it all ever so slightly wrong. As if a part of this particular jigsaw was still missing. And if she examined what that might be, (and she only ever did this for a short while, it being such an embarrassing experience) it seemed to be very closely allied with – um – Sex. She had swapped her husband for a new bedmate and while this new bedmate showed no interest in tying her ankles to the bedpost or going at her with the back of a hairbrush (thank heavens) he had other games, other requirements. Like her wearing waspies and corsets and suspender belts and high heels and gloves. Bloody hell, she thought when she first saw them – *gloves* – how could they possibly be appropriate? And wasn't anyone in the whole world out there happy just to lie down one on top of the other and whisper you were wonderful and kiss a bit – then proceed slowly to what she seen simulated but never seemed to get herself? Apparently not. Yet again, Marianne always felt as if she had run for a bus when they had sex rather than waited at the stop and read the paper for a while first.

But at least Norman's preferred garments were for her to wear. Just for a moment, when he took them out of his bottom drawer, where they sat in a rumpled plastic bag beneath his hairy old jumpers, just for a moment she thought *he* might be going to put them on and she really was not sure at all that she could deal with that. Being strapped down to the ironing board by Charles was one thing, being lunged at by a man wearing a brassiere was – undoubtedly – another. So it was something of a relief when he gave her a very large glass of white wine and then handed the contents of the plastic bag over to her and sort of grunted that she should put them on. Including the dinky little white frilled gloves. Also something she did rather like – which were spiky high heels – because they made her legs look longer and thinner. This was something of a compensation for the knickers he provided, which were so small and tight that she often wondered if they would cut her up at the gusset. Of course she kept these thoughts to herself, just as she never said to Charles that she found hanging from rope attached to the ceiling a bit boring.

What was missing in all this was tenderness. She had begun to read about tenderness. Madame Bovary had obviously had tenderness from Rodolphe which made her swoon for him; Jane Eyre had great tenderness for and from Rochester though they were both good at disguising it and Edmund's tenderness for the egregiously awful Fanny Price was utterly enviable. Marianne found tenderness in being brought an early morning cup of tea at Norman's higgledy-piggledy flat, if she was lucky. Ah well. As her mother might say, 'It's not the be all and end all . . . Rise above.'

She brought herself back to the sweetness of the moment and to Willa's strained face.

'Mmm,' she said, 'Charles and I might get back together and have some babies . . . That's beginning to appeal to me again. Absence really does make the heart grow fonder.'

She did not dare look up from the Kentucky Fried Chicken carton which she was trying to put right with her fingertips. If she had dared to look, she might have noticed how Willa's stony eyes narrowed at this wholly untrue but nevertheless convincing statement. Charles may well want her back, he may well miss her, but he did not love her with tenderness and Marianne had no intention of returning to that grotty house in Richmond. What was happening in her life now was far too exciting to give up. Despite the gloves and the strangulating knickers.

'Nothing more to say then,' said Willa. 'You obviously miss him a great deal.'

'Probably not a lot more to say,' said Marianne. 'And yes I do. I miss my husband very much.' If you are going to lie, lie big. 'And I think it's best if you go now.'

She picked up her copy of *Eugenie Grandet*. 'Balzac knew a thing or two about deceit.'

At the door Willa turned. For a moment there was a knot in the region of Marianne's heart. Then she banished it. Willa's look was one Marianne had often seen directed at others. It said, 'You'll Regret This.' Marianne remembered it – afterwards. 'The thing is, Willa,' she said, giving a false yawn. 'He's not very good at it, Charles, is he?'

Willa smirked. 'I think it's to do with the person you're humping, Marianne. I thought he was very good, actually. Very good.'

The slam that Willa gave the door shook the entire house. Were there resident ghosts of tweenie maids lying about slumbering deeply after long late nights of washing up, it would even have woken them. It was very satisfactory.

Some weeks later, around the time that Norman broke Marianne's heart by behaving just as selfishly as Charles, except in a more artistic way – by forgetting to come and see her when he said he would, forgetting to talk to her at private views because he was obsessed with talking to critics or dealers or other artists, forgetting to collect her from the pub so that she had either to walk or to accept a lift from a drunken old lecher who was late at the bar on purpose and who wished to squeeze any part of her he could get at, or she must pay for a cab – when all these things and more kicked in and she realized that he was no different from Charles in that she still felt irrelevant and that Charles and the future with him was better in one important regard – comfort – and in a second important regard – security – and anyway he had been going on at her for weeks to go back to him – she decided that she jolly well would do so. It was all too much of a struggle. A horrible home shared was better than a horrible home alone. And Charles, at least, was the devil she knew.

He had left her alone for a while, which was tactics, Marianne decided. It was time to go home. She rang him and asked him to visit. She did not tell Norman. When Norman rang and in his usual I've Got One Eye On The Telly way asked her if she was coming over at the weekend, she made an excuse.

When Charles arrived she was calm and prepared, looking at her best, sitting on the horrible settee with her hands in her lap and a sweet smile of welcome on her face. The hospital told her that they could see no reason for her not to get pregnant but that she should get on with her life, go and do something else, be happy, be calm, and it might happen. On the other hand, it might not. Marianne felt that in the light of the urgency of starting a family, and knowing Norman was as far removed from being a family man as Picasso was from becoming Pope, she'd opt for Charles and security.

'I have decided,' she said, feeling quite grand at having made such a big decision all on her own, 'that I want to come back to you.'

She waited for him to fall to his knees and be tearfully delighted (her little fantasy) but instead Charles gave her an unpleasant little grimace. It was not a smile, it was definitely a smirk. Still she sat there gracefully composed. 'Charles?' she said. 'What do you think?'

There was that smirk again. 'I think it is too late, Marianne,' he said. 'Far too late. For I am in love with someone else.'

'Who?' said Marianne incredulously.

'Whom,' said Charles, automatically.

It occurred to her that her incredulity was not altogether flattering. '*Who?*' She repeated and put her hand to her mouth to hide a shocked bubble of laughter. His smirk was very broad now. And then her heart beat one piercing hit of pain. 'Not – *Willa?*' she whispered. The pain was not to do with losing Charles to the girl who was once her best friend, it was to do with losing the girl who was once her best friend to him. *Him!*

'Close,' he said cheerfully. 'It's Stella – Willa's downstairs neighbour.'

Marianne laughed. It was, after all, laughable. 'The guitar-twanger? But you called her an old hippie,' she said. 'She probably smokes dope and she wears patchouli. You can't stand patchouli. And she's got a child . . . You hate children.'

He ignored this. 'Willa introduced us,' he said.

'You said she was irresponsible and should be reported for having a baby and smoking dope.'

'I've changed my mind,' he said. 'She's kind and helpful and very sweet.'

Marianne could not resist saying, 'Like Dickens's Little Nell?' Or is it Little Dorrit?'

He gave her one of his cross looks. 'Willa said you were incredibly rude to her, too.' He let that sink in for a moment and then added. 'After she came round here to see you she came to see me and she was very upset. I had to help her back to her flat.'

Marianne, indignant at the idea that she had been rude to anybody, said sharply, 'And screwed her again?'

He winced. He closed his eyes like a forebearing schoolteacher. 'No, Marianne,' he said. 'I did not *screw* her. I sat with her and had a cup of tea until she stopped crying . . .'

'*Crying*? Why was she crying?'

'Because you were so unpleasant and she was only trying to help. She was your best friend, you know.'

A response to this did not bear thinking about so Marianne just looked at him as if for the first time. He had frown lines, deep as ski-ruts, between his eyebrows and what she always rather admired as his brooding look she suddenly realized was the stamp of ill-temper. He was also losing his hair. In fact, as she continued to look at him she suddenly realized that she found him most unattractive after all. The handsome, elegant young man whom she met at that party all those years ago had gone sour and old. She waited, her face a blank. Charles was no longer smirking. It was as if he realized that he had lost something. Which, of course, he had. This, she now knew thanks to Norman's lengthy discourse on the subject, was the Zen Moment of Rightness – the point at which the light of truth enters the mind. Charles felt her leave him once and for all, this she saw.

'Well,' he said eventually, 'when the crying stopped it left Willa with a headache and she asked me to pop down and get an aspirin from Stella – and I did – and that's how we met. She came up to look after Willa and I stayed and we had a glass of wine and . . .'

'Willa was miraculously better after three glasses?' Marianne put her hand to her head. 'It's your business. I don't want to hear any more.'

'She earns her *living* by playing the guitar,' he said, with just a hint of pride. 'And she weaves.'

'How cool,' said Marianne. She noticed that he was wearing a strangely lumpy tie the colour and texture of cold porridge and bird droppings. 'Lovely,' she said. 'Clearly she manages to do both at the same time.'

She was out of it. Gone. She had spent a third of her life with this man and never questioned why. She understood that, much as she now understood that he was no longer attractive to her, this was a put-up job. She remembered Willa saying scornfully that Stella was just desperate for a husband – or a nice solvent manfriend – well, Charles was that all right.

'Peace and Love,' she said, and smiled and put up two fingers.

She thought he might hit her.

He was halfway up the grotty wooden staircase, his feet all blown about with crisp packets and soggy newspapers, when he wagged his finger at her. This was the old Charles. Up and running and back. 'Willa's been a good friend to both of us and she didn't deserve the way you behaved towards her. She was only trying to help.'

Marianne waited. He wagged his finger even harder. 'I'm sorry, Marianne, I really am. But you've changed. You are not the girl I once loved.'

Marianne nodded. She thought this was probably true. She hoped it was. Suddenly she felt the fog lift to allow a shaft of wisdom. She was free. Whatever that might mean. She had proposed putting her- self back in prison this evening and the gaoler had rejected her. On the whole, she thought, that was good. Very Good.

When she heard the car pulling away and knew that Charles had definitely gone, she felt emptied out and flat, but also vaguely excited. An odd mixture that made her catch her breath. 'Oh,' she said to the horrible room in the horrible flat. 'Oh.' She returned to the horrible settee and put her hand behind the grubby beige cushion and pulled out a tissue-wrapped package, the wrapping of which she had laboured over so carefully before he came. Her gift for her husband. A way of saying, Hallo, I'm back, and just the way you like me.

She ripped the tissue paper to shreds and pulled out the gift. She smiled as she held it up to the popping gas fire. In the light they glowed and swung and looked extraordinarily foolish and obscene. They were red, velvet-covered handcuffs. Special present for him. Obscene and absurd, just the way Charles liked things. She wiggled them so they dangled jauntily, and she wondered if they would make a good present for Norman. He *probably* liked that sort of thing, too. After all, in her experience *every* man in the world seemed to enjoy tying you down or tying you up.

Out loud she said to the fizzing, popping gas fire, 'Oh well, if there are to be no babies for the time being, I shall just have to do something else now, won't I?'

She curled her legs beneath her on the dreadful settee, settled back into the softness of the Indian bedspread – and picked up another book – this one was by someone called Jean-Paul Sartre. It was, apparently, Book One of *The Roads To Freedom* trilogy. Rather appropriate really. As she settled down to read, she wondered what the next thing, the something else, could possibly be.

HOUSE NUMBER FIVE

(Reprise)
24 Russell Road, Richmond

Not noticeably different from when she moved out, Marianne thinks, closing the front door. Still very much as it was when purchased save for some new plastering where dry rot was discovered and a few new floorboards where wet rot sneaked in. The disgusting bathroom on the ground floor is the same but upstairs there is now a bath and a lavatory, brand new, installed in one of the small bedrooms at the back. They look like shiny startled debutantes in amongst the grime and decay of their surroundings. It is hardly a bathroom in the proper sense. Not yet. Here the floorboards are bare and the walls are still a mixture of old paint and cracks where shelves and ancient fitted cupboards have been ripped out. But the bath – and the wash basin – and the WC – are winking, white, new porcelain (or is it enamel?) and the new hot-water tank in the kitchen means she can bath and bath to her heart's content. True, if she opens her eyes when she does so she stares at horrible surroundings, but it is an improvement, a huge improvement, and anyway, she has come back here from somewhere without a bathroom at all. Nothing like being deprived of something for a while in order to appreciate it all the more keenly when you get it back. Though this does not, Marianne would tell you, necessarily apply to husbands. In the bath if she closes her eyes she simply feels the smoothness of new goods, the cleanliness of fresh fittings. For this she is ever thankful. What are dusty feet and nasty walls compared with these other benefits? Not much.

Every morning Marianne gets up at seven o'clock and goes down-stairs to remove from the airing cupboard the two little balls of bread dough that have proved overnight. She switches on the kettle and lights the old gas stove's oven (still filthy and still unpredictable) and then she knocks up the dough for the second time and puts it back into the airing cupboard, turns on the horrible oven to warm, and then she goes into the upstairs bathroom, spreads out a large (rather threadbare) pale yellow bath sheet on the rough floor. She places her mug of tea (the mug has a printed picture of a young girl running a race and the caption is 'Yes You Can') on the side of the bath for safety, and does ten minutes of exercises. Lotte Berk's exercises, which have the great advantage of being arranged for one who is lying on one's back. Marianne is not the world's sportiest woman and has a distinct tendency to walk rather than run, sit rather than stand, lie down wherever possible. But the exercises are part of her single-life routine. Embarrassingly she recently discovered that she is a lover of routine. Which means, alas, that she is getting old. At twenty-seven she feels positively ancient and the exercises are designed to stop her seizing up altogether. Over the years she has watched her mother sink into her armchair in front of the telly and grow slowly, slowly, more and more immobile. This will not happen to Marianne. Nowadays, along with not wearing a bra and not shaving your legs, you are allowed to say that you do not want to end up like your mother. Rise Above.

After the exercises she sits up on the pale yellow towel, drinks her tea, and returns downstairs to the kitchen. The little rolls of dough have proved and she puts them into the horrible oven. Then she uses the rest of the water from the kettle to put into a saucepan to boil two eggs. She sits at the small half-stripped wonky table in the kitchen – which hardly deserves the name of proper furniture – and waits, sip-ping her second mug of tea. She checks her college timetable which is pinned up in front of her. Today is a good day. Art History and Literature in the morning and she will be free all afternoon. She has an essay to complete on the architecture of Christopher Wren (on the whole she approves of it) and another to begin on Christianity and the Early Theatre (about which she knows very little but is fairly sure her conclusion will contain the word Propaganda).

After lectures she will stay on at college and use the library. By the time she has done so she will be a temporary expert on both of these essay subjects. This is what she has discovered since taking up the course. She has discovered that everyone gets their knowledge from listening and reading – no one is born clever or learned – and she has as much right (and brain) as everyone else to succeed – and succeed well. Nevertheless Marianne keeps to herself her most wobbly of dreams – which seems so overreaching – the dream that she will become a teacher eventually and do that happy thing her lecturers are doing for her now, Make A Difference.

All those conversations about words and quotations that Charles the Separated used to have with his sister Snotty Beryl and her husband Dull Richard who was aiming to get a Chair (to Marianne in those days a preposterous and incomprehensible statement which had both her and her then best friend Willa falling about with secret mirth and suggestions for where he might find one) and her enthusiastic father-in-law Bernard and her kind and quietly brilliant mother-in-law Jean and from which she felt so excluded are no more than veils drawn aside now. There is no mystery at all. The bigger your library, the wider your knowledge, and that – she says to herself crisply – is that.

If Marianne looks back to the person she was when she first left her marriage, she winces. She was formed in girlhood to be meek and spent so long being told by schoolteachers and later Charles the Separated that she was not very bright that she believed it. Only Jean was pragmatic in respect of her brainpower. She agreed with Marianne that all knowledge could all be learned. 'But it's how you apply it, Marianne,' she added. 'It's how you apply it that counts.'

Marianne therefore entered the college she now attends timidly, certain that they would discover their mistake in granting her a place. She was an all-round academic failure from birth really and they would see this and kick her out. She met some of her fellow students (all women, ages ranging from twenty-two to sixty-three) with hesitancy, expecting them to scorn her ignorance – but nobody did. Second chances, that was what they were all here for. Some of the women became pregnant schoolgirls and abandoned their education; some had married and now their families were now grown up; some had just slipped the educational net; others were like her – in jobs that did not fulfil them and at a crossroads in their lives. Some – the daring few – just wanted *more*. The sixty-three-year-old Esme who was aiming to go on to university afterwards was the very Demeter of the Dream. Nobody said to her she was too old. They would not dare. Esme was studying sociology and was determined to go on to university in York. York, it was said in happy whispers, would not know what had hit it. Esme was currently taking flying lessons.

In the same way, nobody said to Marianne that she was too feeble. Nobody even implied it. She breathed out after a while. Took to wearing large T-shirts and leggings and sloppy shoes. To get your brain into kilter you needed comfort. How, she pondered, those women of bygone ages managed to write and travel and perform while wearing the same kind of bizarre outfits that Charles and Norman seemed to like her to wear was unfathomable. It crossed her mind that it would be interesting to consider the gender politics of being tied down or trussed up – but she had no time for that now. She was too busy feeding her mind. It was all right to be ignorant, but it was not all right to stay that way. She realized how right Jean was when she urged Marianne to discover and use her brain. There was no excuse of an oppressive husband now. She was free. Complete Freedom can feel like No Freedom to one who has always been told what to do. It took a while for her to overcome the expectation – indeed, the requirement – to be told what to do, how to live, but she managed it eventually. She and Jean had secret meetings over cups of coffee (made more pleasurable in their secrecy because of the disapproval of her ex-husband and her other ex-in-laws) and they discussed the book list, the seminar list, the other students, what she would do after she graduated. Her ex-mother-in-law became her friend and confidante and better, as she said to herself, than any husband or lover.

Her first mark for her first essay, 'I am a Roman and you are a Greek: Discuss', was an A. Jean said that if she *hadn't* got an A after all the time she spent writing the thing, then she might just as well shoot herself. It was true. Marianne spent every waking moment of the entire weekend working on the piece. The words just flowed, the subject fascinated, and at the end of it she knew she would always be a Greek; she would always be more interested in what the intellect could embrace in romantic, spiritual, visual terms, than in what it could achieve with practical application; she admired the Romans for their clever functional efficiencies and their muscular, pragmatic external life. But while she could marvel at a Roman aquaduct and respect the absorption of local deities in the name of peace, she was quite uplifted when she saw even just a slide of the *Winged Victory* or the Delphi Charioteer, or only a scrap, a fragment read from the words of Sappho. Perfect Beauty. To discover that she had a place in this world of knowledge and enlightenment was a revelation – *And he showed me a pure river of water of life, clear as crystal* – and she discovered something else through the books and the knowledge; she discovered that she was an individual and unique. That she stood in no one's shadow.

Ex-husband Charles seems the tiniest bit miffed about that.

This morning, as with every college morning, she eats the rolls of fresh baked bread – a small indulgence which never ceases to delight her – and she eats the boiled eggs which are something called free-range and a gift from her mother-in-law who knows about such things. Jean and Bernard say that food is a political as well as a nutritional act and they choose not to eat factory-produced, chemically treated, processed, cheap food. It is, they say, a sop for the masses and it will end in tears. The idea of baking her own bread emerged from this concern. Jean also brings her stone-ground wholemeal flour, saying that it is important to feed the body properly as well as the mind. The eggs and the flour and other little treats are a secret gift, as indeed is the eight pounds a month that Jean pays into her account. Bernard – out of loyalty to his son – no longer keeps contact with Marianne, but Jean does. This eight pounds is the sum that Marianne, as a student, is allowed over and above her student's grant before paying tax. Jean – though appearing to be dotty to the outside world – has a monumentally practical streak where the emancipation of women is concerned. 'I always knew you could do it,' she said, when Marianne told her that she had been accepted for college. It was as if someone had showered her with kisses. Or at least what she imagines it might be like to be showered with kisses that do not involve having your hands tied to the bedpost or tottering around in ankle-busters.

Marianne does not mind being shunned by the rest of Charles's family. Her bus passes Beryl's and Richard's house on the way to college and it reminds her of the Sylvia Plath poem about Perfection being Dead. She can see through the open curtains that the pale biscuity walls are still there, still without blemish. If there is a hole in Marianne's life it is that she has not had babies. Beryl and Richard have not had babies either but they are childless out of choice. The struggle in Marianne is that she does want them and very much indeed. This is the only bit of grit in the ointment. Could she live like Virginia Woolf for the rest of her life? Could she find enough satisfaction in the attainment of knowledge and from putting it to good and satisfying use to overcome her maternal biology? Though she agrees, could she make such a decision on the basis that the world is too harsh and nasty a place in which to bring forth life? Or would she still feel the ache of her childlessness? Who can tell? At this stage Marianne certainly can't. She's far too busy discovering this newly erudite young woman she has found.

Jean comes over to see her. She just gets on the bus and doesn't tell anyone. She brings the eggs and the flour and they sip sherry and laugh together as they used to do when attempting to make those Sunday lunches, long ago when Marianne still lived with Charles. Jean helps Marianne with some of her texts and she is particularly good on Virginia Woolf whom Marianne finds – despite her admirable qualities – a bit boring. 'You don't have to *like* her, dear,' says Jean. 'But you must learn to admire her and know why . . . the interior monologue, the lyricism, the realism – it's all there. And you should also – I think – pay homage to the fact she was so underrated for so long. It's only really in the last few years that there have been enough women critics to turn on the torch for her.'

Bit like me, really, thinks Marianne, thought she is sensibly under no illusion that she is a genius. But she is a woman with a brain and she does intend to use it. Down among the women at college it is all right to says such things. Women are no longer worrying sexual rivals or fluffy and naughty mates. Women are OK.

Marianne remembers, long ago, how Jean cited Virginia Woolf's dictum that every woman needs a room of her own and changed it to every woman needs a house of her own. One day, she thinks, I will have that, too. With a proper bathroom, naturally.

These are the things she thinks about as she goes through her routine this morning. And, as usual because – well, who cares? – she leaves her dishes in the sink, cleans her teeth, picks up her bulging briefcase, and leaves the house. As always her step is light, her heart at peace and she shines with the possibilities of the day ahead. It is a strange feeling but she has come to recognize it as one of the world's rarest – it is happiness . . .

Charles is supposed to be happy, too, now that he lives with Stella in the flat below Willa (who no longer speaks to Marianne) but as far as Marianne is concerned he is just the same irascible sneering person he always was – and with her he is furious, furious, furious. He is furious because Marianne – who wouldn't say boo to a goose (watch those clichés, Marianne!) while they were living together – has finally said a big fat No to him. He says she tricked him. He says that he allowed her to move back into the Russell Road house as a temporary measure as it was silly to leave it empty and he was travelling to India for two months. Marianne could move back in and caretake the place while he was away. The world was full of squatters nowadays and Charles was good at thinking ahead. He suggested that she should stay until he returned and made up his mind what to do. He might sell it; he might decide to buy her out of her share.

That is what he says he agreed with her. Allowing her back into Russell Road was only a temporary, practical measure. He is a Roman, She is a Greek, then? Not long before Marianne began college, when Charles arrived back from India where he had, it seemed, had an ecstatic time with Stella and without little Florian (*Florian?*) the toddler, he came to see Marianne in the Russell Road house. He had two small gift boxes with him – one in very pretty, flowery colours, handpainted in Jaipur, apparently, and the other carved rosewood with mother-of-pearl inlay. They would both be suitable for jewellery, he said, and she could choose one. Marianne experienced a little ripple of irritation. So, he could not even remember that he had never, actually, bought her any jewellery, that she never had the money to buy jewellery for herself, that she had never inherited any – and therefore she had none to put in a nice little box. Even their wedding rings were just bought as part of the Saturday morning shopping list.

'I don't have any jewellery,' she said, looking him straight in the eye. 'If you remember. You always said it was frummery.'

'Flummery.' He corrected.

She nearly hit him. 'Flummery, frummery . . .' she said crossly. 'I have none.' How irritating it was that he could still poke at her new-found strength. It was only a pinprick but momentarily it hurt.

Charles ignored her outburst as if she were a squealing child. He sat down at the other end of the apology of a table in the kitchen. He said, leaning forward, priest-like, as if asking for a confessional, 'So now I am back and Stella and I have decided to live together and we'll need a house. We'll put this on the market as soon as possible.' He says it as if he is The Law. So much for the liberated, egalitarian, socialist ideal.

The sobriety of the statement was somewhat diluted by the horrible table giving a lurch as he set his elbows down firmly and placed his hands together like a bishop with the two index fingers shaped like the steeple of a church. When the table lurched it had the unfortunate result of his shoving a finger hard up his disdainful nose. Marianne found this very funny and could not pretend otherwise. It reminded her of the man who could play a tune with his nose. From *Monty Python*. She said so. Charles used to like *Monty Python*. It was one of his great saving graces. But not, it appeared, now.

'Really?' he said coldly, touching his nose tenderly. If she had waved last week's fish under his nostrils he could not have looked more disgusted.

'Would you like a warm flannel for it?' Marianne asked kindly, staring at his nose.

'No, I would not,' he said, slightly nasally, which made Marianne want to laugh again but she controlled it for the greater good. He repeated, very slowly, 'So we will put this house on the market as soon as possible. Do you agree?'

Marianne nodded. The devil was in the detail. She nearly said this to him but then she considered his satisfaction at yet again being able to correct her use of cliché. He would, too. It was as if he owned the entire bloody English language.

'As soon as it is possible, yes,' she said, lingering over the words.

He looked at her. Possibly the faintest bell rang.

She looked back at him. She smiled her sweetest Marianne smile. 'When would that be, do you think?' she asked.

'Immediately,' he said.

'Impossible,' she replied calmly.

'Why?' He asked, quite reasonably. This was obviously a bit of Marianne's wilfulness coming out.

'Because I have just registered to go to college.'

He shrugged. 'Very good. Well done. What's that got to do with the house?'

'I shall live here until I have finished studying.'

'Oh, don't be absurd, Marianne. That'll be a hell of a long time.'

If he had wanted to make her even more resolute he could not have put it better. It sounded as if he was saying she'd need aeons to achieve anything with a brain like hers.

She nodded, managing to remain composed. 'The usual amount of time for it, yes.'

'So?'

'So you'll have to wait.'

He went very pink. 'If it's a college they must have halls of residence.'

'They do.'

'Well then, you can move into one of those.' He stood up, walked about a bit, gestured wildly at the grimy walled kitchen, stared up at the cracked and peeling ceiling, stamped the back of his heel against the chipped enamel of the old cooker. 'You don't need a whole house to yourself. For God's sake. All you need is a room.'

'No, Charles,' she said, 'That was Virginia Woolf and fifty years ago. This is now and I need a whole house . . .'

She nearly added 'and a decent bathroom' but he would probably pounce on the words and say she was mentally deranged. She had never forgotten *Gaslight*, Patrick Hamilton's ancient film about a husband making his wife mad so that he could commit her to an asylum and get his hands on her lolly. The last straw for the poor woman was when he arranged for the gaslight to go up and down of its own accord whenever he left her alone in the dim, formidable house. For some reason it had made a powerful impression on Marianne. Something to do with the wife's blind faith in her husband made her uncomfortable. Best keep quiet. Perhaps she was a little unhinged where bathrooms were concerned but they represented happiness, privacy, being safe and warm and naked and getting what you want. She had not forgotten that she was in a clean, sweet, pretty bathroom when Charles took away her happiness by saying he would move her to this dump. And she had let him, as if she were just another piece of his furniture.

At this very moment she could see quite clearly in Charles's eyes that he'd love to commit her. Get her sectioned. If they had been living fifty years ago, he might have succeeded.

'You're looking at me as if you think I'm mad, Charles.' She could not resist saying it. Charles had never been the same since he saw a green-fleshed, wild-eyed, naked Glenda Jackson rolling around in a railway carriage and Tchaikovsky's cholera-ridden mother boiling in her bath in *The Music Lovers*. Threatening women. Ken Russell had much to answer for.

Charles bullied, he cajoled, he yelled. He said that They (so *they* were a They, now) had to get a house in a decent area, and soon, so that little Florian – *Flo-ri-an!* – could go to the right sort of school. Something to do with catchment areas which she knew nothing about since in her day you went to the nearest school and that was that. 'The catchment area is important – and it means,' said Charles, 'that I will need more money out of the house sale that you will need.'

Her turn to blink this time. 'Why?'

'Because good schools are in expensive areas. And it doesn't really matter where you live. You could get a flat near your college. Where is it, by the way?'

'A bus ride from here,' she said. 'A very short bus ride and I'm staying put. We sell when I'm ready and not before. After all, I lived in that crappy basement in Notting Hill for ages while you had all this and you've done bugger all, Charles. Bugger all.' She looked about her. 'You could at least have painted these walls. Or finished the bathroom . . . She felt tears welling up – of fury, of frustration, of contempt. How could she have believed in him for so long. How *could* she? She pointed wildly about her – at the decay and the dirt and the cracking walls. This is where I came in, she thought. Out loud she said. 'Do you know what you are? You, Charles, are a hopeless bloody *bodger*.'

'I have a career,' he said, 'My time is somewhat taken making a success of that. If you remember.'

'Well then,' she countered, 'you'll have lots more money than I will for a house in the right catchment area, won't you?'

The statement, unassailable in its truth, left them both silent. She for the sheer audacious truth of the deduction, he for his surprise at the same. In their marriage Marianne was not known for her logical debating skills.

He opened his mouth, closed it again, and then cleared his throat. She said, overdoing it she knew, but she just could not stop, 'Stella's flat is very nice. You'll be quite comfortable there. And you'll have a built-in babysitter with my old friend Willa upstairs. Perfect.'

'Selfish,' he said.

'Yes,' she said. 'And you'll just have to wait until I'm ready. Like I waited for you when you did your degree.'

'But that was different,' he said.

'Why?'

She prayed he wouldn't start on about the economics of the thing. When they were married and living together and he wagged his finger at her on the matter of domestic sums, she took it all in, drank it all in. It was right, it was the way of the world, men had careers, women had temporary jobs and then had babies – except where she was concerned the babies never came and the temporary job suddenly stretched for all eternity. Boredom for ever on the other side of a make-up counter explaining the virtues of matt powder and liquid mascara. She worked with women who were what she would become. They slapped on the foundation to try to re-create the glow of youth and they were peevish and bejewelled and their hair stank of lacquer. She once had a dreadful image of herself as a bent old crone still attempting to sell lipstick to aspiring debs of sixteen. Once she bowed to Charles's logic and she hid the pain of knowing that she had failed at her only reason for existence which was to provide the next generation. Two or three at least of those little, cuddly pink things with no hair and toothless gums. And she could not even manage one. Oh, the shame of it. But now – *now* – the mere fact that Charles could earn so much and she could earn so little made her angry. Really angry. And all for a little bit of paper that said he could remember facts.

'Go on Mr Left-Wing, Right-On Politics,' she said scathingly. 'Give me one good reason why?'

Now Charles looked as if he had been punched on the nose. He sat down slightly dazed and then immediately stood up and then sat down again. She felt dizzy watching him but that was probably also the sudden feeling of power that crept up on her. He came up close and she could feel his spit as he spoke. 'You realize, Marianne, that you would have been nothing without me. *Nothing*. It was me and my family who made you into something. And now you do this.'

She folded her arms and nodded at the kitchen door. 'Go,' she said. 'Now.' She was afraid she would begin to cry. In her heart, in the very depths of her, she knew that what he said was true. She would have been nothing, nothing . . .

'Think it over,' he said, walking away from her, up the passage towards the front door. He said it through set teeth, there was spittle on his chin, she had never seen him so angry. And she shivered. She knew her husband. It would be very unpleasant. Whatever was to come would be truly nasty. He had that streak in him – Jean said he had changed after babyhood – and it could be dreadful. She wondered if it was all worth it. What about going back to being the old Marianne, the comfortable, amenable girl he married? That would be easier, her weak-willed inner voice told her. She could just say, Oh all right then, and he would be pleased. It would be settled. Easier all round.

'I'm going to see a solicitor,' he said, opening the front door. 'And by the time I've finished with you, you'll be nothing again. *Nothing*.'

She dashed up the passageway after him. 'Good idea,' she spoke loudly to stop the voice that was telling her to submit, submit. 'That's what I did,' she said. 'And he – the solicitor – seemed fairly convinced that there wouldn't be a problem with my staying here since you and the guitar-twanger are co-habiting. It makes it something of an open-and-shut case. Even if it weren't for your little adventure with Willa.'

'Finished?' he asked.

He had a look of triumph about him that made her shiver again and she waited for him to say to her, 'Ah, but you've got someone, too. You've been sleeping with someone else. I know all about that.' But he didn't. The miserable truth was that he did not even *consider* the possibility. Who, after all, would want this piece of nothing? Any idea of submission by Marianne vanished. For his low opinion of her he was paying the price. She would keep quiet about Norman. Compared with her education, he was not important enough in her life. Educating herself was everything.

Literature taught you many things. Madame Bovary would have been a great deal better off if she had owned her house as an independent woman and taken lovers discreetly – and learned to live within her means. At least her own upbringing and marriage had taught Marianne this. She was capable of living on very little and a student grant held no fears. To be financially independent. What power. Though she sympathized with Emma Bovary, she saw her as a fool for love. Marianne would never, ever, be that way again. Love was a word that represented inequality and she had done with all that. So says Marianne to herself as she confronts Charles in that dingy hallway – and she means it. She will learn, later, that the heart is a pushy, resilient little muscle and will not be dictated to.

Norman she had put into perspective and kept him there. He was far less important than her college work. Though he was exciting and different and moved in the rarified circles of red-wine-swigging intellectuals he had faded from the foreground of her life and was secondary. He did not like it very much – who would? – but she was determined and now that she was independent and nearer to being his equal she could easily put up with his bedroom peccadilloes. They were nowhere near as bizarre as Charles's and at least with Norman she was allowed to keep her hands free throughout which was some improvement. In the meantime it was all perfectly pleasant and what more could she want? It would end, eventually. She therefore, in her heart, did not feel she was cheating when she told the solicitor she consulted that there was no one, no one at all. 'Good,' the solicitor said, 'Then we can pursue him on grounds of adultery.'

'Very Good. Thank you,' she had said, as she removed the solicitor's hand from her knee.

Charles was now at the front door, ready to leave.

'So,' she said, 'I expect your solicitor will want to get in touch with mine. He's quite local.' She told him as much as she thought he ought to know about the legal advice he had given her – but not about the fondled kneecap, obviously – and Charles was absolutely silent. Now they were standing – squaring up seemed more like it – on the doorstep. She was about to add something apposite – like See You At Philippi – But it was drowned out suddenly by the noise of the jazz from the neighbours next door. She pushed past Charles, boldly ran into the front garden, leaned across the fence and rapped hard and loud on their window. Enough was enough.

'Will You Shut Up,' she told them. 'Be Quiet. I'm trying to divorce my husband.'

They heard only the rapping on the glass and not the words. Their front room window sash was pulled upwards and they leaned out. 'Sorry,' they said, smiling and speaking together. 'You should have told us.'

'Ah,' said Glenys coyly, to the thrum of *San Francisco*. 'Back together again, I see. Isn't that nice, Bertie?'

By the time Marianne gave up trying to get them to turn the music down Charles had gone. Only the gate clacked where it had been pushed open with great force. She heard the revving of an engine, their poor old car, somewhere in the distance. She went to the gate and latched it. So, she thought, it's over. Really over. It was odd standing there on the path of the house that once held all his dreams and destroyed all hers. She looked up at the scruffy front elevation. She could not love the place but she could use it. And when she had used it, she would move on. It was a good feeling. It was self-determination . . . with a little harmless bending of the truth on the side.

Back indoors she considered the term Self-determination and the icon of the process, Germaine Greer. A confusing woman who once demanded that women take control of their lives and then posed naked in a magazine. It was sexy and provocative and no different from Charles's nudie magazines and left Marianne utterly confused. Feminists, she thought, did not sell their bodies; they used their minds. But the Greer photograph changed those boundaries and threw her into the fog again. Ah well, education would probably help. In her final year she might take Philosophy as an extra and see if that helped. In his cups Norman was scathing about Germaine Greer. Called her a blue stocking and spoke the term as if it were in line with Caligula. Nice, kind men who really believed in equality were pretty thin on the ground. Or they were just thin. With beards. And wearing sandals. Nineteen seventy-four – an inauspicious date for the changes she hoped were to come.

It was lucky that Charles chose that night to call and not the previous one when he would have found his mother sitting upstairs on the squashy old settee in the huge sitting room sipping sherry and chatting away perfectly happily. Just as well also that he did not notice in the kitchen, or connect with her, the dark-brown-shelled eggs that were so wholesomely produced, a loaf of dark-brown moist bread that was wholemeal and rich and like cake, and a bottle of light-brown sherry that was none of these things.

This upstairs room had been decorated while Charles was still in residence – by Stella, presumably, who should, it was clear, have stuck to guitar-twanging. In much the same way that a newly iced cake, if dropped on its head and then returned right way up to its serving plate, could be said to be decorated, this room was *interior decorated*. In which case, thought Marianne, she would rather offer twenty quid to her half-blind granny to have a go. The entire space was painted in crimson and black and a peculiar shade of green that – according to Jean her mother-in-law – held no dominion over nature whatsoever. If the black silk lampshades and the flushed crimson walls had anything to do with it – the guitar-twanger was every inch the perfect, compliant bed companion for Charles. She did not, of course, share this gem with her ex-(or soon to be)-mother-in-law as they sat on the squashy settee that night.

Marianne liked the big, grand upstairs drawing room now she no longer needed a large bedroom for herself. She liked the space and she liked being so high and seeing more of the sky, even if she did feel quite ill with the colour scheme. Some days she thought she might change it but she was so taken up with registering for college and enjoying her new-found space and time that the idea of doing anything of a sensible domestic nature seemed silly. For once she was going to follow her needs rather than conform to the needs of others – and concentrate on her brain.

'Odd taste,' remarked her mother-in-law. Apparently gazing about her at the decor.

'Yes,' said Marianne cautiously, 'But Stella's probably much more exciting than I am.'

'No,' said Jean. 'I meant the sherry.'

'Do you think Stella is right for him?' Marianne asked, surprised at the question.

Jean sipped her sherry and looked around the room. 'Hmm,' she mused, 'Time will tell. One thing is for sure. You weren't.'

And that was an end of it.

'If I married again I think I'd like it to be someone like Bernard. Nice and kind and helpful and respectful.'

She was a little taken aback by Jean's hoot of disapproval.

'All that glisters is not gold, dear,' she said eventually. 'I've learned to manage him, that's all. I've done it so well that he thinks he's managing me. So he's *manageable* maybe, but he's not – and never has been – *easy*. I take that as a personal insult.' The narrowed eyes were only half smiling as she spoke.

'But he does the washing!' said Marianne. She could think of no higher paean. For while her experience of living with a patriarch was nil she knew enough from friends' parents and the behaviour of her uncles, that men did not usually attack the washing-machine or go out to the shops like her father-in-law. Marianne's own mother spoke of Bernard's prowess in kitchen matters as both lucky for Jean and yet somehow unmanly. Another confusion.

'And he irons,' she added, as if that clinched it.

'And Mahatma Gandhi wove cotton,' said Jean crisply. 'To show his humility. But he was also the Big Cheesecloth in Indian politics. Real emancipation comes from political change. Not ironing. And certainly not from wives finding ways to *manage* their husbands.'

'I never learned to manage Charles at all,' said Marianne.

'One thing I will say' – she leaned forward, tapping Marianne's arm for emphasis – 'is that power and all that accompanies it is never given up willingly. No. We've a long way to go before we can say we're equals. It's over to you lot now. Let's see where you are by the end of the century.' She did not look entirely convinced that Marianne and her contemporaries were going to achieve full throttle either.

Marianne said, 'Are you angry that I left Charles?'

Jean raised her glass to Marianne. 'No, dear, I'm not angry that you left my son. But I should be angry – very angry – if you wasted the opportunity.'

She leaned back against the settee as if exhausted and her eyes now had a faraway look that might have been to do with the sherry, might have been to do with anything really. She said, 'Bliss was it in that dawn to be alive – But to be young was very Heaven . . .'

'Coleridge?' hazarded Marianne.

'Nearly,' said her mother-in-law. 'Wordsworth.' She refilled their glasses, sat down again, and said, almost by way of conversation, 'By the way, dear, have you got yourself a good solicitor?'

How Marianne managed not to tell Charles that night that it was his own mother who recommended the solicitor she would never know. It was the sort of thing you did in Marianne's family. You shouted anything and everything to hurt. You did not show diplomacy nor regard for anyone else. The heart drove the head in

Marianne's family. In Charles's family – or in some of it at least – the head drove the heart. Another confusion. Family loyalty should come first, surely? Who wanted a mother who didn't stand by you? Changing the way you thought nowadays was an exhausting process. Sometimes she wished with all her heart she could stay the same – unenlightened and free to be ignorant. But she must march on. Jean would be there prodding her if she didn't. How lovely it would be to stare Charles straight in the eye and say, 'I have Jean's blessing,' but she must not, she would not. Let her education speak for itself. No need for any other form of revenge. With Charles she had begun the process. And Bliss in that dawn it certainly was. Her mother-in-law had handed her a baton and for once she'd hold on tight and win.

She went back into the horrible kitchen and saw that Charles had left behind both of the Indian boxes on the horrible table. She took off her wedding ring and placed it carefully inside the prettier box of the two. And the other, she decided, she would keep for paper clips. Be getting through a lot of those from now on.

When Marianne finally came home from college late that afternoon she indulged in another favourite ritual. She liked to make tea in the afternoons – proper leaf tea in a china pot with milk jug and cup and saucer set out on a tray. She liked to take it upstairs and sit and marvel at how nice it was to come back to her own quiet space. Even if the place looked, structurally and decoratively, like a bomb site (the room was exactly as it was when she first moved back in though now she scarcely noticed the squashed cake aspect of it). There was just something so pleasant about finding her dishes exactly where she had left them and the traces of crumbs on the horrible, rickety table still waiting to be wiped away. Marianne wondered if she was going a bit mental. Since when did people enjoy seeing their own mess untouched? But she did. Something to do with independence, she decided. Odd. But nice. The rest of the world and its worries paled and faded. There was nothing in the universe more important to her than finding her brain. Nothing. She had not seen Norman for nearly two weeks and she felt a twinge of guilt about that. But only a twinge.

The bedrooms of the houses opposite were not yet lit in the gathering evening darkness. She kicked off her shoes, she put her ancient

Julie Driscoll 'Wheels on Fire' on the slightly wonky turntable – and she turned up the volume. It would never be loud enough to compete with the Munt's state-of-the-art sound system – but it wasn't bad. Marcus had built it. And then he gave it to Marianne when he built another one.

'Gave it to me,' she said to Charles very sternly, as she saw him preparing to remove it to the guitar-twanger's flat.

'You, me,' he shrugged. 'What's the difference? Anyway, you don't want it.'

And until that moment what he said was true. But there it was again, his overwhelming certainty about what she wanted, how she would behave. 'Yes, I do,' she said. And she folded her arms and stood guard over him until he put it down.

Suddenly it seemed so easy. Stand up for yourself and you'll probably win.

Now, as the music began to fill the room, she suddenly and most uncharacteristically (those morning exercises were quite enough) felt the need to do something physical. There was not much furniture so she tried a cartwheel which was more or less successful, except she forgot to stretch her legs. She tried another, this time pointing her toe and keeping her knees rigid. Better. She narrowly avoided landing in the fireplace. Just as she came rolling round for the third attempt, her body windmilling past the windows that looked out at the other houses, she saw the astonished face of the old man opposite. His mouth made a perfect O and his eyes rolled with her. He was old and he might die, she thought. And immediately crashed into the far wall. So might she . . . Keeping her head low, she crawled beneath the window towards her tea tray. She poured herself another cup and sat on the floor beneath the window with her back against the wall. She felt perfectly free. She was no longer someone who was required to behave. Let others worry about what she did, she was just going to enjoy doing it. She popped her head above windowsill level, and waved.

Marianne's recent undertaking was not to live her life by the word *ought* any more. She knew that she *ought* to telephone Norman this evening, but she did not *want* to. There just wasn't enough time for everything and right now she preferred to read Gombrich, or Milton, or Tacitus; Art, God and *Germania* were more compelling than the idea of a boozy night out with a lover. Blue stocking she truly was.

What was odd about college – and in particular the writing of essays – was that by the time she left the library, or her desk at home, her eyelids would be drooping, her eyeballs would be pink and pricking, her shoulders would feel strictured and tense from sitting hunched over books, and her brain would almost ache. Yet she had never felt happier. Nor, even more weirdly, had she ever felt more full of energy. Hence the cartwheels. She peered above the windowsill again. The old man had gone. She turned on another of the stupid black-silk-covered lights, respectable again. Best not to overdo living the dream where he was concerned.

Marianne was still sitting on the settee, still sipping her tea when Norman rang. She told him about the peculiarity of being both exhausted and full of energy at the same time.

'Happens when I'm working, too,' he said. Rather dismissively, she felt. 'Seems a shame to let all that good energy go to waste.'

She did not take the hint. The suggestion that her good energy was best used in the bedroom and his good energy was best used in the pursuit of sculpture seemed to sum it all up. I must be vigilant, she told herself, or I'll lose the race.

To lighten the proceedings she told him about the old man and her cartwheel, which was a mistake.

'When am I going to get the chance to see your knickers again?' he said with understandable resentment.

If she really worked at it she could get all her college stuff out of the way by Saturday afternoon.

'Tell you what,' she said. 'Come round for a meal on Saturday night.'

'In or out?' he said.

'In. I'll cook.'

'*Good.*' In the tone of voice that contained suspender belts and scarlet-leather ankle-busters. A voice that dreamed of eating hurriedly or perhaps not even bothering, and making love in odd positions, of drinking too much, of her going down on him, and up on him, and very likely roundabout each side of him. It dreamed.

And it meant ragged Sunday morning and a wasted day. Which was not what she had in mind. There was a way round the wasted day. If she invited some of her friends as well, whom she had also neglected – Marcus and Ruth for example – and a couple of new friends from college, it would be a controlled environment. Not dinner

146

for two and bed but a nice, warm get together over bottles of wine and simple food and lots of talk. And maybe a bit of sex afterwards but not a night of running up and down stairs making whoopee after Southern Comfort highballs. Marcus and Ruth would be shocked at how little she had done to the house. Pity they couldn't see the interior decorating of her brain.

Norman assumed it would just be the two of them. It was easier that way. He probably wouldn't come if he thought there were other people involved and she would have to see him another time. An *ought*. Anyway, she liked to listen to him. He was interesting and thoughtful when he had an audience. She took the tea tray back down to the kitchen and looked for the cookery books. There were two. One by Elizabeth David which Marianne found in a second-hand bookshop and one by a woman called Marguerite Patten who looked like her Auntie May in the photograph – blue-rinsed, and plump arms over a white pinny. Marguerite Patten wrote very clearly and suggested no-nonsense dishes.

There were also some cookery cards. Three little card-index boxes full of them. A wedding present from the didact Beryl who fancied herself as a latterday Elizabeth David. She had painstakingly and resolutely made Marianne this set of recipe cards – all in her perfect italicized handwriting – all written in what Beryl fondly thought was Elizabeth David's vernacular, but which was, in fact, more like a prating schoolteacher. 'How to use up egg whites: Waste not want not.' Or 'Arnold Bennett omelette: This omelette is called Arnold Bennett omelette because it was first made for Arnold Bennett in Paris in . . .' Marianne felt humbled by them when they arrived and she never used them, though Charles did sometimes. It was another needle under her skin that he had thought fit to leave them with her. 'You'll need these more than me,' he said when she pushed them at him. So they stayed. Only later did she realize that the ineffable guitar-twanger was a vegetarian. Beryl was a meat-eater in every sense of the word.

'Well, Up Yours,' she now said to the recipe cards as she shoved them to the back of the cupboard. Bugger off, Beryl, she thought, as she consigned them to hidden darkness. She let her fingers slide – regretfully – over the Elizabeth David and fished out the Marguerite Patten instead. This she did on the basis that she would need to cook something very simple as well as interesting. She was not, she knew, very good at this sort of thing. On the few occasions that she and Charles had *entertained* she had been his second in command – shopping, preparing, washing spoons, laying the table – all under his aegis. And somehow it had always ended up with the finished result being entirely to his laurels. Ex-best friend Willa – before she went into betraying mode with ex-worst husband Charles – always said of Charles that he was playing at being a bossy chef and that he was not that good, he just thought he was. Marianne realized that this reflected the way he was as a husband, too. Willa also used to say that if Marianne had ever been given the freedom of the kitchen (what kitchen, Marianne wanted to know, I've never *had* a bloody kitchen) then she would be just as good as anybody else. Willa meant as good as herself. But then, Willa had every right to mean that, for Willa was good. Very good. Much better at *entertaining* than Beryl who lacked generosity. Even Jean – who ate like a bird – said she tended to come away hungry from her daughter's table.

Jean was not very good at cooking either but she did not seem to mind or see this as a lack in herself. At least Jean provided excess even if it was sometimes a bit odd. She had been known to roast bits of apple in amongst the potatoes or bake entire onions in their skins and then serve the blackened oddments still in their smoking overcoats. But at least there was enough to go round (an unkind person might say this was a drawback). It used to worry Marianne that her mother-in-law referred to her occasional offerings as *interesting*. Her mother-in-law did not, like Marianne's mother (good, plain cooking and plenty of it), see it as a woman's duty to be good in the kitchen. Not at all. And Willa had no inkling of duty but wore her considerable culinary skills as if they were just another extension of her femininity. She certainly seemed to have seduced Charles with them. If only, thought Marianne, flicking through the cookery book, if only Willa had not picked on Charles, then they would still be friends and she could have rung her up and asked her to help on Saturday night and they would have had their usual fun. If Marianne was missing Willa this much, how much more would Willa one day be missing *her*?

Pride and shameful childishness crept in despite itself. Marianne wanted to produce a meal every bit as good as Willa's. She suggested to Fornax and Matergabiae, the bread-making goddesses, that they might like to help although she hoped they could extend their skills to something a little more exotic. So far as she could find there was no goddess specifically engaged in the finer art of cookery. This, thought Marianne, was comforting and said something quite interesting; obviously the ancients were far less bothered about a woman's culinary gracenotes than her practical abilities with weaving and spinning and smithying to keep the community warm and dressed and shod. Not that Marianne could do either – but then, she was a Greek not a Roman.

Arachne
Aclla
Chih Nu
Eileithyia
Frau Holle
Giane
Gnatoo
Habetrot
His-Ling Shih
India Rosa
Isis
Istustaya
Ix Chebel Yax
Ix chel
Kanene Ski Amai Yehi
La Reine Pedaque
Myrmex
Minerva
Moirae
Naru-Kami
Neith
Paivatar
Penelope
Philomena
Potina
Papalluga
Rana Neida
Saule
Sreca
Sunna
Sweigsdunka

Tatsuta-Hime
Valkyries
Wakahirume
were all good at metalworking and blacksmithing to keep the horses
shod and the community tooled up.

Brigid
Dactyls
Ishikore-dome
Lohasur Devi
Moye
Nyamitondo
made Pottery to give the community something to eat and cook from.

There were more goddesses involved in music, dance, art, poetry,
sorcery and shamanism, many more than in more practical, domestic
skills. Which was encouraging. So who needed Bearnaise sauce?

Even though Marianne chose the less sophisticated cookery book
of the two. Marguerite Patten ventured into certain foreign areas.
One of these was Russia. A Russian dish, thought Marianne, would
be different. And so rare that if it went wrong no one would ever
know. She read the text. 'This dish,' wrote the dear grey-haired old
Auntie May lookalike, 'is very simple to make but requires the best
ingredients.' Marianne – on a wave of enthusiasm – chose it. If she
had the best of ingredients then it was far more likely to be a wild
success. Beef Stroganoff. *Boeuf Stroganoff*. Which required fillet beef,
onions, mushrooms, herbs, brandy and sour cream. Marianne wasn't
entirely sure she had ever eaten all those things in one go. It was usually served, so the book said, on a bed of soft noodles.
Straightforward enough, thought Marianne, now that the Chinese
had opened a supermarket in the town. Beef Stroganoff and noodles
it would be. Though where she would get the money to buy fillet beef
and brandy . . .

But she would make soup to start. It was cheap. It was also something she was good at, soup. Mother-in-law Jean was good at it too –
she said that it was to do with the preparation and that they were
both good at it because they had patience and could talk for hours
while doing what soup needed – the chopping of vegetables, the simmering of flavours. The slowness of it all suited their temperaments.

Beryl used to throw up her hands in despair at them. 'Why not use a Kenwood Chef?' There was no answer to that.

'She misses a lot of sensual pleasure that way,' Jean said once, some years ago, and sighed. Marianne kept quiet.

The dish *boeuf Stroganoff* was also on the wedding present recipe cards with a long preamble about the origins of the dish. Beryl obviously felt that no kitchen activity was worthy of standing alone – it required some form of academic hardship. 'Named after Count Pavel Alexandrovich whose Chef devised it for a cooking competition in the nineteenth century. The Stroganovs were one of Russia's grandest families . . .' There was a whole paragraph about tin mines and land acquisitions etc. She shoved Beryl's handwritten card back in its box. Now she knew the secret of having so much information. You just looked it up in a book. It didn't mean you were clever – it just meant you knew how and where to look. Beryl, she thought, I have found you out. She patted the recipe cards. One day she would burn them.

The house smelled delicious. What with the scent of the slowly bubbling soup and the mixture of smells from the fried onions and mushrooms – it was truly delectable – and a great relief. Marianne was so shocked when the butcher told her how much fillet beef cost that she nearly fell over. She would have to take out another mortgage. But she remembered her mother talking about 'a nice bit of skirt' and how the manager of the Co-op butcher's had winked and said, "'S what we all want, love. A nice bit of skirt.' So she rallied, looked the butcher firmly in the eye, and changed her order. He, unlike the manager of the Co-op butcher's, did not wink or pass remark. That was liberation for you.

Marianne bought it in a piece – it looked all right – nice and red and lean. She decided that she would just cook it longer and more slowly. It would do a treat, said the butcher, who was not the best butcher locally but sited over the bridge where houses, and therefore meat, was cheaper. So the longer cooking was now happening in a heavy iron saucepan, once the property of her mother. The pan was simmering on the back burner of the horrible stove, the smallest burner and one she had never used before. She had to pick the gunge of years out of the holes with a matchstick before it would light. If only she'd had a microscope for further investigation she could have compounded her disgust at the domestic arrangements she had to contend with while helping Lister with his inquiries.

She poked at the meat, which looked fine. The flame was still low, the juice was bubbling gently, all was well. The soured cream stood sentinel, still in its little white pot, due to go in at the last minute.

The guests were upstairs in the weird sitting room. Trying not to look at it, probably. Whenever Marianne took anyone up the stairs and into the room for the very first time she always put up her hands in Pontius Pilate mode and said it was nothing to do with her and everything to do with Charles's guitar-twanger. Always a nice moment to see the relief on their faces.

Gathered together were Marcus and Ruth, Molly and Susan from Marianne's group at college, and Susan's husband Alex who was a history teacher and a lay preacher and had the look of one who is thoroughly good but can't resist the odd joint occasionally. Molly was divorced and short and dark and very full of opinions. Susan was tall and slender and fair and almost whispered her words. She was quite Christian, too. It was a motley group but none the worse for that. They were her friends and that was fine and easy.

Then Norman arrived.

Marianne let him in with a bright smile, quite forgetting that she was wearing an old apron. For a moment after she opened the door this seemed not to matter. Norman's face was lit from within by a wonderful light of lust and from without by at least two glasses of red wine. He gave a slightly puzzled blink at the apron and her bare feet, but went on leering gamely. And then he heard voices coming from upstairs. It was an interesting moment. It had something of the Leonardo or Rembrandt Studies of Grimaces about it. One minute he looked quite young and fresh, the next he looked quite old and crumpled again. Sometimes Marianne was glad that the sex thing had passed her by in all its obviously extraordinary forcefulness. She could take it or leave it and the Mystery of the Big O was still a mystery to her. But for Norman – why, look at him – it had knocked ten years off his age, and put them on again just as quickly. Mystery of Mysteries. Oh well, she would sort him out later. Suspender belt and ankle-busters and that curiously padded waspie thing and he'd be fine.

Norman had brought two good bottles of wine with him. The labels said 'Côte de Beaune', which he said was very good. After he heard the voices from upstairs he looked at these bottles as she cradled them in her arms and quite clearly wished he had not given them away. Even more so when Ruth went stomping along the upstairs landing to the bathroom and stopped and peered down at him. 'Oh,' she said. 'You're here.' It was curiously devoid of meaning. Could be she was cross to see him, could be she was pleased to see him, could be she was indifferent. He glared at her and then at Marianne. Marianne smiled. 'A few friends over. Some from college. You'll like them.'

He wouldn't. Norman was not put on this earth to like anybody very much. Bit like Charles, really. Maybe she just chose difficult men. Or maybe they chose her? She'd think about that later.

Norman gazed, refocusing his desire on the bottles in her arms. 'This is great of you,' she said. 'And I've found some *incredibly* cheap red stuff in the local off-licence, just over a pound a bottle,' which seemed to make him want to cry. She led him towards the stairs, still holding on to his bottles tightly, and they ascended. Ruth came out of the bathroom and looked him up and down. Marianne gave him a little pat in the small of his back – and left him to it.

'Got to check the oven,' she said. 'Introduce yourself. Ruth?'

Ruth frogmarched him away.

Everything in the kitchen seemed under control. She finished setting out the table in the horrible dining room where she had used Gloy paste to stick bits of old wallpaper back to the wall – but she planned on using only candles for the lighting so that was all right. She kicked the log that smouldered in the grate. Marcus usefully informed her that the chimney undoubtedly needed sweeping and she said that she thought, instead of painting the upstairs sitting room those sickly colours, Charles could at least have made sure the fires worked – at which Marcus looked anywhere but at her, he being neutral.

There was enough noise of voices coming from upstairs to mean that her guests were not sitting in silence, though God knew what was being said. Norman was good at insults when he'd had a few and Ruth wasn't backward in coming forward either. She called everyone to the table and they all seemed relatively cheerful. Molly had eyes only for Norman. 'An artist,' she said to Marianne. 'A real artist. Coo.'

Norman had obviously denied himself nothing in the cause of

blunting his disappointment and with a full glass of the very cheap wine he came down the stairs last of all, trailing his feet, holding a bottle by the neck and looking very sulky indeed. Marianne tinkled a laugh and kissed his cheek like a good Stepford Wife and sent him on his way. All she cared about was that the food would be good and that the evening would be a success.

In the dining room she seated the guests (putting Ruth and herself on the wonkiest chairs because they knew how to balance with one heel stuck out) and then went into the kitchen to fill the soup bowls. Swift as a slightly drunken arrow, Norman was at her side. She felt his breath on her neck as she bent over the bowls. 'Later,' she whispered.

'You're a cold woman, Marianne,' he said, and went back into the dining room. Am I? She wondered. Well I can't help it and it's probably for the best.

She carried the bowls of soup through on a tray and Ruth said, 'Oh, Norman, you might have helped.' To which Norman said, very good-naturedly really, 'Fuck off.' Marcus laughed in a nervous, liberal way. Ruth just looked at Norman as if he was a two-year-old (which in many respects Marianne thought he was) the others wittered into their soup and the whole exchange set the tone for the evening nicely. Ice broken, courtesy of artistically delivered obscenity. Excellent.

When the soup was finished Marianne removed the bowls to the horrible kitchen sink and lifted the lid off the simmering pan of beef. She tried a piece. 'It will melt in your mouth,' said the recipe. It did not. It stayed in her mouth. She chewed it whereupon it still stayed in her mouth. She turned up the heat and went back into the dining room.

'It'll be another ten minutes,' she said. And filled everyone's glass.

Alex then said something about Society and Art and wasn't all this stuff about Centres of Excellence like the Tate and Covent Garden cruel when people had no homes. At which Norman snorted so loudly that they all jumped and started talking at once.

'Shut up,' he said, quite pleasantly. 'Art nourishes. Listen. People want to aspire to something. That is what sculpture, great painting, great writing, great buildings, great anything gives the poor and oppressed. A glimpse of their souls.'

Ruth said that was really very pompous and outmoded and *masculine.* Tell that to the starving refugees.

Norman said that if there was no great art then there was no civilization and therefore there was nothing worth struggling towards existence for.

Molly just fluttered her lashes and leaned her body towards him and Marianne prayed Norman wouldn't similarly lean towards her and say Not My Type, Dear, which she had seen him do to women in the pub.

Susan, the Christian Diplomat, jumped out of her whispering mode and said nervously, 'I wonder who is the more creative – women or men?' Which, if it was designed to pour oil on waters, didn't. In fact, it was a vermilion-with-scarlet-knobs-on rag to a bull.

Norman laughed sardonically as if he knew more than even the Almighty but it was beneath him to speak. So much for being interesting and thoughtful. The table became enraged at the very idea that there was a difference. Norman just sat there saying 'Michaelangelo, Leonardo, Donatello, Holbein, Rembrandt, Rubens, Cézanne, Picasso, Braque, Mondrian, Rothko, Brancusi – until Ruth said, 'Oh, do stop sitting there and reeling off names and say something constructive . . .' Which he proceeded to do. And which the women, and a rather half-hearted Alex and Marcus, attempted to defend.

'You are defending the indefensible,' said Norman. 'Men have always made the greater art. And I believe they always will.'

'Bridget Riley?' said a hesitant Susan.

'Bridget Smiley,' said Norman contemptuously.

'But you're judging greatness by your masculine yardstick,' said Marianne.

'So does everyone else,' he said.

'Isn't that because all the critics and pundits and whatnots are men?'

'No, sweetheart,' he said scathingly, 'it's because they are heavyweights. Where's the female equivalent of Robert Hughes?'

Marianne came close to throwing her soup over him. Trouble was, he was right.

Marcus, who perhaps had a sixth sense for soup throwing, said that *he* liked Diane Arbus, and they were off on the subject of photography versus painting.

'And the worst thing in the whole business in all that dead-eyed Peter Blake stuff when he can't even paint from life but has to do it from a ruddy photograph . . .' Norman was in his element and the wine flowed down – it was like being on the Left Bank, thought Marianne, and it was wonderful, wonderful . . . She had moved a million miles from the brainless young wife who kept quiet out of fear of saying something stupid. Good.

Long, long after that night, Marianne would remember with amusement and embarrassment how the evening progressed. Jane Austen's name was thrown into the ring, so were Yeats and Auden, then came Berthe Morisot who was put up to counter Monet by someone – at which Norman and Marcus joined forces and suggested that men had grasped the nettle of modernism, not women – until a voice, which Marianne suddenly knew to be hers, said that was rubbish and what about Virginia Woolf? It was agreed that Virginia had cauterized her so-called femininity in order to succeed: she had not had children (Marianne swallowed hard); she had not enjoyed the act of male penetration at all; and scoffed at the penis (Marianne felt she could get to like this woman); she had focused on her work to the exclusion of . . . Marianne sat there and smiled and listened enraptured. Imagine saying the word penis out loud at a dinner party *in context*.

Then Susan, who most uncharacteristically had been banging her fist on the table (which had Norman banging his fist too so they had quite a rhythm going) in the name of denying anything by Picasso after 1955 – it was, apparently, all fucking well about fucking after that (*very* unlike Susan) – suddenly stopped and sniffed the air. 'Are you making toast, Marianne?' she said.

It was quite difficult to know if the nice bit of skirt had tenderized or not, given that most of it was burned to the bottom of the saucepan. Marianne did not know whether to laugh or cry. She had a table full of guests (fortunately they had wine, they had conversation, and they had – if what she could hear was anything to go by – buckets of insults to hurl around regarding the merits and demerits of creative icons) and no food for them – or only the top layer of the so-called *boeuf Stroganoff* and now rechristened Burned Stroganoff. Necessity, she thought, is the mother of invention, so she scraped the unburned top layer from the pan and put it into a fresh one. She then opened the back door and threw the smoking saucepan out into the dark night. It seemed to land somewhere to her right and not necessarily in her own garden. In this awful kitchen it seemed appropriate to dispense with used utensils in that way. Washing up was too good for them.

Marianne opened her food cupboard. What her mother called her stores – which sounded like something out of Little Grey Rabbit – only there was never anything like stores inside despite her mother's constant reminding her on the subject. Apparently, according to Mrs Flowers, any member of the family might call at any time, *anyone*, and then what would they think of her if there was only bread and jam? Be lucky to get that, Marianne thought privately, but did not say. Uppishness with her mother was not on the agenda – Mrs Flowers was concerned enough at Marianne's separation from a Good Marriage for a student's life and further disturbance was unfair.

She stared at the nearly bare shelves. A tin of lentils which mother-in-law Jean had given her, packets of tea and salt and coffee; a lonely small mistaken tin of baked beans containing lumps purporting to be sausages and whose twin had been opened, tried and spat out some months previously; a bottle of soya sauce, a small tinned Fray Bentos steak-and-kidney pie for real emergencies, matches, vinegar and . . . Oh Lo! She would never complain about her mother's old fashioned proletarian ideas ever again. Oh Lo! There at the back – presumably just in case dear old Auntie May and cousin Elsie turned up – a tin of Plumrose cooked ham. It stood there, winking at her, like a metal-cased inverted pear with a very pink illustration of what was inside.

Marianne sent up very warm wishes to both Fornax and Matergabiae. She took the tin down, looked at it, marvelled at it, opened it (getting covered in jelly in the process which she scraped off her hands into the fresh pan and then, on licking her thumb, realized that the jelly seemed to be entirely made from coloured water and salt – just as well she hadn't salted the nice little bit of skirt) and tipped it out on to the draining board. She cut the glistening pinkness into chunks and threw them into the pan with the remaining *boeuf Stroganoff*. Then she opened the lentils and tipped them in too. A quick stir, on low heat, noodles into the other pan, a quick boil – and all was ready. She spooned it into a Pyrex serving dish where it sat looking more like her mother's end-of-the-week corned beef hash than something out of Tolstoy. At this point courage was everything. After all, Virginia Woolf couldn't exactly cook, now could she? But Marianne bet she could damn well tell a decent lie.

When she brought the strange feast to the table she set it down before them as if it were roast swan, stirring in the soured cream with what she hoped and intended was a look of supreme confidence. Then she pushed the dish towards the centre of the table, plopped a serving spoon into the centre of it, and sat down looking as innocent as she could possibly look. If she had not checked herself she might have started whistling.

'Help yourselves,' she said, when no one made a move.

'How interesting,' said Marcus. Slithering a dollop of the gloop on to his plate. Marianne said nothing. Silence was everything at this critical point.

'How unusual,' said Susan.

'How did you get that smoked flavour?' asked Ruth with genuine interest.

She could risk a reply to that. 'You just have to know how to catch it at the right moment,' said Marianne. And she smiled at the assembled guests, who smiled back. 'Bit like life.'

Norman was smiling at her. Nothing like having a good shout about everything when you've had a glass or four. Indeed, everyone was smiling at her and presumably feeling much the same. Norman and everyone were all smiling because they were really quite drunk. She had taken a while to re-create her culinary universe and they hadn't even noticed. See where intellectual pursuits can take you, she thought, looking at their flushed cheeks and sparkling eyes and animation. They were seated at the Table of Ideas. Hers. What a wonder it all was. And she had achieved this, just by saying Come.

So who needed to be good at cookery then, Beryl?

Norman raised his – very full – glass and toasted the chef. The chef raised her glass along with the others and silently toasted Plumrose and Mother. Better than goddesses.

'Delicious,' said Norman. 'Delicious.' He put his hand on her neck and tickled behind her ear. She liked that. It was, she decided, one of those sensual pleasures that her mother-in- law recommended. And at least it wasn't her knee for a change which was just getting over the bruising from her solicitor. Perhaps he would reduce his fees for the pleasure.

'Delicious,' Norman said again.

And then his hand slid down her breasts and on to her knee. She laughed out loud. What was it about knees? But he was smiling back at her with that silly, drunken smile of his, and she was smiling back at him with triumph and affection in her eyes, and Oh what did it matter where he put his hand? So long as he didn't try to feel his way under her skull with it and squeeze dry the juices of her brain, she would be fine.

HOUSE NUMBER SIX

12 Sandford Avenue, London

A five-bedroomed family house on three floors with cellar, *c*.1910. Close to the river and all the amenities of this up-and-coming area of London with schools, churches and British Rail within easy walking distance. The house, though sound, is uniquely available for complete modernization and has the unusual benefit for this area of 120 feet of garden. The price is very competitive and reflects the further investment required to turn this property into a first-class home. There is some traffic noise.

It was the first Tuesday in September and that morning Annie returned to school. It had been raining for nearly two days. Coming back from the short walk to Riverview Infants and feeling slightly tearful herself, Marianne arrived home soaked through. Being wet and uncomfortable seemed appropriate, somehow. Darkest before the dawn, that kind of thing. She had lost her umbrella some time ago and her waterproof jacket and hood were no longer waterproof. Indeed, they were pre-Annie, seven years old at least. Also her trainers let in water. Unsurprising since they were as old as you dare let a pair of trainers become before the dustman finds he can whistle for them and they run to him all on their own. Heigh-ho. All in all she was in poor shape so far as outdoor garments were concerned and there was no prospect of purchasing any more. But at least Annie had a proper, new, raincoat, with a sweet little hood, and daisy buttons, and all in daffodil yellow. At least her daughter looked the same as everybody else's children entering the school gates. Marianne felt this with the fierceness of a jungle mother. *She* might have gone to school in her grandmother's old shoes and suffered the taunts and the sneers that oddballs are heir to, but Annie would hold her head up high and march in proudly with her daffodil mackintosh and matching wellies and her proper Start-Rite sandals tucked under her arm.

Sometimes when Marianne looked at her daughter she felt helpless. The world was not the *Playschool* place Annie assumed. One day, no matter how Marianne tried to retain the fantasy, her daughter would find that out. But for the moment she dwelled in marble halls of love – and that was the best you could say. If you were loved as a child then you learned to love yourself and if you loved yourself you made better choices for yourself. That was Marianne's theory. There were enough people of a different experience, including Marianne, to prove the theory.

Her tears in the rain this morning were partly born out of that. Not so much feeling sorry for herself as being aware that yet again she was in the process of trying to change this path of hers. The path of not quite making it, the Nearly Syndrome. There was no need for it. She had proved she had brain enough but brains need action. What was knowing about Greek theatre, Milton and Dryden, Renaissance Masters, Turning Points in History, when you couldn't go out and get a job that earned you a decent wage? Or made you feel fulfilled? Motherhood was only half the required daily intake of satisfaction; housework was hell on earth and not to be borne (like Santayana's history it was doomed to repeat itself) so she must feed the other half of herself. In ten years' time her daughter, on her way out to a club or to Glastonbury or to go camping in Timbuktu would not thank her for saying, 'Darling, I gave up everything for you.' Back came the dampening of the eyeballs at the very thought of Annie going any-where cheerfully without her.

Well of *course* she would feel emotional, of *course* she would shed a few tears. Today was a very important day and not just because it was the much longed-for first day of term. No one knew why it was a very important day except her and the person from whom she was expecting a phone call later this morning. But so it was. Today she stood at another crossroads in the life of Marianne Flowers. The tele-phone would tell her if the right path was clear for her. If it wasn't . . . So, then, the tears were partly to do with fear of rejection. She might never manage to pick herself up, dust herself down, and start all over again if this attempt failed.

At the school gates Annie had turned once, waved, smiled, show-ing the front gap of a first lost milktooth (quite enough to make her mother shed a sentimental tear anyway) and *run* into the playground on her little round legs. All about her Marianne was aware of wailing six-year-olds, clinging to their mother's rather fashionable jeans or skirts and making it quite clear that their mothers were *wonderful* and that they would not be parted from them and would fight to the end to stay close. After her one wave, Annie never looked back. Glastonbury and Timbuctoo next stop. The only thing Marianne could do was leave the scene and tell herself that she felt good about having a child who was so well adjusted, when a part of her, the inner, secret, wobbly part, really wanted a child who would cling to her and vow that she wanted only to be with her mother, for ever and ever. If you had that sort of effect on your daughter then maybe you were justified in not doing anything else . . . *Look, look how important I am*. Wrong way round. Parents were supposed to affirm their children, not the other way.

Oh well, tears or not, rain or not, bugger it, that was not going to happen. Marianne and Norman, another quick and practical wedding fitted between moving house and giving birth, had bred an independently minded creature. Well balanced was the way she liked to describe Annie. Well balanced was the way everyone described her daughter. Which wouldn't mean a bag of beans in later years when other children rallied around their ageing parents with chocolates and flowers and gratitude, and Annie was off somewhere going up the Amazon and doing something amazing and quite forgetting the address of her mother's horrible old folk's home. It was to be hoped that it would never come to that. The horrible old folk's home. Marianne's mother had seen her last days out in one of those. That dreadful, never to be forgotten, fixed, dead stare she developed: at the beige carpet, the dusty rhododendrons beyond the window, at nothing. Marianne shuddered. This morning's telephone call – due at eleven o'clock – only another hour and a half approximately (*only*) could settle all her future worries. If the call was positive then Marianne's future was bright. If the call was positive then Marianne need never end up lonely, unfulfilled and dead-eyed in an old folk's home. She might only be in her mid-thirties but such were her abiding insecurities. This house didn't help. It was yet another in one, long line of the great unloved.

Rats' tails of very wet hair dripped down her back matching the tears on her cheeks as Marianne went slowly up the stairs to find a towel. She would not receive her important telephone call with madwoman's hair. Irrational, of course, but women who stayed at home with their children sometimes became irrational, especially if they lived in a great unloved. It's a well-known fact, she told herself. She started to dry her hair in the horrible bathroom and banged her elbow on the pipework. Norman rather admired this pipework, so convoluted and chunky and dramatic was it. Marianne loathed it and consequently never remembered until too late. Her elbow was permanently bruised. Swearing helped ease the tension and certain colourful words rang off the lumpy walls, but it made no difference. Mostly she forgot about it but today, when so much was at stake, she saw the horrible bathroom again, as if for the first time. How many of these had she endured throughout her life? Four, five? Please make the telephone call a good one. *Please.*

In an objective way, it was extraordinary how little concern the builders of this house showed for its inmates' personal lavations. Here was yet another bathroom that was small, meanly lit and cramped into the side recess of yet another scruffy house. It might as well not have a window at all, for it faced only next-door's brickwork and was dark and miserable and designed quite clearly as an afterthought in a house so large. Presumably the Edwardian family who first owned the place still used jugs and bowls in the bedrooms rather than risk too much use of the chunky, sculptural plumbing in the new-fangled bathroom. How strange it was that everywhere she had ever lived had only offered minimal and grotty space for ablutions. Or was she inventing her own nightmare? Was this a dark existentialist dream? Was she only living in her own imagination, hence making up nasty bathrooms – or was the explanation much more pragmatic? That she had never been associated in a domestic sense with a partner who gave a fig for the smallest room. Or the biggest room. Or any of the rooms. For Marianne the personal value of home and house went deep whereas she only had partners who gave a fig for themselves. Focused figs. Clever figs. Figs who did not need a house and a home to reflect their place in the world. It was almost believable that she brought this condition upon herself for neither had she been associated with a partner who earned enough money to pay someone *else* to give a fig. That was more like it. When she pushed Norman hard they replaced the stained old bath with a nice new one, and they had papered the walls in that singing blue found at its best on the walls of ancient Roman Villas but nevertheless it was still small, it was still dark and it was unseductive. With determinedly vicious pipework. How tiny it was. How unfathomable the architect when he built it at a time when the British Empire was an expansive land on which the sun never set. The swinging of cats in bathrooms in 1910 must have been a very unfashionable pursuit. Very.

When Annie was tiny and slept during the day Marianne attempted once or twice to take the advice of various motherhood magazines and 'have a long, soothing, pampering bath to restore yourself'. This was perceived to be a great deal more beneficial for mothers than taking a short, heart-starting shot of sherry to knock yourself out. They reminded their maternal readers that 'time for yourself as a woman is really important'. After a couple of attempts at lying in that hellhole with her eyes closed and the bubbles popping all around her and a glass of Guinness on the side (she was still breastfeeding) – she gave up. Much as she might try to imagine herself in some scented heaven of perfect white porcelain and sunlit walls, she knew she was lying in a small bath, in a pinched bathroom, where, if she wasn't careful, when she got out to dry herself she'd bash her shins on the wash basin or brain herself on the brackets. No lingering here then and, alas, no lingering here now. Particularly this morning. Keep busy, keep busy, and you won't have to count the minutes until the telephone rings.

Marianne gave her hair a final brisk rubbing, combed it through. Looked at her face in the mirror (unsure if it was the mirror that had developed a few more cracks and lines, or her) and went back downstairs. And out again. She found one of those disgusting plastic rain hoods – free with toothpaste probably – at the back of the dresser drawer and without a thought for how mad and unstylish she looked, on it went and was tied beneath her chin. It was imperative that she go out again because she was a woman who had given up smoking and so, naturally enough, she was going out to buy fags. No person of serious intent and embarking on a life-changing moment should do so without sufficient carcinogens to get them through.

She gloried in the rain, Oh weak-willed woman, as punishment for what she was about to do. Which was to go to the shop at the corner of the road and squander what little money she possessed on ten cigarettes – of which she smoked five, one after the other, while staring out of the grimy French windows at the back of the house that looked out on to the one hundred and twenty feet of the thinnest garden you could possibly imagine unless it was part of some elaborate plot in a fairy story. Why make it so thin unless it was for Rapunzel's hair to wiggle its way towards the magic motorway at the bottom? It certainly matched the meanness of the bathroom upstairs. It even matched their bank balance, which was always very long and thin and disappearing off into nowhere.

She viewed the grime of the windows with an indifference that was almost satisfaction. More failings as the woman the world would like her to be. She had no housewifely pride. Well, certainly not for this house. To keep this house clean you needed an army of

Money made the difference and let no one say otherwise. With money you could afford either a savage-eyed Polish cleaning lady or a house in a clean part of town. 'Get yourself a job, then,' said Norman, when she complained. But since Annie was born Marianne resisted taking a paid job, and resisted it hard. For one thing she wasn't qualified to do anything that would bring in a large amount, for a second she would have to pay someone to look after her daughter and see all those moments that she would miss, and for a third, she had suffered from not having a mother at home herself as she grew up. So – much to Norman's chagrin – when she sat down and showed him, on paper, what it would cost for her to have a job that required decent clothes and shoes, travel costs and a full-time baby-carer – he had to concede that she was the cheaper option. So much for motherhood: the cheaper option.

But now it was getting near to the time when she must go out and work for money and the only jobs she could get were mundane. Life was disappointing enough without having to get up every day and go to work somewhere dull and uninspiring and she *certainly* couldn't go back to selling cosmetics to idiot young women. She needed to do something that would warm her soul. Didn't everybody, she thought despairingly? Despite his moans and groans how she envied and admired Norman. Focus.

Once, when he won a prize and they both went to the awards ceremony, it was as if they had found their past lives again. He smiled at everyone and drank cautiously before the bestowal of the cheque and she held on to his arm and took the compliments paid to her. There were comments from his old pals – that she had been hidden away for so long, that she must come out more often, that it was good to see them out and about together again.

Norman patted her hand which was still tucked through his arm. 'Yes,' he said. 'You must, you must.'

And for once she did not rise and say that she would if he ever asked her, or something else that was equally sharp if equally true.

She watched her husband as he climbed on to the platform. He wore his old black velvet suit and his hair had thinned and gone grey at the temples, but he walked briskly up the steps and shook the man from Marlborough Park Sculpture Committee's hand like a schoolboy at a prize-giving. It was true. Whatever drove his engine kept him whole and sane and happy. Something of the old, the generous

Marianne returned and she was glad for him. She even blew him a kiss when he was making a short speech about the value of art that was free to all, though part of her wished he would not take this so literally. Free was all very well but she held to Oscar's view that it was better, on the whole, to be rich rather than fascinating. If Norman would sell the odd drawing or maquette now and then it would help. But she kept smiling. Nothing was going to cloud their happy coupledom that night. Banish sourness, she thought.

Then there was a tap on her arm. She turned to find a male face – a very slightly familiar male face – smiling at her a little hesitantly. 'Oh,' she said, for she was not entirely sober herself, 'It's Fuck Pugin.'

The male face laughed, relieved.

'I thought it was you,' he said. 'And what are you up to nowadays?'

'I'm married,' she said.

He looked about him, raised an eyebrow.

She pointed to the stage and said, 'Norman.'

'Ah,' he said. 'To the star of the show.'

She nodded. 'How nice to see you again,' she said cautiously.

'How polite,' he said.

He, too, was wearing black velvet, but it was neither crumpled nor worn at the elbows. The shirt above it was smooth and white and elegant. A far cry from the old corduroy in the pub.

'And you?' she asked.

He handed her a card with one hand while gesturing with the other. It was gesture to move them away from the crowd. She suppressed an unexpected bubble of excitement and smoothed down her borrowed black satin. The card said that his name was Piers Wellington and his occupation was something in a City bank.

'Very dull,' he said.

Her first thought, though shocking, was *very rich*. Also *very attractive*.

'We sponsor the prize,' he said, steering her further away from the podium.

He guided her to the edge of the room where they leaned against a table, took a glass of wine each, and flirted.

'It was so long ago,' she sighed.

'You look even better than you did behind the bar.'

She pouted and fluttered her lashes. A long time since she had done anything like it.

'We used to call you the Renoir.'

'The Red Lion was hardly the Folies bergères,' she laughed. A life-time ago, she thought. Why, then she had scarcely known the painting existed, let alone what it was called. 'I'm flattered,' she said. And she was. More than flattered. It made her tired old heart pump faster.

'It was the Folies with you behind the bar.'

Marianne went suitably pink. Marriage, Annie, Norman, cold old bathrooms, all melted away. She was just her again, a woman in a black satin dress, with a man in a crowded room, and a whole planet full of possibilities.

'I thought you were a penniless writer,' she said.

'I was a Bohemian. I liked all that free love and cheap French wine.'

'You drank light and bitter!' said Marianne, her indignation over-coming her poise.

He laughed and nodded. 'So I did. Well, I liked the *idea* of cheap French wine. The thing was we drank quite nice stuff at home.'

'Fraudster,' she said.

He bowed to acknowledge the fault.

'You were a wide-eyed kitten. Then you left the pub to get an education and never came back.'

'And if I had?'

'I'd have snapped you up.'

'Like unconsidered trifles?'

The speeches and the award were done. Over the shoulder of Piers Wellington, City banker, she watched her husband leave the stage – still with a lightness of step – and make straight for the drinks. He was surrounded by his friends, he was happy and animated. The cheque hung from his jacket pocket as carelessly as if it were a bus ticket. He looked around once, as if to find her, and then went back to his talk and his banter.

'I'd better go,' she said. 'How nice it was to see you again.'

'Polite to the last. Will you give me a call?'

Would she? She might. She felt light-headed and ticklish and it was a dangerous moment. The old Marianne arose from the new Marianne's ashes.

He said, 'Give me your number.'

She shook her head but she said it out loud as she did so – which just about summed up the confusion. He repeated it. As she hurried away – feeling a little dishevelled, possibly from drink, possibly from excitement – she decided that he would never remember it. And that was for the best.

For the rest of the evening she stayed close to Norman. Truth was she did this less to keep herself pure and more to tantalize. In case, just in case, Piers Wellington, City banker, was looking – more to the point, in case he was looking and desiring. It made her happy. The encounter made her happy. And it would not be hard, if he were looking, Piers Wellington, City banker, for him to see that Norman and she were scarcely love's young dream. Norman was animated, drinking, loud, unconcerned with her, and she – who might have remained proud – was not caught up in illicit thrill. When she tried to tuck the cheque more firmly into Norman's pocket, he grabbed her hand. 'Mine,' he said. Then he put his arm round her but for once she did not feel angry and did not make comment. It was his evening, after all, and she had something of her own, too.

Nor did she mind when he needed to be helped into a taxi at the end of the evening and then held upright in place when the taxi drove round corners. The card with Piers's address grew crumpled and creased in her bag as her bag was squashed and sat upon by her award-winning husband. When she took the thing out and put it at the back of the kitchen drawer later, it occurred to her that it looked like she felt.

For two days she waited, hoping. And then he rang. Norman, who was at home, it being school holidays, answered the call. 'No one there,' he said. When it happened again he looked at Marianne suspiciously. 'No one there,' he said, returning the receiver with a gesture of contempt. When it rang a third time, early that evening, and he answered it, he put down the phone and said nothing for a while. Then, just as Marianne was taking Annie upstairs for her bath, Norman called up the stairs 'Who was that fool you were talking to – the one in the poncy suit?'

'I talked to a lot of people in poncy suits,' she said.

If there was an aspect of this artistic, wildish, creative husband of hers that she knew well, it was that he should never be underestimated so far as masculine possessive intelligence was concerned. He knew. And if it went any further he would know. And then this holding situation – this marriage – would be over. Let leash the dogs of war . . . Marianne was not ready to do that.

She threw the card away. No – that was not the answer. That would not be fulfilment. That would merely be lurching into something else that was probably dead ended. A makeshift happiness. She knew that as soon as she – eventually – heard his voice. Piers Wellington, City banker, divorcee (twice) was not the answer to her needs. Not her long-term needs. He reminded her of those occasional men she used to bring home when she was married to Charles. They hadn't been the answer either.

Piers insisted so she agreed to have lunch with him somewhere dark and discreet and she listened to his marvellously charming chat-up lines with delight. Ate the marvellously expensive food, all three courses of it, too. And drank the wonderfully expensive wine. Then she said No. Simple as that. This life in which she lived, this husband, this daughter, this house – they were not to be sacrificed for yet another liaison that might or might not be a happy one. Ruth was right, damn Ruth. The answer – whatever it was – must come from within.

Piers said, smooth as the *beurre blanc*, 'Think about it.' But she threw his new card, the one with the address in St John's Wood – which no doubt (she did hesitate for a moment) had a very nice en suite – into a rubbish bin near her home, and went along the familiar, unloved street and up the path to the grubby front door determined that this time, at least, she would make a good choice. Something else was required. This was her muddle and mess and she must get herself out of it instead of looking around for someone else to prop her up.

Norman's alertness died away after a week or so and when she suggested that they spend some of his award money to stop the leaks in the roof, he agreed. But when she suggested they might do some home improvements, he looked at her as if she were mad. He looked about him wondering and mystified.

'Such as?'

What were white tiles and a new hot-water system compared with the heights of his art? She did not pursue it. If Marianne Flowers wanted a new life or a new bathroom or a new anything for herself, she had to achieve it alone.

Today was the day on which she would find out if she had managed it. Waiting, waiting, waiting. French windows misted over, so close was her breath. Blowing smoke like dragon woman. So tense that her teeth ground together. She must concentrate on something else until the moment the telephone rang. So Marianne considered the garden. It always encouraged thoughts of doing something positive with her life. A quick look at the garden or a short visit to the bathroom, and her resolution was re-steeled. A combination of the two of them was iron in the soul.

She rubbed at the window and took a long and immensely satisfying pull on her cigarette. Garden? Well, you couldn't actually see very much of it – not the long trail of patchy muddy grass (lawn was too grand a word), not the sour, bare soil of the thin flowerbeds (no flowers when they moved in here and none since). She had tried to encourage some blooms in their first season but the plantings choked under the weight of traffic fall-out and junk – oops – *objets trouvés* that gradually arrived over the years. As for the sunken, fissured fences on either side, they were now quite hidden, piled high with Norman's findings. Norman – father of Annie, husband to Marianne and also natural heir to Brancusi. Not necessarily in that order. The surprise of it, she thought, as she stared at the pile of detritus – the surprise of Annie – changing Marianne's life the moment sperm hit egg. The bull's-eye she never thought could happen. Everything went out of the window then, grimy or not, for nothing was more important, suddenly, than this child, this miracle, this unexpected wonder. What was the fulfilment of those Groves of Academe compared with that little soft sleepy thing as she lay in Marianne's arms? Naturally, easily, her life went on hold from that moment.

It was only as the weeks gave way to months and the months to years that Marianne realized that she was standing still in life, that a bab – a toddler, a child – was not enough. It seemed sacrilegious to say so and the discovery wasn't a disappointment exactly, it was a surprise. A newly discovered brain will not sleep for long. But whatever she chose to fulfil, her other half must be something that could be done at home, required no expense, and could fit around her domestic timetable. And there really was only one answer. Unfortunately it was the answer that so many others had tried and failed to achieve. But she told herself that the road to hell in the form of dead-eyed old folk's homes was littered – not with women who failed – but with women who failed to try.

Marianne had learned something on the bumpy old path of life – it was that you had to keep your head down and believe in yourself and try. You tried. And you tried. And if well-meaning friends and family shook their heads and said, 'Dear, dear, Marianne, that's a bit of a leap, don't you think?' You ignored them. You smiled politely and you kept on going. Marianne told herself that if she could do well at college, which she did, she could do well at anything. Even this. And if she didn't, it would not be from lack of trying. She had time and a room of her own. What more, as Virginia Woolf pointed out, did she need?

Well, this morning what she needed was courage. The waiting was dreadful and wonderful. At eleven o'clock she would know. God grant me this one acceptance, she told herself, looking at the all but empty packet, and I shall never buy nor smoke a cigarette again . . .

Ten minutes to go. Back to the garden, quickly. Well – thin as it was, manky as it was, it held a variety of interesting objects. All reflecting that Norman was, indeed, the natural heir to Brancusi, Caro, Donatello – or would be, one day, when he got around to using these interesting and wholly natural items. He spent little time making, much time collating and thinking and one day he would be a great success. She fervently hoped so. Success could be the only reward to make her past sufferings bearable. And his. The Marlborough Park's award gave her hope. The memory of Norman's face when she suggested home improvements did not. It was up to her. Eight minutes to go.

She rubbed away some of the mist from the window. There they were in the putative garden, lined up like drunks at a wedding. All manner of them, all kinds of wild and weird and wonderful items from Nature's stores so that the thin strip of sprouting, muddy soil was no more than an unhappy artery clogged with piles of dried-out sapling trunks, oddly shaped pieces of rusty metal and assorted bits of transfigured, natural bounty. Norman had leaned it and piled it and squashed it against the boarding and more and more arrived every year. Like all true artists, he was insatiable – nor stopped to count the cost.

Nature was, indeed, bountiful. So bloody bountiful, she thought privately, that it was a wonder there were any fallen trees, any bits of old plough, any river flotsam left in the world. Wonders these were, apparently. He liked to stand and gloat over them. Compared with how much he had gathered, he made very few works. Marianne stopped pretending. 'Enough is enough,' she said. 'If you bring one more rotten oar, bit of old planking, dried-out sapling trunk, squashed kettle' – whatever it might be – 'home with you, I'll move out . . .'

When a despairing Marianne crossed her arms and stood in front of him and asked him what on earth he planned to make from such a cross-section of Nature's bounty, he said that he was garnering enough material to make the world's biggest tepee and one day he would. When it was built – and it would only be built if it was a commission – Norman was very stern about that (in vain did Marianne suggest that he build it first and then offer it for sale once it could be seen in all its natural and elegant beauty) – once it was built the garden could be cleared up a bit and some of the other stuff corralled so that Annie could play out there to her heart's content. Until then the mashed-up, thin runnel of soil at the back of the house was his workroom and that was that. Little Annie played, therefore, in the front garden which was about the size of a small double bedroom and which would have been fine if Marianne had not suffered agonies of worry about her daughter being snatched away by some passing stranger, run over by a car because she had tunnelled her way out, or been found with her neck broken having managed to climb up on to the three-foot-high wall. The lack of a safe back garden began to invade Marianne's dreams. When she told Norman he laughed, stared at her and asked her if she was mad. What, she wondered sometimes, would he think of her if she said that she wanted a beautiful new bathroom so that she could lock herself into it, and soak in scented waters and howl at the moon? Like ex-husband Charles, he would possibly privately want to have her sectioned. Surely there must be some men somewhere in the world who were not gay and who enjoyed things like beautiful bathrooms? She knew that if she met one she would lay her dreams before his feet. Perhaps it was Piers Wellington, City banker? Perhaps she had been wrong to put him away from her so firmly. Oh for something positive that she could genuinely call her own. Not long now to see if she was worthy.

There was a very terrible moment some months previously, just before Annie's sixth birthday, when Marianne suggested that Norman might build their daughter a tiny tepee – 'Just look on it as a maquette,' she said. 'Wouldn't it be nice for her birthday?' And Norman had rolled his eyes and found himself quite unable to speak at the thought. So Marianne did. She said, wagging a finger, which was a brave gesture in the circumstances as Norman's complexion had changed to a darkish red glow, 'You are always saying that Picasso was so wonderful when he got in touch with the child in himself and made all those direct, simple sculptures – the fish and suchlike – so why don't you do the same?'

The finger hung there between them. When he eventually did

manage to say a few words they were, largely, spoken slowly, loudly and comprised one – or maybe two – syllables.

'My tepee will be a piece of art, not a bloody *tent* for tea parties! We can go to Woolworths and *buy* her a tent to play in if necessary.'

'With what?' asked Marianne. 'I haven't a pound to my name.'

'Money, money, money,' he said. 'That's all it ever comes down to. Money . . . I didn't realize when I married you that I was getting hitched to a gold-digger.'

As usual, at this point Marianne had a choice. Either she ignored the absurd notion that there might be any bloody gold to dig, or she took umbrage and went for the vernacular. Today she went for the vernacular. 'Hah!' she said, hands on hips like a fishwife, 'Midas, my elbow. Rusty old tin more like.' And they were off. It was over, of course, the marriage, but this would not be acknowledged until the anger between them died away into indifference.

They only ever did it, all this screaming at each other, when Annie was out, and on that day she was playing at the other end of the road at the twins' house. At the posh end of the road where you could hardly hear the traffic at all and where the gardens were sweeter and full of nice things like blossom and flowers and good, green grass. Liam managed bands (which was what you had to call rock groups) and Patty had been something that Marianne did not quite understand in the music business. Then they had twins, a girl and a boy, and they were thrilled with them, acting as if they were the first parents in the world to have such a perfect pair. It was sickening to see the way the two little things were dressed in style just to go to the shops, the way they had a stroller pushchair that was the Rolls-Royce of its kind and the way the nanny who pushed it had dyed black hair, navy blue fingernails and Gothic make-up. That she was called Polly and grew up in Cobham scarcely countered her shocking appearance.

Family as theatre, Marianne thought quietly, but it worked and everyone seemed happy and content. Money, of course, made a difference, as Marianne knew. But so did love. Their house was rambling, full of stripped pine and comforts, pleasant and (Marianne could not help noticing) perfectly maintained. They loved it and they loved each other. Or perhaps they loved each other so they loved it? Visiting them both depressed and pleased Marianne. Depressed her for the comparisons, pleased her simply for the feeling of being welcomed somewhere nice. There was also – and this probably added to her pleasure in the place – without anyone having to think about the cost of it, a glass of good red wine available. And a sit-down at a big, smooth, clean, pine table, and talk and laughter and ease. It seemed to Marianne that the only shadow in Patty's domestic life was that Liam was away so much – his crime being to work so hard that he was sometimes thousands of miles distant and invariably missed the twins' weekday bathtime. Marianne privately thought that this could work very well if, like Patty, she had access to a reasonable bank account, a car to rely on, and a nanny. Whenever Patty said she missed Liam Marianne wanted to put her arms round her and tell her she was lucky to feel that way – but then – that would allow a chink of truth to creep into their relationship and Patty would know that she and Norman were far from happy. So she just nodded sympathetically as if she, too, experienced the same thing when Norman went off on one of his hikes to drag back even more interestingly rotten objets d'art.

There were little revenges. Whenever Patty said how interesting Marianne must find it to be married to a craftsman, she did not defend her husband from the terrible ignominy of such description. If the term *craftsman* were used in Norman's presence he would probably burst a blood vessel. Craftsmen made wrought-iron gates and birdboxes. So it was a particular pleasure not to correct the term. She supposed it would hurt Norman much as she would be hurt if anyone referred to her as his Wifey. If he were sitting with them Norman would say, 'I am an artist not a bloody craftsman. I make things of the spirit. Craftsmen make useful things. I do not make useful things . . . That is the definition of art and that is what I do . . . Art.' But as a little revenge Marianne would merely smile and nod and say, 'Oh yes, his craftwork is beguiling and fascinating', or if she was *really* feeling fed up she would say, 'His handicraft really is very good indeed.' The term *handicraft* would not only have Norman busting a blood vessel, it would have him in orbit for several days.

Once, at another of Annie's friends' parents', a banker husband and a solicitor wife – Minnie of the black satin – who sweetly and innocently asked Norman over the feta and rocket if he would design them some really modern, interesting bookshelves – money no object – made out of some of that interesting stuff he had collected. 'And you can sign them,' added the lawyer, smiling. He had seen a stage set that Norman created in which everything was slightly and fantastically out of true – not so fantastical as de Chirico or Dalí, more like early Leger or Boccioni, as Norman went to great lengths to explain – and it was not hard to tell from this that Norman was a cut above country-fair whittlers. Even Marianne, in all her anger at his selfishness, could not deny his gift. But at this point, when a commission was on the table, even if it was for bloody Boccioni bookshelves, surely Norman could put down his art and take up the shadow of it called craft. If they were not so needy she might have defended his dismissal of the bookshelf idea but the differential had gone on the car which sat miserably in the street outside covered with bird droppings and rusting away so that she walked everywhere and carried the shopping which was heavy and time-consuming and made her arms ache. When she pointed this out to Norman, his sarcastic comment was that she'd have to wait until he won another award – as if she had deliberately caused the problem. She could do with a new pair of shoes – obviously – since she had nearly worn the others out.

Norman laughed at the solicitor's proposal. 'Four bricks each end and planks. That's all you need, pal. Pass the Rioja.' And that was that. The couple looked both mystified and a little hurt – and there were no more mentions of commissions of any kind even though Marianne said how nice a bit of art would look in their perfect back garden. Norman was right. People would spend hundreds of pounds on a table or a wardrobe – but fear to spend anything like that sum on a painting or sculpture. Paperclip money, that was all it was, and what a difference it would have made to their lives. Norman referred to this from time to time and she thought how odd it was that – while she had any amount of art to stick in the garden – she didn't have a wardrobe, only a hanging rail over which she threw an old sheet to keep her clothes from the dust.

The inevitable allusion to Cyril Connolly's pram in the hall was much used within the walls of their house both as fact and as metaphor (the hallway was narrow, the pram was big). In his wilder moments Norman said that Marianne had blighted his life with her bourgeois trappings and requirements – and immediately apologized when Marianne pointed out that one of her bourgeois trappings was their daughter and some of her bourgeois requirements were designed to keep said infant alive. After which he would look hangdog and ashamed and she would soften because, beneath it all, he was seriously dedicated to the purity of the Gaian driven artist and Annie – not to put too fine a point on it – was a great joy that came unbidden to their lives. In other words, the condom broke.

Which was why, one day a couple of months after the prophylactic went bust, Norman was up a Nepalese mountain putting some stones and branches in place and about to go on from there to take up a month's residency in an American colony. And Marianne was taking her finals with what she thought must be exam nerves, because although she did not feel nervous she was throwing up every morning. And the next he was back from Nepal and clutching his glass in a pub while she spelled out his imminent fatherhood. She also clutched a glass and felt a bit wobbly about it all, though on the whole she was pleased. His first words were open and honest and reflected his first thought which was, 'Bugger. That's put paid to Arizona.' Her first words were entirely dishonest and hid another agenda altogether: 'It's put paid to my future career, too.'

He looked at her over his beer as if she was stark, staring mad. 'What career?' he said. 'You're a student.'

'So were you once,' she said angrily.

Thus began their unexpected parenthood.

Despite the marvel of Annie's arrival, the joy they both felt and the pleasure Norman took in the scrap of female humanity that looked so much like him – and the unity their daughter brought in those first months – Marianne recognized the fundamental truth and never could forgive him. The sacrifice was all his. And the rows began. Rows apparently about money but about everything. Largely about the earth mother wanting the best for her young and the Gaian creator wanting no restraints. To which she always said, 'At least you get to *do* your own stuff. I don't even have an *own stuff* to call my own.' Go and work in a shop then,' he once said, pushed beyond endurance and unable to be rational. 'Or a garage – or a hairdresser . . .'

'I am liberated,' she yelled back. 'And being a mother is a full-time occupation. I am not inferior.'

'We eat and we are warm, aren't we? And I provide that. What more do you want? What more can I do?'

Two points of view, both valid. End of argument. Limp and lurch through another month or two before repeating it all over again.

This was the pattern of the years and it was rusting her engine. By the time Annie was up and grown and she was free she would be immobile, powerless, all corroded. Living in yet another crumbling house, being rattled in her bed at night by lorries and screaming cars and the sound – increasingly – of police sirens and her self-respect gone down the tubes.

Even this area was changing. The interesting people – the telly ones who could fiddle their taxes; the legal ones ready for their wigs and silks; the journalists who were moving nicely towards the status of pundit – they all lived half a mile away. Whereas in this part of town down-at-heel people strolled by with lager cans in their hands and depressed-looking foreigners made mournful gaggles on the uneven pavements – it was not fashionable grunge chic; it was more mums who were fat and pasty and dressed from the charity shop and children who ran about with sweet-stained mouths. It wasn't slum stuff – it wasn't poverty – it was just low-income, low-brow despair. Who with money and status and a brain wanted to live so close to the roads and the railway? The underdogs would rise up one day – kill the fat beasts that gave dinner parties and bought shiny new cars, or win the pools and join them in the pursuit of such happiness.

Norman liked where they lived because – he said – it was raffish. Raffish being considerably better than bloody *bourgeois*. Trouble was their home, with its leaking windows and a roof with holes, was part of the raffishness. Presumably he would recognize the downside of raffish only when it touched him directly. Until one day the water dripped right on to his nose. If she were braver with heights she vowed she would wait for a rainy night and then climb up on the roof and gouge out a hole directly above his pillow. Trouble was she couldn't abide heights and would have to do it half-cut on gin which would probably mean *she* would fall through on to his nose.

The thought of another six years of it all before she could even contemplate being free for any kind of career was depressing. Sometimes she tried to convince herself that the chin and the tits hitting gravity did not necessarily mean that you became Invisible Woman or that life was over. But she remained unconvinced. She heard what men said about older women – largely that their aggression and stridency and bids for independence were all to do with losing their looks – and she had a nasty feeling this must be true. They were already gunning for Germaine Greer just because she spoke out about things. And it was already happening to her. She could no longer, in all conscience, describe what took place beneath her eyeballs as *laughter lines* – large, black-beaked birds with size-ten tri-pronged feet was more like it. By the time she had space to change anything she would be over forty and next stop death. It was this thought that galvanized her. Only three more minutes and she would see where the galvanizing had got her.

Occasionally she even found herself thinking that she had been a fool to give up Charles.

Blimey.

Once or twice she came across a photograph of him, or of the two of them together, and she would feel sick in her heart. Not for love but because he was what her mother would call 'well to do' nowadays, living in a big house on the river with the very prosperous looking guitar-twanger who had produced one sprog and was (because Marianne had seen her in Waitrose) about to sprog another. Marianne stood behind a pillar and watched her waddle her way with her professionally highlighted hair and a very full trolley crammed with delicious things like nice and expensive wine and French bread and avocado pears towards a large Volvo with that year's number plate – and something like hatred spread through her system. Deep, excoriating, eviscerating hatred. Try as she would to suppress the thought: It should have been *mine, mine, mine.*

Charles would not know Marianne now. Now she was what he would call a witch. How sweet she was once. How demure she was when she was married to him. And how easy it was to be like that again with a trolley full of Chablis and monkfish. Grateful Marianne, Marianne who was pleased to be given anything and wagged her tail like an unworldly puppy at any kindness. Marianne whose wine-drinking was done in secret rather than at the kitchen table in red-eyed defiance and who was perfectly amenable to being smacked with a hairbrush for no good reason that she could see. Marianne still did not know what it meant to have the Mystery of the Big O but she had given up bothering about that. It was yet another magazine-designated Right that she felt she had forfeited.

Their little house in Eastbourne Road all those years ago. Nearly perfect. While she fitted into it, nearly perfect too, and sweet and containable. Ripped from there by upwardly mobile Charles. Duped then, duped now. The very shame of feeling such loathing for a streaky-blond bit of fecundity with an avocado or two stuck in her Waitrose trolley and a car that went. Perhaps that was the moment when Marianne decided to change. She walked out of the Waitrose car park and knew she could not go on blaming the world.

And then afterwards, when she met beloved ex-mother-in-law for a coffee down by the river (something she did seldom now, for life and friendship move on) and Jean had looked over the rim of her cup at Marianne with such a look of sympathy and sadness that she finally confessed her unhappiness.

Jean nodded and understood. 'Biology', she said, 'and brains are not an easily winning combination.' She squeezed Marianne's hand, a gesture of solidarity. That must be enough. There was nothing she could do beyond that. Their lives had diverged. Jean's loyalties must be to Charles and the guitar-twanger and her adored grandchild and the others to follow. It was inevitable that the deeper intimacy between them should end and surprising, really, that their relationship had lasted so long since the divorce.

When Jean saw Annie for the first time she was fast asleep in her pram, a few months old and pretty as a doll. She touched the baby's tiny, bald head and looked at Marianne and said what they were both thinking. 'She could have been my grandchild . . .' But she had her own grandchild now – one that was walking and mouthing the word Granny and that bond would replace and be greater than this one and that was that . . . Jean was right about biology. Wombs do not always do what they are supposed to do at the time they are supposed to do it. Marianne's had failed her for a while and then taken it upon itself to go all functional just when it was not required to do so. If all had gone to plan and Marianne had fulfilled her duties and desires as a wife, Charles would have made an excellent father and his family would have been a very good family for their offspring to enjoy as they grew up. Marianne would have gone barking mad and hit the bottle, of course, but they would have contained all that behind the Volvo and the nanny. And here, instead, was poor, surprised, latitudinarian Norman – with absolutely no family at all and none required – struggling to take on fatherhood. Wombs – no wonder the ancients worshipped them. Dangerous things.

It was Jean, though, a few years later who, despite the easing of their bond, ultimately put Marianne on another path. Jean understood. Jean encouraged. Always had. They still met in secret occasionally – though rarely – and on this occasion Marianne told her about the Waitrose moment (though she did not dwell on her dark thoughts about Jean's new daughter-in-law) and her sudden keening need to do something with her life. Jean nodded and Marianne, hesitantly, dared to say what she thought might be possible. Jean put down her coffee cup and said, 'Well, I think that's a marvellous idea. Reinventing yourself, just like you did before. I think you could do it

– in fact I'm sure of it.' Jean was the only person to whom Marianne told her secret plan. It was, after all, a plan for a possibility in which many are called and few are chosen . . . Charles.

This was Jean's last gift. She might not be able to help her ex-daughter-in-law with money and mortgages or the refitting of kitchens and bathrooms and the mending of cars, but she could breathe energy, courage into Marianne – and that was beyond rubies. Marianne's own mother thought life was what you got on with. It might be imperfect but if you had a roof over your head and food on the table and a change of underwear, you could hardly complain. You Rose Above. She probably had a point given her own experience, so it was useless and unkind for Marianne to say how depressing it was to still be living in the same kind of malfunctioning shit she had lived in during her childhood. Marianne felt that she had lived in more distressed homes with more damp, dirty, disgusting bathrooms than she cared to count, and unless she changed the pattern, she would do so for the rest of eternity. Love – which obviously conquers all – was an evasive little item after all. She must make do with something more tangible. Kiss the dream goodbye and welcome a new one. 'Oh love,' she sometimes whispered, 'the low smokes roll from me like Isadora's scarves . . .'

As for the emotional requirements, no one could help her with those. Musicians, Poets, Sculptors seldom made partnerships except with their work. They made unions with wives and women, but not partnerships – partnerships, by definition, were equal. Families, on the whole, were burdensome and added nothing to the requirements of their creative mandate. She understood this, knew it bit deep. But for Marianne they were equal and this was the conundrum. How to make the balance. Every time she left Annie with a baby minder or another mother, or even her own mother, she felt both a glorious sense of liberation and a sickening sense of guilt for the abandonment. But it had to be done. She used the time creatively and she never wasted a moment. Time was what the infrastructure of women friends and family members gave her and she made good use of it. The Waitrose moment was A Good Thing. It showed her that she must create a solid rock for her future. There could be no other certainties. Certainties went when she left Charles. Until then her path was mapped out. But here she was with the fulfilment of that dream – a husband and a child – and it was not enough. More was required. Now it made her smile to think that in the great rolling landscape of her life she had cared so much about Willa having sex with her husband. If she had only felt as detached and confident then, as she did now, she would have kept her friendship – which, bugger it, had been there since schooldays – while ditching her husband. She would write to Willa, maybe, and see if they still had something left. But she doubted it. After all, she had committed a very grave error in telling her that Charles felt sick after their night of passion. Marianne – who was learning to turn things on their head and wonder how she would feel in another's place (something that was very helpful during Norman's more erratic moments) – knew that she would be immeasurably hurt if she were told the same thing. Almost certainly you couldn't pick up a friendship after that. Not even wild and fabulous Willa could overcome that insult. No, Marianne had said it to hurt, and hurt it had, and now she was paying for it. When she tried to visit Willa before Annie was born she found she had gone a bit mental – something to do with mind-altering drugs and having two boyfriends one after each other who turned out to be homosexual. Willa opened her door a crack, waggled a feather through the gap, and said that Marianne was giving her the evil eye. Hardly the beginnings of a sistership reborn. Maybe she was different again now. So was Marianne, of course. Very different. No longer the timid one.

In truth, Marianne had never felt so wholly alone. Nevertheless, in that café, with Jean's encouraging smile before her, she found her courage (the courage to fail, the mantra of those early seventies), got up from the table, buttoned her jacket and prepared to begin. If she had to do the thing alone, so be it. She was leaving Jean in a much more profound sense. Family was family, after all, and, for all her liberated ideas, blood was blood, genes were genes, sons were sons. Jean kissed her on the cheek and very firmly handed her a twenty-pound note. Despite Marianne's protestations she said, 'Put it in Annie's Post Office account. Or find a good use for it. And Marianne . . .'

'Yes?'

'This is your Daedalus moment.' She laughed. 'Your Waitrose Epiphany. And you've damn well earned it.'

Marianne smiled up at her. 'Joyce,' she said. *'Portrait of the Artist . . .'*

They hugged, and she was gone.

So Marianne took the money. No such thing as an Annie account existed. All the money they had been given for the baby had gone on bills. So, 'a good use', Jean said. And she had a good use for it, too.

She would make it up to her daughter one day, of course. In the meantime – well – Needs Must.

Imagination. That, at least, she had. As she walked back she drew considerable strength, not to say bile, from remembering the guitar-twanger's expensive hair and expensive avocados and expensive brand new car – and she added lustre to the horrible images by transposing the guitar-twanger to her lovely expensive home where, on her return and groaning with toothsome goodies which the housekeeper unpacked (a little far-fetched but what the hell), she lay in pregnant daze with her feet up on the new sofa (it would not be a settee) – something in eau-de-Nil probably (Marianne's, which was a settee, very definitely, was so old it fell apart at the move to this house) while an expensive cleaner from Poland Hoovered around her. The goad of the imagining added fire to the Waitrose Moment. It got better, much better, for now Marianne saw the guitar-twanger arise from her beautiful and most certainly eau-de-Nil sofa and make her rested way up to a pampering bath in her en-suite bathroom. Also eau-de-Nil. Reflected in the window of the café Marianne saw her own particularly gruesome and crappy bathroom. The twenty-pound note crackled in her hand. She stuffed it in her pocket. On the way home she stopped at the local junk shop. Forgive me, Annie, she said to the air. She bought a typewriter, as crappy as her bathroom in its own way, but it came with several new reels of ribbon. Anger sustained the resolve. Something must be done and it would be. She also bought a good deal of second-quality paper.

When she arrived home she very deliberately went up the stairs to her horrible bathroom which was always in need of a clean (or a bomb) and got on her hands and knees. She cast an unblinking look down at the lavatory bowl. The little hairline crack was dark as ever. And the surface of the plastic bath yielded up no shine. And she imagined, with the full force of her wishful heart, the guitar-twanger drying herself on fluffy, new white towels probably, and smoothing the best aloe vera oil into her blooming belly. While she, Marianne, was down on her knees trying to clean away her sorrows. It was iron in the soul and proved that fate turned on the tiniest thing. A supermarket trolley full of desirable comestibles could change the path of a woman's life, even hers.

Like Anne of Green Gables and her freckles, as she cleaned Marianne hoped that a miracle would occur and a perfect, shining white surface would be revealed. If it happened it would be called The Miracle of our Lady of the Vim. But nothing of a shiny new porcelain nature happened. Of course it didn't. What did happen, however, was that Marianne had an idea. She dried her wrinkled, Vim-roughened hands (in Marianne's world plastic gloves were a luxury), and since there was another hour before she needed to collect Annie, she sat at the tatty old typewriter and wrote her first – somewhat surreal – short story. It came from the past and involved two women in a hat shop and one of the women, ogling the other's husband, killing herself by mistakenly stabbing herself through the eyeball with a hatpin. Sometimes it was hard to believe the amount of memory housed in one woman's brain. She ended it with the other woman buying the hat the deceased was trying on and wearing it in triumph to the deceased's funeral. Nice touch, she congratulated herself. Nice touch.

In the ensuing weeks and months Marianne went to the library and read books with titles like *Write Yourself Into History* and *Get Writing Fiction* and *Successful Novel Writing*. Some of these she brought home. The possibility did not worry her that Norman would be either alarmed or enthusiastic or critical of her attempts at writing. She judged his response entirely correctly. He did not notice. If he came back early and she was still sitting at the machine and the books were in his way he merely lifted them off the table or the chair seat and never even glanced at the titles. If she had said to him across the supper table, 'Norman, what's your opinion about Aristotle's complication, crisis and resolution?' He would have much that was interesting to say, but relate it to his happenings or his installations or his sculptures, or – for a laugh – the quality and quantity of the red wine he was drinking. Certainly not to where it truly belonged, apparently, which was the art of writing well.

Eventually Marianne began to dare to read many, many books on the art of writing that very scary thing, a full-length novel. She read about plot, stream of consciousness, how to tell a story with selectivity so that the mystery remains, how not to have too much mystery so that the reader becomes confused/bored/indifferent, she read about characterization and how dialogue moves the plot along nicely . . . Flat characters and round characters and characters that will do in one sentence. She became entrenched in pundits, obsessed by essayists, daunted by academics and confused by the many and various *How To* . . . books. She heard E. M. Forster's scathing, sardonic voice: 'The novel is one of the moister areas of literature – irrigated by a hundred rills and occasionally degenerating into a swamp . . .' and she imagined herself degenerating into the mangroves and getting sucked under immediately. She decided to give up. Then she decided that she could not give up because she had nothing to lose. Nothing.

But as she sat staring at the blank paper, holding it straight and tight in the roller by her fingertips and suffering a tension so acute she had to remind herself to breathe, she remembered a similar pose in a picture she had seen of Hemingway hunched and intent – and then Rebecca West, Kingsley Amis, Muriel Spark, P. G. Wodehouse, Olivia Manning, D. M. Thomas, Roald Dahl, Enid Blyton – a range of authors so wide and so different that perhaps their only commonality was the typewriter – and it occurred to her that the one thing they all had in common – apart from the machine and the paper in front of them – was that they had to *begin*. There it was, her novel baby, lying in a lonely crib, feeling cold and neglected because, instead of picking it up and breathing warmth into it, she was busy asking questions in everybody's else's nursery. So – gingerly at first – nervously – secretly – she took the infant up in her arms and began to nurse it. It kicked and struggled and wet itself but still she held on tight. Nothing to lose, nothing.

Serious realism, she thought, is the way forward for my book. And the unrelenting telling of how it is. She determined to keep it to this form and she found, much like children, the form had its own ideas. You will do it this way, she told the keys and the paper, but the keys and the paper had a tantrum and would not come out that way. Sparks and quirks of wry thoughts and absurd asides would find their way into the chapters and make them low-brow. Love and sex and loss and pain insisted on being represented. A man might go to the moon or invent the Hydrogen Bomb or write the winning Booker novel about either, but in the end, she admitted, defeated, there is only Love and Sex and Loss and Pain – from Orestes to Iago, from from Chaucer to Charles Dickens, these drive the engine of the world. And laughter. If you could only get that lot sorted out you'd have cracked the literary universe.

She wrote out Pirandello's words: 'When characters are really alive before their author, the latter does nothing but follow them in their action, in their words, in the situations which they suggest to him.' She stuck the piece of paper above her typewriter. Every time her growing child wanted its own way, she read them and loosed its reins.

Since it was not mighty literature she kept her work in progress hidden from Norman. His yardstick were the Greats and she was only Marianne Flowers – and despite herself, despite her very firm ideas on the subject of writing something profound (Joyce and Woolf combined, with, possibly, a touch of Murdoch), she ended up writing something that was only a little bit, if at all, profound. With jokes. Or rather, not even exactly jokes, more like ripples of humour, acidulated comedy. She did not want the jokes, or whatever they were, but they just kept appearing. They even made her laugh sometimes when she wrote them or read them later. She told herself she would remove them later. Once the baby was asleep and could not complain she would whip them out like a spat-out dummy. Delete them. Jokes, clearly, were not art. You did not, after all, burst out laughing when you looked at a Henry Moore family group, or when you read *For Whom the Bell Tolls*.

Throughout the summer she wrote and she wrote. Into the night she wrote, when Annie was asleep and Norman was watching telly (snooker as an art form) or when he was out working late at the school or working late into the artistic night putting the artistic world to rights over artistic rough red wine. Once he asked her what she was doing spending so much time typing. And she said she was writing a book.

'Make it a blockbuster, then,' he said. 'And we can all retire.'

He said it quite kindly with an air of one who likes to pat the heads of precocious small children and send them happily on their way. It occurred her that if he had told her he was working on a major piece and she had said the same to him he would have been outraged. So it is, so it is. All the same and despite Marianne's wanting to keep the whole project a secret, Norman might have shown some curiosity. Really and truly she had become almost invisible. The book would make her solid once more. There were, however, virtues to being partnered by genius, for the upshot of Norman's indifference was to make her all the more determined to write beautifully and engagingly so that the art in his soul would admire and honour the art in hers. Some hopes.

And then – when the summer was nearly ended and the smell of new creosote hung on the air around the school – she read her typescript a final time, and sent it off to an agent. There was no hope that the agent would put it on a slush pile and forget about it, which, at that precise moment, seemed the best solution to a sick-stomached Marianne. She would rather her living, breathing, very warm and well-fed book-baby was not lifted out of its wrappings and examined and poked at and prodded at and made to dance a jig. She did not want this agent to tell her that her baby was too big, too small, too fat, too thin, too sly, too friendly, too, too, too – anything. In short, as she waited by the dirty French windows this morning, she was as afraid for it as any mother might be afraid if she were watching her toddler climbing up a mountain alone. The agent, one Janet Smith (which name for some reason sounded ominously banal to Marianne; in the autobiographies of great authors you tended only to come across paeans of praise to their agents if they were called Rupert or Ezra or Marghanita) had promised to read it by this morning and telephone her at eleven. The agent was a friend of, and next-door neighbour to, Liam and Patty. Which meant there was no hope that she would forget. Simple as that. A connection. How she wished now that she had never asked the blessed woman if she would read her book. Much nicer, much, much nicer, to never know if she was any good at being an author or not. While only she knew its contents, she could dream. When somebody else knew its contents . . . She shivered to even think of it.

She was just fiddling with the very final cigarette when the telephone rang. Marianne jumped and her heart turned over (while, obviously, Charles wagged his cliché finger again) and her stomach seemed to head for her heels. She thought about Charles. Surely she had been happy then, in her ignorance? Not reaching for the stars? Why Oh Why had she ever left him? Why Oh Why had she gone away from that safe, warm, upwardly mobile environment to find herself divorced, in this crap house, shored up by the impossible dream of publishing a novel – of which there were thousands and thousands already. One trip around a bookshop had the effect of making her seriously depressed.

Charles and his horrible sister were right. She was a charlatan, a fraud, a twerp and probably destined only to stack shelves in Sainsbury's. Jean was wrong to indulge her fantasies of being good at something. Charles would not have let her be so silly. Charles would have protected her from such excessive and empty aspiration. Norman might have stopped her except he was so full of excessive, well-placed aspiration himself that he couldn't possibly worry about the little she had – whether it was justified or not. If she *had* asked him to read her typescript he would have groaned (inwardly, if he was kind) and tried to read it and failed. It would be found gathering dust in the workshop or by his bed or near the lavatory – and if she asked him what he thought he would be horribly honest. 'I'm no judge,' he would say, at best, and meaning, 'It's far too light for me because I am a heavyweight of an intellect and you are pea-brained . . . Sweet, but pea-brained.' Intellectual Heavyweights, amongst whose number he could be count-ed, had no time for stuff that slid around on the babyslopes. If it was-n't by Thomas Mann, or Tom Wolfe, or Thomas Pynchon (he always seemed to be reading books by Thomases) then he wouldn't be able to concentrate, could not become engaged. So she had done the whole thing alone, and she would pay the price now when the agent's voice said, 'Crap, dear. Just like all those houses you've lived in. Crap. Sorry. Don't bother again. You're not worth it, you're not talented, you'll never make it.'

She really did feel sick now. These impossible and useless tasks she set herself, like some shadow of Sisyphus' sister. Why meddle with Fate? She walked slowly into the hallway and picked up the receiver.

'Marianne?' said the voice. 'It's Janet.'

Marianne swallowed and tried to sound as if this was just another call. She'd had rejection before – she knew how to take it. Janet now, was it? She was obviously being over-friendly to compensate.

'Oh hallo,' she said, sounding unconvincingly surprised.

'I've read it.'

No matter how prepared she was to hear those words, she was ren-dered speechless. A strange noise came from her windpipe – but nothing you could call human.

'Marianne?'

'Yes. Thank you.' She was already practising how to say that it did-n't matter a bit.

'I love it. I really love it. And I think with a little tweak here and there – you've got a book I can sell.'

Tweaks were things that Marianne would come to know. Tweaks could mean anything, really, from a comma being moved to an entire main character being eradicated with one swift stroke of a pen. But for now – 'Crikey,' said Marianne, when she meant to say, 'Oh real-ly?' in a cool, Hemingway manner. Her brain seemed to have left her skull. Somewhere in the ether behind her she heard Jean's voice say-ing Told You So. And without further ado she sank to the floor, the telephone pressed to her ear. Just in time, she thought, looking down at the worn and ancient carpet on which she slumped. Just in time, she thought again, looking up at the stained plasterwork above her head. Just in time.

'It's very touching,' said the voice of Janet Smith.

I have written Bovary, thought the mind of Marianne. She allowed herself a silent cascade of tears.

'And you have a great gift for comedy.'

What? thought the mind of Marianne, as *Bovary* vanished over the horizon. *Comedy?*

Marianne was aware of smiling – but only weakly. 'Have I really?' she said, 'Got a gift for comedy?'

'I think so,' said the voice of Janet Smith. 'Congratulations. It's one of the hardest things to write, humour.'

'Thank you,' said Marianne. She was close to tears. Partly, obviously, for joy, and partly because she had rather come to fancy herself as the new Flaubert or Virginia Woolf – with Joyceian overtones – a writer of profound meaning, with a fine nose, a good line in knitted suits, round no-nonsense spectacles and an enviably severe view of the world. A writer to be taken seriously; a writer to be pushing out the bounds of twentieth-century fiction; a writer of . . .

'Oh, bugger it,' she said, wistfully. 'I thought I'd taken out all the jokes.'

HOUSE NUMBER SEVEN

6 Gibbon Road, London

Attractive late-Victorian terraced villa offering spacious accommodation, arranged over two floors, comprising 26' double reception room, 18' through kitchen, three bedrooms and bathroom. 35' south-facing garden, mainly laid to lawn. Gas-fired central heating. Offered for sale in good condition and retaining many of the original features and with further scope for refurbishment.

If Marianne thought that, in the matter of love, the low smokes rolled from her like Isadora's scarves, she was quite wrong. If Marianne thought she would move on smoothly from Norman and live as a single, independent, powerful entity as a professional woman and devoted mother, it was not to be. If Marianne thought anything at all it went straight out of the window when a new man entered her life. Complete with trip wire.

In years to come she would look back in wonder at that time – the short time just after she and Norman agreed to part and before she fell into the madness called love and sex and agony and ecstasy – and blink a bit and wonder how on earth she had managed to make such a big and lasting mistake. Her only excuse, which she used to exonerate herself a little, was that she was not experienced enough in the real world of sex and love to distinguish the one from the other so that when The Mystery of the Big O finally arrived at 6 Gibbon Road – along with the firm belief that this new man *was* egalitarian and *would* love her for ever – her whole head turned immediately and no matter how the rest of the world and good sense tried to twist it back, turned it firmly stayed. There is also, as she would come to know, something very seductive about the state of being in love, especially for the first time. Endorphins pump, health abounds, little food is consumed and much daydreaming abounds. It is the happiest state while it lasts and when Marianne moved house Marianne was in that very thing, a happy state. What's in a name, said the Bard. Quite a lot, Marianne might have replied, for this new man called her darling and sweetheart and lover which was a great deal more thrilling and seductive than either her own name (most frequently used by Charles) or You Silly Cow (both affectionately and venomously from Norman). Here was a new start. And when she moved she fell right into it.

The house was over seventy years old when Marianne took up residence, and Marianne, who had been forty, lost a few years. The
house remained over seventy years old but – in the joy of new love
and rosy with endorphins and tinted spectacles – Marianne became
about eighteen. And, as once before at that age, she was prepared to
overlook the fact that in true Marianne Flowers tradition she had
bought somewhere that was crap. So happy with her new love was
she that she could actually laugh at the irony. For this time it would
be different. When she told him that she had only ever lived in horrible houses and that she feared this one would remain the same, he
laughed and squeezed her to him, and as their hearts beat as one he
unfolded a plan. Oh the promises, the promises. The promises Mr
Egalitarian and Forever made.

The happiness factor had to be very big indeed (it was) because if
she had lived before in horrible un-done-up properties, this one was
worse – for it had been *half* done up. Possibly by a blind man with agri-
cultural implements, a grudge and lacking the will to live, she said to
her friends. If it hadn't been for the persuasive powers of the new man
in her life, the bringer of enlightenment in the matter of the Big O, she
would never have considered buying it. But he said, Go For It,
Sweetheart (because he spoke like that) and he said he would help her
turn it into the quality of home she deserved, which was, apparently,
something elegant and stylish and if this were a fairy story he would
also have said a little palace fit for a princess. He said he loved her, frequently. And he made love to her frequently. Non-stop actually, so that
she began to find her knees did not always work as they should. With
all that love and promises under her belt (and the Big O down there as
well) it seemed churlish not to sign on the dotted. What if the window
frames were a-crumbling, what if there wasn't a door jamb that was
straight? Love conquers all. We believe in those who speak to us of love
and Marianne was no different. In years to come she was to remember
Neruda: Love is so short, forgetting is so long.

Her new lover talked in italics about the house's good points.
There was a *very good-sized* bedroom at the front for her, a *decent* room
behind that for Annie, and a small but quiet room which would be
suitable for her *workspace*. She called it a study to herself. When she
said that all her life she had wanted a nice, clean, new bathroom, and
giggled with embarrassment, he understood. *Me, too,* he said. For the
first time she had a man in her life who did not frown on her for being

trivial. A man who could get in touch with his sensual side – and hers. A man who understood the value of brand-new plumbing and, who – along with copper piping and plumber's flux and gaskets and whatnot – understood her plumbing, too.

Most appropriately the Mystery was made real to her right there on the floor of the sitting room of 6 Gibbon Road. How fondly she would look at that particular bit of carpet over the months, how sadly over the years. When they finally rose from the floor of 6 Gibbon Road she showed her gratitude in many happy, tearful kisses, then together, hand in hand, as if walking towards Paradise, they went up the stairs and looked at the very small room that was only big enough for a bath and a half-sized wash basin and a thin, dark window, and they looked at the separate, slightly smelly lavatory next door to it, and they shook their heads. How is it, said Marianne to herself, that everywhere I have ever moved to, the previous owners have used sickly cream paint in thick, careless daubs on perfectly dreadful bathrooms? It was amazing, uncanny. But he would make it all right. *This can be changed, this can be made suitable for you. He understood it exactly, Marianne – the need for a beautiful bathroom – it is something you have been deprived of all your life and it is something you deserve. It is not trivial. Being clean and scented is a lovely feeling . . .*

'He's not gay, is he?' asked Marcus.

How unenlightened mere ordinary men were, she thought.

'Of course he's bloody not gay,' she snapped. 'I've got carpet burns. He just likes good baths and showers and warm places to have them in.'

Ruth looked her husband with an expression somewhere between despair and amusement. English public schools did not do a great deal in persuading their alumni that there was sensual pleasure to be had in the bathroom department.

No, no. He was not gay. He was just in touch with the woman inside himself (which was exactly what current received wisdom required of its New Men) and about as far removed from Charles and Norman as a hairshirt from silk. How wonderful it was to be loved by someone who knew how to roll up his sleeves (over those muscular, hairy, masculine arms of his) and do building conversions. In dread did she wait for him to do what Charles had done and rip and tear and break and hollow – but he did not. He drew plans, he thought things through, he considered, he discussed. He took his time. She saw this as the right way forward. While being a builder in his body he was a poet in his head. Could any woman dream of a more winning combination? A practical poet. She was the envy of what few women friends she now had. Though in truth, a year or so down the line, their eyes would glaze over at the mention of his name. His smell was the most seductive perfume in the world, his voice melted her, his touch lifted her towards clouds of delight. She was hooked.

The Practical Poet liked what she did. To be a writer, and a published writer too, was *marvellous*. For a while she became his status symbol, his accomplished piece of crumpet, his authorial arm candy. Her nose went up in the air several notches. It was such a contrast to be taken out to dinner and told that what she did was wonderful, that she was wonderful, that she felt as if she were now floating on those clouds of delight. 'I am wonderful,' she would tell the late-night mirror if she'd had a glass too many. Her friends said that she looked ten years younger. 'Twenty at the very least,' she would say, hitching her skirts up a bit higher. Her friends began to look askance when she pirouetted into their houses and regaled them so winningly (she thought), so repetitively (they said among themselves), about Him. Eighteen and experiencing first love can be very tedious, they acknowledged. In one who is forty it is troublingly tedious, for Marianne was also eighteen in the amount of wisdom she brought to the proceedings.

'It'll end in tears,' said her friends. But it was only their old heads on old shoulders in old marriages talking, Marianne told herself. She was quite convinced of this love's invincibility. She was the Joan of Arc of the Love Bed. She was the Athena of the Heart. They were simply jealous because she was free, free as the lark now, free to rove and love where she chose. So – really – what did their affluent lives and their affluent houses and their gîtes in France give them that could compare? What was a wonky door frame or a leaking water pipe or a Franco-British campsite in high summer compared with this treasure chest of desire?

It even caused Norman, who had behaved quite reasonably over the separation when it was finally agreed, to show his antlers when she displayed too much of the sparkling eyes and pink cheeks. Although the divorce was agreed and completely mutual he was still only in the limbering-up stages of finding a new love (or muse) for himself and seemed to feel, in ancient Patrician way, that until he had made his choice, his ex-wife should remain in Purdah. He therefore turned up the heat. One evening, shortly before they moved out of the family home and went their separate ways, and when he had asked Marianne to help him wrap some maquettes and she had forgotten and come in late, still pink-cheeked, very sparkling-eyed and ready to love the world, he pounced.

'You never understood me,' he said critically, looking sadly at the pile of maquettes. 'And I certainly *never* understood you, Marianne.'

It did not help that the irony of the statement and her highly strung state made her weep with laughter. Which just about finished any of his future attempts at remaining calm and reasonable.

'That might *be* the problem,' she said eventually. And was off, giggling, again.

'One minute you want to be at home and a good mother, the next you're chasing publishers and throwing everything away.'

She, because she was so happy, let that go. In the old days she would have curled her lip, crossed her arms and said, 'Everything? *Everything?*'

It was one of the oldest, and therefore truest, clichés: once a wife had her financial independence, she could question the basis of her marriage. If the questioning produced unsatisfactory answers, the wife could fuck off out of it. Which was what Norman said to her, quite mildly, one evening, when they were discussing the summer holidays ahead and Marianne suggested that from now on they split their working time between themselves in the matter of looking after Annie. Norman looked at her with utter incredulity and uttered his astonished obscenities. She immediately produced a glass of red wine for him lest he faint. 'Thank you,' he barely whispered. And for some moments he seemed unable to reach the end of a sentence.

'You cannot be serious,' he said eventually. 'It's your job.'

'No, Norman,' she said. 'My job is writing books.'

'That's a sideline,' he said.

'It pays.'

'Pin money,' he said contemptuously. 'Peanuts.'

It was at that moment the door closed for Marianne. There could be no pretending, no going back. Her husband thought of her as lower than a worm. How many more people would do so? How many would she *let* do so?

They started on the dangerous ground of the value of what she did compared to what he did. The subject, though lying as a shadow across their relationship, had never been discussed. He called her books (of which there were now two published) Poisonous Fictions. 'Why?' she asked, genuinely.

'Because you write about . . .' He gestured with his glass as if to incorporate the house, their lives. 'All this.'

'I what?' She asked, wondering how he could possibly consider her talent for writing so banal that she was incapable of imagination. 'They are stories, Norman. I make them up. That's what authors of fiction do. They invent things that are so convincing that their readers believe in them.'

He leaned back and crossed his arms and fixed her with a very beady eye. 'Of course you'd say that.'

'Well, of course my writing is informed by my experiences – isn't your sculpture, your drawing, every concept you have?'

Suddenly the chair came forward, he leaned his elbows on the table and began pointing at her, stabbing the air with every word. 'Don't ever put what I do in the same breath as your pitiful attempts.' Not only had the door closed; by then she had locked it.

'Norman,' she said, 'don't kid yourself. You are not Ted Hughes, I am not Sylvia Plath – and this is not a reprise of "Daddy". We're not that interesting. Either of us.'

'Well, fuck off out of it then.'

Now that her brain seemed to be functioning with reasonable rational accuracy, she understood Norman's dilemma. If he were to accede to Marianne as a creative equal it meant unravelling his world. At least this way, by mutual separation, they retained their right to put their work first. If he had not then left the house in a welter of huff and puff, she would have told him, and meant it, that she was not as good as him and never would be. That would take a few evolutionary aeons more.

They apologized eventually, reaffirmed that parting was best, and all was reasonable. At first. They managed to remain civil throughout the packing up of the horrible house and its horrible contents. Marianne said to friends that this was because neither of them wanted anything because it was all so vile. Friends said whatever the reason they were very lucky and should keep it up. Norman even walked around with a spring in his step (though he might choose to look cast down by the cruel world when he remembered) and

Marianne felt lighter by the hour. They continued to remain civil during the selling of their house. He suggested that sides should not be taken. She agreed.

It was all going perfectly until the Practical Poet broke into her life. Which provoked almost visible antlers in Norman ('Dog in the manger more like,' muttered Marianne to herself, when Ruth and Co. suggested it might be a resurgence of love), followed by a particular night when Norman came back from a colleague's farewell party, somewhat the worse, the very worse, for whisky and wine. Much was said that needed to be forgotten and, given the amount of alcohol he had imbibed, so far as Norman went – it was. But being called a female parasite and a bad mother cut Marianne so deeply that she could not be sensible. Good behaviour came at a price and in this case the price – her humiliation – was too high. By the first light of dawn, as Norman snored in the room next door, she was still so incensed that she took out all the old titillatory gear he used to like – the high-heeled ankle-busters, the frilled waspies, the fishnet stockings, the oddly perforated knickers (she had been wondering what to do with them feeling that the Prospect Hospice shop might be a little out of its depth) and draped them artfully over the pile of black rubbish sacks outside their front gate for the bin men to find. They did. With delighted hootings and catcallings that could be heard right up the street. And when Norman looked out of his bedroom window, and Marianne looked out of her bedroom window, the ribald gestures from the enthusiastic bin men left very little to the imagination. Theirs or their neighbours'. Indeed, the Polish cleaning lady, who was just arriving for her daily slog opposite, crossed herself and continued to do so in the remaining weeks until they moved.

Norman was puce for days afterwards. It was a true betrayal. For a few days Marianne enjoyed the nice, cleansed feeling she was left with and the eruption of laughter at the memory. If she were a male ape she might have gone about beating her breast. Later she winced when she thought about it all. It was too easy, too childish, too cruel by half. Rise Above. They had Annie to consider. Such tricks only alienated. So far Annie had accepted the idea of her mother and herself living in a separate house but that Norman and Marianne were still friends. Nothing must erode that confidence. So she apologized to her puce husband. And he, fairly grudgingly at first, accepted it. Marianne told herself she should feel sorry for Norman, very sorry.

While she was lucky, wasn't she? She had her Practical Poet.

Annie was remarkably accepting of the move and her mother's new love. Marianne took Annie away for a holiday (suggested by one of Marianne's friends who was a counsellor) and then Norman took Annie away for a holiday. A child would have to be in serious emotional straits not to understand the possibilities of such a life. And Norman would still see his daughter regularly, possibly more than he had before, and the hidden cruelties and barbs of the marriage no longer applied now that they lived apart. The pram was gone from the hall, Marianne, too, had her own future to pursue; the worst was over. Norman was disposed to be civil because life was easier that way, and Marianne was disposed to be civil because she was in love and therefore the world must be happy too. Including Norman. Not long after the move was final, Norman eased the whole situation by taking up with (her mother's phrase) a doting young thing half his age who could weld. They met at a bus stop. This made Marianne smile since her meeting with her new love was in much more appropriate and romantic style.

Their eyes met across a pile of poetry books in the Charing Cross Road, and it was love, immediate love. Or so she told herself afterwards. He had pale, sea-green eyes (searing, she decided, also later) and a nice thick, curly mop of black hair that was in very obvious contrast to Norman's thin, long, wispy salt and pepper. They reached for the same book. Later he told her that he had done so on purpose. These were the days of new confidence. She was wearing her Furstenburg crossover, bought in defiance of everything when her first advance cheque arrived, she had a light sun tan and for once she felt perfectly up to the mark and unusually emboldened. Instead of taking her hand away, looking down, scampering off, she stood her ground.

Are you reading Shelley?

She nodded that she was.

She wasn't. She had picked it up randomly.

Art thou pale for weariness / Of climbing heaven / And gazing on the earth, / Wandering companionless?

Yup. You bet she was.

And so, it seemed, was he.

She told him that she was an author. He told her that he was a poet. They were both impressed. No alarm bell rang when he asked her if she was published and she said that she was, and when she asked him if he was published he said that he was not, not quite. No alarm bell at all. Poets had a very difficult time of it. They exchanged telephone numbers. Both were still living with their spouses but both were about to divorce. It was a perfect, perfect world. When he touched her back as he ushered her out of the shop and into a nearby café, she felt a dangerous tremor up and down her spine. In retrospect she wished someone had stood in front of her and waved several large red flags and suggested no surrender, go home. Instead she sat opposite him, drank two cappuccinos which may have been the cause of her heart racing – and said she would meet him for dinner the following weekend. By the time she left the café she thought he was the best looking man she had ever seen, the most *simpatico*, the most quietly stylish. Which was the moment the concept of searing eyes arrived.

But what she told herself that day on the ride back to her horrible old house in Sandford Avenue – which she was looking forward so much to leaving – was that this could be fun. It might not come to anything, but if it did, she was in full control. She knew her path, which was to finish her third book – she was well on with it already – give it to her publisher, and then move into her new house. She had not, at that stage, found a new house yet, but she was very hopeful that the right one would present itself, very hopeful.

The Practical Poet showed his practicality by offering to help her look. He was good at property, he said, with those green eyes of his ploughing through her. Marianne's faith in him became rocklike. She was in the perfect position to start a brand new life. And what this woman needed in her brand new life was fun. Fun, that was all. Care and attention. A bit of looking after and a bit of looking after back. Mini-breaks. Flirtations. And a new reason for pretty underwear. And with a bit of luck this one, if he was a poet, would have more of a poetical thrust about him and he wouldn't want either to suspend her from the ceiling and hit her with a hairbrush as a sign of true love, or to have her cavorting around in curiously constricting undergarments while reciting Racine. Both she and the Practical Poet agreed, over their second cappuccino, that it would be diplomatic not to mention each other to their current spouses on the grounds that it might (a) be a bit early and upset them and (b) get in the way of the two of them getting to know each other first. This was a relief to Marianne as, frankly, if Norman thought a bit of Ann Summers over the plastic binbags was a betrayal, how much more of a betrayal would he think it if she declared that she had met – and rather taken to – a lovely, sea-green-eyed poet?

It took Norman about a week to guess. Apart from the sparkling eyes and pink cheeks the moment of clarity came, apparently, when she stuck on her earphones and sang the entirety of the Carole King *Tapestry* album, not realizing that she was doing so at full-lung capacity and very early in the morning. Annie could sleep through anything. Norman could not. 'Will you stop screaming out those lyrics. Who is he anyway?'

Marianne removed the headphones. He repeated the question so she answered him honestly, and with dignity.

He gave one of his unpleasant little laughs. 'And now you'll have to learn to enjoy that alien thing called Sex. Hah!'

Alien thing? She supposed it always was. It was another betrayal.

But there was no learning involved. When she discovered the Mystery of the Big O and she discovered as she panted and blinked and twitched and groaned exactly what she had been missing all these years, she thought that hers was the greater betrayal. Bugger Charles and bugger Norman – and bugger all those little encounters in between – how could she possibly have spent forty years not knowing? How could she have had two husbands and *they* not know that *she* didn't know. And, come to that, how did men manage to gain thousands of years of ascendancy over her sex if they couldn't tell when a woman was faking it or not? No wonder everyone went on and on about sex. She was probably the only woman in the entire western hemisphere who remained ignorant of such a wonderful truth. *Together we will make this new house of yours beautiful for you . . .* he said, as they slid back down to the floor again. I've certainly christened it, she thought happily, and from that moment onwards she was putty in his hands . . . Charles.

The downstairs double reception room had no fireplaces – just holes where the fireplaces once were. How murderously Marianne pondered on who could have removed the original beautiful mouldings and tiles. The eighteen-foot-long kitchen (two rooms knocked through, or – as Marianne preferred to term it – bashed through with a pitchfork) with French doors at the end had a distinctly rickety look about its timber window frames and creaking wooden floor and slightly cracked walls. Poor shell of itself, she thought. With all its good innards taken away and tat put in to replace it.

Once the house would have comprised a front parlour and a little back room with a small kitchen and scullery downstairs – a house fit for Victorian Pooters to rent while they dreamed of moving to the more salubrious neighbourhood of Tooting or Putney. They would, Marianne decided (her imagination being engaged by such things instead of applying itself to starting a new book), be upwardly mobile and saving hard to better themselves. To achieve this they would eat scrag end and call it roast lamb, they would not light the fire unless pneumonia threatened, they would walk because a tram ticket was a heedless luxury and Mrs P. would do without a char. So tense would all this scrimping make their lives that they would find it hard not to brain one or the other with an (unused) fire iron. But outwardly they would appear absolutely respectable and beyond reproach. Their aspirations would take them, presumably, to three floors in a better class of neighbourhood – and worth the threadbare struggle. So long as they kept their lace curtains spotless, their front step scrubbed, petunias and pansies in the windowboxes and were never run over by a tram with the shameful revelation that every single piece of their underwear was darned and stitched to near extinction, they could carry on the game. And when they arrived in the better class of neighbourhood and the three-floor house? Why then they would be miles apart and sour and unhappy and wonder, on their deathbeds, what it had all been for . . .

When she told her new love of these surmisings, he put his finger to her lips.

Only happy endings, Marianne, he said. *Only happy endings . . .*

Marianne, so happy, felt invincible. She was an author with a place in the world and what if the place was currently a run-down house in an even worse part of town than usual, when you could walk into a room and be confident in what you were? What was a house that looked as if it had been put together by men with Rotavators when you had a folder containing some very fine reviews? Nothing. Absolutely nothing. It was rather unfortunate that the Practical Poet had still not – quite – found a publisher for his cutting-edge and coolly modern poetry – something he felt keenly and something that, after a while, and being in love, made her behave in a diplomatic fashion about her own success. But he would find a publisher soon. Of course he would. And then she could revert to being confident in her own right again. One had, she knew (she had done enough of it), to nurture the masculine ego, for it was not long since the days of the cave.

Anyway, he was so wonderful, so talented, so clever with his hands as well as his brain that he didn't need that kind of success to tell him where his place was in the world. Did he? Sometimes she found herself gazing at his sleeping head on her pillow and feeling as if she had eaten several pizzas on the trot. Full.

We will transform it all. It's easy. When my new flat is finished we'll start on this.

Yes, of course. He had bought a place to live, why would she expect him to move in with her? And he must first attend to that. Then he would begin on her house. She had no fears about such a plan. They had time.

In the front room upstairs, the room that was going to become *the mistress bedroom,* she imagined the Pooters' cheaply bought brown wooden double bed with its ancient springs. She imagined the painted floorboards and the bit of lino in the middle of the room. And in the fireplace, the only original one left in the house, she could see fading tissue in red or blue, and maybe some dusty paper flowers. It helped to try to imagine such things because she really did not like the house very much and she hoped that when it was re-designed she would come to love it. She also did not like its situation, which even green-eyed poets could not transform. It stood at the end of a particularly scruffy cul-de-sac with a view of a brick wall in front. And she did not care for the people who lived in the flats over the back who were avid believers of what they read in the tabloids (she often heard them pronouncing on the mysteries of finding a bus on the moon or the absolute truth that by the year two thousand and something they would be overrun, overrun). They spoke – loudly – of Pakis and Froggies and were barely civil to the mixed-race postman. They reminded Marianne – if she let them – of her own roots that came from such narrow-minded, vaguely nationalistic stock.

When she told him of her fears, that she had yet again bought somewhere that was crap to live in now and would always be crap to live in, he tapped her on her nose and told her to *trust me, trust me, trust me.* Which she did. This time she had promises. *We will make it perfect for you.* She should have noticed then that even though he was in love he did not say, *We will make it perfect for us some day.* If she dared to think about *that* side of things, it was to be reassured that when he and she had lived apart for a while – when they had both explored their own space – they would finally live together like normal people in love. Marianne was fed up with being unconventional. She wanted, where possible, to be like everyone else. All the same, despite her understanding, it worried her, if she let it, that he now lived in a mansion flat – big and spacious and white and in the process of being exquisitely transformed by him – in the heart of Hampstead where everyone was a beautiful person? Artistic. Wealthy. *Cool.* That word again. And where none of his acquaintances had to worry about living within walking distance of a school as none of them had, or wanted, children. By now she had met his ex-wife, who was seriously in love with someone else, so there were no obstacles, none at all. They had the rest of their lives to build whatever they wanted. *Let's take our time, Marianne.* To which, much like the question about Shelley, she lied and said it was a very good and sensible idea of which she completely approved.

After a while she gave up denying to herself that she was besotted, and yielded. Fevers, night fears, lonely tears and all. When she began asking him why he had not telephoned her, or come to see her, and when she spent the times apart from him in an agony of jealous imaginings, she dared to admit that she was lost. He was always relaxed, always plausible when her doubts spilled over into words and she always ended up feeling a fool. It astonished her that a person (her) could be so overtaken by love. Part of her, the writer's part, looked at the machinations of it with curiosity, while the ordinary human side of her just suffered. It was an uncontrolled experience. No matter how you make yourself look on the outside, what was happening on the inside was the truth, and unchanging. She was – wrong word, surely? – doomed.

At the same time she began to realize that he was perhaps a little different from her starry-eyed hopes. The signs were there but she tried not to see them. Ever since she told him, fleetingly and in the barest detail, about her childhood and her childhood home, he seemed a little less caring. They were walking by the river, hand in hand, and she was happy. She said, laughing, that if it all went wrong tomorrow – well – she had loved every minute of the comfortably off life and could probably go back to the low life without it killing her. 'It's a coat I wear,' she said. 'But I could get by on the smell of an oily rag again if I needed to.'

She saw him wince. His hand slackened. 'Not that I ever will,' she said quickly. 'Not that I'll need to. Ever.' Marianne had not yet caught up with the age of Thatcher.

For the first time she was connected to someone who thought of money and status as objects in themselves rather than as means to personal or creative fulfilment. She buried the impulse to challenge him about it. Marianne quickly learned that if she wanted to keep this lover happy she must not challenge anything and she always complied. He talked so much about money and the loss of it. How his family had once been rich but the money was wasted on fast living. He spoke of this with anger and his sea-green eyes hardened. Marianne smiled and said, 'How old-fashioned of them to behave that way.' Which was the only sensible response from a woman who had stepped from one class into another and who felt charmed by the privileges of life. 'Anyway,' she said comfortably, 'you've made it without them. You stand in your own shoes, as Confucius would say.' He did not seem very impressed with Chinese sages. Nor with her achievement. He did not like poverty, he did not like unappetizing houses, he would not want to know that she had grown up in a horrible house (with a horrible bathroom) as well as spent her adult life living in them, too. He was a stylish man with a stylish home of his own and a sense of his own good breeding and was understandably unlikely to be interested in her low-class past. None of this was said; all of it was felt. Even if Marianne was not writing anything at the time, she was still an author with an author's second eye.

As the months flew, then crawled, then staggered by, she became more and more absorbed by this love, more and more absorbed by the peculiar, electrifying delight called sex, more and more miserable when she was apart from him. How humble she felt that he had picked her to be his *amoureuse*. He was beautiful, the charm of a million goldfinches. Women swarmed about him and she felt afraid of them. He was wholly admirable, desirable, clever – he could climb mountains and make shoes and cook cakes and recite poetry – and he looked like a film star in his dinner jacket. These were but a few of his golden attributes. She was nothing by comparison. Three books written, yes, and a fourth to start – but what was that compared with him? The fourth book languished. Part of her felt she had played herself out, that she was not really a writer at all, just a lucky parvenue. She began to think that perhaps it was a fluke that she was published in the first place. And when she told him that it had come about because friends of hers had a neighbour in the business, he just nodded and said, *Yes, yes, that's how it's done.*

Marianne felt like a plate-juggler. She had a daughter to look after, she had a book to finish, she had friends she must not neglect, she had a house that was still the same as it was when she moved in and wakeful misery in the middle of the night. But, more important than all of these, she had a lover who needed to be kept happy and whose happiness would be complete if his poetry was accepted by a publisher. This, then, was the goal. This, then, was something she could achieve that others could not. She must try.

'When are you going to make my window so that it opens?' asked Annie.

'Soon,' she said. The Practical Poet ignored the question and tickled her daughter instead.

'Squirt,' he said.

'Squirt yourself,' said Annie back. They got on all right.

But the window should be mended. Marianne – a tiny bit of the old Marianne – rang a local builder and asked him to come and look at the sashes. He came. He submitted a quotation. She could afford it. Time to take charge. She accepted.

And then the Practical Poet went very strange. His lovely lips went oddly thin and his melodious voice was harsh.

If you feel you want to do it on your own – then do.

So she did not.

He read his new poems aloud. They were technically perfect – rhythms and assonance and pace all mixed together to make a fine word machine – but she looked for the heart in them, found none, and decided that not only was she a parvenue author, but she couldn't fathom poetry either. But she knew people who could.

Her publisher was giving a party for a poet. She had not been to a publishing party for a long time. He no longer wanted to go with her, he almost mocked her. *It is your world, Marianne, not mine . . . that's obvious.* She did not choose to go to such parties alone. Once he had loved to walk into literary gatherings with her. Then, one day, he refused. 'When you walk into those places,' he said, 'they know who you are. I'm just tagging along. Mr Marianne. And I never want to end up as plain old unknown Mr Flowers, Marianne's sidekick.'

She was astonished. 'No one could possibly think of you like that.'

But he was quite firm about it.

But to this one she determinedly took him. 'There will be people you should meet,' she said. On the way she kept the pot of his interest boiling. 'I'll tell them you are a poet and they'll want you.' She could not conceive of anyone on the planet not wanting him.

'It will be my good turn to you,' she said, 'Because of the good turn you are about to do for me.'

And what is that?

'Why, my house,' she said. 'You are going to finish the plans and make it beautiful for me.'

Years later, when she was still having nightmares about him, she would recall that exchange about plain old Mr Flowers in her dreams. But instead of her saying 'No one could possibly think of you like that,' she dreamed that she had said, 'I don't see why not. Enough women walk into their husband's worlds and are known only as an unknown Mrs Something.' It comforted her to dream it right.

Marianne was convinced that the stumbling block to getting the renovation of her crap house under way was his lack of a publisher. Therefore, that night, she ushered him around and, as a latterday Ancient Mariner, stopped one in three, or two, to introduce him. It was all very unfortunate. Because she had been so long away from such parties, all people wanted to ask was, 'When is your new book coming out?' and to ask her where she had been for so long. Then her editor whisked her away to the other end of the room to talk about novel number four and she watched in painful agony as he stood there, tapping his foot, looking at his watch, lips thin, until she returned to him. And they left.

'Sorry,' she said. 'Poetry is difficult. But we'll send it off to some people and that will be better.'

Maybe.

Nothing very much happened to the house. She held on to the promises and when she suggested she might start some decorating herself, he took her by the hand and into the bedroom. It was certainly more fun than painting skirting boards but when it was over and he was gone – *I have to get up early tomorrow* – so had her momentum.

Part of Marianne, the dark, hidden part that crept out sometimes in the middle of the night, told her that she might be fêted at the odd publishing party but she was also Marianne Flowers and Marianne Flowers had always lived in crap houses. It was all Marianne Flowers deserved, probably. When she visited friends who had nice houses, in nice places, with nice plumbing and proper gardens, she looked at it all as alien territory. Deep down and underneath herself, Marianne knew her success was tissue thin, she was a flutter of rice paper underneath. This house, and her lover's cooling interest in her vocation, proved it. She heard the call, knew all the hymns, but she was too far gone to pick up her crap house and walk. *One day, Marianne, it will be transformed*, was said in the days before he saw right through her. She deserved no better, really.

Even the horrible loud proles at the back of the house had a greater expectancy than Marianne. They did not contemplate their navels over what their place might be in the world – they just accepted that some people enjoyed *Don Giovanni* and Titian and Proust whereas they preferred the Shopping Channel. She watched them sometimes from her small, scruffy, dirty-pink painted *workspace* at the back of the house. They just got on with their lives, which were mainly about smoking lots of cigarettes and eating lard sandwiches and discussing the merits of either flogging and hanging, or returning everyone whence they came – and notable breast sizes.

Marianne might have moved on from lard to olive oil but in her heart she knew she had not moved on very far. Knowing a quotation from Shakespeare or Shelley was hardly a ticket to the *haute monde*. This house reflected that. Only a person who was crap would buy a place like this. Marianne wallowed. It was all that was left to her, self-pity.

Fortunately Annie was developing an independence of spirit and had a naturally cheerful nature. The great truth about pre-teens was that they were entirely and absolutely self-absorbed. This burden, this love she suffered for her poet, this frightening thing, was Marianne's alone. Just as well, she thought, for mothers must not be seen to be weak. So far as Annie was concerned there was but one person at the centre of her universe and that was herself. And the telephone. The hours she spent on the telephone with any one of her interchangeable friends were the hours when Marianne, mostly alone nowadays, could sit, staring at her horrible walls, and wonder and fret and do nothing.

She was now authorially dumb. Day in day out she sat in that dirty pink back room that grew dirtier and dirtier and she pretended – to her publisher, to her agent, to her friends, to anyone who asked – that she was doing something constructive. Instead she was watching and listening with repelled fascination to her neighbours over the back. She envied even them. Yes. Despite – in the case of the men – their shaven heads and horrible large bellies which they wore like

Exocets, or – in the case of the women – their thick short necks above bright-blond cropped hair and apparently square bodies (all of which brought Brueghel to mind), she felt envy. She felt it, too, for their even larger voices which they used to foghorn their lives to the world. They enjoyed each other's company (whereas no one cared for hers) and they were *confident*. They were determinedly bigoted and determinedly sure of themselves in their bigotry. They wore baseball hats and iridescent trainers and T-shirts with vulgar messages (If you can read this you aren't pissed enough . . .), they ate very big pizzas on Saturday nights and they sat out on their steps in the summer farting and laughing and belching with pleasure and glee while their barbecue smoke drifted its tantalizing, carcinogenic and arrogant (we have a social life, we do outdoor things together, we are loved and we don't give a stuff . . .) way over the back fence. Horrible people, they were. Delighting in their ignorance. Daring in their racism. Never picked up a book. Never watched Wim Wenders. Never looked at a Turner sunset . . . But even they – salting her wound – did up their dwellings. They might be only yellow-brick flats and not very elegant – but done up they were. Whereas she – she was defeated on all fronts for the Practical Poet, quite suddenly, went walkabout. One minute he was looking at paint charts, the next he was sounding cold as ice on the telephone and asking for *space*. It was the end, of course, though she pretended not to see it.

Of course he was cold. Of course he would leave her. Of course she was not destined to live in comfort and beauty. It was as if an old, familiar blanket had wrapped itself around her once more. An old familiar blanket smelling of damp and decay and unwholesome plumbing smells. Her life. 'I understand,' she said, meaning who would want to stay with her for longer than they could possibly help?

After this she became fascinated by the view from her rotting window. Her neighbours would not tolerate such conditions, either physical or emotional. They were always doing something about something that was done to them. If a husband left a wife, if a wife left a husband, if a girl cheated on a boy, if a boy cheated on a girl, they screamed it – they railed against it – they made sodding well sure that the gods knew they were much displeased with the way Ciara or Jason was carrying on. They considered themselves worth it. Certainly (an entire Saxa factory pouring into her bleeding heart) they considered themselves worth a new bathroom suite and if only she had never raised her eyes above

214

the dais and left their world behind, she, too, might have been lying most cheerfully in a brand-new highly coloured bath or flushing a lavatory complete with acrylic pilasters. She would be none the wiser (or snootier) that there was pure-white porcelain to be had. She saw these bathrooms arriving, she saw the crap carried out and the new stuff carried in. Plastic baths light as gossamer, retro basins grotesquely resembling something found in a Victorian boarding house, silver snake-like towel radiators with scales etched into their sides. Cheap and vulgar maybe. But they were *new*.

Obviously she was depressed. Or going mad. But envy them she did. How she wished she had never been shown another way, never met Charles or Norman or the Practical Poet. Bathroom fittings, kitchens, all went in to the flats at the back. Never a one went into her house. Such things sure took the edge off one's contemplation of *The Four Quartets* and *Ashes and Diamonds* and a love of Mozart.

You should have the very best.

His first gift to her? A large bottle of Badedas. Such irony.

'Oh –' she said, enchanted, for it was *very* expensive and the sort of thing she saw looking quite at home in other people's bathrooms. She remembered that she had opened the lid and sniffed it and closed her eyes in ecstasy. And how it looked distinctly odd in among all the grimy scruffiness of the Sandford Avenue bathroom. It definitely, she told him, turned up its nose to be there. How he laughed at her witticism. How he sympathised. *Poor you, poor you, poor sweet you . . . You are worth it,* he said again.

Until now it had not occurred to her to evaluate the phrase Fallen in Love. It was just something you said. But the appropriateness of it amazed her.

Fell was a pretty accurate term. Never before had she realized that *falling in love* was such a perfect description of the procedure. *Falling* implies making a mistake which you cannot rectify before you hit the shit.

Her fall, she slowly realized, was about as big as Lucifer's and quite as devastating. She, too, went straight from untouched heaven to the pain of a living hell. Which hell, she was reliably told by those of her aquaintance who had been there before her, was commonly known as being head over heels in love with a bastard who cannot commit. Never before had she known anything like it. It had already eclipsed her writing. It eclipsed her friends. It eclipsed her own life

215

and now it threatened to eclipse her life with Annie. Without him she lived as one in the dark. She understood Bovary perfectly now. She understood Jane Eyre, Cleopatra, Norma singing out her pain. She knew why people declared they would die for – or of – love. And did. She was never whole when he was elsewhere. She also knew, but suppressed the knowledge – clinging on as millions before her and millions to come would cling on – that once it gets to the 'I need space' stage, the party's over. Certainly, on the rare occasions they spent together, she dared not mention his promises about the house.

The last time they went away together was in high summer and they went to Lindisfarne. By now she was something of a wreck, what with the insecurity and his coolness and occasional heat (which kept her on her toes – or *dangling* was how her friend Ruth put it). Lindisfarne was so still and spiritual that she found it healing and he seemed to find the same. Unfortunately she could not stop crying. If she was happy, she cried. If she was miserable, she cried.

You will be happy, Marianne, I promise. I promise.

She bought him a copy of a medieval jug which was found when they excavated along the coast. There was something poignant about this simple, brown pot being so revered and spotlit in a museum. He was delighted. He liked nice things. The jug, in its simplicity and quiet brownness, was *cool*. He would put it beside the plate with a face painted on it from Venice, the turquoise candlesticks from Portugal, the small prayer mat from Tunisia.

But after that he seemed further and further away than ever and she began to berate herself for not finding him a publisher. That must be at the heart of it. How it must irk him to do layouts for magazines and book jackets and all that design stuff, without ever finding himself represented on their pages. But when she told him how hard she had tried she suddenly realized, from the look on his face, that she had said the wrong thing. To have tried so hard, and for the poems still not to be taken, meant something that neither of them could possibly contemplate . . . It would have been quite funny if she had dared to laugh.

One day – not long after Lindisfarne – when she was nearly dead with fear for she had not seen him for over a week – she rang him and she cried. She was forty-two years old and blubbing like a teenager. She disgusted herself but she begged him not to leave her alone for so long, to tell her what was happening in his life, to help her with her house which was slowly disintegrating around her. She did what she vowed she would never do – she said it was his fault she was here, living like this, that he had persuaded her and that he must take responsibility.

Very well. I had no idea you were so desperate about it all. Of course we must get started.

And a few days later he arrived at Gibbon Road with a man. The man was burly, in his fifties, twinkle-eyed and rough-brown faced. *This is Bill. Bill is my builder and he's going to do your house. I've talked it through with him, I've sketched a few things out, and he's come to have a look and give you a price. He's very good, Marianne, I have used him often in the past.*

Bill walked around with them. Bill sounded extremely confident. She liked him. She even flirted with him a little which was a strange feeling, another of the lost pieces of Marianne. Bill said, 'A pretty bathroom for a pretty lady,' at which she blushed and he twinkled. Pretty came from a very far-off land. The Practical Poet, who had flirted his way through any social occasion they shared nowadays – even culminating in throwing the wife of one of her oldest friends over his shoulder after a dinner party and running off down the road with her. On that humiliating occasion all Marianne could do was listen to the delighted screams as they faded into the distance, look uncomfortably into Danny's astonished face, and remember that it used to be her he threw over his shoulder and made scream with delight. Her poet took her by the elbow, led her to the kitchen away from Bill, and said that it was stupid to lower yourself with builders because you needed to keep your distance and your dignity. They were employees. Marianne said she was very sorry. She kept to herself the shocking realization that it had been a long time since she had felt even a little bit attractive. And even Annie, in her new-found poise, no longer threw her arms around her neck and told her that she loved her more than chocolate.

Annie had grown up in other ways, too. When Marianne said that at last the house was going to be just the way they wanted it, she was unimpressed. 'He's never kept a promise yet,' she said. Almost cheerfully. One virtue about her daughter, and all her daughter's contemporaries' rooms, was that floors and walls and any available surface was completely covered. The decorative quality of the space held little interest to its dreaming, rebellious occupant. Just as well.

For inevitably . . .

About a week later, quite out of the blue, he suggested they should have a day out together, *en famille*. This was unusual but welcome. Annie was bribed to come. The suggestion convinced Marianne that whatever coldness had settled around them was gone for good. Men were odd, everyone said so, and this one was no different. She sang as she packed a delectable picnic, and she was still singing when they set off. She was singing something by the Eurythmics. *Love is a stranger in an open car . . .* The Eurythmics were *cool*.

By the way . . .

They were well out of London and heading for the Downs. She stopped singing.

. . . about the start date for the work on the house.

In the back seat she heard Annie give a contrived yawn and say, 'Here we go . . .'

I've been asked to manage the rebuilding of one of the flats in the block. They've seen mine and like it and they'll pay . . .

She relaxed. That was good. It was good for him to be singled out. It was even better that he would be paid for it.

. . . and I'm going to use Bill and his men.

'But Bill's doing mine.'

I've asked him to do this project first. It's money, Marianne.

'But what about mine? I'm paying him.'

Yes but you're not paying me. And let's face it sweetheart – you've waited this long – another few months won't hurt – will it? I mean – it's business.

'Stop the car.'

(Annie's shocked face in the back. This really was the height of uncool parental behaviour.)

'Stop the car.'

We're in Sussex.

It's a betrayal. A betrayal.

She wept.

Thin-lipped silence as he turned the car around and drove them home again.

'I never want to see you again.'

(She meant it.)

Annie said, 'Told You So.'

Worst bit: Eating that picnic in the horrible kitchen with the horrible, noisy proles over the back showing off noisily with how happy they were.

Best bit: Finally getting off to sleep at about five a.m. after blubbing like a teenager (under the covers so that Annie wouldn't hear).

For three weeks she managed it. And then she rang him. He was cheerful. *It's not what you think, Marianne, it's just that it's a lot of money and business is business. It's something I'm good at. If my poems had been published . . . I don't want to be typesetting other people's for ever. You wouldn't turn down a writing job, now would you?*

Chance would be a fine thing. She still had not written anything of any value (except private, agonized diaries and poems and letters to him, of course, reams and reams of letters to him) for so long she felt she had fallen off the authorial map. Already she was using up some of her house alterations fund for living expenses. All her energy was tied up in this.

She said she was sorry, Oh so sorry. They became a couple again. Possibly a more semi-detached couple.

You really do understand? I need my space.

Marianne grew very good at pretending. And all the plans that he had sketched, and the paperwork from Bill, was pushed to the back of a drawer. She felt it humming there malevolently whenever she passed by. But she said nothing, she watched her tongue, rocked no boats, accepted his absences and his moods. He seldom stayed the night with her any more though their sex life had never been so good. She made sure of that. If it weren't for the fact that she sometimes felt it was a clever, mechanical process the way they came together every time, and that it was more a point of honour for him than an expression of love, she might have been happier. But there was just something in the self-satisfied look on the Practical Poet's face, as if he had a secret, as if he knew something she did not. He did. He knew how to play her.

After a few of these visits and her lonely morning wakings, Marianne became bored with being miserable. It was entirely one-sided and got you precisely nowhere. And you could lose a lot of friends. Her editor rang her and with an immense effort of will Marianne stopped feeling sorry for herself for long enough to realize that – in some respects – she was very, very lucky. People could lock you up and throw away the key, but they could never destroy your talent. And if you were blessed with a talent it was unacceptable to waste it. She might have been destined for a future that included travelling on the tube every day to a job she loathed – many did – but she was lucky. Instead her destiny was to be an author and in order to be an author she must write. If her editor – that poor, semi-defeated being who rang from time to time – was to be believed, there were people out there waiting for her to deliver another book.

Marianne only semi-believed this – but that was better than nothing.

So she stretched her arms, stretched her toes, took one last look at the dingy, unpainted ceiling above her – and rose from her bed with her mother's ancient wisdoms ringing in her ears. Rise Above. Look on the bright side (a phrase surely calculated to make the really depressed seek a gunsmith immediately). Count your blessings. *Count your blessings.* Oh dear God they were so appallingly smug and awful that they were funny. Marianne cheered up. She laughed a little as she dressed. Such platitudes. But they were comforting.

She felt a tingling in her finger ends and a stirring in her brain. If he had other fish to fry, then so did she. That very morning, with the sun dappling the nicely silent flats at the back (it was too early for them) Marianne began work on a new book. The exact nature of it was unclear to her but she thought – if nothing else – that she now had plenty of material to fictionalize in her own life. If there was nothing else at home in the creative department then she would fall back on Love and Sex and Loss and Pain. With jokes. It would have to do. She sat at her desk for three hours and wrote four sentences. Very short ones. But at least it was a start. And when, most unusually, the Practical Poet rang to say that he would be over again that evening, she felt the tiniest, most fractional blip of irritation. This was soon lost in the usual breathless delight in seeing him for two nights, so rare an event, and what that might mean in terms of their future together – but the sentences were real, they were alive, and they came confidently out of that secret chamber of hers called author.

The next morning the tingling in her finger ends was stronger. She sat up, blinked at the pale light, looked with sadness and love at the pillow beside her and his sleeping head, leaned down and smelled his special smell, and resolutely swung her legs out of the bed. Downstairs she made coffee and kept the four sentences of yesterday firmly in mind. Whenever she wavered and started to think black thoughts, she pulled herself back to the new book. It was an exhausting wrestling match but when she slipped back into bed and tapped him on the nose to wake him and handed him his coffee, she felt she had won the first round.

When he said, as he was leaving, *You don't mind, do you? I've got such a lot to do.* She said that she did not mind at all. And probably because she meant it, he wavered. He looked at her hard with his sea-green eyes and he said, *Are you cross with me?* To which she could comfortably say that she was not. *You are.* 'No, no,' she said, as he was dressing. 'You go. I've got to get on with my work, too.' She stretched her arms and smiled at him and yawned pleasurably. 'I've got an idea for a new book,' and she reached out with her toe and touched his leg. 'Began it yesterday. I'll ring my editor today and she'll be pleased.' She rubbed his knee. 'I think they'll like it. They've waited long enough. So go on, be off.'

That's not very nice.

He said it seriously.

But she had learned a good few lessons and did not take the bait.

He left. She ran to the car and leaned in and kissed him, suddenly feeling anxious. 'I love you,' she said. He tooted the horn (which may or may not have been the semaphore version of her declaration) and drove away. Later, with Annie safely off to school, Marianne went into the dirty pink room, moved her desk away from the window so that she no longer stared hopelessly at the flats and their occupants, and began to work. She was relieved and pleased to discover that the process of writing was the same as the process of driving. No matter how long you were away from it, you never forgot. Like driving, it was also a liberation.

She wrote for over an hour, adding considerably to the four sentences and with the familiar pleasure of losing herself – and then the doorbell rang. Down she went, humming to herself, which was new, and opened the door. There stood the Practical Poet.

My car's broken down and I've got to get to an architectural reclamation place near Slough.

'Take mine,' she said. And reached for her bag and the keys.

He smiled that smile of his. *It's a nice day. I thought you might like to come with me.*

She overcame the second little rise of irritation. 'Of course I will.'

When he asked her on the journey if she had been working she said that she had. But only a little. *Good,* he said, and she wondered if he was referring to the fact that she had worked, or that she had worked only a little. 'Did you ring your editor?'

'Not yet.' She changed the subject and asked him how the flat conversion was going.

'Very well,' he said. 'Client seems happy.'

Good, she said.

The day went. She took him back to his garage in the late afternoon where he removed two ornate Victorian wall brackets from her car boot – and left her. *Thanks.* The horn tooted again. She stood on the garage forecourt feeling deeply miserable and deeply ashamed. This should not be happening. Back home she found Annie and assorted friends sitting watching television with packets of crisps on their laps and gallons of Ribena at their elbows. She knew that she should remonstrate but she had no heart for it. All that sugar, all that salt. Instead she went into the kitchen, closed the door, and stared bleakly around the horrible room, which stared back at her equally bleakly. Upstairs and downstairs the house breathed and creaked and shook its finger at her for her folly. Squandering your talents it said, losing your mind. She knew it was true. Still she said nothing and prayed to the ancients to keep him for her.

She rang Ruth. Ruth was helpful about the crisps and Ribena on the grounds that it could have been hash brownies and vodka. They met for a drink. 'Has it ever occurred to you,' asked Ruth, as they sat in the Café Rouge – Marianne miserable, Ruth bright and matter of fact – 'That he's playing with you?'

'Why would he do that?' she asked.

Ruth shrugged. 'Must be quite nice to have a tame woman. Or even two.'

She stopped speaking to Ruth for over a week. Truth hurt. Two?

Are you working this morning?

'Yes.'

Could you pick something up for me later today? I'll get it from you tonight.

She was useful to him. Anything was better than being ignored.

'Of course. Will you stay to eat?'

It'll be late.

'That's OK.'

She abandoned the dirty pink room for the day. She collected the package for him and then went shopping for delectables. He liked delectables. But when he arrived it was nearly midnight and he had clearly eaten already. He had garlic on his breath, and wine, and his hair smelled faintly of cigarette smoke.

Sorry. Couldn't wait. Stopped off and bought a hamburger.

She asked no questions. Did not dare. At least he is here, she told herself. Dumb cow.

For then, predictably really, she discovered that the neighbour's building job, the expensive flat conversion – the job that he needed to take because the whole world was against him and his poetry, and he did not want to rearrange people's advertisements and illustrations and dull prose for ever – was required for a female who was wealthy, single, thin and shagging him.

She was told by a friend. Or rather, a friend, apparently mentioning it casually on the phone to Marianne, asked if she and the Poet were still together. Of course they were. Marianne was firm. 'Why?' She wished she had not asked. The friend said that she had seen him and a woman in circumstances that made said friend wonder if he was being entirely faithful. Marianne immediately remembered Charles and the image of his promiscuously wandering hands and said, 'Thank you.' And put down the phone. She did not really believe it. Not him. Why would he?

Beyond all shame, she spied on him. And she saw, from the darkness of her car as she watched the lit windows, that it was the truth. After which she was bewildered. She was bruised. She was bemused. She was still unconvinced. Why would he? She wondered over and over again. By the time she reached home she was certain she had not seen him slide his arms around someone's waist. Trick of the light, might be his sister, his ex-wife – anyone.

She went back in daylight. Very early. She waited for over an hour, walking up and down the side street, getting odd looks from passersby, kicking stones. It would not happen. But it did. The two of them left the building together, he tossing a bag of rubbish into the skip behind which Marianne skulked. Apparently they had eyes only for each other or the sight of a woman with a pale face, glittering eyes, scattered bun of slightly greying hair, creased jeans and T-shirt which looked as if they had been slept in – because they had – would surely have drawn some kind of reaction. Eyes for only each other. While Marianne had eyes only for *her*. Gimlet eyes observing the creature. Would that they could screw her full of holes. Rich, dark and thin, she thought, like the best chocolate biscuits. Like the best anti-heroines. Witchlike. And the witch with the hooked and warty nose stole him away. After they turned the corner and were out of sight she leaned her back against the skip and wept and wept and wept. The *her* did have a slightly hooked nose – not unlike Queen Victoria's – but it was wart-free and unusual and attractive. Marianne felt her own. Just a stub. Couldn't even get that right.

She waited for his confession, his goodbye. But he did not tell Marianne, he was not truthful. Never had been. Marianne gave him opportunities. She asked him if he was still happy were her. *Yes. I like it this way.* Perhaps, she wondered, with hope, it was a fleeting affair? He would come back to her. But when he went away to Paris for a long weekend, she knew. He barely made an excuse, saying that he thought he might get a translation for his work over there. Rubbish, she thought. His work is not good enough. She almost said so but instinct said it was not yet time for such cannon.

Perhaps he thought they would just wither away – one day she would stop being in his life and he would be free without any of that nasty confrontational nonsense. In divorces, Marianne read, it is still mostly the women who bring the action. A man will do everything, short of climbing over his rival to find space in the marital bed, to avoid conflict. And if a wife finds a stocking in his briefcase it is likely he will wonder, very convincingly, how the very devil it got there. In the same way, Marianne reckoned, did the Practical Poet assume that the end would eventually come of its own accord and that he did not need to do any more than behave as he was behaving. Ostrich man.

Lobster woman. Gradually, over the days, waiting for him to tell her the truth and waiting in vain, Marianne began to boil. Slowly, like a crustacean in a pot, she grew hotter and hotter, and quieter and quieter with him. When he visited, words helped. Fake, shame, pinchbeck, phoney, cheat . . . Under her breath she said them as she poured their wine or stirred their soup. Then, one evening – when he telephoned her to say that he would not be over to fix the dripping tap (which he had volunteered to do a fortnight since and which volunteering had stopped her neighbour's husband from kindly fixing same) – the heat got to her. She drove to Hampstead again, she parked her car away from his window, she rang his doorbell. Now she was the Goddess Thermidor. She was light on her feet, black in her heart – somewhere between Dame Ninette de Valois and Gertie Lawrence as she entered – balletic and a bloody good actress. Lobster hot and spines brittle.

He let her in. He looked nervous. It was most unusual for Marianne to call on him – and never unannounced. His sea-green eyes were dark. His mouth had vanished. Her beautiful Ganymede twitched with vexation and alarm. Marianne entered, smiling, and she twirled for him and kissed him softly on the cheek and said how happy she was to see him as she walked past him into the vast white room. She had brought with her a bottle of geranium oil. 'Shall I give you a massage?' she asked, flirtatiously. She began unbuttoning his shirt. He began backing away from her. *Not now, thank you.* She went on smiling, touching the buttons, crooning to him and saying how much she had missed him recently.

'You know it never occurred to me that I could just come over and see you but – here I am . . .' She pressed her fingertip to the top of the open bottle, rubbed a little on his forearm. Geranium oil would always be the scent of betrayal.

He looked pale. She remarked it. 'Are you eating properly?' she said. She was beginning to enjoy the ballet, the play, her audience. The telephone rang. He reached for it. So did she. Now he was scared. She knew. Marianne, too quick for him, picked it up and listened. The female voice said something coy. 'Fuck Off,' said Marianne. And put down the phone.

He looked ashen.

He made noises but no finished sentence emerged from those missing lips.

She sat on the black-leather settee, crossed her legs, crossed her arms, wiped the excess oil from her fingers along its sleek arm and said, 'Well?'

He played dumb. It seemed unlikely that he could speak anyway. How strange for him, she thought, that a poodle should turn into a tiger.

Um? He said. Marianne?

Oh, that hesitant, boyish, naughty grin – produced to win her as it always did. He'd be quoting Shelley next.

She dropped the smile, dropped the playfulness, uncrossed her legs and sat up straight, arms folded. Nurse Gladys Emmanuel after Arkwright has taken one liberty too many. 'Don't,' she said. Her voice was a shriek of scratching glass. 'Just *don't*.'

I'll get us a drink.

She waited. And while she waited the telephone rang again. And again she reached it first. 'Which bit of fuck off did you not understand?' she said, without waiting for the voice. Sweet heaven it was. It could have been anyone. From the look on his sheet-white face, it could have been someone important.

'Who is this?' she said.

A masculine voice said nervously, 'Sorry, wrong number,' and hung up.

Look, Marianne . . .

The telephone rang again.

She picked it up again.

'Who is this?' asked the same voice.

'This,' she said, 'is the angel of justice with the flaming sword of retribution. And you?'

He rang off.

'Where's my drink?' she said sweetly. And began drumming her fingers on the black-leather arm of the stylish, bachelor sofa, tracing the oil marks. They were satisfactory.

'How very nice this place looks,' she said. 'How perfectly done up it is. Not like mine. No, not like mine at all. Do you know that my house is still exactly the same as it was when you persuaded me to buy it and you said that I could leave the organization of it all to you?'

Now just a minute, Marianne . . . I never said . . .

Alzheimer Man.

'My drink?'

She was pleased to see that his hand shook as he wrestled with the corkscrew because hers were shaking too. She bought him that corkscrew, come to think of it, from Heal's. He admired its shiny style and simplicity. She went over to him, and took it from his hand, and finished opening the bottle. She had never felt angrier nor so right. Years of simmering now spilled over and she was angry with him, angry with herself. She went to the casement window, which was ajar, and she dropped the corkscrew out – it made a little tinkling sound as it hit the flagstones below.

He made another noise. He managed to say, *Marianne – are you mad?*

To which she very comfortably replied that yes, she was, very. Extremely angry as a matter of fact. Like Alice, she said, I'm growing.

She ignored the drink he held towards her and went into the clean white and stainless steel kitchen and took the replica brown pot off the windowsill. Lindisfarne. She removed the artful dried twists of straw arranged in it and brought it back into the living room. And dropped it out of the window. It made quite a noise as it joined the corkscrew. He blinked like Bambi. His eyes had never looked more beautiful. Power charged through her. Suppressed rage, desire, misery – everything – sent a spark into her guts. She took the Venetian plate and stood on it. It broke into four satisfying pieces. He was on his knees, aghast. Aghast. It was all she could do to refrain from busting the turquoise candlesticks over his bent head – but instead she cracked them against the fender of his perfect fireplace. Then she took one of the shards and ran into his spotless, pure white bathroom, and ran it, squeaking and shrieking, along the surface of the bath. Authors, she thought to calm herself, were allowed to live a little on the edge. He stood behind her, watching.

My God, Marianne. Why?

'You know.'

Finally she took up the small prayer mat from Tunisia and ran a knife through the heart of it. He had tears rolling down his cheeks. So did she. 'I'd have liked to have kept it,' she shrugged. 'But I don't want any reminders of you. None at all.'

She stayed for another hour, frankly terrorizing him, and his telephone, and then she left. Under her arm was a thick file of all her letters and poems and notes sent to him over the two years they had been together.

'Those are mine,' he said.

'Author's copyright,' she said, and marched out with them.

Author.

When she reached home her legs gave way and she sank on to the first stair. Annie was staying with Norman so Marianne was free to howl, rage, sob, scream. She considered. And did none of those things. She even thought, momentarily, of the hook on the back of the door. 'Nooses give,' she said. 'So you might as well live.' And she put the thought away. Instead she wondered what a heroine of hers would do in the same circumstances and she decided a heroine of hers would do something perverse. What would you normally expect of a broken heart? Misery. She therefore rose from the stair and made a very determined agreement with herself that this new book of hers would be a comedy. It was the best way to hit back at the world that she could think of. Black comedy, it was true, but a comedy nevertheless. Let the night take up the pen and write the private misery, so long as the day was given over to how funny the world and its people can be.

Over the next few mad, sad, bad months she worked, and while she worked, she recovered. For the first time in her life she lost weight, lots of it. Silver linings, she told herself, as the dawn filtered through her bedroom curtains and the pain began again.

'I hate this house,' said Annie.

Marianne, losing the reasonableness of adulthood, could only say, 'I hate it too.'

Annie stared at her coldly. At fourteen it was not acceptable to be in accord with a parent.

'We will move one day,' Marianne said.

'When?'

'When I am ready.'

The only consolation (apart from the odd man – usually very odd – who slipped through her life and out again) as the months gave way to years was that so far as she knew the Practical Poet never did get published, and if she ever caught a glimpse of him he was no longer beautiful. He was getting fat. He was still with Rich and Thin but he had a very hang-dog look about him which might mean he had met his match. Perhaps he had found that a woman with money is not necessarily a fool. So which one of us is the poodle now? she thought. Once, at a party, he smiled across the room at her and something inside her felt a twist of emotion. But it was gone in a moment. It was replaced with a heartfelt gratitude that she was free.

Still in the crap house and rapidly moving through her forties she considered her options. Balefully, truth to be told. She missed her orgasms. She had waited a long time for the Mystery to reveal itself, and now the bringer of the gift had gone. Just her luck to fall in love with a man who understood both practical plumbing and women's plumbing, and who then withdrew both sets of services. It was hard to trust again. At eighteen it was easy, but not now. Everyone agreed that Marianne had had a lucky escape. 'You always were attracted to difficult men,' said Ruth.

'And lunatics,' Marianne added. One is mistress of one's own choices, she thought sadly.

Solo love or sleeping with strangers – nothing helped. The heart and the sex were odd little items and given to making their own way in the world. The advice that she dished out to Annie if there was an exam to take or a tooth to be filled, she now applied to herself. Concentrate on something you really like to take the place of the horrid thing.

Well – there was taramosalata. There was the feel of cashmere on her bare skin. There was lavender oil in the bath after a long, difficult day. Greater and grander than these, there were Monet's gardens at Giverny which she visited with Norman years ago, Annie remaining quietly asleep in her pushchair. Marianne never forgot that day since, with Annie asleep, she could yield herself utterly to the experience without having to offer ice-cream, answers and attention. Norman told her how he related to the idea of Monet just painting, painting, painting water-lilies while a war raged beyond his garden gate (Norman was probably waiting, waiting, waiting for the Third World War to strike so he could be found making up his *tepees* while children cried and roasted beyond *his* garden wall) and she could let her mind roam while all that beauty and sublimity shimmered before her. Now she remembered it with pleasure. The whole experience – the sleeping child, the cool spring light, the almost benign husband, and the place – was truly orgasmic. Like Lindisfarne, it was healing in its beauty. Art could do that. Holy places. Rise Above.

Not long after this helpful revelation, and just as she seemed to be in recovery from the Practical Poet, her beloved Jean died. This was her first real, visceral loss and it punched a hole through her newly mending heart. She was not invited to the cremation. Indeed, she heard of the death only from Ruth and Marcus. So she wrote. She received Charles's curt note confirming same, and denying her presence. She could almost hear Jean whispering in her ear, 'Well, they would ban you, wouldn't they, seeing as how you've gone and become an author. My dear, they always liked to think of you as thick.' Which whispering gave her some consolation. The spirit of Jean continued, 'You and I used to laugh and have so much fun together. Let that be enough. Our secret.'

She rang her ex-husband after receiving his letter and had a worrying moment when she thought she'd developed Tourette's Syndrome – all she wanted to do was be as loud and rude as possible. She contained it by swearing silently to the wall and asking him how the rest of his family was. 'Very well, thank you,' he said.

'Oxford or Cambridge material, I'll be bound,' she said, eager to be conciliatory.

'Probably. Certainly Rufus will.'

Rufus?

'Oh, good. That's nice for you. Annie's a little devil at the moment.

Can't get any sense out of her about what she wants to do. Most of the time she's barely talking to me,' she said gaily, thinking it was a great exaggeration, but what the hell. Teenagers survive.

Charles made a noise of disapproval. 'Did you want something else, Marianne?'

'It's about Jean,' she said. 'I am so sorry. She was absolutely wonderful to me.'

There was a very sharp breathing noise from the other end of the phone. She rushed on, managing to suggest that a lot of water had, surely, flowed under the bridge . . . And she waited for him to point out the error of her ways with any cliché he chose. He said nothing.

She tried. 'After all,' she said carefully, 'A funeral is a funeral, so to speak.' She could hear his disapproving intake of breath down the wire. 'Marianne,' came the sonorous reply, 'it is not a funeral, it is a *cremation.*' She gritted her teeth. 'I could stand at the back,' she said in a humble voice. But Charles would not be distracted.

'My mother would not have wished to be laid in earth.' He let that sink in before adding. 'I and my family will never forgive you.' Marianne was puzzled. All of them? Why? For what, she wondered? For not begging for more when he used to string her up from the doorway?

In respect of this last she'd been *obliging,* hadn't she?

What more did he want?

Louder Moans?

And she had thought that was love.

'I loved you,' he once said, after their divorce.

To which she said that he had a very funny way of showing it.

She remembered that now.

'I loved your mother,' she said.

'You are forfeit that right,' he replied.

It was like taking part in very bad Ibsen.

'Oh, bugger off,' she said, and put down the phone.

The memory of Giverny reminded her that she could be somewhere else, just as beautiful, and celebrate the Passing of Jean by herself. She decided on France again, this time the south. Nice would be exactly the right place. Marianne had never been but Jean went once and said that it was enchanting – blue and white and yellow and warm. And the art was very heaven. Nice it was then and certainly, Oh certainly, it would be another orgasmic experience to add to the list. Curious to experience it in the name of one's mother-in-law, now dead, but one took what one was given.

Marianne wrote a short eulogy by hand (it seemed too like her fictions to type it) which began, 'You believed in me when I could not believe in myself. You gave me good things when all I felt I deserved were bad things . . .' Ah – who cared if it was sentimental? Who would ever know? She would commit it to the sea when she got to Nice. Or float it from a hilltop. A tangible something to remember the moment by.

It was her first leisure (if you could call it that) visit to anywhere since she and the Practical Poet parted and she expected its aloneness to be strange and painful and some of it was. Not least the silly little ordinary things like having no one with her to hold the luggage while she went to the women's room and the butter-fingered nature of dealing with passport, ticket, heavy case and cold-eyed airline staff – and, of course, the moment when she turned to make a remark about something amusing to find there was no one there to receive it. But much of it was pleasurable, and much of it got easier as she slipped into solo mode. I can do anything was her new mantra, to keep the butterflies of panic away. I can even find my way from the airport to the hotel alone.

If she was looking for some kind of sign that this place was the right choice, she found it in the benign warmth and the lazy brilliance of the south. Even the seagulls floated and dreamed rather than flapped. Marianne took it as a metaphor for Jean and was certain that this was the perfect time and place to honour the spiritual moment of departure for someone whom she loved, who had loved her, and who had always believed in her. Standing on the hill at Cimiez after her first viewing of the Matisses, she told Jean this. Her handwritten eulogy floated away on the breeze and then she quoted the whole of the The Tired Woman's Epitaph. Its engaging rhythm encouraged the few walkers who came past to linger, and listen as if she were declaiming Homer or Shakespeare. Which would have made Jean smile . . .

> Here lies a woman who was always tired
> She lived in a house where help was not hired
> Her last words on earth were: 'Dear friends I am going
> Where washing aint done, nor sweeping, nor sewing;
> But everything there is exact to my wishes;
> For where they don't eat there's no washing of dishes.

I'll be where loud anthems will always be ringing,
But, having no voice, I'll be clear of the singing.
Don't mourn for me now; don't mourn for me never –
I'm going to do nothing for ever and ever.

Whatever heaven Jean was in, Marianne hoped it was full of books and comfortable sofas. Above the Franciscan monastery (Jean liked Franciscans) the sky was a scintillating blue, the landscape a sharp green and rich brown with yellow light dancing on leaves. Matisse colours. The symmetrical, perfectly manicured Italianate gardens were a much more fitting place for Marianne to mourn than the Putney Crematorium and those sour old relatives. Charles, by banning her, had done her a favour and, accordingly, she wrote and told him so. A postcard from Nice. 'Having a lovely time here with Jean. Best wishes to all, M.'

Afterwards, back in London, the family wrote a terse note – and it was from *the family* all of them, as if they were Mafioso or something – suggesting that it would be appropriate for Marianne to return the Victorian silver manicure set that Jean had bestowed upon her on the occasion of her wedding. Marianne, with dignified spirit she fancied, wrote back suggesting that she thought it would be most inappropriate to return them. And kept them. She doubted if Charles would ever forgive her for that, either. How very glad she was that she had visited Cimiez instead of sitting in a brick-built structure with Charles's guitar-twanging wife giving forth with the Rodriguez. Yes – very definitely – a bit of an orgasm there all right.

Life was not set to be easy for the next few years so it was probably just as well to jettison lovers for the time being. They took so much energy. And she had motherhood and authorship to perform. Annie, in particular, needed care and attention.

Whatever is wrong it is your mother's fault and you will never, ever, forgive her for wanting to be with someone else when you were always, always, her little girl, her best, her own darling, and *enough*. Before him.

Annie doesn't have to say any of this to Marianne, though she does say quite a lot along the lines of teenager versus parent – with knobs on the knobs – as do all the rest of the girls she hangs out with. Looking back Marianne realizes that she never rebelled against anything. She was too busy trying to do the right thing and not being noticed. Well, she was making up for it now. Now she is beginning to feel marginally better about everything – now she can get up in the morning and actually think it might be a day worth living through – Marianne recognizes the psychology of it all. Time will heal, she says to herself. At least he has not crushed the hope from her nature. She tries to laugh as much as she can and she tries to *think positive*: One day I will have a beautiful, beautiful, house and a beautiful, beautiful bathroom and quiet neighbours and a view that does not embrace somebody else's front bedroom (front) somebody else's busy life, gross belly and barbecues (back). With her talent she has a good chance. Surely this is more than enough? It is.

The Practical Poet, a great one for pontificating in matters of the psyche, and who has been to both group therapy sessions and one-to-one counselling (which, on being told, Marianne chose to think indicated a sound, healthy approach to understanding his life and which she now realizes indicated an unsound, unhealthy, fucked-up meandering confusion) said that she had to *learn to love herself*.

If he were here in this house with her now she would tell him that it was a much better idea if he learned to *love her first* so that she could relax enough to have a crack at his suggestion. But he isn't here. She is. And she is working again. At least horrible houses don't matter when you are sitting at your word processor because you forget everything around you in the world you have created.

Her editor was pleased with the book. It made her laugh, she said. Now they want another. And after that, probably another. It's harder for her to write now than it has ever been, but that's life and that's books. They do get harder because – in theory – they get better. Marianne is assuming, in that positive way, that is the reason it gets harder. And she's grateful the talent for words and stories hasn't gone away completely. When love flew in writing flew out. All those years. Too many years. Looking back she can see that he was jealous. Simple as that. How could she *not* have seen it? Because she has only just learned to value what she has herself.

When you are in love you are not wise, and when you are wise you are not in love.

So said some sage old Roman. Quite right. But love for your child supersedes everything, in the end. One of them had to go – blood was thicker than water – in the end it was no contest. But Marianne could have wished for a bit more recognition that it was not the easiest solution in the world. It might be the *only* decision – but that does not necessarily mean it is the *easiest.* Sylvia gave up. Finished collating her poems and then shuffled off the mortal. Marianne will not. But she can understand the temptation. When you split yourself in two each part is weak. Men were just so much better at it. Didn't have to work at it. They just were. Focused.

Back to thinking about Virginia. Funny, Marianne wrote in her diary, how a woman is called obsessive if she wants a career. Nobody would call Marianne obsessive if she went off to Sainsbury's to stack shelves every day – seven hours a day, every day, which is a great deal more time than Marianne ever spends on her writing. It's as if – because she works from home – it is indulgence. She is at home – yet she is not at home. Friends get cross when she doesn't answer the telephone during the day. Marianne says feebly (because she is hurt and puzzled) that it is her job, that she must keep on working, that she is doing it to keep a roof over their heads and that – yes – she likes writing her books but that – no – it is not something she chooses to do on a whim. Did George Eliot suffer this? No. Did Jane Austen suffer this? No. Did Virginia Woolf? Muriel Spark? Enid Blyton? Georgette Heyer? Rumer Godden? And why did they not suffer it, pray? Because they either had no children or they had nannies. She was trying to do her best. They'd be coming for her with crucifixes and garlic soon. The Assias and the Didos of the world. Soon it will be time to move on one last time.

Her Punjabi neighbour is kind, though. She has wisdom and sees the strain. She has a shrine for Marianne in her living room. It is lovely, with candles and fruits and plastic flowers. Renee (which she is called, strangely) has obviously heard, or felt, some of the pain coming through the walls. She offers Marianne milky tea and puts a hand on her arm as she leaves. Her eyes hold some of Marianne's pain for her. She is a thoroughly good woman. On the other side is a Catholic family. They pray for her. They have told her this. They, too, have heard things. They, too, do not condemn. So she is bounded on both sides by good spirits. In more ways than one where the Catholic family is concerned when they return from their regular trips back to the home country. Their poteen is lethal. A wonder drug. For the short while it fizzes around her system, Marianne feels part of a good, loved world. The next day it is always the same loveless world again.

Thank God – whichever one is prayed to on her behalf – that she is a success in some part of her domain. For the rest? It is Marianne alone.

When her new book is published she is surprised to get many letters from many women (and some men) who identify, or understand, or simply enjoy her new work, relish the blackness behind the humour. These letters and compliments are the grace notes of her life. It is this life that one of the broadsheet journalists wishes to write about. Can she meet Marianne and will Marianne give her an interview? Of course she will. She is flattered. Also she thinks that she *does* have a story to tell. Her own. Triumph over madness, success over distractions, the race run and won – or at least the silver medal.

The journalist is nice, sympathetic, without ill-will, wanting to write well of Marianne. The interview is frank and covers her whole experience – from childhood, to teens and marriage and divorce, college, family woman, divorcee and crumbling idiot where the love of a bad man is concerned. It all goes into the pot. Why not? It's all true and there is no point in being interviewed about her life if she is going to lie. She ends by telling the journalist how she feels that where she lives is a metaphor for her life and that it is her aim to live in a comfortable, clean, well-arranged house that she can enjoy. With a bathroom to match. This will reflect her psyche. The journalist smiles but Marianne says that No, she is serious. A fresh bathroom represents something special in her life. You can quote me.

The interview is published. It is long and it is accurate and it makes her sound quite interesting (though she knows many people have lived lives like hers). She is pleased, Sally the journalist is pleased, her publisher is pleased and the book trade is pleased. Her mother would have been thrilled if she had lived to see it but she died long ago, when Marianne was in the middle of being a first-class mess. This was rising above all right. Marianne's family in general is a little less than pleased at the interview's honesty. But on the whole they are supportive. It is, as she says to them, her life anyway. And the photograph is not too bad. Just a bit jowly, but then, she is in the second half of her forties now, and jowls indicate the overall southward plunge of one's youth. She feels good about everything. At last.

. . . And then . . .

. . . Oh then . . .

It was just about the nastiest thing that could happen.

'Maybe,' said a scandalized Sally when she rang, 'that is why it happened. Because you are at a high point?'

Seemed consolingly logical to Marianne. 'Yes,' she said, narrowing her eyes at the mirror in the hall. 'You could be right.'

Someone had written a very nasty letter of complaint to the newspaper about Marianne and the interview. Saying that it was invention: that Marianne was manipulative, a bad mother, incapable of proper loving relationships, and that her mother-in-law had never been that close, that her mother-in-law had never said any of those things, nor done half of the things Marianne claimed – especially that she had never been supportive of her daughter-in-law at the expense of her own son. There should, said the writer, be a retraction by the newspaper if there was any justice in the world.

My eye and Betty Martin – wrote Marianne in her diary – that was some diatribe. A wonder she didn't also write that Marianne was a liar when it came to liking baths, that she never washed, that she kept coal in hers.

'From whom,' asked Marianne, perplexed, 'did it come?'

'From someone called Beryl Bingham,' said Sally. 'She's an anthropologist, it seems.'

'*Beryl?*' said Marianne, wonderingly rather than angrily. 'Who is not only an anthropologist but my ex-sister-in-law.'

'Ah-ha,' said Sally. 'She doesn't say *that* . . . Shot herself in the foot there. Disingenuous to a fault, I'd say.'

'But I haven't seen her for years. How strange.'

'From the sounds of the letter,' said Sally, 'she's been seeing a lot of you – probably in green-eyed dreams. God help the world of anthropology if this is the state of their pundits.'

'Why should she be so angry when I said such nice things about her mother?'

'I'll send the letter on,' said Sally. 'And you can judge for yourself.'

Dear Ms Sampson

Your Interview with Marianne Flowers, People Page, 2nd May

I write with some disgust at the blatant bias of your interview with Ms Flowers. I know the family of whom she speaks and I can assure you that the woman in question, Ms Flower's ex-mother-in-law, would never behave in such a disloyal and uncaring fashion against her son. Ms Flowers is not to be trusted. Her background is such that she holds many grudges. She is manipulative and scheming and would do anything to further her career, including giving such scurrilously false answers to your interview questions.

I know that she has a difficult relationship with her own daughter, and had a deplorable relationship with her own mother, so it is perhaps not surprising that she should invent such episodes. Nor has she managed to sustain any lasting relationship with a man and although she might give the impression of being a wronged woman where her ex-husband is concerned, I can vouch for the fact that she would have been nothing without him. Her education and deprived family background were not conducive to having a balanced approach to life. It is unforgivable and hurtful to abuse this family so. I think both you, your newspaper and Ms Flowers should apologize. Some aspiring novelists will do much to gain notoriety and court publicity and this is clearly the case here. One would wish that Ms Flowers could have been blessed with enough talent to make such dishonest behaviour unnecessary.

Yours sincerely,
Beryl Bingham, BA, MSc
Royal Anthropology Institute

There was also a note attached from Sally Sampson.

By the way – she may be an anthropologist, but she isn't a great one. She's never won any awards though she went in for the Huxley Memorial Medal on occasion. Must be the journalist in me but I checked up. Sounds like a disappointed woman . . . Very . . . Want me to find out and dish the dirt?

Marianne's hand shook as she held and read the letter. But it did not shake from pain or rage – it shook from mild laughter and amused astonishment. In a way having such a letter written about her was something of a peak. The crown on her somewhat jolting journey. She was now *notorious*.

'I have really and truly arrived,' she said out loud to the horrible, dingy kitchen and even the horrible, dingy kitchen seemed to smile. It was an absurd letter, vicious yes, but also absurd. Surely only someone who had never experienced motherhood could possibly expect the teenage years to be anything other than *difficult*. As for having a deplorable relationship with her own mother, it was such a misuse of such a fine, strong word that Marianne could not take that seriously either. The root of deplore was *plorare* – to weep over – and she had certainly never been moved to do that, nor had her mother. Got a bit irritated on one or two occasions, maybe, but never struck down with deep grief.

Whether it was bravado, or whether she really believed the letter was too silly to bother about, was a question she set aside. There were too many other, much, much more edifying things to think about. A future to celebrate. Out of the darkness comes forth light.

She stood in her pokey back garden.

'Here's to you,' she said, raising a glass of champagne to the sky. 'And despite Beryl's best efforts – here's to you, my beloved, inspirational Jean.'

What did it matter that the sky in question huddled over yellow-brick flats full of pink-plastic bathroom suites and empty pizza boxes and people with loud voices revving cars, and pea-brains kept warm beneath baseball caps while they watched gormless television? What *did* it matter? She, Marianne, was not one of them. She made her own pizzas and always, *always*, if she watched gormless television – she at least did it without a hat on.

She drained the glass so that the bubbles made her nose itch and out came a wonderful, awe-inspiring, head-clearing sneeze. Deafening. A celebration of a sneeze. Somebody over in the flats gave a little shriek and asked what the hell that was? To which his beloved wife, or girlfriend, or sister, replied 'Only that saddo single living over the back. Drinking on her own again . . . Poor cow.'

Marianne laughed and went back indoors. She'd be out of here one day soon. She no longer needed to stay. School would soon be over for Annie, and there were no husbands or lovers who required her to remain. Her servicing days were done. Writing was like dentistry and carpentry and any other skill. Universal. You could do it anywhere, if you could do it at all. And so she would move away. Who knew what life would chuck at her when she did – but at least she had her arms open wide to it all. She could have what she wanted at last, she could have anything . . . She would say Yes. Yes. Like good old Molly Bloom. Good old Marianne Flowers. Yes, Yes, Yes, Yes, *Yes*.

HOUSE NUMBER EIGHT

The Pasture House

A charming period property, believed to date in the main from the early 1800s, which has been recently extended to create a comfortable and stylish family home but which still leaves scope for the new owner to extend and improve. The property is built of part brick, part lime-rendered and washed elevations under a clay-tiled roof. A particular feature is that a number of the rooms benefit from either double or triple aspects, some with views to open farmland. The property is presented in reasonable condition and is set centrally in its own gardens half a mile outside the village of Warmer in the heart of the Wiltshire countryside.

Marianne was sitting in the truly horrible kitchen of her newly purchased, very old house, sorting through boxes, waiting for her visitors. Outside the rooks mocked her as they always did. They swooped and circled around the trees in the woodland at the back of the house parading their nests and their mating games so that the noises they made all day long until dusk were like several hundred demented virgins experiencing their first orgasms. Since in the human world of Marianne Flowers such things (both virgins and orgasms) had become somewhat thin on the ground, not to say entirely vanished, it was mockery indeed. But Marianne also mocked the rooks. It was a battle of feathers over flesh which she intended to win. One did not, she mused, move to the country to be kept in a permanent state of neurosis about what a bunch of old rooks enjoyed while she did not. They must understand who was boss. There they were, permanently bound to the cycle of birth, rearing and loss with never a thought about pleasure and self-expansion, while she was free of the cycle of birth, rearing and loss (Annie came back quite regularly enough for Marianne to wonder if she had ever, really, got married at all) and could now attempt – at last – to give in to pleasure *de gustibo*.

Some evenings, smiling slyly, she would sit out on the cracked old pavings at the back of the house, facing the woodland, and wait until all the rooks were quiet and quietly panting for a moment, all worn out from their smutty-sounding shenanigans, all settled on their nests and turning the telly on and telling each other about their busy days and wondering when the eggs would hatch and whether the Buzzards at number 13 would announce the Third World War on them, and then Marianne would clap her hands, loudly, so that the quiet harmony of the rookery would erupt in a squawking and cursing and a welter of feathers and broken nerve ends and high-pitched complaint. Affronted, as they tried to resettle themselves, the birds would eye her beadily and she would eye them back. One of us most definitely must win, she thought, and it had better be me.

Marianne knew perfectly well the dangers inherent in moving alone to the country. You could go mad. But then, so you could in a crowded street in London. Here she might well be going mad – but if she was she was a happy fool. She would give those rooks – and anyone else who disturbed her new-found equilibrium – short shrift. The rooks, in particular, she would give a good run for their money. They were a metaphor. In all her other houses she existed like the houses themselves – crumbling, unassertive, insecure, wet. Very wet. The climb towards self-belief and the removal of wetness was not over but it had at last found a secure footing. The job now was to make it to the top. Including rook-control. And this would be harder than it sounded. She might be a woman of some renown and accorded many praises (as someone once said on Radio 4) but this did not, necessarily, cut the mustard in terms of inner certainty. Women of much more renown and many more accorded praises went to the wall thinking little of themselves: Marilyn Monroe, Judy Garland, Sylvia Plath, Dorothy Parker, Janis Joplin all faced that midnight mirror and found themselves wanting.

Bravado is a good state and tends to be fleeting. So when the newspaper's editor finally sent on to Marianne the original of horrible Beryl's defamatory letter, she was not surprised that she felt chilled and unnerved. It was one thing to have held a faxed copy of the thing and laugh at it – quite another to hold the original. It was as if the poison had seeped into the ink. The letter arrived, just before she moved to the country, and when she read it again she immediately felt the old Marianne creep up on the new. She put the horrible thing away, but still it hummed and buzzed at her. She showed it to no one, especially not Annie. You did not share such things. It made them all the more real if you did.

When Marianne moved she packed it, and today she had taken it out again and re-read it, taking in each nasty word. When she looked up from the careful script of the signature and looked about her at this house, she suddenly saw that it was no different from all her other houses. Bodged, battered, broken. The people who lived in Pasture House down the years were not, it was clear, in the business of interior design, or even interior maintenance very much. When

Marianne first saw the place, she felt confident and positive about buying it because there was nothing and no one to stop her from putting it right. Obviously from the way her hands shook as she held this offensive thing it did not take much to knock her confidence. Now she wondered, the chill in her spine again, why she always ended up in places like this. And although there was a perfectly sensible answer – i.e. because beautifully done-up houses in desirable places cost more than you could ever afford, dear – there was also the implicit simile – that she was no better than she ought to be and therefore doomed to perpetuate living in places that reflected this. Perhaps what underlay her enthusiasm for Pasture House was that she recognized her twin – yet again – and was comfortable with it. In short, when the estate agent brought her here, Marianne looked at the cracked old brickwork and uneven floors – and felt perfectly at home. Send her one poison-pen letter, give her one nasty jolt by telling her she is something discovered on the bottom of your shoe, and she thinks it is probably true.

This releases a rush of relief inside her so that she finds herself nodding and saying with triumphant conviction, 'I know, I know. I've *always* known I was shit.' It might not be the natural state of mind of Woman in General, but it was certainly the natural state of mind for Marianne. It was the easy option. Like an old cardigan rather than a smart, new, untried jacket. Or that damp, decaying familiar blanket again. She must change. If she did not achieve change with this house which was – she privately decided (having done all the packing herself and never again) – to be her final resting place, she would never achieve it. The tip of the Eiger of life was nigh. Feminism might teach you many things but it did not teach you how to deal with the vileness of some women to women – an aspect of the gender pool that Marianne continued to find very strange. Well might Virginia Woolf write in her diary one of the great understatements of all time, that 'friendships with women interest me'. What she really meant, of course, was that Katherine Mansfield had betrayed her by apparently praising her in a review, but actually making her sound just a fuddy-duddy old dullard. Well, if Virginia could be crestfallen and depressed by such a betrayal, how much more would she have suffered had Katherine written poison *to* her?

Getting the rooks under control was as good a way as any to start the campaign for reinstatement of her self-esteem. Start little. She knew the pitfalls of starting big. Once, and only once, years ago she attempted to start big and it got her into big trouble. Marianne attended a meeting of a feminist group in Surbiton. It was held in one of those large, dauntingly untidy, confident houses that Marianne knew she would never own herself and it was owned by an ardent, articulate member of the group. Although the women's movement did not have leaders, of course, you could have fooled Marianne. The group favoured *supportive criticism*. It did not go very well. Newly divorced from Charles and flexing her wings she was severely *supported critically* for failing to *learn to accept a compliment as her due*: For failing to accept that she was praiseworthy. Marianne made the mistake (having said no thank you to the shiny speculum that was idly making its rounds – which refusal had not been very well received) of saying that she *would* accept a compliment – when she felt she was due one – only at the moment – well – What Had She Done To Deserve It? She would never forget the look the ardent and articulate non-leader gave her. Marianne had definitely, definitely failed. The ardent and articulate non-leader – to prove this did not matter at all – then gave Marianne one of those very odd hugs, which were supposed to make her feel loved by the sisterly universe but which felt all dungarees and no kindness, and told her that she had *survived* and was a *woman* and that was enough. The speculum was again pressed upon her – in the spirit of seeing the mysteries of her innards – but Marianne thought she had quite enough mysteries in her life to be going on with and she did not want to discover any others. She refused again and was told, very patiently, that they all understood. Then everyone joined hands and hummed. Whereupon she came out reeling into the Surbiton night air and felt even worse about herself than when she went in. She was not, at that stage, entirely sure that she *had* survived, as a woman or as a wife or as anything else. About the only thing she could feel confident in was that she definitely was a woman – and what went round in her head to do with that was 'Vanity, thy name is Woman.' Which would certainly have finished the feminists off. The whole experience shook her and now, remembering it, she was glad to know that the path upwards was directed by personal belief, not group therapy.

Over the years, if she remembered the incident at all, she smiled about it, but today she felt a hot surge of anger. How formed she was by her marriage to Charles. How shaken by her divorce. And how very deep went his words 'You would have been nothing without me.' It had taken over half a lifetime to put those to the back of her emotional drawer. Now as she sat in her new home, surrounded by boxes and dust, waiting for friends and family to descend and stir her (and the dust) to activity, she remembered the way it was. She was the original Female Eunuch. And Charles should have married Germaine Greer. '*She's* got a body as well as a brain' was what he said of her. Marianne shut her eyes and shivered, remembering how the words cut her – to be non-intellectual was forgivable, but to be physically imperfect as well was a very terrible fate. Poor him, she thought at the time, Poor Charles with such a dud of a wife.

It was, thank God, different now. But Charles, though he pretended otherwise, was only a plastic egalitarian. He was pretty traditional really, a man who needed to control his woman (hence, presumably, the penchant for bondage) and who also forgot that he had several millennia of male ascendancy behind him in which to consolidate his place in the world. Marianne grew up in a time when every single area of power was run by men and every single area of servitude was staffed by women so it was no wonder she was amenable. She still remembered the awful shock of arriving at the fertility clinic to be confronted by a man in a pinstriped suit who laid her down on a very hard bed and kept telling her to relax as he groped her most private parts. No wonder she was pronounced infertile. Annie didn't come along until six years later – it took her that long to obey the pinstripe and Let Those Muscles Go.

All those years of moving from house to house, none of which she had chosen because she cared about them or because they were what she wanted but because they were forced upon her (no, no – she *allowed* them to be forced upon her) by circumstances – economic, of course, and to fulfil her husband's dreams, or to be near schools, and to have the right number of bedrooms, and to be near Annie's friends and her own – as it proved rather shifting – social infrastructure – went deep. But now, here at Pasture House, she had made a choice. The choice was hers. 'Fail again,' said Beckett, 'Fail better.' Perhaps that was as much as she could hope for. There was no contract in the human condition to say you would be happy. Alive, yes – happy, no. This was her best chance. A home she had chosen out of love for it and which would, perhaps, achieve that Practical Poet's careless advice – that she should learn to love herself. It was better than the speculum anyway. Her job was to make Pasture House sound and healthy and loved and to try to be very happy in it.

Sounds on the gravel. Cars arriving, voices; she stood up, smoothed herself down, pushed the offensive letter to the bottom of a box, and went out to greet the day. There were Marcus and Ruth by the gate, staring around critically. This was their first visit. She wondered idly if the boxes they were unloading contained cleaning materials with which Ruth was preparing to clean the ancient Aga. How familiar and nice that would be. And there was Annie, struggling with a very large bunch of flowers (where the hell were the vases packed?) and here she was, Marianne, mistress of the house, opening the wonky front door, waving, smiling, looking, she hoped, completely relaxed despite the fact that the house had a look about it of preparing to fall sideways. If they did not see the beauty of potential, if they could not see that the setting was enchanting with woodland and fields surrounding it and that the quiet lanes and shimmering trees were a little bit of paradise – she would send them on their way. The one thing she knew she had, because you cannot create anything – frocks or books or happy offspring – without it, was vision. She must hold on to that, and cherish it. Out she went.

When she found the house it had people living in it. Well – possibly people, possibly Hobbits. Two little people, a man and a woman, who had a strange, elf-like look about them and who had strange Frodo-like ideas regarding interior decor. They had created a series of dungeonesque rooms with little dark, wooden doors all over the place that looked as if Gandalf would pop out at any moment. It had rough, dark stone floors as brutal as any prison's; it had interior walls deliberately set with flints to give it the charming look of a dungeon interior. It had dried-blood-red walls with dark, dark paintwork around the windows – and a touch of the Northanger Abbey or Thornfield Hall in its bits of Gothic ironwork (installed, at a guess, c.1996). Plaster was stripped away from the old range to reveal shoddy, sooty brickwork above which Gandalf or Frodo had placed a couple of guns in pride of place. They had many dogs, several cats and, from the state of the attic after their departure, a few long-tailed friends as well. Despite the dogs and cats.

It took a great deal of vision – and a considerable amount of madness – to buy it. It was a house that had asked for bread and had been given stones. Full of neglect, bodgery, corner-cutting, ugliness, makeweight ideas and dark sorrows. Yes, it truly was her architectural alter ego.

The estate agent was understandably thrilled when she said she would buy it and the survey was absolutely appalling – but she was delighted to hear from the surveyor that the roof was sound. 'Just like me,' she found herself saying cheerfully, thinking of her brain. He gazed at her in astonishment. This compounded his view of her which was, she knew, and to put it kindly, eccentric.

Upstairs she compounded the eccentricity even further by sitting on the edge of the very discoloured and unpleasant bath, gazing joyfully around at the scrubby decor, the pinched window, the unwholesome basin and w.c., and saying, 'Oh yes, this is absolutely as it had to be. Exactly right. Couldn't be worse. I can make something of this all right. I certainly can.' She saw him also looking around and trying desperately to see the same. And she saw him fail. What he liked, he confessed later over a cup of tea from her flask, were new properties. Why, there was a lovely one about a mile from here. She could have moved into it and not have had to do a thing.

'But you see,' she said, holding out the packet of biscuits and going all dreamy so that long after he had taken one she continued to hold them up to his nose, 'I don't want what someone else says I must have. I want to make this my own. Ever since I was a girl . . .' And she told him all about the grand house where she wore camellias in her hair, sat in a gloriously huge bath, and met her future husband.

He listened politely as he would if she was about to pay his bill, and she saw that she had completely fazed him. So she just smiled and offered him another biscuit which he looked at very suspiciously.

The bathroom. Get that right and the rest of the house would unfold its comforts and its pleasures. Like the spine of a strictured, misshapen body, a good bathroom would be the domestic and sanitary equivalent of applied Alexander technique. She would then really be like Alice. Like Alice she would grow until she was so tall and so powerful she could peer into the rooks' nests and tell them exactly what was what. Fortunately she did not say any of this to the surveyor, who was by now, presumably, wondering what she put in her tea apart from Assam.

When Annie first saw it she just said, 'Crikey, Mum.' And then shut up. By then the house was signed and paid for. Annie was diplomatic. And about to be married and living elsewhere. Happy. It was hard not to feel that old medieval conformity – that when a daughter marries she becomes the responsibility of someone else. Whatever ancient paths still lurked in the maternal breast, Marianne certainly felt free. Later Annie said that she approved, but she was grudging. It is not easy to see one's parent grow wings when they should be in retirement. Marianne imagined how she would have felt if Dora had suddenly upped sticks and bought a bungalow in Bournemouth – much the same as her own daughter, probably. Slightly miffed at the effrontery.

Even before she owned the house officially the vendors cheerfully cleared out their stuff, gave her a key, and scarpered.

'I'm not surprised,' said Norman when he saw it.

His curiosity got the better of him when Marianne invited him down, and he accepted immediately.

'It's got a nice pub near by,' she said. A useful reinforcement if all else failed.

He only had eyes for the woodland. She promised to let him know if any of the maple saplings fell down. He was still building tepees, some two-dimensional, some three-, but the difference was that nowadays they were selling. She was glad they were no longer married. With the money he made he bought himself even more tepee material and was slowly moving into two-dimensional, wall-hanging structures which were more domestically acceptable. The scope on a tepee for decoration was unlimited, which made them very nice objects to own, too. Good. She might buy one from him one day – that'd show him.

Where he lived, in a once scruffy and now fashionable part of London called Hoxton (which he found mortifyingly respectable), his house had a bathroom in which you mountaineered to get to any of the facilities. There had once been an oven in the kitchen but it was now buried under yards and yards of assorted canvas. He was in creative heaven and she did not have to suffer it. Perfect.

They sat on the cracked paving stones at the back of the house, red wine to hand.

'I'll move in properly after the wedding,' she said.

'You'll go mad,' he said cheerfully, 'with all this quiet.'

That was before she introduced him to the rooks.

Aside from the Hobbits the house had suffered from serious neglect and other people's silly ideas about how a house in the country should look. Apart from the flint walls and gothic everything, the even more previous owners, who were presumably on an inner-city escape route, had put up horrible *faux* beams (really disgusting thin things with woodworm and old nail holes) which were all right for little subsequent elvish beings but no good at all for anyone over five foot seven. To bang one's head on a real beam is careless, to bang one's head on a *faux* beam is infuriating . . .

But even Norman, despite hitting his head twice, acknowledged that somewhere beneath all of the rustic travesty the house had charm. Immense charm. Like me, perhaps, Marianne thought with amusement. But best not say it.

'Are you moving anyone else in?' He asked, second glass gone down.

'No,' she said. 'Well – not yet.'

'Then you'll definitely go mad,' he said again, even more cheerfully. How nice it was that he would soon go home to Hoxton. A little of Norman went a very long way. And no doubt he felt exactly the same about her.

It was perfectly possible that there would be someone of the masculine variety in her life again but at the moment she – and the house – were not conducive to this. If a he did materialize, Marianne would want him to be a bit higher than five foot seven and until she had dealt with the disgusting beams, anyone taller would be rendered insensible over a weekend.

'It might be nice,' she said, stretching her legs out over the nasty, broken paving stones, 'to be one of a couple again.'

Norman, third glass down, said even more cheerfully 'He'd have to have the patience of the entire Apostlehood with you.'

She put her chin on her hand and gazed at this ex-husband of hers. She was very fond of him really and he was not without knowledge of her. What he had just said was probably true.

'And the kindness of King Wenceslas,' she said, 'And the looks of the Delphi Charioteer – dressed and undressed . . .'

'And from the look of this place, Marianne, he'd also have to be rich as Croesus.'

'Norman,' she said, a little irritated, '*I'm* the owner. The bills will be mine. All he's got to do is . . .'

But the rooks started up again, loud and furious, drowning the rest of her sentence. They rose from the trees in a flurry of wings and beaks and made no bones about their discords. Just as well.

'You'll have to do something about those things, Marianne,' Norman said.

'I intend to.'

One night, not long after Norman's visit, she realized that she did not have to just think about doing improving things, she could just get on and do them. So she unscrewed the beams from the ceiling and carried the flimsy nonsenses out into the – garden was the wrong word – site or plot or overgrowth in which the house sat would be better – and she burned them. How they crackled, how high the flames went into the dusky sky. How furious the smoke made the rooks and how the rabbits scattered. It was a bonfire of hobbit vanities, a sacrificial flame for Marianne and future happiness. No more false fronts, no more faux personas. For she would be happy here, she would, or die in the attempt. With the enormity of the task that presented itself (she studied the rather large cracks in the outer walls) she thought this latter a distinct possibility. Hold on to the enchantment, she told herself, you are going to need it. Later she wrote the word ENCHANTMENT on several bits of paper which she spread around quite liberally in drawers, on walls, under chairs. She knew she would need the reminders.

The first thing that enchanted her when she came to view Pasture House was the location. It was set in the middle of an acre of ground which backed on to woodland (and rooks) and south-fronted to open farmland – with not a baseball cap or a pizza delivery boy or a drunken night reveller in sight – no one in sight, actually – no neighbours to be seen, the nearest, breeders of lurchers, lived a good five minutes' walk away – so she just saw the sky and the fields and the open road. Once the single house was two small farm cottages – rude huts – and now that they were conjoined and made larger, they had an air of surprise about them. Much as Marianne would have been surprised, at the age of eleven, if she was told that she was worthy of investment, that she could achieve much. She knew her place then, and these cottages once knew theirs. Both of them had grown with the years.

The cottages were originally built in the early days of Enclosure, somewhere around the beginning of the nineteenth century, when the local landowner needed to expand his workforce. He could afford to be both benign and blessed with common sense. Proper farm workers' cottages would both improve the value of his land, and improve the quality of the labour he hired. So he built a substantial dwelling on the big hill near by where he housed his steward and his family, and he built another decent little house at the bottom of the hill by a stream, where he housed his gamekeeper, and then he cleared an acre of woodland and built two small adjacent cottages of flint and rubble on a plot equidistant from the other two houses. Each would have one large upstairs room, and a kitchen and living area below with a substantial range for cooking and heating which fed into a decent chimney. The range was built out of poor-quality bricks and soon cracked with the heat. These poor things had been stripped and exposed in their paucity by one or the other of the previous owners. Marianne would cover them up again and hide their shame.

Originally there would have been a dirt floor but after a year or two, the clay being what it was, the landowner set down flagstones in each place. She imagined the cottagers bobbing a curtsey and wishing he had given them wooden floors instead. Years later the Hobbits had taken up the wooden floors to lay horrible, rough tiles, as if the peasants of yore liked living in darkness and discomfort. What fools the town dreamers of country living were. She was surprised that they hadn't ripped out the bathroom. Not until a hundred years after they were built did the cottagers' privies become sanitary – until then they were dug out at the rear, in the woodland. Nice enough when the bluebells were out, grim when snow and ice were on the ground. Water came from a well at the front and each cottage had its own pump. When, finally, mains water was connected, somewhere around the early 1930s, the small byre or sty attached at the back became partly a bathroom and partly a scullery and washroom, with – grand improvement – a copper boiler for laundry. Marianne laughed at the idea of reproducing this in its new form as *the utility room*. There was nothing new under the sun – only pretensions.

More than a hundred years later, when land had dwindled and risen and estates were chopped up and sold and then amalgamated and adapted, the two cottages were turned into one substantial dwelling for the local gamekeeper. It was in this form that Marianne had bought it. At the back of the combined cottages he had kept his pheasant pens so that the land, what might have been the garden, resembled a miniature Saxon burial site with mini-long barrows. Marianne remembered the potential artistic tepee parts that had dashed all hope of her garden when she was with Norman – and the vile proles with their cars and farts and barbecues that had stopped her enjoying the postage-stamp patch at Gibbon Road. After them, turning a bit of lumpy ground into a proper garden would be easy.

She spent a lot of time thinking about the past in the first days at Pasture House. Something to do with all those boxes she had filled and either dumped or transported. The Practical Poet's poetry, which she thought she had thrown away turned up at the back of the eaves cupboard in London. Surprised to find it, she sat, cross-legged, on the floor of the attic and read her way through it. Truly it was unappetizing, mundane stuff.

> Bones crunch underfoot in the cemetery
> As I lie you down upon an ancient stone.

Fortunately they had never done that though he had once or twice said how interesting it would be to make love in a graveyard. She winced to think that she had nearly gone mad for love of him. A graveyard – Oh really. And she was over it – of that she was very sure. It took a while.

When, a year or so later, she was told that he had sold his lovely flat and moved into something altogether grander and more expensive and much, much more fashionable, with Rich and Thin, it still hurt. She saw that night through the end of a bottle and came out of it the next morning with a first-class hangover and cursing him. But later still she invited him to her book launch and he came. That hurt too. He arrived with a posy of her favourite anemones and bought three of her books, which he asked her to sign to various names. For the one dedicated to Rich and Thin she drew such a flourish at the end of her signature that it broke the pen nib. Already, by then, he had begun to grow a little around the waistline and he was no longer the fresh-faced boy-man she had worshipped. It took a few more sightings, a meeting or two over the years, for her to realize that she was finally and irredeemably over him.

Having destroyed so much, it seemed unnecessary to destroy this last souvenir – his poetry. She would return it. That was fair. And it would be good to be sure and certain, before she made this final move, that she was really whole and free of him. One never knew what lurked in one's psyche, she told herself darkly. It would not do to get down to the rural life and find a vestige of regret for him in her heart. She wrote him a note. 'I'm moving and I have a whole file of your poetry. Would you like it back? Hope you are well. Marianne.'

He arrived two days later. He stood on the doorstep, larger and greyer but smiling. 'Can I help?' he said. And he marched in to take charge. She could scarcely get her breath as he strode past her in the hallway, already rolling up his sleeves. That was how he was when she first met him. How sad.

'It's all right,' she said, but faintly. 'The removals men are doing most of it and Ruth and Marcus are coming tomorrow.'

'I'd like to help,' he said.

She could, quite sincerely, have brained him.

All those years when she would have fallen to her knees for such a moment. Now here it was, just when she needed it. This was Zen. You let someone go and – like the flight of the arrow – they come back to you.

'Thank you.' she said. What else was there?

It was very, very extraordinary. As if he was trying to be what he should have been before. He humped furniture, packed boxes, removed electrical fittings, fitted her old freezer into her Punjabi neighbour's lean-to (with much weeping from both Marianne and Renee so that they all ended up laughing and drinking her strangely sweet milky tea).

When he left it was after midnight. On the doorstep she handed him the file of poems.

'You might like to keep them,' he said. 'I have copies.'

'No,' she said. 'I shall be living out of boxes for months because of all the building work. There isn't room.'

'What are you having done?' he said.

'Everything,' she said. 'But slowly. I'm not going to rush into anything.'

'Very sensible,' he said, suddenly pompous. And would have said more, no doubt.

But she put the poems gently but *very* firmly into his hands and said goodnight.

As he drove off he tooted. It was then she knew she was cured. For instead of thinking sad thoughts at his going and the memory of all those other toots, all she thought, with sharp irritation, was that he would wake the neighbours. And probably always had.

It was during the visit of Ruth and Marcus to help her finish packing up the old London house that Ruth took Marianne by the elbow for a turn around the non-garden. Ruth was still probably the kindest woman you could hope to meet and the bluntest. She had arrived, as she always arrived in Marianne's houses, ready for action. Just as before, like a warmth in her life, there was Ruth with the Vim. It was a symbol of friendship, Marianne was aware of that, and she put aside her irritation.

'You can't leave it dirty for the people who've bought it,' Ruth said firmly.

'Why not?' said Marianne. 'The people I bought it from left it filthy for me.'

They stood by the crumbling back fence that divided the flats from the postage stamp.

'Can't wait for you to see the new place,' said Marianne cheerfully. 'It's even filthier.'

Ruth said, 'We're looking forward to it.' She was looking serious. Lecture coming up, thought Marianne.

'I wanted,' said Ruth awkwardly, picking at the top of the crumbling fence, 'to ask you something. Now that you are so settled and happy again.'

This was new. This was capable, reliable, confident Ruth sounding hesitant. Marianne had a sense of what was to come. There had been vague rumours, the odd reference . . . And Ruth was sterling, trustworthy, non-judgemental, a good friend – and not just to Marianne. St Ruth of Assisi. Ruth was also, still, despite the years, despite rebuttals, a good friend of ex-husband Charles and ex-best friend Willa. Willa the Great Deceiver. Willa whose folly with Charles when Marianne was young and foolish began it all. She supposed she ought to thank her – clever, funny, scheming, untrustworthy Willa – for kicking her out of her rut. All the same, there were other, gentler ways to do it. Willa was, very definitely, the kind of best friend you were best not keeping.

The memory of seeing her husband with Willa, all that misery, and being made to apologize, and eating bloody éclairs, came back full force. Willa deliberately brought Charles and his guitar-twanger together out of pure vengeance – how could she have known it would all work out so well? When Marianne touched the name of Willa it still held the trace of a bruise.

'What?' she said to Ruth.

'It's Willa.'

'Thought it was.'

'She's had a rough time.'

'Two children by different men sounds like fun to me.' It did. Despite all the muddles and the messes over the years, there was still something enviably unorthodox in Willa's way of life.

'She's living in Putney.'

Marianne laughed. That was quite funny really – Putney being so proper. 'And?' A substantial RSJ settled across her softer parts. She had a feeling she knew what was coming next. The rumours were fairly specific.

'The boys are married now.'

"Yes?'

'She living on her own. She's drinking.'

'Aren't we all?' said Marianne.

Ruth did not laugh. Of course she did not. 'She's trying to give it up. She could do with a friend.'

'No,' said Marianne.

'I think she would like to see you. At least talk to you again.'

'No,' said Marianne. 'Try Charles. He's good at that sort of thing. Could help her with her Shakespearian quotations. And any other requirements.

Ruth removed her hand. 'That's not like you,' she said, sadly.

'She sent my letters back to me unopened when I had Annie. Two of them. It was her writing. Return to sender.'

'Well, she could do with you now.'

'No,' said Marianne. 'I don't want to see her. I don't want to open all that up again. She's not safe. I've survived. I'm about to move from here and make a new life. So – no.'

And that was an end to it.

'And don't cluck,' said Marianne. Ruth made another noise like a mother hen. 'And when you do come down I will introduce you to my rooks.'

When the move was complete and she sat alone in the new horrible kitchen in the lamplight (because the house looked better, like all her houses before this one, in dim wattage) and the rooks were finally silent, she decided that if she could quell the rooks, she could quell anything, including the beating of her frightened heart. To move to the countryside, to uproot herself from London after living there all her life and to put so much store by its success was frightening indeed. There was consolation. On the few occasions she had made momentous decisions – leaving Charles, going to college, becoming an author – she had simply held her nose and jumped. No sitting down with calculators and lists and long discussions into the night with sensible worthies. She just did it. And here she was again. Just doing it, just as frightened. Making big decisions was not comfortable and never would be – it was a bit like gambling, she thought, the greater the stakes the greater the reward. A sort of stud poker of life. Speculating while the deal is in progress.

The next day, her first full day in Pasture House, she wrote in her diary: 'Authors are permanently surprised at what is stored in their brains. Things I never knew I knew, memories I never knew I stored. Images and words and conversations suddenly bubbled to the surface today when I sat at my desk and started to write. It was all to do with quelling those raucous birds.'

Her desk no longer looked out over yellow-brick flats, but across a sunny field of half-grown wheat. Here she could see the rooks playing and wheeling about but she could hear their cries only faintly. Faint was good. Entirely silent better. What would shut them up?

Then came the incongruous image of an object that might scare them into silence. An object that she remembered from her childhood. An object she had forgotten about but which, in its own way, illustrated the way it was to be a boy and what was forbidden, or considered irrelevant, if you were a girl.

The incongruous image was a football rattle. A proper, stoutly built, heart-attack arranger which was owned by the boys who lived opposite her when she was growing up. For a while it became the most desirable thing on earth. It was made of wood, huge and heavy, and you held it above your head and whirled it so that the ratchets made a noise to waken the dead. When they set off for the Chelsea match and passed her house the boys would give the blue and white rattle a whirl and make a noise so loud and shocking that

256

it set the streetlamps ringing. If she was at home her mother always clutched her pinafore breast and rushed to the window to see if the Third World War had started and Marianne would dive under the dining table with her fingers in her ears. It was exciting, it was powerful. To make such a noise – and legitimately – was highly desirable. But she was never allowed to use the great, clumpy thrilling thing. Not once. 'It's not for girls,' they said. 'You'll break your skinny arm.' And she believed them. Now she realized that their arms, then, were just as skinny as hers, even if they did grow up later to be more muscular. She might have grown up a bit more muscular, too, if she'd been allowed to do those muscular things. That rattle was something she craved for years. She had forgotten all about it until now. A couple of turns of a rattle like that would tell those rooks who was boss. So Marianne was keeping her eyes open in junk shops and local auctions for one just like it. In the name of the success of the project, she chose to ignore the strange looks she got from the owners of said junk shops and auction rooms when she told them what she wanted. 'For your son, is it?' One of the dealers asked. She let him think so. There was a limit to how much eccentricity one lone woman could bear. She was told, triumphantly, that she wouldn't be allowed to take one of *those* into a football ground any more for reasons, according to this particular Lovejoy, ranging from hooligan behaviour to the war on terror. She nodded meekly. Sometimes the old ways were best.

Noise was a surprising feature of the country. Marianne was shockingly alert for the first few weeks after she moved and often found herself sitting bolt upright at some devil's hour of the morning when a passing pea-brained pheasant decided to greet the day with its enraged shout, or the feckless wagtails began their long day's journey into singing very loudly to protect their foolishly positioned nest. It was a whole new aural experience. Gone were the sounds of the baseball-capped bovver boys and their late-night swearing and slamming of car doors (how many doors did their cars have, she would lie awake in London wondering? Eight? Ten? Fifteen?) and replacing it all was the indigenous sound of country life. If the nights were given over to the calls of creatures, the days were more functionally broadcast. Tractors, guns, bird-scarers, trucks of squealing piggies and trailers of bellowing cattle rattled like gunfire over the bumpy lane. Postmen whistled as they roared by in their jolly, red

257

vans and cyclists grunted and shouted to each other as they hurled themselves at the hills. Helicopters chopped their way to the country estates of London businessmen and at weekends they flew their bi-planes, risking their bodies in death-defying swoops as during the week they risked their cash. Occasionally, above it all, came the hope-ful sound of the wind as it riffled through fields of ripening wheat – soon lost to the throb of an engine. It seemed perverse to want to silence one of the legitimate, natural country noises. We have been here for a thousand years, the rooks could reasonably argue, but she could argue back that she had never been perverse in her life before and from now on she meant to encourage it.

Of course it was safe in the country. Here, if she clapped her hands to shock the rooks into silence they didn't immediately come round to her front door and threaten to punch her car headlights out. And rooks certainly had community honour. Rooks knew that if they damaged or upset another rook in its nest, the whole community suf-fered. It was always One Out All Out whenever they were disturbed. Drove her mad. Reminded her of the old days in pubs when if one girl stood up to go to the Ladies then all the other girls stood up and went with her. It was called sisterly solidarity, it confused the boys, and it meant you could discuss the merits and demerits of the evening – and the boys – in private. Rooks also rose simultaneously. And like those girls, they made a fusspotting chatter and a rumpus about it. In her book of birds it said that rooks were a highly gregari-ous lot, breeding in large colonies and forming well-developed, cohe-sive communities. Unlike the Carlsberg-swigging London mob whose sense of a well-developed community was the old Latin tag *Noli defecate in tua soglia*. Sometimes she pinched herself in the night to reassure herself that she had really got away.

When Marianne casually mentioned the football rattle to Annie, her daughter replied indulgently, 'A football rattle? Mum, you're crazy.' She then smiled at her mother as if her mother was quite old and rather senile. Exactly how she equated her role as daughterly nanny with having a mother who was also still writing and publish-ing reasonably complex novels was another of those mysteries of their intimacy, but, verily, their roles were beginning to reverse.

'I'm not mad,' said Marianne. 'I'm benign and sane. It's better than shooting and it sounds just like a machine-gun.'

Annie laughed. 'Win the rookery and you win the world?' The next stop could be getting sized up for the asylum. Put like that it sounded madness indeed.

'Don't be ridiculous,' she replied, feeling as ruffled as the rooks. Marianne tried a more deprecating tack. 'It was when I was a girl, you see . . .' she said. 'The football rattle . . .'

Annie smiled. 'You told me about it. When *I* was a girl.'

'Did I?' she said, wonderingly.

Annie nodded. 'You said that rattling the thing was something you'd set your heart on doing just once – and nobody let you.'

Marianne blushed. As she had completely forgotten the rattle, so she had completely forgotten telling any such stories for her daughter. She tried to nod and look as if she remembered it very well. Every memory of bringing up your child was supposed to be precious; mothers were not supposed to forget things like that. She said out loud, 'Sorry – head like a sieve.' Charles – who would have pounced on so ignoble a cliché – had completely gone. About time.

'You told me about it when I was struggling with my A-levels.'

Struggling? thought Marianne. Her memory of those revision days at home was something quite different. Each to their own view of history as Tacitus would say.

'You said the exams were like the football rattle. Mine for the taking if I had the balls.'

'I did not say balls.'

'I paraphrase.' Annie smiled. 'But it's what you meant.'

'Did I now?'

'You certainly did.'

It was Marianne's turn to smile. 'And you did,' she said.

Annie nodded. 'And I did.'

They chinked their glasses. Annie took a biscuit from the tin. Who but her daughter was still child enough to want a Hobnob with her Sauvignon? Annie had a faraway look in her eyes – she was thinking about something that her mother could never know. Like Marianne, she had her own tastes, her own life. She was married, she was successfully beginning a career that was neither about writing nor about sculpting (much to Norman's astonishment) and she was nobody's fool. All the same Marianne found it unnerving that Annie had arrived for this little visit without her husband.

'Nothing wrong, is there?' asked her mother anxiously.

Annie looked at her with what would once have been called An

259

Old-Fashioned Look. 'Ben and I are married, Mum. Not joined at the hip. Anyway – I just want to see you. Get it?' She looked stern.

'I get it,' said Marianne.

Odd that her daughter could marry someone who liked to curl up on the Saturday sofa watching motor racing and that her daughter did not take it as a personal affront. He liked motor sport, she didn't. He stayed in, Annie went out. Altogether more relaxed in their confidence this generation of young women. It would have gladdened her ex-mother-in-law's heart.

'Do you remember Jean?' she asked.

Now they were walking through the bluebell woods, looking for the first primrose, admiring the first sprinkling of green on the trees. All good country-dream stuff. There was the faint smell of the pig farm on the air mingled with the smoke of early bonfires. And the rooks were sleeping.

Annie thought. 'Vaguely,' she said. 'I remember sitting in a café somewhere and you and she were laughing about something.'

'That's her.'

'Your mentor.'

'Annie,' she said, 'you have no idea what a naive young woman I was all those years ago.'

'Well, it was like that then.'

She said it as if in those days they had barely invented the wheel – and in a way, Marianne thought, so far as women were concerned, they barely had.

After her daughter left, driving off up the hawthorn lane, tooting her horn and making the rooks wake madder than ever, Marianne thought that she really must do something about that letter of Beryl's. She was just not at all sure what. The spirit of Jean was sadly quiet on the subject. Should she go and see her? Confront her? Let her tyres down? Write a scathing piece about envy in the *Guardian*? She had still never told anyone about it, partly because she did not want even to acknowledge the existence of such a piece of poison, but also because of a real sense of shame that she should have occasioned it. The letter was in one of the boxes piled up in the kitchen and still humming and buzzing away. She knew exactly which box. One day she would be ready for it. Meanwhile, she had a house to rebuild, bathrooms, kitchens, bedrooms to create. Forget the horrible thing, it could buzz and hum away until she was ready to do battle with it.

My house, she thought, mine, hugging herself as she gazed – without embarrassment – at a brochure about superior sanitary ware and lost herself to thoughts of close-coupled Victorian top – or side-handled flush with a feeling of ancient Greece in its fluted features . . . Perhaps Sappho had bathed in just such a tub. Then so might Marianne.

She remembered the opening of one of Annie's favourite childhood books:

> A hill is a house for an ant, an ant.
> A hive is a house for a bee.
> A hole is a house for a mole or a mouse
> And a house is a house for me.

You had moments of happiness and moments of sorrow. Of course you did. Life was, like the weather in Ireland, mixed – and mostly different kinds of rain. But it seemed to Marianne, and she kept this thought to herself and away from jealous gods, that the periods of sunshine were getting longer. The trick was to remember this when the darkness came in.

She waved at Ruth and Marcus but neither could wave back for all the bags and paraphernalia they carried. They both had a look of determination about them and Marianne was glad that she had asked Annie to come down, too, for moral support. You never quite knew how the first sighting of Pasture House would take people for it was in need of a great deal of vision, a very great deal and she was still a little fragile about the immensity of what she had done. Deep breath then. She waved and smiled. Annie was down alone again (Grand Prix time, obviously) apart from what appeared to be half a plant nursery in her arms. Marianne stepped out of her broken, old front door and put all thoughts of the horrible letter out of her mind. It was back in its box and there it would stay.

'Grand Prix,' said Annie. Marianne smiled and asked her to take the flowers indoors and try to find a vase among the boxes while she gave Ruth and Marcus a guided tour around the plot. Almost immediately she and Ruth lost Marcus somewhere near the front porch. He was last seen bending down and poking about with a stick in his hand. Familiar sight. They turned towards the woodland and just at that moment the local squire's bird-scarer went off and the rooks made their overtures and beginners in the matter orgasms *en masse*.

'Oh dear,' said Ruth. 'A rookery. Noisy beggars. They'll drive you mad.'

'That's what Norman said. But I'll see to them,' she said. 'Just as I'll see to everything else. Get it organized the way I want'.

'Big job,' said Ruth.

'Not for superwoman. By the way – you don't know anyone who's got an old football rattle, do you? I have a plan.'

Ruth promised to bear it in mind. They walked to the edge of the woodland. Ruth had that look about her again. Marianne put her arm through hers. 'I've put the past down,' she said. 'And you know Willa will find someone to look after her. She always did and she always will.'

'Maybe,' said Ruth. 'All the same . . .'

Marianne guided her back towards the house. 'The Aga is very old and very filthy,' she said. 'You'll love it.'

They walked back towards Marcus who was inspecting the drains. 'Bad,' he said. 'Very bad.'

'All will be well,' said Marianne, 'When rebuilding begins.'

They had done up a few houses in their time, those two. 'We'll help,' they said. 'You will talk it through with us, won't you, Marianne? Before you do anything foolish?'

'Oh, but I've got a surveyor and an architect and a builder. This time I'm *paying* someone to do it properly.'

Their silence said it all. Being solo was hard for a woman, and Marianne had made it so. Shame to need a surveyor and an architect and a builder when she could have had a husband to do it for her if only she had behaved more wisely. Still – she *would* go and have it all her own way.

'So let's go in and have a drink.'

Annie was standing by an open box, still holding the flowers to her chest, and reading Beryl's crumpled letter.

'What on earth is this?' she said to her mother.

Marianne took it, read it once more, said, 'Absolutely nothing.'

Very quickly, as if ripping off an Elastoplast, she tore it up. Then she ran up the stairs and flushed it away down the horrible lavatory in the horrible bathroom. She had finally discovered where it belonged.

At the first burst of the rattle, the rooks were silenced. Glorious triumph. But like all her triumphs, like all triumphs since Caesar's, it was short lived. For at the mighty sound of the cracking of the ratchets, it seemed that all the dogs in Christendom began to bark. She had quite forgotten that her nearest neighbour bred lurchers. Jumpy things, apparently, dogs. The rooks might be cowering now but five minutes' walk away was nothing to a pack of sharp-eared, complaining lurchers. So there were some things that she still could not win. Maybe a little humility in life really was no bad thing. So long as it was tempered with the occasional dash of pride. In her last novel, *Between the Acts,* Virginia Woolf created a country pageant as if to say that art could impose order on the muddles of life. It only worked in books. In reality rooks, dogs, people, all went their own way, as Marianne was now happily going hers. But at least it was her way. At least in Pasture House she had enough potential success to be going on with, she felt. She would, she was certain, be content with that.